the
LIE
that
BINDS

AMY ARGENT

Turning Tree
Press

ISBN (paperback): 978-1-7369405-4-9
ISBN (e-book): 978-1-7369405-5-6

Cover design by Mayhem Cover Creations
Illustrations and Turning Tree Press logo by Jared Pace
Edited by Susan Atlas

Turning Tree Press
First Edition

Sue, this one's for you!

BOOKS BY AMY ARGENT

THE EMBRACE TOMORROW DUET

Come Back Tomorrow

Whatever Tomorrow Brings

CHAPTER ONE

It's like high school holds two different worlds, revolving around each other and never touching; the haves and the have-nots. I guess it's a good thing. High school is supposed to prepare you for the real world, after all.

– Lauren Oliver

HOLLY

It's really freaking cold. And not the brisk, refreshing chill of winter, but wet—the kind of cold that just seeps into your bones and saps whatever strength of will you have to do anything other than lie in your bed under a mountain of blankets. But the best part? It's the middle of September. In Amarillo in the middle of September, I'd be swimming and wearing flip-flops, not shivering in my boots and the warmest cardigan I could dig out of my winter clothes box. *Where the hell did I move to?*

As I pull into the parking lot, I see the other students hurrying into the building to escape the wetness that permeates the air—all five hundred

1

and forty-nine of them. At Palo Duro, there were twice that many just in my junior class.

Getting out of my car, I turn the collar of my all-weather jacket up but resist the urge to bury myself in the fleece-lined hood. It's my first day here —I don't want to advertise what a wuss I am in the face of this freezing nightmare. They'll find out soon enough the first time it snows.

Crossing my arms as I walk briskly across the parking lot, I give myself a good shake. This is my first day at a new school, and moving here was the right choice. Dad always wanted to live in Oregon, and ever since Mom passed, I could tell he needed to get away from the constant reminders of what's missing from our lives. And he's always wanted to be chief of police in some tiny little town instead of just another officer in Amarillo, so I need to suck it up, put on a happy face, and brave the petty miasma that is high school.

I make it to the safety of the main office with only a few curious glances, but my cover is blown by the kind-faced older woman behind the desk.

"Oh! You must be Holly Ross. It's so rare that we have new students come mid-term—I'm sure you'll be the talk of the town!"

Every head in the office snaps up at her bubbly outburst, and my cheeks flare so hot that I now know what supernovas feel like at close range.

"O-okay." I stammer, and the woman continues on as if my face didn't just explode.

"You're in Mr. Harper's homeroom; here's your schedule and locker number, and you'll get your books as you go through your classes. Make sure to check in with all your teachers—I'm sure they'll make you feel right at home! Oh, and if you need anything, come back and see me."

I give her that frozen smile people give when all they want is to get away, and I beat a hasty retreat. As I duck out the office door, I rear backward as the obnoxious seafoam green of the lobby tilework nearly overwhelms me. I was so caught up in finding the office, I didn't even notice it as I came in. *Well, hello, nineteen seventy-two*, I mumble as I make for the hallway full of lockers, heads turning as I go. It's almost time for the first bell, so I ditch my bag and hurry off to my homeroom.

The room's about half full when I get there, and although all eyes are on me, Mr. Harper declares he'll introduce me to the class after the announcements, to be sure everyone's here. *Oh joy, wouldn't want anyone to miss out on their chance to ogle the new girl and snicker,* my sarcastic side pipes up, but I merely nod and try not to trip as I make for the back of the room.

As I pass, a girl with a long, brown ponytail and butterfly-shaped glasses gives me a warm smile, and I can't help but return it. She seems nice and looks like my usual crowd, but things are gonna be different this time. I have to focus. I have to figure out how things work here in the land of frozen nineteen seventy-two—who's the "in crowd" and who wishes they were.

The back of the room gives me the perfect vantage point to observe. All the groups are here: the nerdy boys with their not quite styled hair and thick-rimmed glasses, the rockers in their ripped jeans and Stones t-shirts, the druggies . . . well, you just know who they are by that vacant look in their eyes . . . Is that girl with the spiky black hair a Goth? I scan the room again. *But where are—*

My thoughts are interrupted by the loud arrival of the group I was looking for. Three guys in letterman jackets strut through the door like they own the place, followed by three tittering bimbos. *Now, now, just because they're showing boob-crack and sound like dying hyenas does not mean they're stupid,* I remind myself. *You're going to try to befriend these girls. You have to—it's the only way to join the popular crowd.* But Jesus, don't Henleys have buttons for a reason?

I shake my head and focus on the guys instead—I usually can relate to them better anyway. *Two blondes . . . nice! The one with the curly hair isn't bad, and that one with the blue eyes is cute, but he kind of looks . . . plastic, like a Ken doll.*

And then it happens. A god walks into our midst, and I seem to be the only one to notice. Time stops and as a ray of heavenly light falls on his caramel hair, I swear I hear angels singing . . . or is that the druggies listening to some rave music? Who the hell cares? Right now, all I can see are deep blue eyes and wild sex hair, and my God, just looking at his jaw makes my throat dry. Is that because I'm drooling, and any remaining moisture in my body has gone south for the duration?

He's *gorgeous*. It's the only word in my brain and the only one likely to be there when I look at him. Unless, of course, it's chest hair or stubble or naked—*Jesus*! Gorgeous drops his books onto the desk two in front of me and snaps my mind back into the present and away from my amazing porno fantasy. But I'm still staring—*shit*! *Eye contact!* Those incredible eyes force mine down to my notebook because I'm not able to take in the full blast of his beauty. To him, I probably look shy, but in reality, I've lowered my eyes in reverence. *Um . . . reverence? Exactly when did I start worshipping creatures who think spitballs should be an Olympic sport? What the hell happened to me in the last five minutes?*

I try to compose myself as Gorgeous turns toward one of the bimbos and hits her with said Olympic projectile. She's pissed, but the smile he flashes almost makes me swallow my tongue. *How can she stand to be that close to him without licking his jaw? Argh, come back, porno fantasy!* But this is reality, and I know I need to stop lusting over what undoubtedly *has* to be some other girl's man-meat.

As Mr. Harper calls the class to order, Gorgeous turns to the front, and sanity douses me like a bucket of cold water. *Wow. I can't let that happen again.* Obviously, not getting past first base, and even that over a year ago, has caused some kind of chemical imbalance in my brain. I'll have to be careful when I'm around Gorgeous lest I slip back into horndog Holly mode. I have more important things to do today.

I dodge a bullet after announcements—Mr. Harper completely spaces on introducing me, but I'm not so lucky for the rest of the morning. Government, English, calculus—I'm paraded in front of each class and forced to say something about myself as my face achieves heretofore unknown shades of crimson. I honestly have no idea what I've said, but I suspect it involved cattle ranches and tumbleweed, as I'm sure they expected. *Brilliant. Just the first impression I was hoping for. Let's all go befriend the lone-*

some cowgirl. The first time, the popular kids survey me, but after that, they don't even feign interest.

Gorgeous turns up in my English class right in time for my introduction, looking all sexy in his blue and green plaid button-down with the top two buttons open, chest hair just peeking out—"chest h-h—chest high! That's how tall the tumbleweed can be!" *Oh my God, please shoot me now.*

I don't really talk to anyone through my morning classes. I return any smiles I come by, but I'm too busy figuring out where things are, prepping for the next round of humiliation, and observing the popular group to really have time for anything else.

Curly-boy doesn't seem to have a girlfriend. Ken-doll favors the overly bubbly one with the curly blonde hair, but they haven't been very handsy, so I can't tell if they're really attached. Maybe it's all in Bubbly's head. And then there's Resting Bitch Face, the recipient of the homeroom spit-ball. I swear she's only smiled twice all morning, and both times were at Gorgeous. I had to disguise my snicker as a cough when she smiled at him in calculus, and he looked right past her. Anything going on there is *definitely* all in RBF's head. But Bubbly seems like she'd be okay to talk to, in a purely superficial high school girlfriend kind of way, and possibly that Katie girl too. Hers is the only name I can remember so far.

One more class to go before lunch—chemistry. *What kind of idiot schedules a class where you're likely to end up reeking of chemicals right before lunch? Then again, I suppose it's better than right* after *lunch,* I muse as I offer my pass to Mr. Metcalf. He's a short guy with glasses, and he reminds me of Danny DeVito, but his smile is warm and reassuring.

"Holly! So nice to have a new face in class! Here's your textbook and lab workbook, and I have a seat for you over here with . . . where's Nathan?"

I glance up and see an empty lab table before me and lots of blank stares.

"Amber, is he here today?"

Resting Bitch Face (aka Amber) graces Mr. Metcalf with a bored look. "He was in last period."

Okay, so he's got to be one of the popular kids since Metcalf asked Bitch Face, but Ken-doll, Curly, *and* Gorgeous were all in calculus and none of them are here now, so I have no idea which is Nathan. *Fabulous.* This is like one of those SAT questions where there are four people in a row, and they give you details about each, and you have to figure out who's sitting next to whom. *I hate those things.*

"Well, never mind, Holly. I guess you have the table to yourself today," Metcalf says, frowning as he ushers me to my seat.

Thankfully, he doesn't put me through another painful introduction, so I have both peace of mind and time to focus on the big moment in my day: lunch. I'm going to approach the popular kids and try to make friends. I'm not encouraged by what I've seen so far, but even if they're assholes, being with the "in" crowd has more benefits than I can count. *There has to be at least one decent human being among them, right?*

The period flies by, and before I know it, I'm in the caf walking toward the popular table with my tray. I chose a veggie burger with carrots and celery, just like Bitch Face and Bubbly, and I follow them to the table where Curly, Ken-Doll, and Katie are already sitting. I take a deep breath and try to push down the butterflies in my stomach, but the influx of air only seems to make them flutter faster.

As I open my mouth, all the air in the room is stolen by Gorgeous as he arrives at the table. It's as if all the molecules of oxygen have flocked to play in his unruly honey-brown locks, and the rest of us aren't fit to breathe now that he's here. My eyes go wide as he runs a hand through the spell-binding chaos atop his head, and he slides smoothly into an unworthy plastic chair. I want to be that chair so much it *hurts.*

But now the entire table is staring at me, and my practiced, cool introduction is mocking me silently from between the strands of Gorgeous's freshly fucked hairstyle.

"Um . . . hi. I'm Holly. Can I sit with you guys?" comes out of my mouth in the quietest, shakiest voice possible, but I follow it up with what I hope is a confident smile. I scan the faces staring back at me. Curly and Ken-doll are eyeing me up, waiting for the girls' responses. I can't look at Gorgeous,

or I'm going to combust, so I shift my gaze to the girls instead. Katie's look is neutral, Bubbly looks confused, but Bitch Face has her eyes narrowed like a lioness contemplating her kill. *Oh hell.*

She sniffs delicately and looks down her nose at me, her gaze fixed on my chest. *Are my boobs too small for this club?*

"What's up with your shirt? Are you advertising for where your dad works?" She fires off the words, dripping with disdain and sarcasm.

I'm wearing my 7-Eleven t-shirt. Retro was all the rage back in Amarillo, and honestly? This might be the coolest shirt I own. Or at least, it was when I wasn't in the land of western bumblefuck with a side of ass backward.

Everyone here will probably be wearing them after I've gone off to college, or popped out a few kids or something, and I'm dying to retort, "I guess you guys aren't ready for this yet. But your kids are gonna love it," a la Marty McFly in *Back to the Future*. But I don't. Instead, I drop my eyes to the floor, and through my lashes, I can see Bitch Face's smirk.

She knows. *How do they always know?* Is there a secret handshake for the popular club? A tattoo? Do they all have the dark mark on their forearms? What is it? If we normal people could just figure it out, we could break in undetected, but somehow, I don't think that's going to happen today.

And why, why *did I look down?* Why can't I maintain eye contact and say the things I'm thinking? Why do I always have to collapse in on myself? *Dammit!*

My cheeks are on fire as I stammer. "No, I—"

"Nah, her dad's the new chief of police. That must be her own part-time job," Ken-doll says, earning an approving look from Bubbly.

"Does Daddy need some extra money because busting booze parties doesn't pay that well?" Bitch Face asks with a smile, and now the whole group is grinning and elbowing each other.

"No, Bitch Face, I don't have a job, my dad is just fine, and this shirt is awesome. It's you morons who are behind the times and clueless." But the

words stick in my throat like they always do, and instead I shake my head as tears well in my eyes. I need to leave. *Now.*

I turn on my heel amid the laughter and exit the caf with as much dignity as I can—I don't even look to see who else might be watching. Disgusted with myself and my pathetic attempt to fit in, I dump my tray in the trashcan by the door. *I* hate *veggie burgers!*

What was I thinking? I should've known those bitches would see right through me! If only I'd had the confidence to pull it off and come back with some snappy retort so they'd know I wasn't to be messed with. *Dammit!*

I spend the rest of lunch in the bathroom, swearing at myself and wiping away angry tears . . . and accepting my fate. I'm not going to be one of the popular ones at this school. I had my chance, and I blew it. Now I'll have to try to figure out where else I can fit in—*if* I can fit in. I cringe at the thought of being an outcast. High school is hard enough even when you're *not* a pariah.

PE is miserable—Bitch Face and Bubbly spend most of the period pointing and laughing at me, although even *I* have to admit my attempts at volleyball are ridiculous. French and physics pass by in a blur as I try to regroup and pull myself together. Butterfly smiles at me again, but she must have seen the event in the cafeteria because she seems to know better than to approach me today. Maybe tomorrow I'll try to talk to her.

Finally, I make it to the end of this disaster of a day, and I almost take a full breath as I shove my books into my locker. All I want to do is go home, forget this ever happened, and start over tomorrow, trying to befriend the people I should have looked for in the first place.

I slam my locker door, then nearly jump into the next county as I spy Gorgeous tossing his books into his own locker three down from mine. He closes the door, and I know the instant he feels my open-mouthed stare. He rivets me to the floor with those vibrant blue eyes. *Is he really about to talk to me? Could this day actually turn out okay?* He looks surprised and almost panicked for a second, but then two other junior

boys walk by, and one of them bumps his shoulder. His lips part, but his smile isn't angelic; it's leering and wicked.

"Headed for the wrong ranch today, eh, Cowgirl? Maybe tomorrow you'll figure out where you belong—the losers aren't hard to spot around here."

The eavesdropping boys chuckle, and Gorgeous laughs—his voice is even more fluid and velvety than I'd imagined, but the sound and the words are so hateful that, for a moment, it doesn't compute, and I let him saunter away as I gaze after him, my jaw still on the floor.

Fuck my life. Gorgeous is an asshole too.

CHAPTER TWO

No one can make you feel inferior without your consent.

– Eleanor Roosevelt

HOLLY

There are fewer stares today—I guess I'm not as shiny and new as I was yesterday. Bubbly (who I'm now considering renaming Bubble Butt) snickers as she walks by my locker, elbowing Bitch Face.

"I guess Holly doesn't have to work today."

I huff in frustration, but there's no point in turning around. I'll only provoke them to new heights of bitchdom.

"They're assholes."

It's a quiet murmur from my left. *Butterfly.* I glance over and can't help but grin.

"I'm Megan Wembley. Don't let them get you down. There *are* actually some nice people here in backwater Oregon."

I chuckle as I gather my books. At least she's aware she lives on the arse-end of nowhere.

"I . . . um, I liked your shirt yesterday. I thought it was cool," Megan says, looking down as her cheeks redden.

So she *had* been in the caf when I made a complete fool of myself. *Lovely.* But her dark brown eyes hold nothing but sincerity as she watches me.

"Thanks. That's the kind of thing everyone in Amarillo was wearing before I left."

"Which means it'll probably be the 'in' thing here two years after we graduate," Megan says, and I can't help but laugh with her. Butterfly is cool. I should have known to zero-in on the geeky ones first—they're my tribe.

I follow Megan into homeroom, but as she goes by Ken-doll's desk, he throws out his foot and trips her. She falls forward, landing hard on her hands as her books scatter.

"Well, *Weeble*, I guess you *do* still fall down." Ken-doll sneers as most of the room laughs.

You asshole! I scream in my head, but my lip just trembles as I narrow my eyes at him.

"What are you looking at?" Ken-doll demands, and I break under his stare, bending down to help Megan gather her things.

"Are you . . . hurt?" I whisper as I give back her notebook. I know she's not okay, so there's no point in asking.

"Fine," she murmurs, head down as she slinks to her desk.

I follow her, sitting in Gorgeous's seat in front of her instead of heading farther back to my own. She glances up, clearly surprised I haven't ditched her, her cheeks finally starting to cool as the rest of the room's attention shifts elsewhere.

"I wasn't surprised you tried to talk to them yesterday. I'd be one of the popular kids if I could, too," Megan says, sniffling.

"Aw, to hell with 'em. They're just a bunch of snobs anyway," I tell her, and she chuckles as she wipes away the last of her tears.

"So, who are the decent people around here?"

She smiles and gives me the lowdown. "Well, some of the guys are nice—I have art with Eric, and Justin is really sweet and funny." She nods toward two dark-haired boys: a smaller one and a larger one with glasses, both of their heads bent together over a comic book.

"And I usually talk to Lucy. She's really into music and great to hang out with . . . as long as Mercury isn't in retrograde."

I open my mouth to ask her what that means, but the words die in my throat as the tiniest Goth I've ever seen wanders into the room. *Aren't they supposed to be all tall and willowy?* This one can't be more than five feet, and instead of long, drowning black hair, hers sticks up in cute little spikes all over her head. She's a Gothlet.

She sits down next to Megan and gives a lackluster, "Hey," and I have to cover my mouth to conceal my grin. She's adorable, but I'm sure that's not the look she's going for. She's wearing a tight little black dress that barely covers her hoo-ha, with thigh-high black tights and platform black leather boots that have more buckles than Hannibal Lecter's straitjacket. Her spiked dog collar precisely matches the double-spiked cuffs on her wrists —because even if you're emo, you can still be fashionable, right? If Marilyn Manson had a cheerleading squad, she'd be the perky little captain . . . *except Goths aren't perky, are they?* Maybe she'd be the lead moper.

"Lucy, this is Holly. She's new," Megan says, as if that weren't obvious.

The Gothlet looks me up and down, her dark eyes settling on the buttons of my blue and red plaid shirt.

"Tumbleweed," she mutters, and I drop my face into my hand.

"I don't even know what I was saying yesterday. I get so nervous when I have to get up in front of people."

The Gothlet raises one side of her mouth in what could almost be considered a smile. "I hate that too."

What else could we possibly have in common? I scored on my first attempt, so I decide to keep shooting.

"So, what kind of music do you like?"

The Gothlet's eyes go all round and glowy. "Right now I'm hooked on Cold Showers and Drab Majesty, but my all-time favorite is The Cure."

"The Cure? Aren't they from like twenty years ago?" I blurt out the words, my tongue engaging *long* before my brain.

The Gothlet's eyes go wide, then narrow to slits. *Jesus, I think she might actually cut me.*

"Um . . . what I mean is they're timeless. Classic."

The Gothlet continues to squint at me but slowly nods.

Megan leans forward and whispers to her. "Chris was an ass this morning, but Holly helped me."

So Ken-doll's name is Chris. He doesn't look like a Chris. Definitely Ken . . . or maybe Justin—a blonder version of Bieber, that is.

The Gothlet's look turns fierce as she purses her lips. "He's such a bastard. Why can't he just leave us alone?"

"Is he always like that?" I ask, although I'm pretty sure I know the answer.

"Yeah, he and his evil minion Nathan," The Gothlet replies.

Great. I'm sitting with Nathan in Chemistry. *I can't wait.* "Which one is Nathan?"

"He's not here. And look; neither is Ryan. I wonder if they decided to skip today."

"Probably." The Gothlet grumbles. "At least our day will be quieter."

And as The Gothlet predicted, it *is* a quiet day, which gives me time to learn everything I need to know about navigating Tillamook High. I learn where all the classrooms are, which teachers are strict and which are just plain mean, and that Mrs. Gibbs, the Spanish teacher, is screwing Mr. Metcalf, who teaches chemistry. Whether his wife knows is anyone's guess, but apparently, Gaudy Gibbs is completely shameless.

I sit with Megan and The Gothlet at lunch and learn who's who among the students, too, but the ones I really need to know are the bullies and the petty bitches. I had the bitches nailed—Amber, aka Resting Bitch Face, and Erica, aka Bubble Butt, are the main ones, but Katie Norris is one of them too. And the bullies are Chris Newman, aka Ken-doll, Tyler, Sean, and, of course, Nathan. Apparently Ryan is often with them, but he doesn't really tease anyone. Chris and Ryan are the jock basketball stars, and all of them often hang out with the senior guys because Nathan's brother, Evan, is a senior. Now here's the bad part. Since both Ryan and Nathan are absent today, I don't know which one is Curly and which one is Gorgeous. I shouldn't even be thinking about this because Gorgeous was a jerk yesterday, but . . . he *could* be Ryan. Maybe he was just having a bad day. Maybe I looked at him funny, or he's protective of his friends.

A desperate cry erupts from some dark, moist place between my legs. *Please, for the love of all that is holy, let Gorgeous be Ryan!* I have no memory of Curly's body—he could be a centaur for all the notice I took, but Gorgeous . . . ah, Gorgeous has the body of a god! I spent three periods yesterday staring at the bulk of his shoulders, and the fine, muscular, inward cut of his arms, peeking out from under his rolled up sleeves. Those arms have played basketball. Those arms have dribbled the ball up and down the court, glistening with sweat as the muscles ripple in and out and up and down and—

"Earth to Holly! Where are you?"

The answer, "Just south of the waistband in Gorgeous's basketball shorts," will clearly *not* do. "Um . . . just thinking about our physics assignment."

"I don't think I have a dreamy smile on *my* face when *I* think about physics," The Gothlet says, elbowing Megan.

Well, I almost told the truth. I was thinking about *physiques,* which is close enough to physics.

"Come on, Holly! Who do you have your eye on?"

Jeez, am I that transparent, or is she psychic? "No one! I just got here, and I've barely talked to anyone!"

"That look had *nothing* to do with talking," Megan says.

"Let her go, Megan; she'll give herself away," The Gothlet says, sniffing delicately. *The Princess of Darkness is entirely too perceptive. Shit. Now I have to limit my ogling too.*

"Come on; let's go to study hall." *Maybe I can read about something more pleasant—like the Spanish Inquisition.*

The day passes quickly, and I don't ask either Megan or The Gothlet which of the mystery boys in my head is Gorgeous. After they caught me daydreaming about Gorgeous's um . . . *assets,* and knowing that I can't manage to ask the question without suddenly and rather closely resembling a tomato, I'm sure they'll know he's the one I want to give my virginity to. *Holy shit, where did all these hormones come from?* It's like seeing Gorgeous flipped a switch I didn't even know was there.

That night, I dream of a certain brown-haired jock who happens to be the star basketball player for Tillamook High. I'm a preppy little cheerleader, and after he wins us the state title game, he falls into my arms and goes right up my ridiculously short skirt and—

I startle awake, panting like a poodle in heat. I *need* to know if this guy is a total asshole before my fantasies get any more out of control than they already are. *Me? A cheerleader? Wow.*

I'm a nervous wreck by the time I get to school, but I don't have to wait long. Gorgeous is in the hallway surrounded by a large group of junior boys. They're giving him high fives, and The Gothlet rolls her eyes as we walk by.

"Look, Nathan is showing off again. He gets to stay home from school whenever he wants to."

Oh hell—Gorgeous is Nathan! This revelation hits me hard, and I can feel my chest contracting, but I have to maintain the conversation, or I'll give myself away.

"His parents know?"

"Yeah, they know. They even sign the notes for him."

"Why would they do that?"

"Don't know." She shrugs. "His brother Evan never takes days off like that. Maybe it's because Nathan's the baby."

"Seems more like a jackass to me," I murmur, still reeling from the blow. Gorgeous can't really be *that* bad, can he? What did The Gothlet call him? Ken-doll's evil minion? *Shit, that doesn't sound good.*

And why would his parents let him skip school? This guy sounds like bad news all the way around, the rational part of my mind says, but the hormone-driven, she-devil part is still focused on how good he looked in that striped shirt and sunglasses and how the fly on his button-fly jeans is folded to reveal two of the three buttons.

"Nice of you to join us, Nathan," Ken-doll says as Gorgeous passes him in homeroom, both of them snickering. The bitch brigade titters, and I shake my head. How did I ever think I could even *fake* fitting in with them?

I settle down and try to put Gorgeous out of my head, and it works for most of the morning . . . until chemistry. I got so caught up in English and calculus that I actually managed to forget about this nightmare, but seeing him hits me like a sucker punch as I walk into the room. He's sitting at our table with his feet up on my chair, a cocky grin on his face.

Megan gives me a nudge from behind, and I walk over slowly to stand beside our table. *Move your feet, asswipe*, goes through my head, but all I manage to say is, "Um."

Gorgeous looks up, and it takes everything I have not to gasp as my throat goes desert dry, and my cheeks flare to level: raging inferno.

"Problem, Cowgirl?"

Jesus Christ, really? Wasn't it bad enough to endure that for one day? I don't know which is worse, Tumbleweed or Cowgirl, but it seems my first day blatherings are going to haunt me forever.

"That's . . . that's my seat." I stutter, barely resisting the urge to face-palm.

"So it is. Why don't you sit down on it, and I'll give you a ride," he answers, wiggling his foot suggestively as he points his toes straight up in the air. "Hmm . . . never mind, I just cleaned these sneakers."

Tyler laughs and elbows Ryan as I slide into my seat. Ryan grins but shakes his head.

Okay, asshole, your name just went from Gorgeous to Jackass, I resolve as my brow furrows, and my traitor heart begins to ache. I am *not* going to cry.

I let my hair hang over the side of my face and do my best to ignore him, but he's not done yet.

"I see you found your people," Jackass whispers, nodding toward Megan and The Gothlet.

Screw you, Jackass flies from one side of my brain to the other, but as usual, it just can't escape its mental prison. Instead, I turn my head farther away from him.

"Hey, *Weeble*, I heard you did more than wobble yesterday."

"Fuck you, *asshole*." Megan fixes him with a glare, and my estimation of her goes up an order of magnitude. She's *much* braver than I.

The room is suddenly silent as Megan's words seem to magnify and echo, and as I look around, everyone is either staring at Megan in shock or looking to Jackass for his retaliation.

"You'll pay for that one." Jackass sneers, angrier than I thought he'd be. *He knows he's an asshole, right?* If the shoe fits, shouldn't you wear it with pride? But for a fraction of a second, his eyes seem almost . . . sad. But it's gone in a flash, and I wonder if I even saw it at all.

"What are you looking at?" Jackass snaps at the room at large, and eyes scatter like cockroaches escaping a blinding light.

But mine don't. I watch Jackass out of the corner of my eye, and as soon as the attention is off him, when I expect a satisfied smirk to slither onto his face, he braces his forehead against his palm, elbow resting on his desk, and scrunches his eyes shut as if he's in pain. *What the hell?*

He straightens up as Mr. Metcalf calls the class to order, and I shift my gaze so he won't know I saw him. Beside me, Megan takes a shaky breath, and I turn my head and grin at her. *Way to go, Butterfly.*

But as soon as I face front again, I can feel the presence of Jackass beside me. I'm not quite near enough to feel his body heat, but sitting this close to him, my heart is racing and the sweat is gathering on my palms. *But he really is an asshole*, my rational mind says as hormone-driven she-devil whimpers. *I don't want him to be an asshole; I want him to swallow my tongue.*

I'm disappointed.

I had really hoped he was better than all this high school crap, but I guess he's just one of the boys. The stupid, immature, holier-than-thou jock boys. Sighing, I vow to write him off as that ache in my chest returns.

At lunch, I sit with Megan and The Gothlet, and Justin and Eric join us too. All anyone can talk about is Megan going off on Jackass.

"I can't believe you did that!" Justin exclaims as Megan blushes.

"Yeah, no one talks back to Nathan!" Eric chimes in.

"She was great," I tell everyone. "She stared him down until he blinked. He had *no* comeback."

"He will," The Gothlet says, her eyes fixed on the popular table. Bitch Face has her head on Jackass's shoulder as he's talking, but he looks pretty annoyed by it. Ken-doll and Tyler are nodding as Jackass speaks, and Erica casts a glance over her shoulder toward our table. It wouldn't be any clearer that they're talking about us if they were holding a freaking neon sign.

"No one messes with Nathan and gets away with it."

CHAPTER THREE

We are bound by the secrets we share.

– Zoe Heller

HOLLY

My morning is uneventful until I get to chemistry. Friday is lab day, and since each table seats two, that makes Jackass my lab partner. *Awesome.*

I want to hate this guy. He's a jerk, he makes fun of my friends, and he represents everything I hate about high school. But as I walk into the room, the air in my lungs turns solid, and my heart takes off like a jackrabbit. My cheeks heat, so as I sit down, I lean over to play with my shoelace for as long as I think I can get away with it to allow my blush to fade. Maybe he'll be an ass to me, and my stupid hormones will knock it off. The warmth between my legs seems to disagree though.

As soon as I take my seat, Metcalf starts explaining today's lab, and I zone out, watching Jackass. He's leaning forward, but he somehow looks relaxed as he twirls a pen between long, dexterous fingers. His sleeve has slid down, and I stare at the bracelet he's worn every day this week. *What is it, anyway?*

Occasionally, one of the guys will wear a shark tooth necklace or some Rasta beads, but Nathan's the only one I've noticed who regularly wears anything other than a watch.

It looks sort of like an ID bracelet, but as I look closer, there doesn't seem to be anything engraved on it. It's a square piece of silver metal that curves around his wrist, held on by a black braided band that looks almost like a shoelace. The band goes through the silver square on one side, over its surface, and then back out a hole on the other side, and the two ends of the band come together in a silver clasp on the underside of his wrist.

Jackass suddenly glances at me and follows my line of sight. He drops his pen with a clatter and tugs his sleeve over the bracelet, casting an almost guilty look at me. *What is that all about?*

"Miss Ross?"

"What?" I answer automatically, as chuckles erupt around the room.

I can feel Jackass's eyes on me, so I keep mine on Mr. Metcalf as my cheeks sear with heat. *Shit, what did he ask me?*

"If you were paying *attention*, you'd know I asked you to go choose your reagents for today's lab," Metcalf says, looking down the bridge of his nose.

I grin sheepishly and scuttle to the back of the room.

As I make my way back to our table, I mentally prepare myself for the onslaught of abuse from Jackass. Every time he's ever spoken to me, it's been to say something snide, and I just gave him the perfect opening.

He's fiddling with the Bunsen burner, but he glances up as I place our chemicals on the table.

"Do you want to go first?" he asks, fixing me with those deep blue eyes and a neutral expression.

What the hell? Who are you and what have you done with Jackass?

I narrow my eyes at him, my head spinning as I try to figure out his game. He stares back at me, his brow furrowing, and suddenly, I get angry.

"What's the matter? Can't come up with anything awful to say?"

"Huh?" He stammers, leaning back a bit in confusion.

"Is it my lucky day or something? Or did you suddenly forget how to be a jackass?"

We both draw in a sharp breath. *Did I just say that out loud?*

For a second, Jackass looks as if I've struck him, but then he clenches his jaw so tightly, I swear I hear his teeth grind together.

"I was *trying* to be nice—"

"Why bother? You're an ass to all my friends. What makes *me* so special?" My eyes widen as the words tumble out of my mouth, and his do too as he takes a long, slow look from my head to my midsection and back again. My skin heats and prickles under his gaze, adrenaline thumping through my veins as anger breaks into waves of desire.

He leans forward so he's mere inches from my face—so close I can feel his breath on my cheeks.

"Absolutely *nothing*."

The words pierce me, freezing my heart and every drop of blood in my body. I can't move, can't think—I just stare, and his cruelty seems to ricochet back at him because he turns away and brings his hand up to shield his eyes.

"Just . . . stay the fuck away from me!" His ultimatum sounds like a growl, and I bite my lip to keep it from trembling as I gaze down at our lab instructions.

It takes me a good five minutes to thaw out enough to focus on anything other than the fact that Jackass basically called me garbage. What the *hell* just happened? Did he actually try to be nice, and I got in his face about it? *Me?* I've *never* uttered the snark that goes through my head. It's always stuck there, even when I want to fire it at someone. But he made me so mad! Why does the only guy I've ever been truly attracted to have to be a jackass? Why can't I lust over a decent human being?

The rest of the period lasts seven lifetimes as Jackass and I shove the lab sheet back and forth, making our separate observations of the chemical reactions and not even daring to look at each other. *What an asshole.* Maybe I *should* make an effort to stay away from him because this shifting from mooning over him to wanting to tear his head off is even making *me* dizzy!

As soon as the bell rings, Jackass flies out of his seat like the hounds of hell are on his heels, and I'm not the only one who notices.

"What was that about?" Megan asks as she strolls up to me, books balanced on her hip.

"I'm not sure, but I think this class is going to ruin my Fridays," I answer, gazing at Jackass's retreating back.

～

Against my better judgment, I spend the weekend puzzling over the dichotomy of Jackass's behavior, and I conclude that more data is needed before I can figure him out. So on Monday, I watch him. I watch him pal around with Ryan and be shamelessly hit on by Resting Bitch Face. I watch him bully guys younger and older as Ken-doll's wingman and make crass remarks to girls. I watch how he smiles, but it never seems to reach those piercing blue eyes of his. And I watch how the eyes of half the girls in the school seem to follow him, but *his* eyes seem to shy away from mine. *Interesting.*

On Tuesday afternoon as I make my way to my locker after physics, the junior/senior hallway is in an uproar. Groups of boys are clustered around their phones, laughing hysterically. The popular girls have smirks on their faces, but the rest look slightly horrified. *Uh oh. Which poor girl is the target this time?*

The Gothlet darts in front of me, eyes wide as saucers, and grabs my arm. "Have you seen her?"

"Seen who?"

"Megan! We need to find her before she sees!"

My stomach drops into my shoes. "Sees what?"

The Gothlet takes a gulping swallow as she hands me her phone. I breathe in sharply and nearly drop the thing. It's a picture of Megan in only a bra and leggings. But the humiliation doesn't end there. There's an arrow pointing to one of her boobs and a caption that says, "Training bra: clearly not needed." On the other side, there's an arrow pointing to her nearly flat stomach, captioned, "Whore handles."

Fuck.

Me.

"Scroll down," The Gothlet whispers, clutching my arm.

The next picture is Megan sitting down, gym t-shirt on, and her knee drawn up and bare from the pant leg she just removed. Her panties are pink cotton with an arrow pointing to both front and back —"Worn out" and "Insert here."

Jesus Christ on a pogo stick.

"Who?" A tidal wave of anger overwhelms the tears stinging my eyes.

"Rumor is Chris or Nathan."

I turn and glare at Ken-doll, but his back is to me, and he's surrounded by most of the senior boys, laughing and making lewd comments. Tears of frustration roll down my cheeks. There's nothing I can do to humiliate *him*. Anything I say will only make things worse for Megan and likely make me the next target. The other boys surround him like the outer wall of a fortress; their approval of his jackassery is disgusting.

I heave a frustrated sigh, trying to hold my temper in check. "Let's find her," I tell The Gothlet, and we leave the drove of douchebags behind.

We search every bathroom and the empty classrooms, both of us calling and texting her as we go. By the time we make it back to our lockers, the halls are all but deserted, and we've had no luck finding Megan.

"I bet she saw it and ran," The Gothlet says, shaking her head. "I'll drive by her place on my way home and text you if I find her."

"Okay. I just have to pack up, then I'll head out too."

The Gothlet gives me a sad smile as she turns away, both of us understanding what kind of hell tomorrow will bring. *Stupid boys and their need to put others down to raise themselves up!* I slam my locker shut with a bang as my temper flares . . . and there's Jackass, standing in front of his locker.

It feels as if the Big Bang happens again inside my chest. All my emotions —sorrow, disappointment, humiliation, fear, hurt, frustration, and an unbelievable amount of anger—rush together and explode outward in every direction.

"Hi, Cow—" Whatever he sees stops him cold. "What?"

"Was it you?" I take two threatening steps toward him, barely containing my fury.

"Was *what* me?"

"Don't play with me, Jackass; you know exactly what I'm talking about!"

His expression was merely curious before, but now his eyes narrow. "No, I really fucking don't, so either tell me or leave me alone."

"This!" I yell, shoving my phone in his face. His eyes widen, and he snatches it out of my hand.

"Where did you—"

"It *was* you, you asshole! How *could* you!" I scream. As he stares at the picture, his eyes widen even farther, and he gasps as all the color drains from his face.

"Where—"

"You are the biggest *douchebag* I've ever known! How could you humiliate her like this?"

"But I—"

"*Fuck you*! You're just like the rest of them!" I yell, swiping my phone from his hand as he backs away, staring somewhere over my shoulder. He doesn't seem to be paying attention to me, which makes me want to murder him.

"Mister Popular! Everything's perfect in *your* life, so why do you have to go around making other people's lives miserable?" I poke him in the chest for emphasis.

That snaps him out of wherever he was, and his eyebrows draw together as he glares at me. "My life *isn't* perfect," he says, teeth clenched, but I hardly pause long enough to let him finish.

"Of *course*, it is!"

"Holly, you have no fucking clue—"

"You guys are such assholes! You go around putting everyone down and making them feel like *shit* just to make yourselves feel good! What kind of a horrible human being *does* that?"

Jackass winces as my words rain down on him, but when he looks up, there's fire in his eyes. He takes a deep breath like he's trying to calm himself, and I go ballistic because I *want* him to lose it.

"Holly—"

"You and all your perfect friends! Nothing *ever* goes wrong for you! You have no idea what it's like to be different or alone! You—"

"You know *nothing* about me, so shut the fuck up!" he roars, stepping forward and getting right in my face. I can feel his breath as it comes in gasps—his face is bright red, and there's a vein bulging in the middle of his forehead. He looks as if it's taking everything he has not to hit me. He brings a clenched fist as high as his waist, then storms off down the hall, leaving me fuming in his wake.

I wasn't done yet.

I take off after him, breaking into a jog as he whips open the door to Mrs. Gibbs's room and storms inside.

Fuck that asshole; he's going to listen to every damn word I have to—

But Jackass isn't standing there, ready to round on me and continue right where we left off. He's sitting on the floor with a faraway look on his face.

I don't want to hesitate, but the hair on the back of my neck is standing on end. *Something's wrong.*

"Nathan?" I say, taking a tentative step toward him.

His gaze snaps to mine, and there's terror in it, and embarrassment.

"J-j-just g-g-go, H-h-holl-y-y." His stuttered words are barely audible as he lies down on his side on the floor.

I stand there, confused and undecided, flummoxed by his odd behavior. I know he really wants me to leave, but something tells me I shouldn't.

Then his whole body stiffens, and I freeze, unable to look away. He throws his head back, eyes closed, the tendons in his neck standing out rigidly, but he doesn't look to be in pain. He doesn't look to be really conscious either. And then, with a cry, he starts convulsing.

I watch in horror as his body jerks uncontrollably. I'm unable to move. His head hits the floor with a thud, and suddenly, I'm propelled into motion—I slide across the floor and put my knees under his upper body, instinctively turning his head to the side and holding it as his body twists and writhes. As I hold him, I can only see the whites of his eyes, and his lips are turning blue. I don't know who's shaking more violently, him or me.

And then, as suddenly as they began, the convulsions stop. Nathan goes limp against my knees as he gasps for air, his lips regaining a little pink with every breath. He moans a little, but his eyes don't open.

What the hell am I supposed to do now?

I pull out my phone, but I don't have his brother's or his parents' numbers. I'm about to dial 911 when, with a flash of intuition, I reach for his arm, grasping the bracelet on his wrist. Now that I can examine it closely, I see the small caduceus in the bottom corner. I turn it over, and printed on the back in large black letters it says:

Nathan Harris
Epilepsy
ICE: 503-555-2017

I dial the phone number with shaking fingers, and a moment later, a woman answers.

"Hello, Julie speaking."

"Mrs. Harris? This is Holly Ross."

"Yes, how can I help you, dear?" I can hear the confusion in her voice.

"I'm with N-Nathan, and h-he just had a s-seizure." The line goes dead for a moment as we both absorb what I've said.

"Oh my God! Is he all right? Is it over?"

"Y-yes, I think so. He stopped shaking a minute ago."

"How long did it last?" Her tone is urgent.

It felt like an eternity, but I try to make a realistic guess. "Um, a minute or two?"

"Thank God," she says. "Where are you?"

"We're in Mrs. Gibbs's classroom at school."

"I think Evan is still there somewhere. I'll call him, and he'll come and get Nathan. Can you stay with him until Evan gets there?"

"Of course." There's no chance I would leave him alone like this.

"Okay, I'll call Evan now," Mrs. Harris says. "Are you all right?"

"Y-yes. Just . . . a little scared."

"I understand, dear; that's normal. If Nathan wakes up before Evan gets there, he's not going to know what's going on. Just tell him that everything's okay, all right? Thank you for staying with him."

I don't know what to say.

"I'll call Evan now. Sit tight."

"Thank you," I answer, and I disconnect the call.

Nathan's still lying on my knees, but he's beginning to move around a bit. I stroke his hair gently, and his eyes snap open.

"You're okay," I whisper soothingly, but the look on his face tells me he has no idea where he is, maybe even *who* he is . . . and certainly no idea who *I* am.

I continue to stroke his hair and talk softly to him, and he closes his eyes and seems to relax again.

We stay like that for about five minutes until Evan comes barreling through the door.

The sound makes Nathan jump, and he rolls to a sitting position.

Evan's on his knees beside him in a heartbeat, his arm curling protectively around Nathan's back.

"Hey, bro, are you with me?"

Nathan looks up at him and nods very slowly.

"Let's get you home, okay?" Evan asks him, but it's more of a statement than a question.

"Okay," Nathan mumbles, bringing a hand to his forehead. "What happened?"

"We'll talk about that later," Evan answers, putting an arm under Nathan's knees as he stands, lifting him easily. As Nathan lays his head against Evan's chest and closes his eyes again, Evan looks down at him and sighs.

As he stands, Evan looks at me for the first time. His displeasure is easy to read, but he takes a deep breath and says, "Thank you, Holly," as he walks out of the room.

I sit there and shake for I don't know how long. I can't process what just happened. Slowly, my brain begins to unfreeze, and I pull myself off the floor and into one of the desks.

Oh my God, Nathan has epilepsy. I just sit there for a while and let this knowledge seep into my consciousness. And then, I slowly start to think and puzzle it out.

Obviously, he's had it for at least a little while since neither his mom nor Evan were surprised about what happened. If this was the first seizure he ever had, his mom would have flipped and sent EMS, not Evan. His mom *did* seem surprised it happened at school, though. *Maybe he doesn't have seizures at school?* How could that be? I think about Nathan's "vacation" days, and suddenly, it clicks into place. He isn't spending those days playing hooky; he's not in school those days because of having seizures. I wonder if there's some way he knows he's going to have one, and that's why he never has them at school.

Is it possible I'm the first person at school to find out about this? This isn't the kind of thing high school kids would keep quiet. If anyone knew Nathan has epilepsy, it would have been whispered to me as he walked by sometime during that first week of school, probably even the first day. All the juicy gossip on everyone else was passed to me that way. And people would treat him differently. If they were nice, they would just walk on eggshells around him, waiting for the next time he falls down on the floor. If they weren't nice . . . I shudder to think about how cruel kids can be about things like this. *No, there's no way anyone knows.*

So, Nathan has a secret, and it's a huge one. That must be why he lost it when I accused him of being perfect. Everything I know about him is now cast in a different light.

One thing is certain though. He's going to be furious that I know about this. But even with how much it terrified me, I don't wish I hadn't been here. The thought of him having to go through that alone, with nobody knowing where he was and that he was in trouble, and no one being there to comfort him afterward—it's more than I can stand. He's been a jerk, but this afternoon, he was just a boy, lost and frightened. No one should have to go through something like that by themselves.

Chapter Four

Don't judge people. You never know what kind of battle they are fighting.

– Unknown

NATHAN

I jerk awake as the light seeping through the blinds stabs at my aching eyes. *Shit, I must have had a seizure yesterday,* I think as I throw my arm over my face. My arms and legs feel like lead as I haul myself up to lean against the headboard, my head humming with the persistent dull ache that will last for most of the day. I never admit just how messed up I still am the day after a seizure—Mom would flutter around me like a mother hen, and Dad would come up with more tests to run. *Nope, I'm better off keeping those details to myself.*

Leaning my head against the wall, I reach back in my mind for the last thing I can remember. I never know exactly what happens when I have a seizure, so I have to gather the pieces of scattered memory and fit them together like a jigsaw puzzle.

Evan's car. The last thing I remember is Evan waking me up . . . to get out of his car? *What the fuck was I doing—*

The fuzzy images assault me before I can finish my thought—Holly bitching me out, taking off to get my Spanish book, the aura for the seizure, then—

"Mom!" Yelling makes my head throb, but that's nothing compared to the pounding of my heart as I pant for breath.

Oh fuck, *no. No, no, no, no, no, no,* no!

I jump when Mom touches me, barely holding back the panic that threatens to engulf me. My chest is tight, and the lack of air is making me dizzy.

"Nathan, are you—"

"Did I have . . . a seizure at school?" I gasp, gripping her arm as I squeeze my eyes shut.

"Honey, you need to—"

"*Did I?*"

"Yes."

My chest tightens a little more, but I have to keep going. I have to *know*.

"Was I alone?"

Silence.

"Evan!"

I can't open my eyes because the room was spinning when I closed them, but I know Evan's here. He always is.

A heavy sigh. "You were in Gibbs's room. Holly Ross was with you. No one else."

"Holly called me. She must have looked at your bracelet. Evan brought you home."

Holly. Pieces of yesterday fly at me in an unrelenting loop, making my heart pound and my head spin. I'm breathing as fast as I can, but I just can't get enough air.

She knows. Holly knows! Oh God, oh God, everyone *will know!*

"Nathan, you need to calm down." Evan's voice, but I can barely hear him as the world seems to go to pieces around me.

And suddenly, terror explodes at the base of my spine. *No, no, no, no, no, no, no . . .*

"Mmmmom . . ."

Ow! I groan as I roll over, my head pounding and my bladder screaming. I have no idea what's going on, other than if I don't pee soon, I'm going to explode. Sitting up is agony—I'm so exhausted that my legs shake as I stand, and a wave of dizziness hits me. Somehow, I manage to stay on my feet, trying my best not to think of anything but my goal of getting to the bathroom.

The wall holds me up once I reach the doorway, and within seconds, there's a strong arm around my waist and a head poking under my shoulder.

"What are you doing up?" Evan asks, modulating his voice to a whisper when he sees me wince.

"Bathroom," I mumble, and he supports me down the hall and deposits me in the doorway.

"Are you okay to do this by yourself?"

I nod, moaning and clutching the side of my face as the pain throws me off-balance. Evan squeezes my shoulder and closes the door behind him. I do my business in a daze, and when I open the door, Evan's there waiting for me. Normally, I refuse when anyone tries to help me this way, but I'm so bone weary that I gratefully throw my arm over his shoulders and stumble back to my room. I make to fall into my bed, but Evan sits me on the side instead, producing two Tylenol, a PowerBar, and a Gatorade.

"You've got to be hungry. You haven't eaten since lunch on Tuesday."

My hands shake as I reach for the Tylenol and Gatorade, and after I toss them back, Evan thrusts the unwrapped PowerBar into my fist.

"What time is it?"

"Eleven. On Wednesday night."

"Shit," I mutter as my mind starts looking for the pieces.

"Don't think about it."

"What?"

"Until tomorrow. Don't think about what happened. Just go back to sleep, and we'll work on it in the morning. I'll help. I promise."

Work on what? "Evan, what are—"

"I'm serious, Nathan. Finish that and go back to sleep. You can hardly keep your eyes open."

I want to argue with him, but I just don't have the energy. And Evan usually shoots straight with me—if he says not to worry, I trust him.

"Okay," I answer, hoping I can finish chewing before I fall asleep.

I wake with a gasp, my hand flying up to clutch at my head. The pain is blinding, but as much as I want to curl up in a ball, I know my roiling stomach will never tolerate that much movement.

"F-f-f-fuck . . ."

"Nathan?"

Dad. Of course, it's Dad.

"How are you feeling?"

His voice is calm and soothing—his bedside-manner voice, the one he always uses when something's wrong.

"My head. God, it hurts. What happened?"

"You had a seizure two days ago, and then yesterday, you had another one. That's why your headache is worse than usual. I want you to take some codeine and rest for a while longer. Then we can talk about what happened."

Jesus, two days in a row? That hasn't happened since freshman year. No wonder I feel like I've been hit by a train.

"Son?"

I open my eyes slowly, and in the semi-darkness of my room, Dad's concerned gaze meets mine.

"There you are. Let's take the edge off that pain."

I raise myself onto my elbow, still gripping my head, and swallow the pills Dad hands me with a lukewarm glass of water.

As I lie back down, Dad grips my shoulder—he knows better than to go anywhere near my head. "Just relax and try to go back to sleep. Every-thing's going to be fine."

Something's really not right, but I'm hurting so much that I can't focus enough to figure it out, and I really don't want to. Just trying not to vomit is taking everything I have, and as soon as the fuzziness from the codeine hits me, I pass out again.

～

"Nathan."

"Nathan, it's time to wake up."

I roll to my side, curling up and pressing my palm to my forehead. The ache is there, like I've had a seizure, but I can't remember . . .

Holly.

The last three days, or what I can remember of them, come flooding back as my stomach rolls and my chest solidifies.

No...

"Son, try to stay calm. If you start to hyperventilate again, you could have another seizure—"

"I went to school today, Nate. No one knows anything. Holly must not have told anyone."

"What?" Evan's words break through my escalating panic attack.

"No one knows. It was just a normal day."

I uncover my eyes to find Evan inches from my face, kneeling on the floor next to my bed. "Are you sure?"

He exhales sharply and smiles. "I'm sure. I was there all day, and no one said anything. You know there would have been talk if anyone knew."

"Was Holly there?"

"Yes. She didn't talk to me, but she looked . . . confused. I think she was looking for you."

I roll onto my back and press my palms into my eye sockets.

"How are you feeling?"

Like my world just ended. But I know that's *not* what Dad wants to hear.

"Hungry. Tired. But my head is much better than when you gave me the codeine."

"That's good," Dad says, massaging my shoulder. I open my eyes, and Evan hasn't moved, but now I see Dad on his left and Mom on his right, hovering over me.

"Can you eat something?" Mom asks, the hope and the need to take care of me unmistakable in her tone.

"Yeah." My thoughts are still whirling, wondering how the hell this happened and why the whole school doesn't know yet.

Mom lifts a tray from the floor, holding my usual post-seizure fare: peanut butter and jelly and a Gatorade. If I've slept for a long time or the headache is bad enough, I often wake up nauseated, but PB and J is almost always a sure thing.

Ev stays where he is, and Mom perches on the edge of the bed while I eat, but Dad remains standing—a harbinger of the questions to come. Mom holds back until I'm on the last bite of my sandwich, but just barely.

"What happened?"

My head is still aching, and all I want to do is hide from that very question. *How did I have a seizure with no warning?*

"Nathan?"

I close my eyes and huff out a breath. *There's no way they're gonna let me avoid this.*

"I don't know. I got . . . angry. *Really* angry. And I went to get my book, and then the aura for the seizure started."

"You had no other warning?" Dad asks, absently studying the books on my shelf, but I know he's much more focused than he looks.

"No. Nothing."

"So what did you do?" Evan asks, his words clipped.

"I only had a moment, so . . . I just lay down on the floor."

"Alone."

It's not a question, but I answer anyway.

"Yeah." *Oh fuck, here it comes.*

"Why would you do that? You know what could happen if no one's with you," Mom says.

Evan huffs out a breath as he stares daggers at me. Mom doesn't get it, but *he* does.

"He doesn't give a shit about that. All he cares about is that no one finds out."

Anger flairs in my chest. "What did you want me to do, Ev? Walk out into the hallway so everyone could *watch*?"

"Well, if you hit your head on the floor and die, then what will it matter who knows and who doesn't!" He rages at me, getting to his feet.

"Boys!" Dad's sharp tone cuts between us, but we're still glaring, breathing hard.

Dad catches my eye, and I look away, crossing my arms as if that will ward off the lecture.

"Nathan, you know better than that. Evan's right—you could have hit your head; you could have choked—what if no one had found you? You should be grateful Holly was there to save you from your own stupidity."

"Grateful? Now the whole fucking school's gonna know!"

"Language!" Mom snaps, but I don't care. My mind is back on the consequences of what happened as I drop my head into my hand and take deep breaths.

"I *told* you! She didn't tell anyone!" Evan yells.

"Yeah? Well, that doesn't make any sense! She *hates* me, and now she knows something about me that would set the whole school talking! Why *wouldn't* she tell *every*one?"

"I don't know! All I know is that no one knew anything today. I watched and I listened, and it was just like every other day."

"Maybe she's waiting to do it in front of me."

"Nathan! I can't imagine this girl would do something like that. She sounded so worried for you on the phone," Mom says, covering my hand with hers.

I shoot Evan a look, and he shakes his head a little. We both know there's no point in trying to explain to Mom how cruel teenagers can be, and even if I did manage to convince her, it would just make her more upset.

"Son, I think you need to rest this evening so you'll be ready to go back to school tomorrow. I'm sure you can talk to this girl and sort it all out."

Dad's got a little bit more of a clue than Mom but not much. But he's right—my head still hurts and I have no energy, and tomorrow is gonna be the day from hell.

"Sure. I think I'll just lie here and watch TV for a while."

Mom looks pacified; Dad, concerned but willing to give me space; and Evan? Evan shakes his head and walks out of the room. *He'll be back before long.*

I channel-surf for a while, but my thoughts keep going back to what happened, and I have to fight to keep the panic down. *Why the hell did I have a seizure with no warning? Will it happen again? Is Holly going to tell everyone?*

Things had been going so well. I hadn't felt afraid like this since it all began—when I didn't know what was happening to me. The thought of living with that uncertainty again sends a shiver down my spine. I honestly don't know if I can handle it.

I startle as the hulking form of my brother blocks out the light from the hallway.

"That really *was* a dumbfuck thing to do, you know."

I glare at him, but I know better than to say anything. He's already pissed, and I'm not feeling up to a rumble right now.

"Just . . . keep your phone in your pocket from now on, okay? I know you used to—"

"I still do. But I had already put it in my coat before I saw Holly, and I stomped off without thinking."

"She laid into you about Megan, didn't she?"

I can feel my cheeks heating as Evan stares me down.

"Speaking of dumbfuck things to do—"

"Honest to God, Ev, I had no idea that's what he wanted them for."

Evan crosses his arms and raises an eyebrow at me.

"Seriously! He's got a crush on her—everyone knows that! I thought he wanted them . . . you know, for himself."

Evan snorts out a laugh. "If that's what he's looking for, he'd be better off with *Playboy*."

"No kidding."

"I'm sorry you're having such a shitty week."

"It's probably going to get shittier," I tell him, my thoughts returning to Holly and the much bigger problem I have to face tomorrow.

But Evan just grins at me. "We'll figure something out. I don't think Holly's waiting until you come back to say something. If she were gonna do it, she would have done it already."

I shake my head, staring down at the blanket. "I don't get it."

"Try to get some sleep," Evan says as he turns to leave. I want to tell him that's all I've done for the past two days, but I know I'm not gonna last much longer. Sadly, it's probably better this way. If I wasn't wiped out from the seizures, I'd probably spend the whole night freaking out.

CHAPTER FIVE

A secret is a kind of promise . . . it can also be a prison.

– Jennifer Lee Carrell

NATHAN

"Nate, get up. Being late isn't gonna make your day any better." *Fucking Evan. Does he have to remind me before my eyes are even open that it's gonna be a crappy day?*

I haul myself up to sit on the side of the bed, and I actually feel pretty good, physically. The heaviness in my limbs is gone, and my head sort of hurts, but not really. The tight ball of worry in my chest won't let me take a full breath, though, and as I get ready, I keep dropping things.

When I finally make it to the kitchen, I can feel the looks shooting like laser beams behind my back between my family members, and I bite my lip, trying to contain my irritation. The juice glass slips from my trembling fingers, and suddenly, I'm surrounded.

"I'll clean that up, honey."

"Nathan, was that—"

"*No*, it wasn't." I grate the words out, turning to face the concerned expression of my father. "I'm fi—"

"He's nervous." Evan, the wonder douche of helpfulness, blurts out. "He's still worried Holly's going to tell everyone his secret."

I whirl around, ready to lay into douche-boy, but I find myself chest to chest with my father.

"I want you to take some Xanax this morning, and carry some with you for later, in case you need it. Stress could bring on another seizure, and that's the last thing you need right now."

"Dad—"

"I'm not asking, son," he says, grabbing another glass for me and pouring the juice with his surgeon-steady hand. He retrieves the pills from the cabinet, holding one out to me and dropping two more into a little pill container. *Dammit, I hate taking meds at school.*

"Fine." I pop the pill in my mouth, slam the juice, and swipe the pill container off the counter. The kitchen is stifling, and if I don't get out of here, I'm gonna say things I'll regret.

Douche and I ride to school in silence—my anger and frustration surround me like volcanic rock, ready to blow at the slightest disturbance, and I'm pretty sure he can feel it.

I'm out of the car the second it stops moving, but I slow down as the school building looms in front of me. For the first time, there will be someone here who isn't obligated, through love or the law, to keep my secret—the secret I've had since the summer before my freshman year of high school, and that, with my family's help, I've guarded and kept flawlessly. *Oh God, is today finally the day?*

My breath starts coming in shallow pants, and I stop at the bottom of the steps, trying to get a grip. *Breathe. Maybe Evan's right, and she's not gonna tell anyone. You're only hurting yourself by freaking out, and you're putting yourself at risk for another seizure.*

I draw in as deep a breath as I can and climb the steps, hoping to make it to my locker without talking to anyone.

But every look makes me paranoid. Every glance, every stare from a girl who's probably just checking me out—every time, that little voice in my head screams, *do they know?*

"Have a nice vacation, Harris?"

I look up to find one of the sophomore boys, whose name escapes me, grinning and winking at me.

"I was actually sick this time, dumbass." I push past him, ignoring the shocked expression on his face.

As I walk into homeroom, Holly's gaze meets mine, but she quickly looks down and away. My cheeks heat, and I swallow thickly . . . *But wait, is she blushing?* Why the hell is *she* blushing when *I'm* the one who was drooling on the floor in front of *her?*

I sit down, my heart thudding a mile a minute in my chest. She could do it now—tell everyone—and there's not a damn thing I could do about it. *Look normal. Breathe normal. Don't draw attention to yourself.*

"Hey, Harris! What the fuck, man? Where've you been for the last two days?" Chris leans over the back of his seat, fixing me with a curious stare.

My stomach churns as I stare back, considering my options. I could tell him I was on "vacation," but I usually only do that for one day at a time, and it'll likely lead to more questions. *Considering that right now I feel like I'm gonna throw up . . .*

"Stomach bug," I answer, wiping the sweat from my brow.

Out of the corner of my eye, I see Holly's head snap up, and my heart flies, but she merely stares at me, her expression unreadable.

"Ew," Chris says, recoiling a bit. "I think I'd rather be at school."

Ryan's been listening the whole time, and he gives me a sympathetic look. I nod back, and that icky feeling flutters through my chest. I hate lying to Ryan, but it's necessary—just like all this other shit I do.

I missed so much being gone two days that school distracts me for most of the morning. That is, until I walk into chemistry.

Holly's already sitting there, fidgeting with her notebook and doing anything but looking in my direction. Like this morning, she looks . . . nervous. *Two days ago, she ripped my fucking head off, but now, she can't meet my eyes? Unless . . . oh fuck, is she worried I'm gonna have another seizure right here in the classroom?* My heart sinks as the familiar feelings overtake me—I'm a time bomb. Just like my family, she thinks I'm made of glass now, ready to shatter at any second.

As I sit down, I squeeze my eyes shut, *hating* how it feels to be weak, different, and *alone*. I slam my binder open, giving what rein I can to the anger coursing through me. I never wanted this—not at all, but *certainly* not here.

"Um . . . Nathan?"

I hear her, but I'm still breathing heavily and trying not to throw my binder across the room. *You should be nice to her—she's holding your life at this school in her hands,* the voice of reason whispers in my ear, but I can barely hear it over the thud of my heart.

"Yeah," I answer, staring straight ahead.

"Are . . . are you all right now?" she asks timidly, and my anger morphs to confusion. I just can*not* figure this girl out. One minute, she's all shy and quiet, and the next, she's glaring at me in reproach or chewing me out. *And why do I even fucking care?* She hangs out with the misfit crowd, so I shouldn't even be talking to her.

"I'm fine." I push the words out through gritted teeth.

"I was worried when—"

"*I said I'm fine,*" I repeat, and she pulls back as if I've slapped her.

"Oh," she whispers and turns back to her notes, letting her hair fall over her face.

My fingers curl into a fist on top of my thigh. I want to stand up and scream how *not* fine I really am, how much I hate this situation I'm in, and how scared I am that she's going to ruin me with a slip of her tongue, if she hasn't already. But I can't do any of that. As usual, all I can do is sit here and pretend. I close my eyes and focus on my breathing as Mr. Metcalf starts his lecture, and within a few minutes, I'm able to take notes and push it all aside for the rest of the period.

As soon as the bell rings, she scurries out of the classroom before I can even begin to come up with what to say to her, and I feel like I blew it. But the worst part is, thanks to my wonderful conversation skills, I still don't know if she's told anyone. *What if she didn't tell the whole school? What if she told one or two people, and it's slowly spreading around?*

By the end of the day, I'm positively twitchy, so I pop the Xanax Dad gave me on the off chance it'll actually calm me the fuck down. Ryan falls into step with me as I head for the parking lot. Usually, that's a good thing. Ryan and I have been friends since riding a two-wheeler was cool, and we've always been close . . . or at least, we used to be. Now, we're as close as I can let anyone get who doesn't know my secret.

"Hey, you okay?" he asks, sounding honestly concerned.

"Yeah, I've just been sick."

"So I heard. Did you really take those pictures for Chris?"

And here's another country heard from. "Yes," I answer tightly.

"Dude, why? Pranks are one thing, but that shit was way over the line."

"I didn't know about the captions, all right? If I'd known he was going to humiliate her like that—"

"What, and the pictures weren't humiliating enough? Whose idea was it? I didn't hear about it, so I'm betting it wasn't yours."

"No."

"Why do you do his dirty work, man? I've never understood—"

"It was a bad idea, okay? I didn't think it through."

"Tell me next time. I'll help you think it through."

My chest gets that empty feeling as I look at him. I'm so accustomed to it that usually I hardly notice, but today I'm . . . scared, and I wish I could say that to just one person. But I can't. It's bad enough I have to deal with Holly's accidental knowledge.

"Yeah, sure."

He gives me a piercing look, but he doesn't say anything more. *I wonder how much of my bullshit he actually sees through.*

I'm nearly to Evan's car when I see Holly standing beside hers, and it's as if my brain makes some kind of self-preservation decision without my consent. I veer to the right, arriving just in time to put my hand over hers so she can't open her door.

"Who did you tell?" I glare at her, every fiber of my being demanding an answer.

"What do you mean?" She takes a step back from me.

"I said, *who did you tell*?" I get right up in her face so she flinches and jumps back.

"No one!" she squeaks.

"No fucking way."

"Honest, I haven't said anything!" she reiterates, her eyes wide.

"Jesus, you really don't have a clue, do you?"

She looks at me blankly.

I sigh in annoyance. "You've got the hottest fucking piece of gossip in the whole school on the tip of your tongue, and yet you say nothing. *Nathan Harris* has epilepsy. Let's all watch the freak-boy have a seizure," I add sarcastically.

When I look up, her hand is covering her mouth.

"Why would I tell anyone that?" she whispers.

"Why wouldn't you?" I counter her words, staring at her with open hostility. "Because that's what high school kids do! You're supposed to tell everyone you know how weak I am and how you saw me out of control. Or you're supposed to tell me you'll keep quiet if I do something for you, like take you to the prom or some shit. What you're *not* supposed to do is stare at me like I'm crazy when I'm telling you what a normal girl would do in your position!"

"I would never do any of those things."

"Why?"

"Because it's none of their business," she says quietly.

I'm sure my mouth is hanging open. I stare at her for a full minute, trying to understand this sometimes brazen, sometimes bashful creature before me, but none of it makes sense, and I'm so tired of dealing with all of this today.

I turn tail and stomp off to Evan's car in a huff, throwing my bag into the back seat and myself into the front seat forcefully. As I slam the door, Evan glances over at me, grimacing. "I take it that didn't go well?"

"No . . . yes . . . fuck, I don't know!" I growl in frustration, flinging my head back against the headrest. "That girl makes no sense to me at all!"

"Is she gonna say anything?"

"No."

"What did you have to do to buy her silence?"

"Nothing! That's the whole fucking problem! She told me she wasn't going to tell anyone, pretty much because it's the right thing to do. Who the hell *does* that?"

Evan is silent for a moment, considering. "Do you believe her?"

"I guess?" I reply, shrugging. "What choice do I have?"

46

Evan sits quietly for another few minutes, and I can almost see the hamster running on the wheel. The little guy seems to be getting tired. "What, Evan? I can smell the brain cells burning."

"Well . . . what if you gave her something she didn't ask for?"

I sigh heavily. It's been a rotten, stressful day. I'm tired and my head hurts, and my jackass brother wants to play the riddle game rather than just tell me what I should do. *Perfect.*

I cover my face with my hands, massaging my forehead with my fingertips. "Could you just fucking tell me what you think I should do? I really can't handle the twenty-questions method of getting to your opinion right now."

"What if you went out with her?"

I drop my hands and turn to stare at him in open-mouthed astonishment. "*What?*"

"She's cute and she has a nice body. Go out with her. Convince her you like her, and date her for a while."

"That is the batshit craziest idea you've ever had! Why would I want to do that?"

"Think about it, Nathan. If she's your girlfriend, she's not going to want to do anything to hurt you. And if you're with her all the time, you'll know she's keeping quiet."

"But—"

"Come on, when was the last time you dated a girl? And I'm not talking about that shit in the janitor's closet with Amber Watson; I mean *really* dated a girl?"

"That's not the point—"

"You're right, it's *not* the point, but dating once in a while couldn't hurt your image, and getting laid would certainly improve your disposition."

I snort and shake my head. This whole conversation is completely insane, and yet for some reason, I feel the need to continue to argue with him.

"She'd never go out with me. She hates my guts. This whole thing started with her calling me out as a colossal asshole for what I helped Chris do to Megan."

"She doesn't hate you. It may take a bit of doing to convince her to like you, but I think you're already on your way."

"And how do you figure that?"

"Dude, give your big brother a little credit for experience with girls. You've already got her sympathy. And she knows something about you that almost no one else does."

"I know," I say through clenched teeth. "That's the fucking *problem*."

"I *know*, dumbass, but if you'd just shut up for a minute and *listen* to what I'm trying to tell you—"

I cross my arms like a petulant toddler, but I remain silent.

Evan nods his approval. "You can use what she knows to get her to like you. Tell her something related to your epilepsy that makes you different from everyone else. Girls like things that are different. And if it gets you more of her sympathy, too, that's even better."

"I don't *want* her sympathy," I mutter, scowling.

"No, what you want is for her to keep your secret for you, and now you need to decide how far you're willing to go to see that it happens. I would think a little sympathy and the potential to get between her legs isn't too high a price to pay."

"I don't know, Ev. It doesn't seem . . . well . . . right somehow."

"Look, I'm not suggesting you intentionally hurt her or anything. Just . . . keep her busy for a while until the novelty of this wears off. I'm sure she'll get bored with you after a while and decide to move on, and that way she won't be mad at you, so she'll still keep your secret."

"Why is she gonna get bored with me?"

"Because she's a smart girl, and you're a butthead."

My fist flashes out and catches his bicep, but I think it hurts my knuckles more than it hurts his arm. He just chuckles and shakes his head.

Now that I think about it, maybe it *isn't* such a bad idea. Holly *would* be loyal to me if we were dating, and it would get Amber off my back. She's been pining for me for two years now and making her way around the block while she waits. But I'm not gonna hit that—not ever. And Holly *is* kinda cute. She has those big brown eyes and long hair to match—I have a thing for brunettes . . .

"Hey, lover boy, you workin' the details already?"

I startle and look over to find Evan staring at me, a wide grin plastered across his face.

"Fuck you, Evan." Brilliant response, but I'm distracted right now.

"Just think about it? I really think this is the best way to get what you want."

"I'll think about it."

CHAPTER SIX

To know a man's secrets is to discover his weakness, and thus control his will.

– Jeremy Aldana

HOLLY

I watch Jackass's retreating back, still trying to catch my breath. He flew over here like an avenging angel, eyes glowing like some freaky Halloween ghoul, the red tints in his hair seeming to intensify with his fury. *Jesus, that was hot.*

But as my heart slows down, it starts to hurt. *Did he really think I would tell everyone or try to blackmail him? What kind of shallow bitch does he think I am? Is this really what he's used to dealing with?* Resting Bitch Face comes to mind immediately—yup, this *is* what he's used to dealing with. That skank would have his favorite hoodie, his class ring, and his dick on a keychain if she knew his secret.

It's sad, really.

God, I'm so messed up right now. I'm still furious with him over the pictures, but every time I want to march up to him and tear him a new one, I just keep seeing a defenseless boy convulsing on the floor at the mercy of his own body. I Googled epilepsy as soon as I got home that day, but there are so many different types and so much information, and I have no idea what he has. *Where was he for two days? Was he sick like he said, or was it seizure-related? Was he so afraid I'd tell everyone that he stayed away from school?*

Fuck. It doesn't matter. What he did to Megan was despicable, and his own problems are no excuse. As I start my car, Evan drives by in front of me, and Jackass is slumped down in the passenger seat, looking miserable. The pang of sadness that pierces my chest just makes me want to kick his ass for ever showing me that he's not perfect. *Damn him.*

"You ready?" Megan asks, her books clutched in her arms to head for Monday morning homeroom. It's been a rough few days for her, but what Jackass and Ken-doll did was so over the top that most of the girls have been sympathetic, and even some of the guys. But not the popular crowd, of course.

As I shut my locker, Jackass materializes beside me.

"Holly?"

I close my eyes for a second, debating, then I hear Megan's angry huff beside me. I turn away from Jackass and head down the hall.

"Holly!" he calls, and I glance over my shoulder, starting to walk faster as he struggles to catch up.

"Holly, wait! Please?"

I slow my pace, but I don't turn to look at him. "What do you want, Nathan?"

"Can we talk?" he asks, bending down to peer at my face to try to get me to meet his eyes.

"We *are* talking." It seems my fucked-up head has decided that sarcasm is the order of the day.

"Two minutes," he says, dropping his gaze to the floor and then looking back up at me, but his chin isn't quite as high as before.

I sigh heavily, but he continues to stare into my eyes, his jawline soft, his posture submissive—almost defeated.

"Please."

Dammit.

As I turn to face him, I see Megan's shocked expression a few feet ahead of me.

"I'll be along in a minute, Megan," I tell her, and the hurt in her eyes is unmistakable. *Great.*

Anger flares in my chest, but I follow Jackass into the little hallway that leads to the art room. As he turns around, he runs a hand through that glorious hair. I know it's likely a nervous habit, but the Sultan of Sarcasm who seems to be in charge of my head today plants the idea that he did it because he knew it'd drive me wild. *Asshole.*

"What?" I snap at him, but he just stares at the floor for a moment.

"I . . . I wanted you to know I'm not the one who edited those pictures of Megan."

I snort and shake my head.

"You don't believe me?"

"Why would I? You knew what they were when I showed them to you."

Jackass's cheeks turn red, and he jams his hands into his pockets.

"See? Guilty as charged."

"Fuck!" This time his hand rakes through his hair more forcefully. "All right, dammit! I took the pictures and gave them to Chris, but I didn't know what he was going to do with them. I had no idea he was going to humiliate her like that, or I wouldn't have given them to him."

He looks up at me, and I can feel my eyebrows reaching for my hairline. *Is it possible he really didn't know?* "Well, what *did* you think he was going to do with them?"

"Um . . . well . . . I thought they were for, um . . . *personal* use."

I narrow my eyes at him, thinking hard. *Personal*—"Ew! That's disgusting!"

"Yeah, but guys do stuff like that, and no one would have ever known. What Chris did was . . . awful."

I do a double take as all the horrible things I've ever heard him say run through my mind. "Is it more awful than the way you guys have shamed girls in the past? What the hell's the difference, Nathan?"

Jackass heaves a sigh and closes his eyes, his brows pulled tight in a wince. "Look—fuck, Holly, I don't want to argue with you! I just—I'm sorry, okay? I never meant to hurt anyone."

Dammit, he really does *look sorry.* I want to hate him for this right now, but my resolve is fading fast. Truth tends to wash away things like that.

"I'm not the one you should be apologizing to. You should apologize to Megan."

"You're kidding," he says, looking at me as if I've just asked him to eat shit. *Well, I am asking him to eat crow . . .*

"No, I'm not. She's the one you hurt here, not me."

"Well, you're the one who went ballistic on me . . ."

Now it's my turn to flush with embarrassment. "I'm sorry about that. I shouldn't have—"

"Are you sorry because you saw me have a seizure or because you chewed me out?" he asks, looking resigned.

"They're not really related. I'm sorry because I made assumptions about you, and I shouldn't have. You were right; I don't know anything about you."

"Do you feel bad for me?"

"I don't know," I answer. I guess in some ways I should because of the seizures, but nobody likes being pitied. The look of shock on his face makes me pause. "Should I?"

"Um . . . no. I guess not," he says, searching my face.

"What?"

"You might be the first person I've ever met who doesn't," he answers, looking more vulnerable than I've ever seen him.

It's too much because, right now, all I want to do is pull him into my arms and shield him. I cross my arms in front of my books to prevent them from winding around him.

"Will you apologize to Megan?"

"Holly—"

The bell rings, and it's as if we've both been doused with cold water. He straightens up, and I grip my books tighter.

"Think about it, Nathan. If you're truly sorry . . ." I say before I turn away, leaving him behind with both of our truths for company.

Jackass doesn't talk to me in chemistry, but the silence feels thoughtful, not hostile. Ever since Tuesday, the vibe I feel between us is different—the heat is still there, but the distance and the anger don't seem to be. Regardless, I have nothing to say to him. He hurt my friend, and he's obviously not sorry, so there we are.

As I'm packing up my books after my last class, Megan walks up to me in a daze.

"Are you okay?" I ask, only half-paying attention.

"Nathan . . ."

Okay, now she has my *full* attention.

"Yes?"

"Nathan apologized to me for taking the pictures."

"He did what?" I can't have heard her right. There's absolutely *no way* Jackass actually did what I asked him to do. It's inconceivable.

"He apologized to me. He said it was wrong, and he was sorry, and he wouldn't do anything like that again."

"Shut the fuck up!" The Gothlet pipes up from Megan's other side. "Was he high?"

"No," Megan answers, still spaced out. "He was just . . . nice. Sweet, even."

It takes me a second to realize it, but that pull on my cheeks is my own doing—I'm grinning so widely it's almost painful.

A locker bangs open three down from mine, and the smile freezes on my face as Jackass's eyes widen. His bushy eyebrows draw together, and I nearly choke on thin air as my heart seems to warm and expand. I close my eyes and drop my chin as heat sears my cheeks.

I bet he thinks that smile was for him. Well, it was, but he wasn't supposed to see it. *Oh fuck it all, I can't believe he actually acted like a human today.*

I leave with Megan and The Gothlet, but as we turn the corner, I catch Jackass staring into his locker, a goofy little smirk on his face. *What the hell is he up to?*

~

When I walk into chemistry the next day, Jackass is already sitting there leafing through his notebook.

"Hi."

I'm lowering myself into my chair when the sound of his voice from beside me drives all thought from my head, and I thump down hard on the seat, nearly tipping over backward.

Jackass grasps my forearm, but he lets go as if I'm on fire the second he realizes he's touching me. My skin prickles. I can feel every individual hair jump back up as if they're reaching for him, so I rub my hand over the spot self-consciously.

Did he just? And then he—I stare at him dumbly, still rubbing my arm until he glances down, and his cheeks turn a delicious shade of crimson.

"Usually when someone says hi, you say hi back," he says, his tone sharp.

Well, yes, but not when that person has never said hi before and they're acting all weird and confusing and you're attracted to them but they're an asshole and—

"Hi."

I stare at him, trying to adapt to this new version of Jackass who offers social pleasantries instead of insults, and his handsome face morphs into a scowl.

"Fuck," he mutters under his breath. "I'm not gonna fall apart, you know."

"What?"

"I'm still me. I'm the same person you sat next to before."

No, you're not, because now you're talking to me. "Before what?"

"Before . . . last Tuesday. It's not gonna happen again. I just wanted you to know that." It sounds like something good, but as I look into his eyes, all I see is sadness.

"Not ever?"

"Not here," he says firmly, ending the conversation.

The silence stretches on as we both stare at our desks, so I break it with what's been ricocheting around my head for the last eighteen hours.

"You apologized to Megan."

"Uh . . . yeah," he answers, but his gaze pins me in silent accusation. "I told you I was sorry."

"Yes, you did, but I didn't think you actually meant it."

"Maybe you don't know everything there is to know about me." He fires back at me, and it gets my dander up.

"I think I know more than most."

He tenses, and if humans could smell fear, I know this place would be reeking right now. He swallows thickly as his hands curl into fists. "Yes," he says quietly, and I know I've royally fucked up his attempt to have a semi-normal conversation with me. *Shit.*

I want to fix it somehow, but it's like I've walked into one of my mom's flowerbeds. Even if I take the shortest path out, I'll still be trampling things, so I just sit there until Mr. Metcalf starts boring us with his lecture.

Jackass steers clear of me for the rest of the day and the next one too. I want to say something to him, but I can't get, *"I'm sorry I assumed you were going to be a dick, but your moods change so quickly it makes my head spin,"* to sound quite right in my head.

So I try to distract myself. We have a big English paper due next week. *Maybe if I go to the library, I can kill two birds with one stone.*

The room is empty when I enter, but I honestly didn't expect anyone to be here. Most kids fly out of the building like bats out of hell within five minutes of the final bell—*God forbid any more knowledge get into their heads than is absolutely necessary.*

I peruse the shelves, considering just reading something for fun, but dammit, that paper isn't gonna write itself. I locate a copy of *Dr. Faustus* and start looking for the similarities to Shakespeare.

Just as I'm really getting into what I'm reading, the library door swings open, and Jackass struts in like he owns the place. He freezes and his eyes widen as his gaze falls on me.

"Hi," I say, trying not to grin at how flustered he is.

"What are you doing here?"

I furrow my eyebrows. "Studying. This is the library, you know, right?"

He smirks and looks down. Then I'm the flustered one when his bright blue eyes glint with mischief. "You're getting better at the saying hello thing."

"I've been practicing."

He walks across the room, setting his bag on the table catty-corner to where I'm sitting.

"What are *you* doing here?" *Do boys actually do homework?* I think I may have caught a rare event in the wilds of high school.

"I'm waiting for Evan to finish at football," he says as he sits, pulling out his physics book.

"How long is his practice?"

"Until five," Jackass answers. "I usually have plenty of time to get my work done."

"That's a long time to be stuck here. Why don't you just drive yourself in on the days he has practice?" *He's a doctor's son—surely he has his own car.*

He stares at his book for a long moment as a blush slowly colors his cheeks. Oh *shit*.

"You don't drive, do you," I say, but it's not really a question.

He bites his lip and closes his eyes, and he takes two deep breaths before he speaks. "I don't have my license," he says, playing with the edge of his book. "I'm not allowed to drive."

I stare at him, trying to comprehend what just happened. He could have told me he was lazy today and didn't want to drive. He could have told me it was none of my business. Hell, he could have blown me off entirely and changed the subject.

But he didn't.

Instead, he told me something that no one probably knows. The *second* thing I know about him that no one else does.

"Is that because—"

"Yes. It's because . . . I have epilepsy." He says it quietly, as if the words taste funny in his mouth. I wonder if he's ever uttered them out loud before, other than when he yelled them at me.

"I'm sorry; I shouldn't have followed you that day—"

"It's okay; don't be sorry. I never thanked you for what you did. I shouldn't be alone when . . . that happens. I could choke or hit my head—"

"You *did* hit your head," I tell him, and Jackass buries his hand in his hair. "That was when I—"

"What?" he asks, looking as if he could vomit any second, and my heart squeezes painfully in my chest.

"That was when I held your head on my knees . . . until it stopped."

"I can't do this," he mutters, and he's up and out the door before I can even blink.

I stare again, but this time at the empty space where he was. *What the hell just happened?* It seems like I'm thinking that almost every time we see each other now—*will I ever understand a single thing this boy does?*

But I do know one thing.

For some reason, he's actually trying to talk to me.

CHAPTER SEVEN

Nothing makes us so lonely as our secrets.

– Paul Tournier

HOLLY

The next day in chemistry, we exchange hellos, but the look on Jackass's face seems to say, "Please don't talk to me," so I don't.

At the end of the day, I'm not sure what to do. I've checked out *Dr. Faustus*, so I don't really need to go to the library, but I still want to. I want to see if he'll be there again and if he'll talk to me. *You shouldn't be doing this*. Yeah, but it's just talking. *What can it possibly hurt?*

When I get to the library, it's empty, and instead of choosing the front and center table, I sit at the one in the back of the room and off to the left, a little behind the last bookshelf. That way, I'll be able to see him if he comes in, but he can ignore me without any trouble if he chooses to.

About five minutes later, I hear the door open, so I make a concerted effort not to look up. The rustle of his bag pauses for a good thirty seconds, but then it resumes and gets closer until the flutter of my heart tells me he's standing over me.

"Hey," he says, and I pretend to be startled, but I can't seem to maintain the pretense when I meet his eyes.

"Hey."

"Change of scenery today?" he asks, thumbs hooked in his pockets, relaxed but somehow, not.

"I thought maybe you wanted to work alone."

"So you sat back here?"

"Yeah."

His eyebrows furrow, and he cocks his head to the side, and whatever wasn't relaxed in him seems to let go a bit.

"Do you mind if I sit with you?"

Heat surges through my chest, fluttering over my lungs and singeing my throat. *He wants to talk to me! And he's waiting for an answer.*

"N-no . . . I mean, yes, you can." My cheeks warm as I stumble over my words.

He sits, but he doesn't pull out his books.

"Were you as bored in chemistry as I was?"

I miss a beat, not expecting him to start a casual conversation, but just as it's getting awkward, I recover.

"Totally. How is memorizing a bunch of chemical reactions *ever* going to help us in real life?"

"And Metcalf found it *so* fascinating."

"You know, I just thought of a real-life application—meth. If you planned to set up your own meth lab, today's lecture would be vital information."

Jackass laughs, and my breath catches as his face is transformed. I've seen him laugh when he's with the boys, but what's happening now isn't even close to the same.

"Do you think that's why he was so into it? He's actually the Walter White of Tillamook?"

We both crack up, and after that, the conversation flows easily to the latest rumors about the other teachers. It's a small school, so everyone knows everything about everyone else's business, and Jackass is a fountain of knowledge about it all since he grew up here.

He looks so . . . different when he's sitting here talking to me. He's relaxed in a way I've never seen, and believe me, I've been observing him quite closely for *weeks*.

"Do you really think he's boning her?" I ask, and Jackass makes this gasp-laugh sound as his look turns incredulous.

"What did you say?"

"Um, I asked if you thought he was boning her." *What did I do to make him look at me like that?*

His eyes sparkle with mirth as he grins at me, and my heart beats a staccato rhythm in my chest. "That's what I *thought* you said. I've never heard a girl use that word."

Is he serious? He looks serious. But I guess, now that I think about it, it's not really a word most girls would use, or if they do, not in front of a guy. I'm not really a flirt, but damn, he set me up so perfectly. I wonder . . .

"Well, I guess I'm not your average girl."

"No, you're certainly not," Nathan says matter-of-factly, shaking his head. And then he freezes, and his eyes widen a little. He looks down to hide his surprise at his own words, but he can't hide the blush that spreads from his cheeks to the tips of his ears.

We both jump as the door swings open, and Evan pokes his head in.

"Nathan, what the fu— Oh! Hi, Holly."

"Hi," I answer as Nathan scrambles out of his chair.

"I'll see you tomorrow," he says curtly.

"Here?" I ask, completely forgetting in my oh-my-God-I-think-he-just-flirted-back haze about the dozen other places I'll see him before the end of the day.

"Uh . . . yeah," he answers as he walks out the door behind Evan.

And I realize with a start that in my head, he's not Jackass anymore—he's not even Gorgeous; he's Nathan.

The next few days seem to fall into a pattern. During school, Nathan doesn't talk to me overly much, but his smiles are a little freer, and he never says anything nasty. Yet every afternoon when we meet in the library, we talk like we're the best of friends. He doesn't even pretend he's going to do homework, and my English paper was handed in days ago—we just sit down and talk as if we've been doing it forever.

He loves college basketball and 30 Seconds to Mars. He hates the chicken patties the caf serves on Thursdays and the way Mr. Harper grinds his chalk into the board. He can't wait to see *The Dark Knight* and the Summer Olympics. Movies and music, rumors and dirty jokes, but never once does he ask about my family or past, nor does he talk about his. It's intimate but superficial at the same time, and that's probably good because out in the real world, we move in different circles, and I know it can't be any more than this.

At least, I don't think so.

"Come on, Nathan, they sucked. They could have replaced Hayden Christensen with a two-by-four, and the acting would have been the same."

"But, Yoda fighting with a lightsaber! That right there makes it all worthwhile."

"The romance was so cheesy though."

"It's *Star Wars*! Who cares about the romance?" Nathan exclaims, exasperated, and I can't help but laugh.

"Boys." I huff, shaking my head. "It doesn't matter what shit gets destroyed. If Padme and Anakin don't get it on, then there's no Luke and no Leia for the *real Star Wars* movies."

"You're hopeless," Nathan declares, mirroring my posture.

"I guess we'll just have to agree to disagree," I tell him, not backing down one iota.

"Shit! It's five-thirty," Nathan says, his eyes on the wall clock. "Evan should have been here by now."

He pulls out his phone and rings his brother, but he swears again when he gets voicemail.

"I bet that douche met up with Lori and forgot to tell me. Cocksucker."

I bite my lip to keep from laughing at his "brotherly love." "I could give you a lift home . . ."

He tenses—I can see it in the slight rise of his shoulders as he breathes in—but it only lasts a few seconds before he blows out a frustrated breath.

"Um . . . yeah, if you wouldn't mind."

A lump forms in my throat, and my spine tingles. *Does he not want to be seen with me? Is that what this is?* Other than Evan, no one knows we've been meeting in the library after school.

Before he can get up, I lay my hand on his arm, and he stills, his eyes rising instinctually to mine.

"Why do you meet me here every day?"

He draws in a sharp breath, and his cheeks bloom like roses in the space of a heartbeat, his eyes wandering down to the buttons on my shirt.

"Nathan?"

"I don't know. That first day we just . . . and Amber and Katie would never talk about *Batman* or *Star Wars* . . ."

He glances up at me, then away. "You know me better than they do. All of them."

He looks shocked at the words coming out of his own mouth, and he's not the only one. *How the hell does he figure that?* Most of the time, I feel like I don't know him at all.

"Are you ready?" he asks a little too quickly, as if he can't wait to get away from this conversation.

"Sure," I tell him, gathering up my things.

He follows me to my beat-up, old Chevy, and I brace myself for the abuse I'm sure is coming. It's a nineteen eighty-five Impala—a beast of a thing that was once a police squad car. Even my dad takes pot shots at it. But Nathan doesn't say a word. He just gets in, and when I join him, I notice his knee is bouncing.

"You'll have to give me directions," I tell him as I pull out of the lot, but he's staring out the window, lost in thought.

"Hey." I put my hand on his knee, and he jumps, taking a sharp breath in.

"I'm sorry. What did you say?"

"Are you okay?"

"That's not what you said."

"No, but it's more important now than what I said."

Another deep breath. "I'm fine. I was . . . somewhere else."

I want to ask where he was, but the bounce is back to that knee, so I don't. "I said you'll need to give me directions."

"Oh. Right. I'm off the River Loop."

Nodding, I head up the one-oh-one.

He's quiet for a few moments, but I can feel his tension growing. His knee has stopped, but now his fist is slowly bouncing off the ancient armrest. *If he keeps that up, it's liable to fall off.*

"Things would be so much easier if I could drive," he says as if to himself. But he didn't say it to himself; he said it out loud for some reason. To me.

"Have you ever?"

"Driven? Yeah, I know how; I just can't do it legally."

"Is that true for everyone who has . . . what you have?"

"No," Nathan says, both hands now clenched in fists on his knees. "Most people who have what I have can control their seizures with medication. There's a drug that's basically a cure for most people, but it doesn't work for me."

"If the drug worked, then you wouldn't have any more seizures?"

"That's the idea," he says tightly.

"So how long would you have to go without a seizure before you could get your license?"

"The state of Oregon says you need to be seizure-free for three months," he answers as his gaze fixates on his knees. "I can't go more than three weeks without having one."

"You're kidding." I blurt the words out thoughtlessly, and he grimaces.

"I wish," he says, shaking his head. "I fought hard against it in the beginning since my, um, seizures are so predictable, but the state decided there was too much danger of them becoming unpredictable. I guess they were right."

"What do you mean, 'predictable'?" Now that he's talking about it, I might as well try to get all the information I can.

He shifts his shoulders—I get the impression he's uncomfortable talking about this. I'm about to tell him he doesn't have to tell me when he speaks up again. "Well, what I have involves more than one kind of seizure. There are little ones, and then there are the big ones, like the one you saw, and the little ones always happen before the big ones so I know when a big one is coming."

His explanation is simple enough, although he's avoiding the details carefully. Unable to suppress my curiosity, I press further. "Is that why you miss school so much?"

He looks up at me quickly, the surprise evident on his face. He furrows his brow for a moment, but then he relaxes again. "You don't miss a trick, do you?"

I smile at him smugly, and he chuckles.

"Yeah, that's right. The little seizures happen in the morning on days when I'm going to have a big one, so I stay home those days. I guess if you know my secret, it's not hard to put it together. I'm just not used to anyone knowing, so you caught me by surprise."

I have one more question, but I know I'm probably pressing my luck. "But . . . the day I was with you . . . it didn't happen that way, did it?"

His eyes widen, and fear and sadness wash over his face. He looks down again as he always seems to do when he's talking about something that bothers him. "No . . . that day I had no warning. That's only ever happened twice before and never anywhere near school." He pauses and bites his lower lip, but he seems compelled to continue. "And then the next day, I had another one at home without warning."

"You're scared, aren't you?" I say softly, reaching out and touching the top of his hand.

He pulls his hand back and makes a fist with it.

. . . and I've gone too far.

"Let's talk about something else, okay?"

And just like that, the window into Nathan's thoughts slams closed. *Shit.* My curiosity is nowhere near sated, but at least I got something. Actually, quite a few things.

"Turn here," he says after a few moments, and I turn down a heavily wooded drive. After a few minutes, a house comes into view, and I gasp. It's three stories tall and the most modern architecture I've seen in western bumblefuck. All right angles and smooth lines, the house is a mix of wood and stone. It looks as if a giant punted it here from LA, or maybe Geneva.

As I pull around the circular drive, he already has his bag in hand. "Thanks for the ride, Holly," he says quickly, and he's out the door before I can put the car in park.

I watch him take the stairs two at a time, still marveling at the house, and he pauses with his hand on the doorknob. He turns and gives a half-hearted wave, and I know I've been dismissed. It says, "*Get the hell out of my driveway*," in no uncertain terms, and I can't help the tightening in my chest, cursing myself for a fool as I drive away.

By the time I wake up the next morning, the sting of Nathan's dismissal has mostly faded, and I'm again confused as hell about what's up with him. One minute he's opening up, and the next he's shooing me away like a stray cat. But I can't help the tidal wave of warmth that washes through my chest at just the thought of seeing him again. It's Tuesday morning, and I'm sitting in homeroom with The Gothlet, listening to her go on about The Cure—well, I'm nodding and smiling in all the right places anyway—but my head is a thousand miles away, wondering when Nathan is going to walk through that door and what he'll be wearing today. Until suddenly, the bell rings.

And there's no Nathan.

Ice shoots down my spine.

Maybe he's just late—the jock boys often are. But as I look in front of me, Ken-doll, Ryan, and Tyler are all present and accounted for. When they're late, they're never late *alone*.

Ken-doll jerks his head toward Nathan's desk and furrows his eyebrows, but Ryan just shrugs back at him. Ken-doll smirks and shakes his head.

And I realize then that I'm the only one in this room, the only one in this *whole damn school*, who knows that Nathan isn't playing hooky today. I'm the only one who knows he's sitting at home, waiting to have a seizure—

or maybe he's had one already. My stomach gives a sickly flip, and I scrunch my eyes closed as images of Nathan convulsing play on a loop in my head. And with a gasp, I realize he's right—I *do* know him better than anyone here even though I've only known him for a handful of weeks.

I know the secret that defines his life.

And as I wander through my day, I really start thinking. *What must it be like to have to hide all the time, to fear everyone finding out that something's really wrong with you? How does he cope with it? How* long *has he been coping with it? Is it lonely?*

He's the one who started talking to me in the library—maybe he *is* lonely. It's a startling realization, considering he's always surrounded by the jock squad. I'm quite familiar with the feeling of being alone in a crowd, but I never imagined it might be that way for one of the popular kids.

A million more questions flutter through my mind, and I realize I want to know the answers, not out of morbid curiosity and not because he's sex on legs.

But because I want to know *him*.

It was lust in the beginning, and then when I saw him have the seizure— argh, it *was* morbid curiosity *and* pity for a while there, but now? I feel like I want to help him bear this if I can because, for some reason, I know it and no one else does. Now that I've gotten closer to him, I want to be his friend. It's a curious sensation, and it brings a different kind of warmth to my chest. It's still lustful, but it's so much *more*.

I know I can't have his body, and I can't be the girl on his arm, but maybe I can have this. Maybe *we* can have this.

Chapter Eight

Secrets are generally terrible. Beauty is not hidden—only ugliness and deformity.

– L.M. Montgomery

Holly

As I sit in homeroom, I'm on pins and needles waiting to see if Nathan will show today. I almost went up to Evan and asked about him yesterday —I even considered asking the school secretary if he was out sick—but in the end, I just kept to myself and worried.

It's creeping toward eight o'clock, and everyone, even the stoners who are habitually late, is in their seats, and I'm about to dash out into the hall to look for him when he comes ambling through the door.

Relief washes over me in waves, but it's short-lived.

He looks like hell.

The slight purple shadows under his eyes are deeper, and his perfect, unblemished skin looks washed-out and pale. He moves to his chair as if he's wading through deep water, and when he sits, his face scrunches up in a wince.

I glance around the room, but no one else seems to have noticed Nathan's entrance. They're all talking and laughing, waiting for the bell so they can go off and be bored to tears for the next eight hours.

Does he always look like this the day after a seizure? I have to admit I don't know. Maybe I wasn't really looking before. Just like no one else in this room is looking now.

Ken-doll claps Nathan on the shoulder and says something to him, and Nathan glances over, grinning as he replies. But the minute Ken-doll looks away, Nathan's eyes close, and his brows knit together. *He's putting on a good show; I'll give him that.*

I watch him through English and calculus since we don't sit close enough to talk, and he continues his performance. It's quite convincing unless you're watching closely. It's the little things that give him away—how slowly he turns his head to answer Ryan's question, how often he rests his palm against his forehead, how he grips his desk as if it's the only thing holding the earth in place. If I didn't know better, I'd say he was drunk or hung over.

Finally, it's time for chemistry, and as I expected, I beat him to our desk. He trudges in a few moments later, putting on his plastic smile as he approaches.

And I can't help the way my eyes narrow at him, my mouth set in a firm line. Anger flares in my chest, sudden and searing.

His brow furrows, and he slows his approach, cocking his head to the side.

"You don't have to do that with me. I know where you were, and I know something's still wrong, so just cut the crap."

His eyes widen and then narrow, but he drops the façade completely as he slides into his seat. He's angry, but I swear his shoulders are a bit less over his ears.

He rests his forehead on his palm as I've been watching him do all morning, and for a moment, pain and fatigue seem to flow out of him. My heart clenches, and guilt tastes bitter on my tongue.

"I'm sorry," I mutter quietly. "I don't know why I snapped at you like that. I'm just . . . What is it?"

Nathan tilts his head and side-eyes me. "Headache. I always have a killer one the day . . . after."

"Did you take anything?"

"Doesn't help," he answers, eyes still closed. "It usually goes away by evening."

I know better than to suggest he go home. He misses too much school as it is.

"Listen, Metcalf's probably gonna drone on for a while. Why don't you put your head down, and I'll give you my notes later."

Nathan lifts his head and searches my face for a moment, then frowns. "Nah, I can't do that."

"Why? You're allowed to have a headache once in a while without people thinking—"

"—that I'm not right in the head?" Nathan finishes with a raised eyebrow.

"Well . . . yeah."

"Um, I guess you're right," he says, laying his head on his arms and finally seeming to surrender to the fact that he feels like shit.

Warmth floods my chest as I look at him . . . and I like it.

Nathan doesn't show up for gym class, and I sincerely hope he went home or at least to the nurse's office if he was still in as bad a shape as he was during chemistry. I don't see him again for the rest of the day, but I still find myself in the library after school, just in case.

After a few minutes of staring at the clock like an addict waiting for their fix, I give myself a good shake and take out my Spanish book. Nathan turns up fifteen minutes later, his hair sticking up in all directions as he falls into the chair across from me.

I raise my eyebrows, and he blushes adorably.

"I, um, fell asleep in the nurse's office. I didn't know the day was over until she came and kicked me out."

He puts his head down on his arms, face turned in my direction and eyes closed, so he doesn't see my smile. He's not hiding from me anymore.

"Is it still as bad as it was?"

"No."

"But it's still there."

"Yes."

"Why don't you just go home?"

"I miss too much school."

I chuckle. "As if you give a shit about that."

He cracks one eye open and stares at me for a few seconds, then closes it again.

"It'll freak my parents and Evan out, and they'll annoy the hell out of me. There's nothing they can do."

I smile again at his honesty.

"So . . . what happened yesterday?"

He draws in a sharp breath, and his arms shift as his fingers curl into fists.

"You don't have to—"

"No, it's okay," he says, relaxing his hands but not opening his eyes. "Um, so I told you I have little seizures on the days of the big ones, right?"

"Yes. Are those . . . similar to the big ones?"

73

"Sort of. They're called myoclonic seizures—it's like, have you ever been almost asleep, and then you jerk awake?"

"Sure."

"That's exactly what a myoclonic seizure is, except I'm awake when it happens."

I cock my head, not quite understanding, but of course, he can't see me, lying there with his eyes closed.

"Um, I don't think I get it."

"It's an involuntary jerk of a muscle—usually in my arm, neck, or shoulder. Yesterday, the first one happened while I was holding a glass of orange juice, so it flew out of my hand. Made a fucking mess everywhere."

"Shit. Was your mom mad?"

"Nah. Usually after I've had the first one, I don't hold anything for a while, but if the first one hits when I'm in the middle of doing something, there's nothing I can do."

"So what happened after the orange juice?"

His brow furrows, and there are those fists again. I can see the muscles in his arms flexing tightly.

"I had four more little ones, and then I had the big one about an hour later." He forces the words out quickly. "Holly, do you mind if I just lie here for a bit? I . . ."

He pauses, not sure how to explain what I already know. "Of course you can. I have Spanish to do anyway."

His arms relax instantly, but the vise grip around my heart takes a bit longer. *Why is he doing this?* He keeps pushing himself to talk about it, well past the point of his own comfort. *What good does it do him? Unless . . .* My heart leaps in my chest, but I'm scolding myself before the thought can even fully form. *You will* not *do this to yourself, Holly. You will not even entertain the notion that he wants to be anything more than your super-secret friend.*

74

And why are you being his super-secret friend in the first place? my self-esteem pipes up.

The answer is instantaneous.

Because he needs one.

Chapter Nine

Nothing weighs on us so heavily as a secret.

– Jean de La Fontaine

NATHAN

Okay, today's the day. I'm gonna do it, I tell myself for the millionth time. The guilt has been growing and growing—Holly deserves better than for our friendship to be a secret, and if I'm going to ensure that she keeps *my* secrets, then I need to get a move on and ask her out.

But something twists in my gut every time I think about this plan. I've gotten to know Holly, and she's . . . nice. She's more than nice; she's a really cool person—one I'd like to at least be friends with. And if I date her and it falls apart, there isn't a chance in hell we'll remain friends, and that really sucks.

And do I really need to do this? Last night, I told Evan I was considering leaving things as they are now, but he just shook his head.

"Do you really think she's going to tolerate being your closet friend for very long? If she does, she's dumber than I thought. And once you go public with this, the rumors are going to start flying, so you might as well get some action out of it and iron-clad assurance that she's not going to talk."

I don't like it, but I've known from the beginning that I'll do anything to keep my secret, including keeping my best friends in the dark and basically taking a vow of chastity. *I've gone this far, so what's a little further?* And it *would* be nice to get my dick wet again—it's been ages since anyone but Rosey Palm and her five sisters came for a visit.

I'm on my way to chemistry, but somehow my frigid feet steer me to the nurse's office instead. I claim I have a headache, and she looks at me with barely disguised pity. I *hate* coming here—it's bad enough when I have to, but today I'm just being a wuss. *Fuck.*

I'll face Holly at lunchtime. Explain, or . . . something.

My heart rate skyrockets just thinking about it, and I try to keep my breathing under control as I fish a Xanax out of my pocket. I nicked it this morning from the stash Dad keeps for me in the kitchen—this is the first time I've considered taking one without being forced in a long time. But it's not as if I could have said, "I'm going to have a panic attack at lunchtime today because I'm going to destroy my social status by eating with Holly so she'll like me and keep my secrets." *Jesus, that even sounds bad in my head.*

Downing the pill with some water from the sink, I lie on the nasty little cot and try not to think about anything.

I jump when the bell rings, rubbing a hand over my eyes as the clamor of hungry students spills into the halls. *Well, that's one way to pass the time.* It's not as if Xanax hasn't knocked me out before.

As I approach the cafeteria, my breathing picks up, and my palms begin to sweat. *I can do this. Why am I so freaked out about doing this?*

I go through the lunch line, then circle back around and wait like the stalker I apparently am . . . until Holly walks in. I want to follow her, but my feet seem to be stuck to the floor.

As I watch, she takes a chicken sandwich and a Coke, and suddenly, she's nearing the end of the line and my chance is getting away from me and . . . somehow I lurch forward. My throat is like a desert. I swallow hard, then manage to whisper, "Hey."

She startles but doesn't turn around. "H-hi."

I put my tray down beside hers so I don't drop it and grip the back of my neck, wiping the sweat away and trying to force myself to breathe.

"Um . . . would you have lunch with me? I mean, like, not a lunch date or anything, just, um . . . you know what I mean . . ."

She whips her head around, and her eyes get really big.

"Wh-what?"

"Um . . . lunch. Will you sit with me?"

She's staring at me as if I just grew another head. *Oh God, does she not* want *anyone to know we're friends?* I always assumed . . .

"Uh . . . it's okay if you don't want to. N-never mind." My cheeks are on fire, and my stomach is churning—all I want to do is hide from her *forever*. But as I turn to bolt, she grabs my arm and—*Whoa! What the hell was* that?

It's as if she touched me with a branding iron, but now it's just little electric tingles. *I must be hallucinating from that Xanax—*

"No, I . . . I want to. I'm sorry. I was just . . . surprised. Um, but what about—"

"Fuck 'em," I say, and it comes out way more confident than I feel. But I did manage to say it, and *wow, look at that smile spreading across her face.* She looks beautiful when she forgets herself and smiles for real.

I pick up my tray and walk out into the main room, passing her table and mine, and I seat us at our own table away from everyone else.

And there's *silence*. I can feel the stares of the whole room, and my cheeks are burning again, but it also feels . . . good. For the first time in three years, I feel like I'm not hiding.

Oh my God, I can breathe again.

I take a full, deep, glorious breath, and it intoxicates me. My head is spinning as I grin at her, punch drunk on how free I feel.

"So . . . what shall we talk about?" I ask, feeling like I'm on top of the world.

She smiles at me again, but it wavers as her eyes dart from side to side.

"Everyone is staring at us."

I glance around, but it's as if this feeling of freedom is a shield from all that, unless . . .

"Um . . . yeah. Do you not want to be here?"

"No, I—"

Mayday. Mayday!

"I do."

Never mind.

A strange warmth spreads through my chest. *Is this what friendship with a girl feels like?* I wouldn't know—I was thirteen the last time I let myself feel anything toward the opposite sex other than lust. But whatever it is, it feels . . . good.

"So, what did you do last night?"

With each question I ask her, Holly relaxes a little more, and the room around us fades away. It's just like the afternoons in the library—we laugh and tease each other, and when the bell rings, I'm amazed lunch is already over.

"I guess we should go," Holly says, moving to stand.

"I . . . yeah." I shake my head, reeling from the abrupt realization that we're in the middle of the cafeteria, not in our own little world in the library.

"Will I see you . . . after school?" she asks, her cheeks turning pink as she stares at her tray. Her swings between outspoken, quirky geek and shy schoolgirl are making my head spin, but something tightens in my chest when she looks down and blushes like that—as if she's so unsure.

"Yeah, I'll be there," I tell her, grinning as she raises her head and smiles wide enough to make that little dimple on her left cheek.

And when the hell did I notice that? I shake my head, but I'm still smiling as she walks away from me.

I did it. Okay. I give myself a mental high five, but deep down, I know I'm just trying to hang on to this feeling of success. The fallout is coming, and I have no idea what's going to happen.

No one has the balls to say anything to me in the hallway, but I can hear the murmurs as I grab my books from my locker.

"Are they dating?"

"Nah, they can't be. He's just messing with her."

"Why would he bother with someone like her?"

I slam my locker door, making three sophomore girls jump and scurry away like the little gossiping hoes they are. *Why am I so angry?*

I storm down the hall, but by the time I get to study hall, my heart is pounding for a different reason. My palms are again slick with sweat—I'm about to be the center of attention, and that's never a good thing. In fact, it's a thing I usually avoid at all costs.

Chris, Tyler, and Ryan are already in their usual seats, and I take my place right in the middle. Holly is on the other side of the room, but I can't look at her. I have no idea what I'd see, and I need all the courage I can muster just to stay here.

"Dude, what the fuck? Why were you slummin' it at lunch today?" Tyler asks, his gaze hard.

I can feel my cheeks heating as my jaw tightens, but I don't respond.

"Yeah, Nate, what's up?" Chris chimes in. "Are you looking to trash bash?"

"She's *not* trash." I force the words out through gritted teeth.

"Ooh, what do we have here? I think Nate likes this one!" Tyler's ribbing sounds innocent, but there's an evil gleam in his eye.

"She *is* a nice piece of ass." Sean speaks up for the first time, and a shiver runs down my spine. "Maybe I'll take a turn with her too."

"She's mine!" My outburst surprises everyone, including me. *Oh shit.*

"For now," Sean mutters, his eyes roaming over Holly in a way that makes my skin crawl.

"Have fun slum-diving, if that's your thing," Tyler says, shaking his head, but I'm still stuck on Sean's words, and my own. Now I have to ask her out because if I don't, they'll all think I'm a pussy, or one of them will do it themselves just to fuck with me, or . . . *what if they think she refused me?*

My stomach is tight and queasy all at the same time, and I feel . . . icky. My eyes are drawn to Holly, but she's turned away from me, her head resting on her fist so her hair covers her face. *Did she hear any of that?* Damn, I hope not. I wish I hadn't heard it.

As I turn to face forward, my eyes fall on Ryan. He was quiet through the whole exchange, and now he's watching me, his brow furrowed and an almost-smile on his face. *What the hell is that about?* I shrug it off and try to get some actual work done. It's still gonna be a long-ass day.

I finally make it to my last class of the day, and I'm about to sigh in relief . . . until I remember who sits on either side of me. *Oh, motherfuck.*

They're waiting for me—both of them staring me down the minute I enter the room—Amber with pure disdain and Erica with barely contained amusement. The nurse's office is looking *really* good about now.

I'm barely in my seat when Amber strikes first.

"Why the hell would you sit with *her*?"

"Oh, come on, Amber, you know he's just playing a game with her. It'll be fun to watch, especially the ending," Erica says, sneering at me.

"I'm not playing with her. We're dating." *If I'm going to have to do this, I might as well get some more mileage out of it.*

The looks on their faces are priceless. Erica nearly swallows her tongue, and Amber looks as if I just told her I'm gay. But then, she gets scary. Her lips purse, her eyes seem to glow this eerie green color, and she raises one eyebrow. *Shit, are those flames around her ears, or am I hallucinating again?*

"Are you?" she asks, but it's a question I know better than to respond to. "That's . . . *nice.*"

I may be seventeen and know next to nothing about women, but I know she thinks this is anything but nice. This is dangerous. Amber is easy to deal with when she's pissed, but when she gets like this . . . look out. She got like this after our little adventure in the janitor's closet, when I refused to take things further with her. I occasionally still hear a whispered rumor about my microscopic dick and missing ball.

"No way!" Erica exclaims. "But I thought—"

"Shut it, Erica!" Amber shoots her a glare before her mask of composure slips back into place. "Nathan can date whomever he wants. I doubt she'll hold his . . . *interest* for long."

Erica's eyes widen, but Amber turns away before she can say anything, and so do I. But I watch Amber for the rest of the period, and whatever is going on in that evil little mind of hers doesn't bode well for Holly, or for me, for that matter.

But all of that fades into the background as the bell rings, and I head to my locker—now I have to go meet Holly in the library and ask her out before anyone I've talked to today finds out I haven't already.

That icky feeling is back. I can't help but wonder if today hadn't gone the way it did, would I still be doing this? *It doesn't matter; you're committed now,* I remind myself. But my steps are slow and heavy as I approach the library door.

When I push it open, Holly is sitting front and center, and she raises those chocolate brown eyes to me as a brilliant smile transforms her face. Warmth begins to spread in my chest, but that icky feeling washes all over it and turns it into nausea, and all I can manage is a weak smile in return. *Fuck.*

Her brows come together slightly, but she says nothing until I'm seated beside her.

Her gaze shifts to the open book in front of her. *Shy schoolgirl time.*

"Um . . . hi."

"Hey."

"How was your afternoon?"

If that isn't the worst question she could have asked, and yet, just like her too. *Well, I acted all caveman about you in front of the guys, and then I told Amber we were dating just to see if smoke would come out of her ears.*

"Um, it was . . . different."

"I know. Everyone was talking about us." Her nervous laugh is a sound I've never heard before.

"What were they saying?"

Her cheeks turn pink as she swallows. "Well, some people asked me if we're friends, but . . ."

"But?"

Now she meets my eyes, and I'm amazed she has the balls to do it. "But most of them asked if we were dating."

"What did you say?" *Jesus, I'm an ass* and *a coward. She should walk away from me just for putting her through this conversation.*

"I told them no," she replies, her eyes darting away.

"Did you want to tell them no?"

"What do you mean?"

Relief and anxiety flare through me as she tosses the ball into my court. Thank God she has the balls not to let me force her to ask me if we're dating—*you are such a dick, Nathan*—but now, I need to man up and get this over with.

"Um, well . . . would you like to be dating? Uh . . . me?" *Christ, you sound like you've never talked to a human before, much less a girl.* "I mean, would you go out with me if I asked you?"

Her eyes widen as we both turn a cartoon shade of crimson.

"Well, are you?" she asks.

"Am I what?"

"Are you asking me to go out with you?"

Oh fuck, what did I say? I try to recall my words, but when I come up empty, that little voice in the back of my head is happy to fill the void. *If she goes out with you, it's going to be out of pity. She has to think the seizures have addled your brains by now.*

"Oh my God, can I just start over?" I ask, too much of a pussy to even look at her.

"Of course," she says, biting her lip.

I take a few calming breaths even though I know she's staring at me. I even reach down to see if my balls are still there, and amazingly enough, they seem to be. *If you don't need to grow a pair, then use the ones you have before they shrivel up and fall off!* Holy hell, I've *never* had this much trouble talking to a girl before.

"I . . . what I mean is . . . Holly, would you like to go out with me?" I haven't said these words since I was twelve, so they feel funny on my tongue. Maybe that's why I couldn't get them out.

"You're serious," Holly says, looking at me skeptically.

"Uh, yeah. Why wouldn't I be?"

"Well, because . . ." As she pauses, her gaze pierces me.

It's as if she can see right through me, and I struggle not to squirm under her scrutiny. *Does she know why I'm doing this? Could she possibly?* I meet her eyes steadily, knowing if I fidget even the slightest bit, the jig will be up. As the first bead of sweat begins to trickle down the back of my neck, she breathes out heavily, her shoulders dropping.

"Yes, I would like to go out with you."

"Really?" *Oh my God, did I actually pull this off?*

"Yes," Holly declares, laughing. Her smile is radiant as she puts her hand over mine, and I expect to feel good, but something lurches in my chest, and the icky crashes over me like a tidal wave. *Oh God, I've made her happy. I am the biggest asshole in the whole, entire world.*

Chapter Ten

The biggest coward is a man who awakens the love of a woman without the intention of loving her.

—— **Bob Marley**

NATHAN

She's beaming at me, but I feel like such a piece of shit, and I've had all I can handle for one day. I know I should sit and talk with her—act all excited because I now have a girlfriend—but I just don't have it in me. I've pretended too much already.

"Holly, I'm really sorry—"

—*more than you will ever know*—

"—but I just feel icky today—"

—*first truth I've uttered in hours*—

"—and I think I need to go lie down."

Her smile fades.

Did I just screw this up? Can she see right through me?

"I'm sorry, Nathan. Do you want me to take you home?"

Oh God, she's trying to take care of me. Nathan, you are a douche canoe. No, it's worse than that—you're a fucking douche cruise ship. A doucheliner. And you don't even deserve this girl's friendship.

"No, that's okay. Evan's usually done early on Wednesdays, so it shouldn't be too long. I'll go wait in his car," I tell her, standing up.

"Okay, if you're sure."

"Yeah, I am." *Holy fuck, get me out of here.*

"All right. I'll see you tomorrow, then," she says, her smile making the bile rise in my throat.

I turn and bolt from the room, not stopping until I push through the front doors of the school. The cool air helps slow my rapid breathing, but my stomach is still churning threateningly. If I don't find a way to calm down soon, I'm going to throw up . . . or worse.

As I expected, Evan drove his gear over to the field for practice, so I find his car parked against the fence on the side of the building. Nobody's around, so I recline the front seat and plug my iPhone into the stereo. I put the window halfway down, and 30 Seconds to Mars soothes me, helping me briefly forget this bitch of a day.

That is, until Evan shows up.

My cord lands in my lap as my music abruptly cuts off.

"I went to the library. I thought you'd still be with Holly."

I crack open one eye just long enough to see that he's turned in his seat, waiting for a response.

His warm-up towel lands on my face, and I nearly gag, bolting upright as I whip it at him. "What the fuck, Evan!"

"Chillax, jackass. I was just messing with you! What the hell crawled up your ass today?"

"I asked Holly out," I reply sullenly.

"Finally! And?"

"And what?"

"And I want to know the square root of pi. What did she say, dumbass?"

"She said yes."

"Great! Then why do you look like your balls are stuck in your zipper?"

I grimace at the image because that *did* actually happen to me once. "I'm just . . . Fuck, I don't know what I am. I thought it would make me happy, but . . . it was a shitty thing to do. I've done shitty things all day, and . . . let's just go home." I pinch the bridge of my nose, trying to forestall the headache I know is coming.

"Hey, it's not *that* bad," Evan says, finally using his "inside" voice. "Think of it as a mutually beneficial relationship. She gets a boyfriend, you get your secret kept, and you both get to polish each other's knobs. It's win-win."

"I guess. I just . . . I don't want to hurt her, you know? She's nice."

"Dude, you're not going to hurt her. She'll get bored with you; you'll see. How many girls did I date before Lori?"

"I lost count."

"Exactly! Holly's young and at a new school. You may have been the first to snap her cracker, but you won't be the last."

I try not to wince as Evan the Emasculating Elephant tramples all over my ego, but he's probably right. Maybe I won't have to hurt her. Maybe we can both have some fun with this, and then she'll walk away.

"I'm not sure why she likes you to begin with, but if you don't settle down, this isn't even gonna last a week. Every time I saw you today, you looked like you were gonna hurl. And you asked her out? Damn, love really *must* be blind."

"Jesus, Evan, don't even say that!"

"What, love?"

"Yes! There's no love here. I haven't even kissed her yet."

Evan shakes his head at me. "Have I taught you nothing?"

"Fuck off, dickwad. I've got this." *But I really,* really *don't.* Thankfully, dickwad stays quiet the rest of the ride home, and he opts not to out my new relationship status to Mom and Dad over dinner. I nick another Xanax as soon as I can and curl up on my bed, hoping that in the land of oblivion, there's no such thing as icky.

The next morning, I'm feeling better about everything.

I'm just gonna be her friend and have fun with this. I'll kiss her; I'll hold her hand—it'll be like Amber and all the others except I won't have to be as careful. And I'm not *going to hurt her.* I give myself this pep talk all the way to school, and it seems to be working—right up to the point when I see her.

She's at her locker, sorting through her books, but her eyes flick to mine and quickly away as soon as I round the corner. *You should stop and talk to her. You asked her out, then ran like a bitch yesterday.*

But as I get closer, I can feel the icky in my chest and stomach. It's not as bad as yesterday, but it's still there. *I'm not going to hurt her. I'm not going to hurt her.*

"Hey."

Even though I know she saw me, she still jumps at my greeting. "Hi. Are you feeling better today?"

"Yeah, much. I'm sorry I ran out on you like that." *But if I hadn't, I would've tossed my cookies on your Spanish book.*

"It's okay. I understand."

Oh God, how I wish you did. The irony isn't lost on me that the one person who I should be able to be completely open with is the one I'm lying to the most.

"You better hurry; the bell's going to ring."

"Yeah, I'll see you in a few," I tell her before I continue on to my locker.

The whispers and stares continue all morning, and I watch as various girls ask Holly if she's dating me. She blushes at the question each and every time, looking down as she gives a timid "Yes." She's always shy schoolgirl with people she doesn't know well. *I wonder why that is.* She's got a kickass personality and brass balls under that skirt, to boot.

The shocked responses she receives get under my skin a little. She *is* beautiful—what's wrong with any guy in this school noticing her, no matter who he hangs out with? I know the reality of how things work in high school, but I'm offended for her that she has to put up with this shit.

By the time we get to the end of chemistry, I've had it.

We walk along in companionable silence until we reach the entrance to the cafeteria. My hands have started to sweat a bit, but my stomach's okay, and a strange excitement begins to spread through me.

As we turn, I take her hand. Her eyes widen, but her fingers entwine with mine almost of their own accord. *Like they belong there.* The warmth I felt last time I touched her begins to spread up my arm, but this time, it isn't a shock; it's . . . comfortable. But it still takes my breath away. I've never felt this way when I've touched a girl before. *Is this the way it's supposed to feel?* It's been so long since I've really been close to anyone I wasn't related to. *I guess it's normal.*

Holly's mouth is still hanging open, so I reach over and cup her chin. "Close your mouth, Holly."

She laughs, but as she bites her lip, her eyes dance.

"Now, no one needs to ask if we're dating," I tell her, and her smile nearly blinds me.

We walk down the steps hand in hand, and the response is similar to yesterday's, minus the shocked silence.

I lead her right through the center of the room to the line on the other side, ensuring that everyone can see us. But suddenly, I'm not looking at them; my focus shifts to her.

She looks . . . relaxed, content even. And her hand seems to fit so perfectly in mine. *Maybe . . .* A wave of confusion with an extra helping of icky rolls over me, and I squeeze her hand without realizing it. Her smile widens, and the nausea I've been playing tag with all morning nearly wins the game, and I have to swallow repeatedly to keep the bile down. *I'm not going to hurt her. I'm not going to hurt her.*

Fuck, I've got to get a grip on this. I've been up and down so much already today, I'm giving myself whiplash and a fucking stomach ulcer. Evan's words ring in my head. *"If you don't settle down, this isn't even gonna last a week."* I hate it when that jackass is right.

By the time we sit down, I've managed to compose myself, and today it's Holly's turn to make *me* feel comfortable. She's still beaming as if I hung the moon, and I focus on enjoying her happiness instead of the reason for it. *Damn, she's pretty when she smiles.*

We talk through lunch just like yesterday, and not a soul comes to bother us. *If only we could be alone like this and not have to deal with the rest of these assholes, this could actually be okay.*

I plow through my afternoon, but I can't bring myself to go to Spanish. I'm sure Amber's been sharpening up her glare all day, and I don't think I can stand to be bitch-brow bludgeoned for an hour without going apeshit on her.

The nurse's office is cool and dark, and it's still that way when I wake up sometime after the final bell. *Holy shit, does anyone* ever *check this room after last period?* I'll have to remember to set my watch next time.

Warmth floods my chest when I see the top of Holly's head through the library window, but it's short-lived because the look on her face is . . . *Ouch.* And as I push open the door, it's more than apparent why—Amber and Erica are sitting at the table behind her. *How the hell did they find out?*

Holly's eyes meet mine, and they soften, but the firm line of her mouth doesn't. Those bitches haven't been quiet as she's waited for me; I'm sure of it. And the icky makes a triumphant return, but this time, it's layered with a shit-ton of guilt.

"Hi, Nathan. We were just talking about you," Amber says, and even *I* can feel the malice dripping from her words. *Fuck.*

"Holly here seems to actually think she's dating you," she continues, Erica's giggle punctuating her statement.

"She *is* dating me, so leave her alone!" Amber's eyes are doing that green, glowy thing again, and I know now why it's green and not any other color.

"Oh, come on, Nathan! You can't be serious!" Her mocking tone oozes superiority, and the urge to smack that smirk off her overpainted face is almost unbearable.

"I mean it, Amber. Fuck off! Go find some jock to screw, if there are any left who haven't pounded your worn out twat."

Amber gasps as her mouth falls open, and as I glance from her to Holly, they have the exact same look on their faces.

"Come on, Holly. Let's get out of here," I say as I pick up her book bag, and the smile that spreads across her face seems to wash away some of the icky this time instead of making it worse.

She follows me out of the library, but I hesitate in the lobby because I don't know where to go. My brilliant plan ended with the twat comment.

"Um . . . do you want to go to my house?" Holly asks, stopping beside me.

New police chief, loaded weapon—he can probably see through teenage bullshit like it's a damn store window. I think I'd rather fuck Amber, and that's saying something.

But that leaves only one other option if I want privacy but not to be thrust into an insta-date situation. *I'm going to regret this; I just know it.*

"Why don't we go to my house instead?"

Holly's eyes widen. "Really?"

"Yeah, why not?" I shrug, trying to be casual.

There are a thousand reasons why not, and my mother is the first nine hundred and ninety-five. Say no, say no, say no . . .

"Okay, sure."

Fuck.

We get into her car, and my mind is going a hundred miles an hour. *What the hell are we going to do at the house? How can I keep her away from Mom? Why the fuck—*

"Nathan?"

I startle, not even realizing her hand was on my knee until she quickly removes it.

"What?"

"Are you okay?" she asks, her brown eyes gently probing mine before she looks back to the road.

"Yeah. Why wouldn't I be?" *Dumb answer. You should have just said yes!*

"Well, your knee was bouncing a mile a minute, and you look . . . stressed. Do you not want to go to your house?"

Are all girls this perceptive? Can't they just . . . think about sucking dick or shopping or something?

"No, I—why would you think that?" *What the hell is my face giving away?*

She glances down at her jeans.

"Well . . . the last time I dropped you off, it seemed like . . ."

Shit. The last time she dropped me off, I was freaking out majorly, and if I could have transported her car with my mind alone, she would have been in Idaho—or maybe Botswana. The icky rolls around in my stomach, and I know lying will only make it worse.

"I haven't brought a girl home in a long time," I say, willing my knee to stay still.

Holly's sharp intake of breath draws my eyes.

"You're kidding."

I shake my head, afraid that if I open my mouth, the real reason might come flying out, which would likely lead Miss Perceptive to guess the reason we're dating.

"I thought . . ."

"What?"

She blushes, and the flip-flop in my stomach has absolutely nothing to do with icky.

"Well, you're one of the popular guys and—"

"And you figured I get around?"

"Um . . ."

Her blush is so intense, it's spreading down the side of her neck, and it takes almost more than I have to keep my hand from brushing back her hair so I can feel the heat of her skin.

"Some of the guys do, but . . . it's never been my thing." *Oh God, how I wish it were my thing.* "I guess I haven't—"

"Found the right girl?"

Figured out how to fuck them and leave them with my balls still intact.

"Yeah, I guess."

She does this shoulder thing that hides her face behind her hair, but her grin is too wide for me not to see it . . . and I realize what I've said. Or rather, what I've said by agreeing with what she said. *Jesus Christ, I just told her she's the right girl. I need to pay more attention and not let the conversation stray onto topics that make me daydream about fucking.*

I plaster a grin on my own face, but she's not looking. Thank God, because I know at this moment, she'd see right through me.

As we pull up the driveway, I'm still trying to calm myself.

Dad should still be at the hospital, and with any luck, Mom's out shopping or something. Maybe we'll be all alone . . .

That brings on a whole different type of anxiety, but I don't have time to even formulate a freak-out because the garage is open and the Mercedes and Beemer are there.

Mom *and* Dad. Are. Home.

Motherfucking bloody hell; karma is a bitch, and she's pissed!

Okay, maybe we can just walk by the house and go for a walk out back, and Mom and Dad never have to—

"Wow, I love your house! I bet all those windows make it so bright and cheerful inside."

Shit. Biggs, Wedge, we're going in. We're going in full throttle. Blowing up the Death Star would be *infinitely* easier than introducing Holly to my mother.

Holly parks, still gazing up at the house, while I frantically scramble to put together a plan.

Kitchen! Mom's usually never in there this early—maybe we can sit at the table and not be noticed for a while and then go out for a walk. *Yeah, that's it! A quick look at the house, a drink and a snack, and out we go. Brilliant!*

We make it through the front door, but as I usher a wide-eyed Holly through the living room and into the kitchen, I catch Dad's eye as he's going up the stairs. His eyebrow only raises a fraction, but that's the equivalent of falling down said stairs in shock for any normal person.

I squeeze my eyes shut tightly, willing karma to give me a break just this once. Just. This. Once.

"Holly, can you go sit at the kitchen table? I'll be back in a minute."

I dash to the bottom of the stairs just in time to hear my dad rat me out.

"Your son has a girl downstairs."

"Oh, tell Lori I said hi if you go back down."

"Not that son."

My mom's jaw hits the floor with an audible crack.

"What?"

"Nathan. Brought a girl home."

I don't need to hear anymore. What I need to do is move. *Fast. Holly will understand if I just grab her by the t-shirt and drag her out the back door, right? That's normal. Of course it is.*

I hightail it to the kitchen, but as I reach the table, I hear a sharp intake of breath behind me. *Holy shit! Did she sprout wings? Use the hovering mother emergency chute? There is* no way *she walked down those stairs.*

Holly's eyes widen, but after a second, I realize she's looking at me, and not June Cleaver on wheels behind me. *Fuck! Breathe, Nathan! And wipe that look of abject terror off your face!*

"Nathan? Oh! You have a guest!"

My eyes roll so hard I think I see my brain.

"Yeah, Mom. This is Holly. She's my lab partner." *And I may have asked her out yesterday for all the wrong reasons.*

"So nice to meet you, Holly," Mom says, extending her hand along with the widest smile I've ever seen.

"You too, Mrs. Harris," Holly responds, blushing slightly.

Mom's brow furrows. "Holly . . . you're the one who was with Nathan when—"

"Mom!"

"Yes, Mrs. Harris. I'm the one who called you." Holly's interruption saves me from having to hear the words.

"Thank you for staying with him. He tends to—"

"I'm *right here*, Mom." I grate the words out through clenched teeth as I struggle to keep my temper and my sanity.

"I know, dear," she says, patting my cheek. She's either completely oblivious to my mortification, or she doesn't give a shit, but either way, it's making my blood boil.

"Have things been going okay at school? I know Nathan was worried—"

"Mom! Holy f—"

"Nathan and I were just about to go out back. He says you have a beautiful rose garden, and I've been dying to see it."

The words die on my lips like a volcanic eruption on pause. I'm holding my breath; all the rage I want to spew at Mom is still. Right. There. But . . . *What the fuck did Holly just say?*

"Oh . . ." Mom seems as bewildered as I am.

"Come on, Nathan. Let's go. It's so nice to meet you, Mrs. Harris!"

Holly waves over her shoulder as she tows me out the door, and I'm so confused that I can do nothing but be pulled along.

My brain finally re-engages when we reach the roses, and I stop, causing her to turn around and look at me.

"I never told you my mom had a rose garden." I stare at her intently, wanting to understand this strange creature beside me.

She glances down now, fingering a leaf of the nearest bush.

"No . . . but I knew you were about to go apeshit on your mom, so I made it up."

I can't help the chuckle that escapes. "Apeshit, huh? Is that what I do?"

"Well, I wasn't sure, but the odds looked pretty good. I didn't want you to get in trouble, and I knew you needed an escape."

Now she looks into my eyes, and my heart gives a lurch as heat creeps up my chest and neck. Her eyes are such a mesmerizing brown—as if whatever's behind them goes on forever—deep and warm and safe.

I step closer to her, drawn as surely as if there's a rope around my waist. And before I can stop myself, I reach out and tuck a strand of soft, chestnut hair behind her ear.

And suddenly, I realize I want to kiss her. And not just because she's a girl. I want to feel *Holly's* lips against mine and listen to her breath quicken. I want to hear *Holly* moan as I touch her and feel her hands on my bare skin.

Holy hell, I . . .

Even my inner voice doesn't know what to make of this one. The silence inside and out is so complete, it's deafening. And all I can do is *feel*. My hand begins to tremble because this scares the hell out of me, but nothing in my life has ever felt this *right* before.

I move just a hair closer, my throat desert-dry but my lips aching for the sweet pressure that's only inches away. I drop my chin, and Holly closes her eyes in response, and . . . *this is really happening.*

Our lips meet, and it's so soft and so gentle, but my body explodes in sensation.

I'm getting hard.

My head is spinning.

My chest is expanding with emotions I can barely even contain, let alone define, and *oh my God, it's never felt like this.*

Our lips seem to move as one, push and pull, taste and tease, and I swear I've died and gone to heaven until her tongue darts out and . . . *motherfucker.*

My tongue is in her mouth and hers is in mine and *Jesus, I can't even . . .*

I jerk as her hands thread between my chest and arms, my skin warming and sizzling as she envelops me in heat and *how do I get closer?*

My own arms wrap around her, pulling and owning and *I never wanna stop . . .*

So I lower my arms, drawing her as close as I can, and *Jesus motherfucking* —"Ohhhh . . ."

My.

Dick.

Oh my God.

Her.

Nipples.

Mmmpphhhawwfffuck. Did I just come in my pants?

I break away, panting, trying with all my might to keep myself from jizzing and roaring and whimpering like a little girl.

And Holly is staring at me in the same state of . . . what the fuck?

I can't, I'm . . . Jesus . . . no, that's not right . . . My inner voice is stumbling, but at least, it's not speaking in tongues anymore, but I *feel* like I could walk on water and climb every mountain and ford every stream and when did this become *The Sound of Music,* and *holy hell, what's happening to me?*

CHAPTER ELEVEN

Falling in love is like jumping off a really tall building; your head tells you, "Idiot, you're gonna die," but your heart tells you, "Don't worry, pretty girl, you can fly."

– Unknown

HOLLY

Nathan just . . . stares at me, and all of a sudden, the biggest smile I've ever seen spreads across his face, and I'm flying. That was . . . I don't even know what that was—the only thing I know is if we don't do it again *right now* I think I might die.

I move forward, and Nathan more than meets me halfway—lips and hands and *oh good Lord* his *tongue*—and everything feels so warm and fizzy and dizzy . . . Now I know what it feels like to be a dropped soda bottle with the fizz surging and building to overflow. That's what I'm about to do—overflow. I don't know where or how, but I can *feel* it. And I don't ever want this feeling to end.

His tongue reaches deeper, thrusting and claiming, and every time he goes deep, something flips in my stomach and floods me with a wave of zinging heat.

His arms thread through mine this time, and I gasp into his mouth as my hardened nipples press into the firm planes of his chest. *Damn! I didn't know just kissing a guy could make them do that!*

The kissing is still incredible, and my thoughts are disjointed, but the movement of his hands slowly down my back commands my attention. His fingers stretch and flex, seeking . . . *Oh my God, what? I'll give him anything.*

And then he's there—hands firmly cradling my ass and pulling me closer until . . .

"Mmmpph." Nathan whimpers into my mouth.

Is that his . . . holy shit! Something warm and hard and—*wow!*—long is pressing against my thigh—I think it's *the* thing.

"Oommpphh." Nathan groans as the thing slides down and then up again.

Yup, definitely the thing—*holy cock, batman! Is it really that big? I didn't know they could get that big!*

The thought of *that*—anybody's *that*—someday trying to fit inside me is almost enough to make me stop kissing him, but the second my focus turns back to him, the pit of my stomach . . . um, lower . . . quivers and melts.

He's *so* into this. I can feel his heart thundering against my chest, and he whimpers and moans every time his *holy cock!* slides against my leg.

Why is he—

"Mmmnnnhh!"

I think lightning just struck.

Between.

My.

Legs.

Ohmigodohmigodohmigod. The holy cock! and my . . . he . . .

And it starts to pulse. It's like my heart has gone south and is beating in that little nub—*do I have a lady boner? Is this what it feels like?*

I don't care what it is; I want more!

Now *my* hands are somehow on *his* ass, and he groans loudly, coming up for air for a second before diving right back in, pulling me closer—if that's even possible.

We're both moving now, my hands kneading—*needing?*—his ass as we rub against one another.

Are those sounds coming from me?

And suddenly, something starts to build. The pulsing in my clit grows stronger, and I feel hot and *so* ready to overflow, and . . .

What the hell?

I tense up as my underwear suddenly feels wet—*really* wet—and it's like I've woken up and realized where we are and what we're doing.

I break the kiss and the friction, and my body is positively *screaming* at me to *get back over there and climb that boy like a tree until something wonderful happens*, but . . .

"We should stop," I tell him, hardly able to believe the words are coming out of my mouth as my mind tries to convince every other part of me that we shouldn't do this. My mind plays to win, reminding me that I need to be careful, that I shouldn't trust him so quickly . . . but God, that felt so *good* and so *right* and . . .

Nathan is staring at me. He's panting like he's just run a marathon as his hand riffles through hair damp from exertion. *Our* exertion.

I realize then that I'm also trying to catch my breath, and my stomach feels like a bed of hot coals—stoked and glowing and just *waiting* for the finish.

"Jesus," he mumbles, looking at the ground as color rises in his cheeks. I'd *kill* to know what he's thinking right now, what he's really thinking about any of this and why he's doing it.

I *want* to believe him, but it just makes no sense that a guy like him would date a girl like me. But I'm still doing this. I'm gonna date him; I'm gonna see where this goes, but we're *not* gonna go all the way. He can't hurt me that much if we don't do *that*, can he?

He grabs my hand and we walk, neither of us saying anything about what just happened, but somehow, that's okay too. He swings our hands between us, and when I look over, he's grinning at me, but . . . it's different. He looks happy in a way I've never seen him before. He stares at me with a look of . . . wonder? And it makes no sense, but my belly does that flip-flop thing, and I grin back.

The wind picks up, and I shiver. It's October and we've been outside for God knows how long, but I never noticed the cold until now. And it's getting dark. Dad will be home soon, and not being there is *not* something I want to have to explain today. *I kissed a boy and humped his leg and lost my mind. That's why there's no dinner on the table.* Um . . . no.

"Nathan, I think I need to go home," I say, staring down at our hands. "My dad will be home soon, and . . ."

Nathan visibly flinches at the word "dad," and I can't help but smirk. *Yup, Dad would have at least loaded the gun today.*

"Don't worry. He doesn't have laser vision, and he can't read my mind."

Nathan chuckles, but it seems half-hearted. *Is he really afraid of Dad?*

"Okay, let's go get your stuff, and I'll walk you out," he says, dropping my hand as we approach the house.

It stings for a moment, but then I remember his mother's ridiculous level of excitement over meeting me. Nathan probably has quite an interesting evening ahead of him while I just get to go home and make pasta. *Jeez, I hope his mom wasn't watching out the upstairs window.*

We breeze through the house, encountering no one, and before I know it, we're standing by the driver's side of my car.

Suddenly, he's holding out a red rose to me, and my insides melt into a puddle of ooey gooey girlishness.

"I . . . well . . . I thought you might like . . ."

Oh God, could he be more adorable? It takes nearly everything I have not to pounce on him and resume scaling Mount Nathan right where we left off.

"I love it! I mean, yes, I do. Thank you," I tell him, trying to keep the quaver out of my voice.

He grabs my hand, eyes focused on my fingers as he rubs them between his. He takes a deep breath, and then those riveting eyes pierce me.

"Could we . . . uh, get together tomorrow?" he asks, dropping his chin and glancing up at me shyly.

"You mean . . . like a date?" I blurt the words out and before I realize what I've done . . .

"Only if you want to."

"I want to." I reassure him with a smile. "What did you have in mind?"

He grins and exhales in a whoosh, and my smile grows wider as his nerves recede.

"Well, it's supposed to be warm and sunny. Wanna go to the beach?"

My eyebrows go up. *Holy shit, a bathing suit? It's October and I'm not ready and—*

"Not to swim. Let's just . . . go walk and take some snacks or something."

"Sure, that's sounds great."

"Okay, why don't you come over around eleven?"

"All right, I'll see you then, and I'll bring the snacks," I tell him.

He moves toward me but stops, suddenly unsure.

"Can I . . . kiss you again? Not like before, just . . ."

And I'm moving forward before he can finish the thought, one hand grasping his shoulder as our lips meet and mold together as if we've been doing this forever. The kiss isn't chaste, but he's not deep throating me either, and I linger, ghosting soft kisses on his lips after he's withdrawn his tongue.

"I'm glad you came over," he says, eyes still closed and a smile on his face.

"Me too."

And I float all the way home.

Chapter Twelve

The greatest prison people live in is the fear of what other people think.

– David Icke

Holly

I roll slowly down the long drive, and finally, the huge stone house appears through the trees. As I pull up, I see Nathan and Evan out in front of the detached garage washing Evan's car, and Nathan's mom is on the front porch reading a book. The boys have music blaring out of the garage so loudly that Nathan doesn't even hear my car, so I decide to go join Mrs. Harris on the porch and let them finish.

As I approach, she looks up from her book, a warm and welcoming smile spreading across her face. "Hi, Holly! It's so good to see you!"

I'm a little leery after the way Nathan reacted to her yesterday, but she certainly seems nice enough.

"It's good to see you too, Mrs. Harris!" I respond brightly.

"Oh please, dear, my name is Julie."

I grin. "Okay, Julie."

"So what are you and Nathan going to do today?"

I glance up at the near-cloudless sky, amazed again at how the weather here can turn on a dime. Yesterday, it was gray and in the fifties, while today is sunny and in the low seventies.

"We're going to the beach. I packed us some snacks and a blanket. I think we're just gonna go soak up some sun."

"What a great idea! I don't think Nathan's been down there in a few months," she says, and I wish I could hear what she *doesn't* say.

We sit in silence for a few moments, watching Nathan and Evan as they work their way toward the back of the car in what I realize is a practiced routine.

Evan drops his sponge, ruffling Nathan's chaotic mass of hair before hauling the bucket over to the hose for a refill.

"Were they always like this? I mean, didn't they ever . . . fight?" I ask, realizing a moment later that I said this out loud and not in my head.

Julie laughs—a sweet, soft sound that echoes the fondness written all over her face as she watches them.

"Oh my goodness, yes! When they were younger, all they did was beat on each other. We were concerned they'd really hurt one another as they got older. . ." She pauses, a faraway look in her eye. After a moment she meets my gaze. "Things changed after Nathan was diagnosed. Evan changed . . . not immediately, but we knew that was the reason."

"When did that happen? His diagnosis, I mean."

She eyes me shrewdly. "Nathan didn't tell you?"

I probably shouldn't be doing this. Nathan nearly went ballistic yesterday when Julie merely skirted the topic of his epilepsy, but I'm *so* curious, and if I can find things out without making him uncomfortable, that's good, right? *Right?*

"No," I reply, shaking my head. "He's told me some things, but he doesn't seem to like talking about it."

"No, you're right; he doesn't. But I don't think he'd mind that you know," she says, winking at me.

"It all began in the spring of his eighth grade year. He started having myoclonic seizures—did he tell you about those?"

"Yes?" I answer, drawing the word out as I struggle to remember the few details he's provided. Thankfully, Julie is more than happy to help.

"Well, those are just involuntary jerks of the muscles—kind of like when you jerk awake if you've fallen asleep in class?"

I smile and nod—*that's right, now I remember!*

"Anyway," she continues, "he started having those, and he didn't tell anyone for a few months, but then I saw him have one, and I knew it wasn't normal. I told Alan right away, and we took him to a neurologist. By then, it was the middle of the summer before his freshman year. They started running tests on him to figure out what was wrong, and while we were waiting for the results, he had his first tonic-clonic seizure."

I cock my head to the side. "Those are the big ones?"

"Yes, like the one you witnessed a few weeks ago. It was the scariest thing I'd ever seen. Luckily, Alan was there, and he knew what to do, but it didn't take long after that for Nathan to be diagnosed."

"Okay, so those are the big ones, and the myoclonics are the little ones . . ." I say, rapidly aligning Julie's story to what Nathan's already told me.

Julie furrows her eyebrows.

"Nathan *did* tell me about the two different kinds of seizures. He just didn't give the big ones a name."

"Oh, I see," she says, nodding. "Well, after the diagnosis, things changed between the boys. After we explained to them what could happen if

Nathan had any kind of head trauma, Evan never laid a hand on Nathan again, but they still weren't friends.

"It was a really hard time for Nathan—he was starting his freshman year, the doctors were having him try lots of different drugs to control the seizures, and he was learning about his . . . limitations. The hardest of all was the fact that he couldn't play basketball anymore," she says, shaking her head.

"He had been a star all the way through middle school. He has an incredible shot. He had one game in eighth grade where he scored forty points. The coaches at Tillamook High had already scouted him, and it was very likely he would have made the varsity team his freshman year. But there was no way he could play after we knew he had epilepsy. The risk of a head injury was just too great.

"So, he had to give it up. He didn't want anyone to know anything was wrong with him, as you know, so he told everyone he didn't want to play anymore. We tried to protect him and tell everyone it was his decision, and we supported it, but the coaches and players still gave him a really hard time. And Nathan just took it. Even though it was killing him not to be trying out for the team, he never said anything when the guys laid into him for it. That was what drove Evan over the edge. From that point on, Evan stood up for Nathan whenever anyone said anything to him, and they became friends."

I'm on overload—a little embarrassed for Nathan by all the information Julie's given me but mostly reeling from the knowledge of all he's gone through. *Holy shit! He was* that *good at basketball, and he had to just give it up? And everyone gave him a raft of shit over it?*

The sounds of laughter and a struggle ring out from the driveway, and we both look over to see Nathan soaping Evan with his sponge while Evan's soaking him with the hose. I can't help but laugh at the two of them— they're incredibly cute together. Julie's laughing as well, and she yells over to them, "Get more on the car than yourselves, boys!"

That's when Nathan notices me; he immediately drops his sponge and jogs over. He's wearing navy basketball shorts and a white t-shirt, which is now plastered to his chest because it's soaking wet. The sodden cotton outlines his pecs and abs in sharp relief, and my breath catches as I stare at his sculpted torso. *I had no idea that's what was under there!* I suspected he worked out, but *damn*. His hair is in its usual state of disarray, but he runs a wet hand through it as he approaches, slicking it back and out of his eyes.

"Hi, Holly! When did you get here?" he asks as he leans against the edge of the porch.

"A little while ago," I say, winking at him to try to calm his nerves.

"Uh oh, have you two been talking?" Nathan asks teasingly but not quite.

"Oh, Holly and I have just been getting to know each other." Julie's offhand reply is smooth as silk.

Nathan frowns, but he lets it go. "Why don't I go change, then we can head out?"

"Sure," I reply, thinking I'd really rather have him just stay in that wet t-shirt . . . I shake my head to clear it and smile at him.

Once Nathan leaves, the conversation turns to me, and Julie asks all the usual "getting to know your son's new girlfriend" questions. She's quite nice about the whole affair—much nicer than I'm sure Dad is gonna be whenever I decide to bring Nathan home—but that's just a daughters versus sons thing, isn't it? Although most dads probably don't have firearms within reach during that discussion—*shit, I'll have to remember to tell Nathan to bring his Xanax along.* Maybe we can slip one to Dad too.

Nathan returns in fresh basketball shorts and a Nike t-shirt, and I stand, eager to avoid a repeat of the pre-rose garden incident.

The tension between mother and son seems low today, though, and Julie just offers us a "Have fun, you two" as Nathan leads me off the porch.

He walks me to the driver's side of my car, but before I can open the door, he turns me against it, hands cupping my cheeks as his lips and tongue bid me hello. I lean into the kiss, flames dancing in my belly as excitement thunders in my chest. My hands grip his waist, beckoning to *holy cock!* to come and nest on my thigh, and Nathan's more than ready to oblige . . . until a wolf whistle sounds from near the garage.

"Goddammit," Nathan mutters, breaking our kiss and resting his forehead against mine. "Remind me to put some Icy Hot in that fucker's jock for practice on Monday."

I crack up, holding onto his shoulders as I shake with laughter, and Nathan's frown melts away.

"You two are major league, aren't you?"

"You have no idea," he says, opening the door for me, and he's still chuckling when he gets into the car.

It's a gorgeous day, so we wind our way along Route 131 with the windows down. Nathan sits with his elbow on the door, chestnut hair glinting in the sunlight as it blows into his eyes, but he doesn't even seem to notice.

I notice because he looks like a centerfold out of *Rolling Stone*—all he needs is a cigarette dangling from his mouth, and he'd give James Dean a run for his money.

We ride in silence for a while, but it's the comfortable kind. I'm about to ask where I should park when a sudden movement from the passenger side catches my eye. Nathan immediately slumps down, blowing out a frustrated breath as he closes his eyes and bows his head. His head jerks to the side, but it's so rapid—I don't think it's quite under his control.

"Fuck." His tone is resigned as he slides a little closer to me on the bench seat of the car.

"What's wrong?"

He doesn't answer right away, but this time, his arm flashes out and almost hits the dashboard.

"Nathan," I say, both a demand and a plea. *This is getting weird.*

He speaks very quietly. "I'm sorry, Holly, but I'm going to have to break our date for today and ask you to take me back home." The sorrow and frustration in his voice cause a lump to form in my throat.

"What is it?"

He sighs angrily as his left shoulder jerks forward. "I'm having myoclonic seizures."

My eyes go wide as panic tears down my spine, and I draw in a rapid breath. *What do I do? Is he going to convulse like he did at school? Oh fuck, I don't want to be here.*

I glance over at him, and there's pain and anger and every negative emotion I can think of written all over his face.

Dammit! I just did what he's afraid everyone else will do! He thinks I'm like everyone else! And somewhere in the back of my mind, I wonder if I really *am* like everyone else, at least a little.

"It's okay; these are the little ones I told you about. Don't be afraid," he says, his voice soft and comforting, as if he's talking to a small child or a frightened animal. The wall he's put up is like a physical barrier between us, and I feel like a complete and total piece of shit.

"I do need to go back home though. Can you turn around?"

"Sure," I reply automatically, mentally shaking myself and doing as he asks.

"Holly, it's really okay. This happens all the time." Despite the pain I've caused him, I can tell he wants to reach out and touch me to reassure me, but he keeps his hands resting lightly on his knees. Again, his head jerks sharply to the side.

"Does it . . . hurt?" I ask, really, really hoping the answer is no.

"No . . . well, unless my arm hits something when it jerks, which is a distinct possibility in a small space like a car. That's why I moved away from the door before."

I ponder this for a moment. "This means you're going to have a big seizure today, doesn't it?"

"Yeah," he says heavily. "I'm sorry about this, Holly. I really am."

"Don't be sorry. You can't control it. *I'm* sorry you're going to have a bad day."

And I really *am* sorry, and not only because he has to break our date. For the first time, I truly understand how little control he has—how much he's at the mercy of his body and has to adapt to whatever situation it throws at him.

"I'll be all right." I can sense his disappointment, but there's something else in the way he says it. An . . . uncertainty. Maybe even a little fear.

"Then . . . why are you afraid?"

"How the hell do you do that?" he asks, irritation creeping into his voice.

"Do what?"

"Read me like that. Sometimes I think you would have figured out my secret even if you hadn't seen anything."

"Does it bother you?"

"Yes," he responds quickly, "and no. With a secret to keep, it always makes me nervous when someone can guess things about me. But . . . somehow I don't really mind it from you."

Warmth spreads through my chest—I must be doing something right because the wall is coming down a little—but I still want to know why he's afraid.

"You haven't answered my question," I say gently.

He raises his eyebrows as he looks at me, and his lip curls into a frown.

"This usually only ever happens early in the morning. I'm . . . concerned about this happening so late in the day."

"You're worried it could happen at school."

"Yeah," he replies, running a hand through his hair. "I don't know what's going on with me. Everything has been so predictable for such a long time now. Why is it changing? It's stressing me out, and that leads to even more problems."

I reach over tentatively and put my hand on his knee. "I'm sorry, Nathan. I wish there was something I could do to help." I can't take back my earlier reaction, but I *can* show him that now I'm afraid *for* him and not *of* him.

I feel his eyes on me, and I risk a glance to find him staring at me with a strange expression on his face. "You already have," he whispers.

There's still distance in the silence between us, but it doesn't feel like a wall anymore—merely the divide between what he's experiencing and what I can only guess at.

I look over at Nathan again, and he's staring out the window. He's perfectly still, except his knee bounces a rapid rhythm. His hands are clenched in his lap. *There's something else.*

"What has you so nervous right now though?"

His eyes flash to mine, and I see fear there—and anger. "You know, this is why I don't have girlfriends."

Ouch. I blink rapidly, stung. I'm silent for a moment, listening to the sound of his rapid breathing as the hurt settles in. "I'm sorry, I—"

"No, I'm sorry," he says, heaving a frustrated sigh. "I'm not used to talking about this stuff. I'm worried about the lead-time on this seizure. Normally, it happens an hour or two after the little ones, but it's so late in the day already."

"You think it's going to be soon."

"Yeah," he admits, running a hand through his hair.

I unconsciously depress the gas pedal a little harder and curse myself for my instinctual "afraid *of* him" reaction, but Nathan doesn't seem to notice. Maybe if I can keep him distracted, it'll calm both of us.

"How do you know when it's going to happen? I mean, when I walked in on you that day, you obviously knew something was about to happen even though you didn't have the little seizures first . . ."

"Yes, I knew. I get a warning a minute or two before it happens."

I wait expectantly, but he remains silent. "Nathan?"

He shakes his head. "The warning is . . . fear. All of a sudden, I feel this completely irrational terror that just about paralyzes me. Then I know I've only got a minute or two."

"Oh," I say softly. I remember the look on his face when I walked in that day, and now I understand. It had nothing to do with me and everything to do with what was about to happen to him. The more I learn about what he has to go through, the more I realize how much more there is to him than I knew. To have to deal with this on top of school and home-work and everything else in his life and to try to keep it a secret from everyone above all . . . "Wow," I murmur.

"What?" he asks, not unkindly this time.

"I don't know how you do it."

"Well, I don't really have a choice, now do I?" he says bitterly, the edge creeping back into his voice.

"You don't have a choice in having to handle it, but you *do* have a choice in *how* you handle it, and I think you handle it well."

His lips turn upward in a small smile. "Thanks," he says quietly.

We're winding our way up his long driveway, and I can tell he's anxious to be in the house. "Nathan, can you please call me tomorrow to let me know you're okay?" I ask as I slow down.

He has the door open before the car stops moving, but he meets my eyes as he closes it. "If I can, I will," he answers, turning away and jogging to the house without another word.

∾

I spend my Saturday reading and trying not to think about what Nathan might be going through. *What the hell happens after he has one of the big seizures anyway?* I saw him right after when Evan carried him out of the classroom, and I know the next day he had a terrible headache, but what happens in between? Maybe he just rests for the day, but my imagination is coming up with too many other possibilities. I hope I can find a way to ask that won't offend him.

He calls on Sunday around suppertime, and as soon as I hear his voice, I know he still feels like hell.

"Hello?" I answer eagerly—I've been waiting for this call for more than twenty-four hours.

"Hi, Holly," he says, his words coming slowly.

"Are you okay?"

"Yeah, just . . . tired, and I have a massive headache."

"So, you—"

"Yeah, about five minutes after you dropped me off."

Holy shit! He could have had a seizure right in my car! The lump in my throat is almost too thick to swallow around; the combination of fear *of* him and *for* him is almost more than I can handle.

Breathe. It didn't happen, and you can't be afraid of him. He needs you to be there for him.

"You don't have to say anything," Nathan says before I can pull myself together. "And if you don't want to go out with me anymore, I understand."

"No!"

There's a sharp intake of breath, and a mumble of "fuck" before I realize *he's* misunderstood.

"I mean, yes! Of course I still want to go out with you! Your seizure yesterday has nothing to do with that." I can almost hear him cringe when I say the word "seizure," but after a moment, the rest seems to sink in.

"Really?"

"Really. I know what happened yesterday kind of . . . scared us both, but I'm not afraid of you." *I really, really don't want to be afraid of you. I'm working on it. Please let me keep trying.*

"Are you sure?"

"Yes, I'm sure. We'll go to the beach next weekend if it's warm, and if not, we'll find something else to do, okay?"

"Okay," Nathan says, and I just know it's the first time he's smiled since yesterday. *Mission accomplished.*

"Holly, I need to go. I still feel like shit, and I have to make it to school tomorrow."

"Go crash and I'll see you in homeroom. And don't let Ryan make you late."

He chuckles, and my heart clenches, but it's a funny little good kind of clench—like I did something right.

"Goodnight, Holly," he says, his tone much lighter than it was when he first said hello.

"Goodnight," I answer, knowing that it really *is* a good night, for both of us.

Chapter Thirteen

NATHAN

Fuck. How is it Monday already? *Oh right. I had a seizure late in the day on Saturday that ruined my date and scared the hell out of me. And it pretty much killed the rest of my weekend too.*

I groan as I roll over, but at least my head isn't hurting. Yesterday's headache was a monster—the only thing I accomplished all day was calling Holly.

What I can only describe as excitement rushes through me at the mere thought of her name—exactly the same way it's been every time since I kissed her.

I enjoy it for a minute because it's new, and it feels *so* good, and it's all mine. *She's* all mine. And I came so close to losing it this weekend, or at least, I thought I did. I should have known she wouldn't dump me because I almost had a seizure in her car. She's already seen me lie down on the floor and have one right in front of her, for Christ's sake.

But the way she looked at me—I could see the fear in her eyes, and I felt so . . . alone. I hated it and I wanted to jump out of her car, but she kept . . . talking and poking and prodding and distracting and fucking *caring* about me until suddenly, I was home, and I didn't have time to freak out before the seizure hit.

I wonder if she had any idea what she was doing—that it was the best thing she could have done for me. A panic attack followed by a seizure isn't pretty—at least *that* hasn't happened in almost two years . . . *Oh yeah, except for the day after Holly was with me at school.*

How the hell did my head get here? Oh right. Holly.

But now my head—both of them, in fact—is in a completely different place. The warmth—and my hand—travel south as I remember the softness of her lips and the feel of her tongue wrapping around mine. *Jesus.*

I've gotten off with quite a few girls, both real and imagined, but no one, not even the best porn flick chick I've ever seen, can get me there as fast as thoughts of Holly. I would have done it last night, but raging headache and raging hard-on tend to be mutually exclusive. I still thought about trying to force the issue, though.

Speaking of the issue, it's forcing itself right now—right up into the waistband of my boxers.

My hand slides over cotton, and I have to bite my lip to keep in the groan as the ribbing bunches and rolls, creating incredible friction. But I don't want fabric; I want fingers, and if I can't have hers right now, my own will have to do—I'll just pretend they're hers.

I touch the pads of my fingers to my lips, mimicking the soft touch of hers as my other hand slips into my boxers and down my length. *Holy mother of fuck, I've never been this hard before, I swear.*

She's kissing me, her tongue thrusting against mine the way I would thrust inside her—and suddenly my hips are moving, and I'm fucking my fist the way she's tongue-fucking me in my head.

The sensation is already building. *Jesus, I'm going to have to get myself drunk and do this just so I can have a few minutes to enjoy it.*

I wanna slow down, but I can't. I'm *so* close already, and everything in me wants to explode like a balloon that's ready to pop.

"Ohhh, Holly," I murmur, and suddenly, it's her pussy and not her hand and—

I squeeze my eyes shut as the pressure mounts—*oh God, here it comes*—

"Nathan! Get up, honey; you'll be late for school!"

Mom's head appears around the side of my door just as my world inverts and explodes, and I can't contain the cry that's torn from my chest as my toes curl, and I pulse hard into my hand.

I'm barely coherent, but the only thought that does come through is, *I am so fucked.*

"Nathan, are you okay?"

Mom's halfway into the room now, and if I don't come up with something fast, come is exactly what she's gonna see—all over my dark blue sheets.

I've already curled on my side away from her in some infallible instinct for self-preservation, so I grab my calf with my non-jizzed hand and grind out, "leg cramp."

"Oh, it must be really bad for you to yell like that. Do you need me to massage it for you?"

Oh Jesus, talk about instant karma. Who needs to wait to burn in hell for masturbating when you can have this happen instead?

"No, I'm fine, Mom . . . I'll be down in a few, okay?"

"All right, sweetheart, if you're sure."

Mom, I have never *been more sure of anything in my life.*

"Yep, be there soon." I force the words out, all while trying to figure out if my head is still on my shoulders and to keep from panting after what was arguably one of the best orgasms of my life.

I lie there for a few minutes, stunned by the force of my orgasm and my own stupidity.

Evan would twist my nipple off for this. What's the rule for whackin' your kraken? Lock the door.

At least no one will ever know.

Once I can breathe normally, and I think my knees won't buckle, I slide out of bed, intent on wiping my hand off before I head to the bathroom.

"Hey, Nate, have you seen my—"

Oh, for the love of God, can't anyone in this damn house knock?

I freeze halfway between my bed and dresser, my right hand still in "jizz hand" position. Yes, "jizz hand" is remarkably similar to "jazz hand," and every guy on the planet knows what I'm talking about.

Including my fuckwad of a brother.

He freezes too, marveling at my outstretched hand. His lips look like they're gonna give birth to something; he's trying so hard to hold in his laughter.

"Evan—"

"Nate, uh . . . I think you're having a bit of a . . . containment problem . . ."

"Evan.

"Get.

"The fuck.

"Out.

"Of my room."

He finally explodes with laughter, doubling over with the force of his guffaws, and I'm seriously tempted to give him my best jizz hairstyle.

"I swear to God, Evan, I'll super glue your dick to your leg while you sleep if you don't get out of here. *Right. Now.*"

He's still laughing so hard, he seems to be having trouble breathing, and right about now, I'd be happy to help him pass out on my floor.

Except that wouldn't get him out of my room.

So I snatch up a tissue, wipe my hand, and then shove him bodily out of my room, locking the door as I press my back up against it, Evan's snickers still echoing in the hallway.

It's 7:10 a.m.

How is it possible for this much to go wrong in ten fucking minutes?

~

The ride to school is a silent war: Evan with himself as he tries not to howl with laughter, and me with my subconscious as I try to resist grabbing the wheel and steering his side of the car into something made of concrete.

Fucking asshole motherfucker. Maybe I'll glue his dick to his leg anyway.

But the thought of seeing Holly calms me somewhat. I still have a girl-friend even if I don't understand why, and it feels . . . good.

I intend to go straight to my locker, but Holly's at hers, and I slip an arm around her waist, chuckling when she startles, and books go flying everywhere.

I've never touched a girl like this in public, and it draws the stares of most of the other girls in the vicinity.

"Nathan!" she exclaims, playfully whacking me on the shoulder as she starts to bend to pick up her things, but I beat her to it, gathering her books and offering them to her from one knee on the floor.

"I'm sorry. I didn't think I'd scare you." *But your boobs did this great bounce thing, and I'd totally do it again.*

"It's all right. Are you having a good morning?"

Totally. I jizzed in front of my mom, and my brother caught me semen-handed. It's been divine.

"Yeah. I'm feeling much better than I did yesterday."

"Good."

Holly's gaze shoots to the floor.

"I missed you," she says to my shoes, and my heart does that lurch thing again, but I know now that it's a normal thing. A good thing. The *right* thing.

"I missed you too," I tell her, and my hands move to her face of their own accord, pulling her forward to touch my lips to hers.

Heat and want explode in my groin, and I can feel myself getting hard, but I don't care. This isn't about that. It's about something else that I'm way too chickenshit to put a name to, so I just let the wave wash over me and bask in the feeling.

"I'll see you in homeroom," Holly says as I step back, and she looks exactly the way I imagine I do—eyes wide in wonder and warmth and . . . want.

"Yeah."

Okay, I do care about my hard-on because my dick is literally screaming at me to rub against her leg, the lockers, something, *anything*, but we're in the middle of the hallway for Christ's sake. *It's going to be torture if this happens every time I touch her.*

This happens every time you even think *about her, you horndog,* head-voice snarks at me.

I'm gonna need to come up with some more times and places where I can play a little five-on-one—

"Nathan?"

I startle out of my internal debate to find Holly smirking at me and Megan smiling over her shoulder.

"Your locker's that way," Holly says, pointing down the hall, and my face is so hot, it actually stings.

I turn without a word and slink to my locker, hoping to God no one else saw me standing there like a lovesick puppy.

Did I just think the L *word?*

Seriously. What the hell *is happening to me?*

I make it through the day without hitting my emergency Xanax, but it's a near thing. Since I started hanging out with Chris and the other jocks freshman year, I've never done anything that wasn't exactly what they expected. But dating Holly? That's definitely cause for strange looks at best and outright abuse at worst.

As I'm heading to my locker, I spy Chris and Tyler on the lobby steps, giving some sophomore girls a raft of shit. Chris gives me the eye, and I click into autopilot, taking my position as his wingman and joining in.

"Yeah, Katie, we all know you fell out of the slut tree—"

I happen to glance over Katie's head and lock eyes with Holly. My heart lurches, but this time, it bottoms out in my shoes. She doesn't look angry, just . . . really disappointed. I've made it a point to disappear when the guys start in on her friends, but what does she expect? I can't just stop being who I am.

"—and banged every guy on the way down."

Holly's lips form a thin line, and her eyes flash as she turns and stalks toward her locker.

Now she's pissed.

Bang!

Really pissed.

She's supposed to come over to my house after school. *Shit. Maybe I should just wait on Evan.*

The fuck you say? my dick cries out. He's been waiting all day for the three b's: bedroom, boobs, and bow chicka bow wow. *You better apologize, grovel—do whatever it takes to fix this!*

Holly and my dick are pretty pissed, but my feet are even colder, and I feel . . . ashamed.

I leave Chris and Tyler as soon as I can, intent on grabbing my stuff and heading out to the stands to watch practice, but Holly's waiting at my locker.

Shit.

I approach with caution. She doesn't *look* like she's about to rip my balls off, but looks can be deceiving. Amber kissed me right before she tried to twist them off that one time—I will *never* let an angry woman within three feet of my jewels again.

She smiles, and I know it's meant to reassure me, but it only puts me more on edge.

"I think I'll just wait for Evan today."

She puts a hand on my arm, and I freeze, my attraction to her and my self-preservation instinct deadlocked.

"Can we talk?"

No, no, no, no, no . . .

"Sure."

You *are a dumbass.*

I follow her to her car.

A pussy-whipped dumbass.

Holly sits behind the wheel, but she doesn't turn the ignition, so I know that whatever's coming, it's going to happen right here and now.

"Why do you make fun of people like that?" she asks, her brown eyes wide and innocent as they search mine.

"I don't know," I reply, staring at my knees. Actually, I do know, but I don't want to tell her—I'm sure she won't approve. When I first gravitated toward Chris freshman year, I'd done it instinctively, but eventually, when I thought it out, I realized that if I was always on the offensive, I would never have to be on the defensive. That was exactly what I needed to keep my secret, so I became Nathan the jerk—cool with all the popular kids but bane of the existence of the geeks, dweebs, and misfits. I don't like it, but it's the role I have to play to protect myself.

"I don't believe you," she says, and it's as if she can see right through me. I consider arguing, but do I really want to push her away? She already knows almost everything.

"That's who I have to be."

"Why?"

"Because the best defense is a good offense," I say, thinking back to Evan's words from so long ago. It was the first time he kicked the shit out of somebody before they could lay a hand on me, and I'd realized his words applied to my social life too.

"I don't understand."

"If I make fun of people, everyone looks at them, and no one ever looks at me."

Holly's eyes widen. "Your secret?"

I nod, feeling the shame that I talked myself out of long ago turn my stomach.

"That's . . . not what I expected."

I raise my eyes to her and she looks . . . relieved?

"What, you thought I was just a jerk naturally?"

She blushes, and I don't know whether to laugh or be insulted.

"You're very good at the front you put up."

That's a compliment, I think.

"I have to be."

"Nathan, don't you realize what you're doing?"

"I'm protecting myself," I answer, but I know that's not what she means. I justified and laid to rest what she means two years ago.

"Maybe, but you're also doing to them exactly what you don't want done to you. You're guarding against your own worst fear by making theirs come true."

Ouch. When you put it like that . . .

"No, I'm not—"

"Yes, you are. And you know you are. You might not want to think about it, but you know."

"How the hell do you know *that*?" I snap at her, suddenly wanting to be anywhere but here.

"Because you're about to tear the armrest off my door, and you're breathing faster."

"Stop watching me!" I yell, and now my breathing really does speed up as the inside of her car seems to close in on me.

"I'm sorry," I mutter, trying to keep the panic at bay and my ass in the seat while all my instincts scream "Run!"

Holly squeezes my forearm gently, and then begins to rub up and down. Her touch grounds me, and I focus on that until the need to escape fades.

"I'm sorry for snapping at you. I try not to let anyone ever watch me that closely because—"

"Because it makes you panic."

"Yeah." I don't think I've ever admitted that to anyone—not even Mom.

"I'm sorry for making you feel trapped. I'll try not to do it again."

I squeeze my eyes shut as shame and self-loathing over my weakness flare, but it's . . . me, and there's nothing I can do about it.

"I can't change, Holly. I can't change my diagnosis, and I can't change how I react, and I can't change who I am at school."

"You're right," she says, still rubbing my arm. "At least partially. You can't change your epilepsy, and I don't know if you can change the way it makes you feel, but you *can* change how you treat people at school. There are plenty of kids who don't make fun of anyone else and still don't get picked on themselves."

"But there's no guarantee." I'm quick to point out the flaw in her logic. "If I'm with Chris, I'm untouchable. No one can hurt me."

"But are you hurting yourself?" she asks, and her words rip open the wound I ignore and have learned not to even feel anymore—the one that festers and grows deeper every time I cut down someone else.

"It doesn't matter. I can't go from being somebody to being nobody." And as soon as the words leave my mouth, I know I've made a terrible mistake.

"Holly, I—"

"No, it's true. I *am* nobody, and you can't go from being nobody to being somebody either. I tried at the beginning of the year, remember?"

"You're *not* nobody," I reply hotly, but I understand what she means. We both know how high school works.

She shakes her head with a sad smile.

"So where do we meet, Nathan? How do we do this when you're one of the most popular kids at school and I'm . . . not?"

"I don't know." I wish I could tell her I don't care what anyone thinks, but it's not true. It can't be true because of my situation. It can never be true.

"Will you at least think about what I said, about trying not to be Chris's minion? For me?"

Her eyes are *so* brown, and when they're a little wet, they look even more intense.

"I . . . yeah, I will," I reply, and the smile that lights up her face as she starts the car is totally worth it.

The next thing I know, we're parked in front of my house. My dick doesn't understand why she still can't come in so we can legsturbate, but my head is way too preoccupied with our conversation.

And Holly knows it.

"I'll see you in the morning, Nathan," she says, and I get out without a second thought.

"Yeah, see you," I mumble, too lost in my own head to even try to interpret her smile.

CHAPTER FOURTEEN

Courage is grace under pressure.

– Ernest Hemingway

NATHAN

I think hard over the next few days, but I really have no solution to either of my problems. I'm afraid to stop being the person I've been for two years, and Holly and I don't seem to fit into any social group as a couple.

But that's a problem for another time. Right now, it's Friday night, and for the first time in what my dick tells me is eons, I'm going to a dance *with a girl*.

Given my . . . *situation*, Evan has agreed to drive Holly and me to the dance with him and Lori. Normally, I would go with Ryan or Tyler, but I have a girl now, and I can't very well have Holly pick me up when everyone thinks I should be driving.

Motherfucker, if I could only drive a car.

I've thought about doing it illegally, but Mom would have an aneurysm if she found out, and God forbid I actually had a seizure behind the wheel, or even worse, Holly's dad caught me.

This whole girlfriend thing draws a lot of attention to the question of my driving that I used to be able to avoid—just one more thing for me to be stressed about. *Dammit.*

"What are you thinking about back there, lover boy?" Evan asks, wearing a grin I'd like to smack off his face. "Going over the birds and bees since yours have been in hibernation for a while?"

"Fuck off, asswipe." I glare at him as my face goes hot, but I say nothing more. It's better he thinks I'm daydreaming about sex than stressing over my limitations.

"Stay out of trouble tonight, will ya? Lori and I have plans."

"Whatever."

I have zero intentions of staying out of trouble—*after the week I've had, he actually expects me to stay sober?* I need a good stiff drink almost as much as I need to jerk off, and that's saying something.

And speaking of stiff drinks, I could really use a double right now. As we pull up in front of Holly's house, I see the squad car in the driveway.

Holly's. Dad. Is. Home.

Oh shit. Oh shit, oh shit, *oh shit.*

I've known since the moment I found out he was the new police chief—I would rather chop my junk up like franks and beans and feed it to the local wolves with a side of freshly pulled toenails than meet Holly's dad. I would even do it more than once, if it were possible.

The air in my lungs starts to solidify, and I take a gasping breath as I grip the armrest for dear life.

Evan glances over at me and shakes his head.

"Do you think you could do us all a favor and calm the fuck down? Assuming Holly's dad lets you keep your dick, nothing bad is gonna happen. No one knows your secret, and no one knows—"

My fist flashes out and connects with his bicep before he can utter the words.

"—anything else they shouldn't, so just enjoy yourself, okay? Holly's a cool girl, and for some reason, she actually likes you. Don't convince her you're too neurotic to be dateable."

I slug his arm again, but this time, there's no force behind it.

"Can Lori even spell 'neurotic'?" I ask, pressing myself against the window to avoid Evan's tree trunk of an arm as it swings my way for a headlock.

"I don't care if she can because she sucks dick like a Shop-Vac, and her tit size has more letters than her name. But that's not the point. The point is, get through this, and then relax."

Evan slaps my knee reassuringly.

"Man up, and show him what you're made of. Shake his hand like Dad taught us, and don't look away. It'll be fine."

What I'm made of is a swirling mass of soon-to-be vomit, hopefully not on the chief's shoes. My whole life is a lie, and I started dating Holly to preserve that lie. A lie on top of a lie that's now grown into something wonderful, but its roots are still rotten and shameful.

And this guy's gonna see it; I just know it.

"Go on now. Go."

Evan's words seem to come from far away, but I obey on autopilot and push myself to stand beside the car on shaky legs.

Come on, Nathan, you can do this. Passing out on the porch will not impress the chief.

My trembling legs deposit me in front of the door, and I can hear the ball-game on in the living room.

He's watching the game. It's not cool to disturb a man and his sports, right? Maybe we should save this for another day.

I turn away from the door, but the thought of disappointed, deep brown eyes stops me cold.

Nathan, man up.

Speaking of my manhood, where the hell is that fucker now, eh?

I would reach down and make sure everything's still there, but I'm terrified that my dick's somehow managed to crawl back inside me.

This is ridiculous.

I turn around and ring the doorbell before I have the chance to talk myself out of it, and my stomach does that swooping thing like when you start going down that first hill of a roller coaster.

"I'll get it!"

Oh shit, here we go . . .

Holly whips the door open, her eyes a little too bright and eager—as if she's trying to hold me together by the sheer force of her will. She nods encouragingly, but her Nathan bolt-o-meter must be going off because she threads her arm through mine and pulls me over the threshold.

"Are you okay?" she whispers, and I think I nod, but it's hard to tell when so much of me seems to be shaking. Her lips curl into a frown. "Let's get this over with."

As we cross the living room, the chief stands and sizes me up as if there's a little table between us and a mirrored wall behind me. He's in his uniform for work, but I almost pass out from relief when I see there's no holster on his hip.

"H-h-hi, sir. I'm Nathan Harris."

Thank God I've had that one memorized for fifteen years and can spit it out without having to think about it.

"It's nice to meet you, son. Why don't you walk me out?"

If looks could kill, Holly would have just incinerated her dad, but as it is, all I can do is gape at her in terror as I follow the chief into the hallway.

His glance over his shoulder stops Holly in her tracks, and she flops down on the couch as if her legs won't hold her anymore. And I'm left to wonder if my chalk outline will be in the entryway or somewhere outside the house.

The chief puts on his gun belt, and while I'm debating if I can vomit *and* piss myself at the same time, he claps a hand down on my shoulder.

Hot breath that smells like bologna blasts my face. "Son, a shotgun and a shovel are child's play. I'll make it look like the bears got ya. Don't give me a reason."

"N-n-no, sir. Never." All my bodily fluids actually *do* stay where they belong but only because I'm paralyzed by fear.

"Good boy," he says, hefting his jacket over his shoulder. I think I see a smirk on his face, but I'm pretty sure I'm having stress-induced hallucinations, so I can't be sure.

The door snaps closed, and Holly appears at my side.

"Are you all right?"

I reach between my legs and give my junk a firm squeeze, both to make sure everything's still there and to try and snap me out of my haze. "Yeah. Um, I think so."

Holly blows out a relieved breath while failing miserably at hiding her smirk. She wraps her arms around me, pulling me close as her clasped hands come to rest at the small of my back.

"I *really* appreciate what you just did," she says, kissing my nose. "I know you've been dreading it, but you did it anyway. Hey—what did my dad say to you before he left?"

Oh, nothing really. He just described my impending sudden loss of life.

"Um, sports stuff." *Hunting's a sport, right? But usually the bears aren't the ones hunting* you.

"Oh," Holly says, not looking convinced, but she lets it go.

We go to Lori's next, and as I watch Evan walk her back to the car, I can tell she's already bitching about something. Some*one* is probably more accurate because I'd bet my left nut it has to do with me.

Evan reaches for her a few feet from the car, but she pulls away and whips open the door, a whirlwind of candy apple red lipstick, thick eye makeup, and way too much perfume.

"Hey, Lori," I say, knowing that affirming my existence is usually all that's needed to piss her off.

"Hey, Na-*than*." She singsongs my name as Evan gets into the car, shoveling the sarcasm into her tone with a backhoe.

"Play nice, you two," Evan says, sighing in resignation.

"We wouldn't have to play *at all* if Nathan would just get his own damn car." Her snappy reply makes me flinch, but that's immediately followed by the urge to slap the back of her head. The sudden lines of pain across my palms let me know how tightly my fists are clenched, but Holly grabs the one closest to her and interlaces her fingers with mine.

"Now, Lori—"

"What? Can't your brother do anything for himself? You're always babying him—now we have to cart him and his girlfriend around too?"

I close my eyes as the anger and frustration come to a boil inside me, but I bite my tongue because there's nothing I can say. She's right—Evan and my parents *do* baby me, but it's not as if I want it this way.

"That's *enough*." Evan's tone leaves no room for argument, but his apologetic gaze in the rearview mirror makes me even more disgusted with the whole thing.

Lori huffs and crosses her arms, but she doesn't say another word.

I open my mouth, intent on at least suggesting that my brother date something that doesn't come from a barnyard, but Holly's lips are on mine before I can finish the thought, much less get a word out. Just as I'm really getting into it, Holly pulls back and puts her finger over her lips. I smirk and shake my head as I disentangle from her hand but only so I can grab it with my other one and put my arm around her. She snuggles into my shoulder, and by the time we make it to the school, her warm breath and soft kisses on my neck have me so horny, I can hardly see straight.

Do we have to go to the dance? Can't we just stay in the car? Or the woods? Or the middle of the fucking parking lot?

My dick hasn't had this much to say since I first discovered porn.

But Holly looks so excited to be here!

I'm excited too—doesn't that count for anything? I'm so excited; all she has to do is—

Which is exactly why we're going into the dance first. Zero to jizz in ten seconds will *not* impress a girl, no matter how much you tell her it's because of her mad skills, and I'd like a few minutes of awesome before you get yours.

But—

"Nathan?"

Holy hell, have I been sitting here having a conversation with my *dick*?

"Yeah, coming!"

No, we're definitely not.

I scramble out of the car, red-faced, and Evan smirks at me from the other side and gives me a "jizz hand" wave.

How does that fucker always know?

Because he talks to his dick too. And in a nicer way than you do.

Did you just turn into a pussy right before my very eyes?

"Nathan?"

Now I'm standing next to the car *looking down at my crotch.*

Oh my God, I have *got* to get this under control.

I shake my head to clear it and take Holly's hand, trying to focus on something other than my recent heart-to-dick . . . head-to-head . . . whatever.

As soon as we're through the caf doors, we run into Justin and Megan. They're standing a few inches apart, but I throw my arm around Holly's waist and tuck my hand into her front pocket as if it's the most natural thing in the world.

What the fuck did I just do?

But Holly molds against me and lays her head on my shoulder, smiling so widely it's as if the sun came out in the darkened room.

And it feels *good*.

I stand with my arm around Holly as the girls chat, and a feeling of contentment steals over me. I've never been able to do this—I've never had a real girlfriend; I've never stood just . . . touching a girl for the sake of doing it—all of my female interactions since the eighth grade have been of the "wham-bam-thank-you-ma'am" variety since I can't ever let anyone get too close. I never really thought I was missing out, but now? Now, I'm feeling in ways I didn't even know existed, and it's as if a whole new world has opened up.

A slow song comes on, and Megan grabs Justin's hand and pulls him toward the floor. He rolls his eyes as he passes me, but he doesn't look *that* unwilling.

And suddenly, I'm staring into fathomless brown eyes that look so hopeful, so eager.

"Will you dance with me, Nathan?" Holly asks in shy schoolgirl voice, and my heart does that thing again, and I *like* it.

I nod because I'm blown away by what I'm feeling, and we get to the center of the floor, and it's dark, and "Use Somebody" is playing, and I pull her to me as her arms lock around my neck and her head rests on my chest, and *oh God, how did I not know about this*?

I hold her. I breathe in the floral scent of her hair, taste the sweet tang of her skin as I place a kiss behind her ear, feel the soft press of her breasts against me. And nothing exists in that moment except the two of us and this *feeling*.

It's growing. It fills my chest, and I can barely breathe, and for once, that's a *good* thing. I have a name for it, but it scares the shit out of me. This was only supposed to be a way to ensure Holly's silence, but it's turned into so much more. It's what I *want* and what I *need* and . . . what I can't live without.

This can't be happening.

Why not? the voice in my head asks. *Why can't you have what the others have now that Holly knows the truth about you?*

Jiminy Fucking Cricket has a good point, for once. Why *can't* I have this? She obviously cares about me, and no one ever has to know how this all started. Why can't it just be that she's mine now, and to hell with everyone else and the horse they rode in on?

There's no reason why it can't.

I squeeze her a little tighter, and the peace that fills me is unreal.

"I hope it's gonna make you notice . . ."

I've never wanted to be noticed by anyone, but now, from this girl in my arms, I want it more than anything.

I hang on to her, reveling in the discovery that I *want* this because I haven't allowed myself to want anything other than for this nightmare to end since I was diagnosed. I have no idea how much time has passed, but I suddenly become aware that another slow song has come on, and Holly shifts against me, her thigh brushing against my erect dick, who's just been biding his time while I had my little emotional awakening.

I gasp and grit my teeth as a wave of *need* nearly overpowers me, and when I open my eyes, Holly's smirking at me.

She presses as close to me as she can, and this time, she slides *upward*.

Holymotherfucker—"Unnghh."

Holly giggles. She actually *giggles*, and dammit, enough is *enough*.

"Come on, I know a place where we can have a little privacy," I say, grabbing her hand and leading her out the back door of the cafeteria.

It's pitch dark, but the arc light overhead illuminates the fine, misty raindrops to the point that they look like snowflakes. Intent on my destination, I pull her out of the light and toward the football field. Around the back of the stands, there's a large brown shed where they keep the mower for the field and the other maintenance equipment.

Even in the dark, I can see her eyes widen as I reach up under the eave of the little roof at exactly the right spot and produce a key.

"Shall we?" I ask, grinning smugly as I open the door and usher her inside. I glance around, then shut the door behind us, pocketing the key. That's the universal signal to the other half-dozen guys who know about this place: if the key isn't there, the room's busy.

Holly stands in the middle of the little space, arms crossed at the wrists while she glances around at the equipment. My goal is for her not to remember a single thing in this room other than me.

I walk toward her, a coy smile turning up the corners of my mouth as I think about what I want to do in the next few minutes. I stop about three inches from her nose, staring into those amazing brown eyes and breathing in the sweet scent of her perfume. I join my hands with hers, my gaze never wavering, and then I move imperceptibly closer. I hear her rapid intake of breath as her eyes flutter closed, and in that moment, I know she wants me as much as I want her.

I close the distance and meet her lips gently, exploring as heat blooms in my chest. She responds by stepping even closer, her fingers tightening in mine as her tongue runs along my bottom lip. I release her—needing her closer still—and run my hands up her back, the smooth cotton of her blouse making the tips of my fingers tingle with sensation. She shivers as I pull her against me, my stomach flipping giddily and my dick twitching as I thrust my tongue deeply into her mouth.

Oh.

My.

God.

Her whole body clings to mine now, her breasts soft and supple against my chest, her heat radiating against my thigh just below where my dick presses against her. I can't help but slide downward—it's as if my dick is following a homing signal to where it wants to be.

Oh fuck, we have got to go further tonight, or I'm gonna lose my mind.

We've been doing the bump and grind every time I can get her alone, but we haven't actually touched each other yet.

I'm so lost in myself that I almost forget what she's doing—her hands are now wound into my hair as we continue to kiss—her lips and tongue exploring me with increasing urgency.

Maybe if I touch her first . . .

My hands slide under her shirt and make quick work of her bra strap, and while I hate like hell to remove my dick from her thigh, my desire to fill my hands with her breasts is even stronger. I break away from her lips as I ease my hands under her shirt, asking permission with my eyes as I slowly make my way up her chest. She nods uncertainly, so I smile to reassure her. *This is going to drive her wild.*

I cup my hands gently under her breasts—her skin is so soft and warm, and the shape is just *so* perfect—my thumbs circle slowly over her nipples, and I smirk as she moans, her eyes closing of their own accord. I want to rip her shirt off and take both of her hardened nipples into my mouth . . . *slow, slow*, I remind myself and lean forward to leave a trail of hot wetness on her neck instead.

Her hands leave my hair and slide down my sides, and I'm so aroused that the mere thought of her actually touching my dick is almost enough to make me jizz.

Keep going; keep going; yes! Now move to the center . . .

Her right hand comes to rest on the top of my jeans, and I quiver in anticipation as I try to keep feathering kisses on her neck.

Her hand slides down, and I gasp raggedly as she touches me. She jumps back.

"I'm sorry!"

In my lust-filled haze, I'm barely aware that she seems a little frightened. "Oh no, Holly, don't be sorry. Actually . . . could you do that again?"

She looks at me uncertainly. "Are you sure it's okay?"

I open my eyes and telegraph my sincerity. "Oh, it's *better* than okay."

"I mean—"

Oh.

Dammit. Not what I want to be thinking about right now.

"Yes, it's okay," I answer, trying to hide my irritation. "Can you do me a favor, please? Just assume I can do everything everyone else can unless I tell you otherwise?"

She nods sheepishly. "I'm sorry. I thought that since we hadn't . . ."

Hold the fuck up. She thought we hadn't gone further yet because *I* couldn't, *not* because she wasn't ready? So we could've . . .

Nathan, you stupid motherfucker.

Who cares? my dick pipes up. *Her hand is* right there, *and so help me, if we don't get some action soon—*

"Don't worry about it. Now, where were we?" I say, molding my lips to hers.

Her hand slides down between us again, and she starts to tentatively rub over the bulge in my jeans.

Oh God . . . it's been *way* too long since a girl touched me like this—since Amber Watson, in fact, and that was during the last school year. I moan against Holly's mouth as pleasure spikes through me, and I can't help but press against her hand and squirm a bit to try and get more friction.

Her strokes grow firmer as she becomes more confident, squeezing a bit as she traces the outline of my dick with her fingers. I try to keep kissing her, but soon, I can't focus on anything but what she's doing to me. I start to pant, my breath catching as she pauses and then releasing on ragged moans every time she rubs her hand down my length.

Some part of me knows I'm going to scare the hell out of her when I come, but that part is *very* far removed from the one that's in control right now. There's no way I could bring myself to ask her to stop. It's just. Too. Good.

As she strokes faster, my breathing accelerates, my lungs trying to keep up with the twinges of pleasure rolling over me, winding me in ever-tighter spirals . . .

I cry out as lights flash behind my eyes and warm wetness spurts onto my stomach, holding on to her as my knees threaten to buckle. The pleasure is so intense—all I can feel is the ecstasy that washes over me in waves. I never want it to end.

I slowly become aware that Holly is very still in my arms.

"Did you just—"

I nod, eyes closed, still breathing heavily and trying to remember who I am.

"Because I was—"

She pauses, and I open my eyes to find her staring at me, eyes wide as saucers. I raise an eyebrow. "You *do* know how this works—"

"Of course I do. I just—"

"You've never gotten a guy off before?" I venture helpfully. She shakes her head.

"Well, you have now."

A smug, satisfied grin spreads across her face, and she leans in and kisses me. Just as things are getting hot and heavy again, and I'm starting to wonder if I can get hard five minutes after getting off, a loud bang sounds on the door of the shed. We both jump, and Holly squeaks in fright.

"Relax; it's not a teacher or anything. I'm not the only one who knows where that key is. Someone's just getting impatient."

"We'd better go, then," she says, still smirking.

What I want to do is slide bonelessly to the floor and lie there with a grin on my face for a good half hour, but that's pretty much out of the question.

"I *guess*." I concede grudgingly.

But before she moves away from me, I run my palm over her center, rubbing my finger right in the middle. Her eyes drift closed but fly open again as I whisper in her ear. "Next time, it's your turn." I chuckle at her shocked expression. *Having a girlfriend is going to be* so *much fun.*

We stop by the bathrooms so I can clean up, then head back to the dance. The minute we walk through the caf doors, Ryan and Tyler are on top of me.

"Where the *hell* have you *been*?" Ryan demands, ready to rip my head off.

"I was . . . busy." My response is cagey, but I clarify it with an exaggerated eye roll in Holly's direction.

"Oh. Well . . . now that you're here, we're all ready to go."

"Okay, give me a minute," I tell him, and he grabs Tyler by the collar and heads back out the door.

Holly has a suspicious look on her face, and I feel as if she's looking right through me as she narrows her eyes. "What's going on?"

"Um . . . guy stuff. I'll be back in a little while," I tell her, putting an arm around her waist and giving her my most charming smile. "Go hang out with Megan and Lucy, and I'll be back before you know it."

She still looks suspicious, but it's not like she's going to stop me, so I give her a peck on the cheek and turn to follow the guys out into the night. *Now for the second best part of the evening.*

CHAPTER FIFTEEN

HOLLY

What the hell is he up to?

I've got a few ideas—*please don't let it be drugs*—but I'm a little miffed that he left me right after we—*oh God, I wanna do that again.*

Heat is still smoldering in my belly from when he touched me . . . there, and I wanna know what comes next. *Really* badly.

He's been so attentive this week and *so* sweet, and I feel like I'm falling even though I know I shouldn't. But he's been so different from the way he was; he's . . . real when he's with me, and it's even starting to spill over into the way he is at school—like when he had lunch with my friends on Friday. Maybe he *is* changing. For *me*.

The thought makes my chest flutter and my heart pound, and I let myself enjoy it.

This is okay. This is good.

~

I spend the next hour dancing with Megan and The Gothlet, although The Gothlet looks a little out of place without a stripper pole in that, um . . . outfit. I swear, if she didn't have leggings on, she'd be flashing us her minge fringe.

The Gothlet and I take a break from dancing, standing off to the side and trying to catch our breath.

I almost fall over as someone drapes their arms over my shoulders, the smell of alcohol so overwhelming that I choke as I inhale. Nathan's lips brush against my ear.

"Hello, beautiful," he whispers, dropping one hand to my waist and squeezing gently.

I lift his arm and spin around to face him, and he rears his head back and squints at me.

"Holy shit, Nathan! How much did you have to drink?"

"Enough," he replies, chuckling, his hands firmly gripping my shoulder and hip as his body sways.

"Too much." I scold him. "If a teacher sees you like this, they'll be calling my dad."

But he's not listening to me; his hand moves up to caress my cheek as his glassy eyes drink me in.

"So soft," he murmurs. "Dance with me," he says, throwing both arms over my shoulders and pressing his body against mine.

"You are in *no* condition to dance. We need to get you out of here before you get caught. Here," I say, maneuvering him backward until his backside is against one of the caf tables. "Stay here while I go find Evan, okay?"

He shakes his head stubbornly, hands pawing at my chest.

"N-n-n-o, s-s-stay here," he says, closing his eyes and reaching down to grip the table with both hands.

Jesus, he's really wasted. How the hell did he even get back here? I have to find Evan and get him out of here as soon as possible.

"I'll be right back; I promise. Lucy will stay with you."

The Gothlet's eyes grow wide as saucers, so I cock my head and purse my lips imploringly. She scowls at me but nods, so I turn my attention back to Nathan.

"Stay, *please.*" I squeeze his shoulder to emphasize my plea. He nods slowly, his eyes still closed.

I spin around and walk quickly across the cafeteria toward where I last saw Evan. The rowdy group of senior boys is still there, but Evan isn't among them. *Shit.*

I glance back and Nathan is still where I left him, staring at the dance floor while The Gothlet stands uncomfortably beside him.

Where else could Evan be?

Suddenly, it dawns on me, and I look over at Lori's group of friends. She's missing too. *Dammit, this isn't going to go well.*

I leave the caf, knowing they won't be anywhere else in the building because everything is locked. The teachers patrol the parking lot, so they won't be back in the car . . . unless they took the car somewhere.

No, Evan wouldn't leave Nathan alone here with no way to get home if he needed to.

The shed? *Maybe, but that place seemed quite busy and in high demand.*

Behind the bleachers? *Yes! I bet that's it!*

It's pitch dark back here since the stadium lights are off, and as I round the first metal beam, there are couples scattered everywhere—splayed out on the crossbeams, backed against the poles, using the stored sports equipment in ways that were *never* intended.

"Evan!"

They freeze for a second, then Evan whips his head around to look at me.

"Holly? What the—"

"It's Nathan."

Evan's eyes widen, and he's moving toward me, Lori completely forgotten.

"Did he—"

"He's drunk. *Really* drunk, and I'm afraid he's gonna pass out right in the middle of the caf—"

Evan goes from scared to livid so fast, it makes my head spin.

"That asshole! I *told* him to stay out of trouble! I'm gonna kick his ass from here to Portland!"

"This is *Nathan's* fault?" Lori exclaims from behind us.

"Can it, Lori! I need to go. Can you get a ride home with Amber?"

Lori huffs incredulously, but Evan is *so* not in the mood.

"Can you?"

"Yeah." Her glare is murderous as she crosses her arms in a brazen pout.

"I'll call you later," Evan tells her as he takes off for the caf with me struggling to keep up.

"Were you with him?" Evan asks, giving me a sidelong glance.

"No! He went off with Ryan and Tyler. I was with the girls."

"I figured."

Thankfully, Nathan is still where I left him, but The Gothlet is gone, and Justin and Megan stand on either side of him, doing their best to hide the fact that he's completely plastered.

"Thank God! We had a hell of a time keeping him here," Megan exclaims when she sees me. "He kept wanting to go look for you."

"Nathan?"

His head swings up at the sound of his name, and he gives me a lazy, lopsided grin.

"*There* you are! I miss-s-s-sed you." He throws his arms around me, his words even more slurred than before.

His weight nearly knocks me over, but I manage to keep us both vertical.

"I missed you, too, but we've gotta go now. It's time to go home."

"But I don't wann-n-na." Nathan whines while dropping sloppy kisses on my neck. "I think we sh-should—"

"Come on, asshole. You're drunk, and we need to get you out of here." Evan's fists are clenched as if he's barely holding his temper.

Nathan narrows his eyes at his brother, but I cut him off before he can say anything.

"Evan's right, Nathan. We need to get you out of here. C'mere, put your arm around my shoulder, and I'll help you."

I seal the deal with a kiss, and Nathan gives an exaggerated nod.

"Only becaus-s-s-se you as-s-sked me to, Holl-l-l-y. F-f-f-fuck that ass-s-s-s-hole."

Evan mutters something under his breath and takes off without another word, leaving me to contend with a very unsteady Nathan.

"F-f-f-fuck," he mumbles. "S-s-spinning."

Shit. He's either gonna pass out or get sick any minute now; I'm sure of it.

The walk across the parking lot feels like it takes ages, but we make it without running into any of the teachers.

I help Nathan into the car, sliding him over on the seat so I can get in. He looks as if he can barely keep his eyes open, and as soon as I crawl in next to him, he lays his head on my shoulder.

Evan walks around the car and gets in, slamming the door so hard that Nathan and I both jump. He turns around and glares at Nathan.

"What the fuck, man? You can't get this drunk on school property and expect no one to notice! You're lucky Holly was here for you to hang on to; otherwise, everyone would've known you can't even stand up right now!"

"Can too," Nathan says, raising his head to peer blearily at Evan.

"We're gonna talk about this tomorrow when you've sobered up," Evan says, the threat clear in his voice.

"F-f-f-fuck you, Ev," Nathan says dismissively, his head lolling onto my shoulder again.

There's silence in the car for a few moments while Evan drives toward my house.

Suddenly, he looks back at us in the rearview mirror. "Is he passed out?"

I bend my head to look at Nathan, and he appears to be asleep on my shoulder. "Yeah, I think so."

"Goddamn son of a—" and the rest is lost under his breath as he shakes his head.

I don't think this was a great idea on Nathan's part, but now that we're away from the school, and I know he's not going to get caught, I don't really see the harm. Everyone has to have some fun once in a while.

"Oh, come on, Evan, don't be a killjoy. Cut him a break. He was just having a little fun."

Evan shakes his head and grunts. "Yeah, come over tomorrow and watch the seizure he's gonna have to pay for his 'fun,' and then we'll talk about what a killjoy I am."

I freeze. "Oh, *shit*! Really?"

Evan sighs. "Every single time. He failed to mention that part, didn't he?"

I nod, stunned into silence. Apparently, telling me what he can and can't do only applies to limitations he's not planning to ignore.

"Why does he do this, then?" I demand, angry with him now for his recklessness.

"To be like everybody else, I guess. There are so many things he can't do. I guess there's a limit to what he's willing to give up."

"Are you gonna tell your parents?"

"Nah, I'm gonna get him to bed and stick around the house tomorrow," he replies gruffly, looking straight ahead as he drives.

I'm silent for a few minutes, thinking about all the things Evan does to look out for Nathan.

"I'll help you," I say firmly.

Evan's eyes flick to the rearview mirror. "What?"

"I said 'I'll help you.' I'll tell Nathan I don't want him to do this anymore and try to convince him that it's a bad idea."

"Why?" he asks, dumbfounded.

"What do you mean 'why'? Because I care about him, and I think he needs to take better care of himself. This is too serious for him to mess around like this."

"Oh," he says, looking distinctly uncomfortable.

When we get to my house, I lay Nathan down across the back seat as I slide out from under him.

"Evan?"

"Yeah?"

"Can you please ask Nathan to call me tomorrow if he can? I know he's done this before, but . . . I can't help but worry."

Evan gives me a piercing look, then glances away.

"Yeah. Yeah, I'll tell him."

"Thank you. And . . . I'm sorry," I say as I shut the door, not sure exactly what I'm apologizing for.

Chapter Sixteen

You are free to choose, but you are not free from the consequences of your choice.

– A Universal Paradox

NATHAN

I awaken to the sound of Evan's voice and his hand on my shoulder. "Hey, you better get your shit together. Mom'll be in here in a minute."

I groan, my head pounding and my tongue stuck to the roof of my mouth. My stomach cramps violently, and I roll onto my side, wrapping my arms around myself as sweat breaks out on my forehead. It takes me about ten seconds to realize I'm definitely going to throw up; it's merely a question of when.

I fling the covers off and hurry down the hall, registering Evan's glare as I pass him. I lock the bathroom door behind me and sink to the floor, trying to will the awful churning in my stomach to stop. As I lay my cheek against the cool tile floor, I hear the conversation outside.

"Where's Nathan?" Mom asks Evan as she stops outside the bathroom door.

"He's in the bathroom. I think he's sick. We came home early last night because he wasn't feeling well—there's some kind of stomach bug going around school."

I feel like complete and utter shit as I listen to Evan lie for me. I truly don't understand why he does it. I was stupid, and I'm prepared to take the trouble that comes with it—I always am—but he never lets me. He always covers my ass, and Mom and Dad have never figured it out—yet. *I have to stop doing this.* I know it's not good for me, but somehow, when I go out with Ryan and Tyler and start drinking, it's easy to forget I'm any different from them—to make believe I'm normal.

"Oh, no! I hope—"

Whatever else Mom says is lost to me as my stomach chooses that moment to revolt. I spend the next half hour wishing for death.

When the heaving finally stops, I brush my teeth so Mom won't smell the alcohol on me and stumble back down the hall. She's there waiting at my bedroom door.

"Oh honey, I'm so sorry you're not feeling well! Why don't you lie back down, and I'll bring you some water," she says as she puts her arm around me, guiding me back to my bed.

I lie down and curl up on my side, my head pounding to the rhythm of my too-loud heartbeat. Mom covers me up and smooths the hair back from my forehead, and I wince in response.

"Can you bring me some Tylenol, too?" I know I sound pathetic, but at the moment, that's how I feel, and if Mom wants to baby me, I'll take it.

"Of course, sweetheart," she replies, the concern on her face and in her voice causing my stomach to twinge with guilt and remorse. She leaves the room, and I close my eyes, wishing with all my heart that it were tomorrow. At that moment, both of my arms twitch violently, warning me that the rest of the day is going to play out exactly as I knew it would. *Dammit.* As if being hung over isn't punishment enough.

When Mom returns, I'm still having myoclonic jerks, and I see the unshed tears in her eyes as she gives me my Tylenol and pulls my desk chair up next to the bed. *I really have to stop doing this.*

~

My Saturday is basically nonexistent. About an hour after Mom tucked me back into bed, I had the big seizure I'd known was coming, and I slept for the rest of the day. On the ironically twisted bright side, at least I didn't have to deal with the hangover.

When I wake up at almost noon on Sunday, I'm dehydrated and starving, but I feel ten times better than I did the day before. I'm a little shaky until I get some breakfast and Gatorade into me, but after that, I almost feel normal. My headache isn't even as bad as it usually is.

As I'm finishing up, Evan walks into the room, pours a glass of orange juice, and stands at the counter, staring at me. *He's sizing me up to figure out if I'm okay now;* I know it, and he knows I know it. I think about feigning further illness because he's just waiting until I'm recovered to lay into me for my adventures on Friday night, but I decide it's time to man up and pay the last piper in the line.

"Go ahead, Evan. I know you've been waiting," I say, resigned.

He glowers at me and takes a deep breath before he launches in. "Do you have *any* idea how worried Mom and Dad were yesterday? Because you were sick *and* you had a seizure?"

"No—"

"It lasted longer than usual. Did you know *that*? It was a full five minutes, and they debated taking you to the ER."

I bury my face in my hands.

"This has to stop. You know you can't go out and tie one on like everybody else and expect to be fine the next day. That's been proven every single fucking time you've done this."

"I know," I mutter.

"And I'm not going to cover for you anymore. The next time you do this, I'm gonna just let Mom and Dad catch you, and then you'll get grounded on top of all the other shit."

"Fine," I answer a little more loudly.

"Oh, and I called Holly for you yesterday. You were passed out on Friday night when I dropped her off, and she asked me to have you call her to let her know you were okay. Of course, you *weren't okay* at all yesterday, but I called her and said you were, so at least *she* wouldn't be worried sick about you. God*dam*mit, Nathan, I'm so mad at you right now I could just—" His hands ball into fists as he shakes with anger, but he chokes back the rest of what he was going to say.

Now *that* rubs me the wrong way. I'm on my feet and in his face before I realize what I'm doing, my hands also clenched into fists.

"You could just what, Evan? Take a swing at me? Well, go ahead! I know I deserve it. Maybe we'd both feel better if you cleaned my clock!"

His eyes blaze, but he keeps his fists held tightly to his sides.

"You know I can't do that." He grates the words out, and knowing the only reason he's holding back makes me even angrier.

"I can't even have my brother kick my ass like a normal guy!" I roar in frustration. My parents show up in the kitchen then, staring back and forth between us as we glare at each other with flushed faces and trembling fists.

"Evan!"

I cringe, knowing that's Mom's opener before ripping him a new one.

"What's going on here? Your brother is just getting over being sick—what are you two arguing about?"

I can see Evan backing down, but I'm getting closer to the boiling point. Of course, they won't get on *my* case about fighting with Evan; it's always the other way around.

"It's nothing, Mom. You're right. Nathan and I were having a . . . discussion, but we're finished now."

I'm literally shaking with anger, but the tiny sliver of reason I have left tells me that exploding isn't going to make things any better. It'll probably trigger another seizure, and I'll be right back where I started from. I turn on my heel and stomp out of the kitchen and back up to my room. I need to do something to calm myself down, or I really *am* going to explode. I look around my room for distraction, but it feels as if the walls are closing in on me. I've been in this room since Friday night. *I need to get the fuck out of here.*

Normally, when I need to calm down and get away from my problems, I hang out with Evan, but obviously, *that's* out of the question today. I think about calling Ryan, but I'm still feeling off and don't have the energy to do anything physical or to pretend I'm perfectly fine. My thoughts drift to Holly. We had a good time on Friday night—before I became a stumbling drunk anyway—and she knows all my secrets, so I don't have to pretend around her. Hopefully, she's not *too* mad at me.

I pick up my phone, knowing I deserve a raft of shit from her, too, but hoping against hope that I won't get one.

She picks up on the first ring.

"Nathan?"

"Hey, Holly."

"Are you okay? Evan said you were, but you never called . . ."

"I'm okay." *Except for wanting to go taunt my brother until he pounds my ass into the ground, go tell my parents what a dumbass I am and let them ground me, and go just plain fucking insane over all this bullshit I have to deal with.*

"Good. I was worried about you."

So was everyone else, but somehow it means something entirely different coming from Holly—something that doesn't feel as if it might suffocate me.

I still have no idea how to respond to it, though, so I don't.

"Um . . . are you busy today? Could we—"

"Do you want me to come over?"

I can hear the eagerness in her voice, but hovering mother plus pissed-off brother will most definitely equal Nathan losing his cool in a spectacular shit show, and I don't want to put either of us through that.

"Um . . . not the best idea. I've been in the house since Friday night, and I really need to get out of here. Could you . . . come pick me up?"

I nearly choke on the words because I *hate* asking her to come get me, but no one downstairs is gonna do me any favors without questions and bullshit.

"Sure. I can be there in a half hour. What do you want to do?"

Honestly? I don't give a flying fuck—as long as it has nothing to do with talking about anything that's happened over the last three days.

"I don't know," I answer, trying to slow myself down. "We can figure it out when you get here."

"Okay, I'll see you soon," she says, and I take what feels like my first full breath since I woke up this morning.

I get ready, then hide in my room, waiting. When I hear her car coming up the drive, I bolt down the stairs, stopping in the living room only long enough to tell Mom and Dad I'm going out.

"Are you sure you're feeling well enough?" Mom calls after me, and I cringe, positively squirming under her overprotectiveness of her seventeen-year-old son, but I grit my teeth and respond that I'm fine, and I'll be back later.

I can't help but smile the moment I see Holly, but it freezes on my face when I hear Mom's footsteps behind me. *Goddammit, she would* never *chase after Ev like this.*

I jump down the porch stairs, and I know I'm running like a bitch, but I can't take one more confrontation today. So I dive into Holly's car like I'm dodging bullets.

"Wha—"

"Just go!" I tell her a little too sharply, but Mom's on the porch now, and I know if we stay here one more second, politeness is going to force Holly to acknowledge her.

Holly hits the gas without another word, and I can literally feel the stress falling away from me as we roll down the driveway. My thoughts tumble over each other, reliving the day and the weekend and . . . everything that's happened over the past few weeks, but they finally land on dancing with Holly on Friday night. I don't realize how fast I'm breathing until I start to slow down.

CHAPTER SEVENTEEN

When you know, you know. And you don't fight it. You don't deny the inevitable. You free fall because you know there's someone there to catch you on the other side.

– S. L. Jennings

NATHAN

We drive to her house, and although Evan and I have picked her up a few times now, this is the first time she's asked me inside.

Holly tugs me through the entryway and right into the cozy little living room. I try not to cringe as my gaze lands on the brown leather recliner in the corner that must be the chief's domain.

"Do you want a drink?"

"Sure."

I sit down in the middle of the couch as Holly disappears into the kitchen, taking in the pictures of little Holly on the mantle underneath one of the largest fish I've ever seen anywhere, much less hanging on a wall. *Priorities.*

Holly comes back carrying a Coke and a water and, given how my weekend went, I know which one's for me.

"I thought you might need—"

"Thanks," I say, taking the water from her hand. I can manage to let her take care of me, but we don't need to talk about it too.

She smiles and sits beside me, grabbing the remote and switching on the TV.

I drink half of my water bottle, and when I pass it to her to set on the table, she grabs my hand and pulls me, maneuvering us so my head rests in her lap, and I'm spread out across the couch.

She says nothing; she just starts running her fingers through my hair, and I heave a sigh as my shoulders relax. No one's ever done this for me except my mother, and that's a completely different feeling. This? This fills a hole —a *need*—I didn't even know I had.

And I bask in it.

I close my eyes, not even caring what's on the TV, and I'm drifting when Holly lowers the volume. *I could get used to this. I could . . .*

I wake with a start, sitting up so quickly I almost hit Holly's chin with my head.

"What the—"

"You were just napping," Holly says, grinning at me.

I pass a hand over my eyes, trying to calm my racing heart. Waking up anywhere but my own house triggers automatic panic that I've had a seizure in public, and that's a tough gut reaction to get around.

"Are you okay?"

"Yeah, fine. I just didn't know where I was."

Her hands find my shoulders and begin to massage again, and somehow, the touch telegraphs straight to my dick. I'm hard in an instant, and it's painfully and visibly obvious as I sit up beside her.

With a sly smirk, she reaches over and strokes up my length, but it feels . . . wrong, and I grab hold of her hand.

"Um . . . actually, can I touch you instead?"

"Sure, but don't you want—"

"Yeah, I do, but I kind of . . . can't."

She tilts her head inquisitively. *Oh fuck, I'm gonna have to explain this. Embarrassment should just be my middle name.*

"The day after a seizure, I'm still not . . . right. I don't know if it's the headache or something else, but . . . I can get hard, but I can't—"

I push my fist forward and twist it.

"—yeah."

"Oh . . . *oh,*" she says as a blush colors her cheeks.

I feel like a freak and a half at this moment, but Holly doesn't bat an eyelash.

"You still have a headache?"

"Yeah, but it's not too bad."

I just told you my dick is broken the day after a seizure, and you're worried about my headache?

"Maybe you should lie back down for a while—"

Yup, apparently, you are. But the embarrassment I was feeling fades as quickly as it came.

"What if I don't want to lie down?" I ask as I turn and claim her lips, my hand sliding up her thigh to let her know without words *exactly* what I want.

Her hands find my hair as her tongue thrusts forward, and I moan as my stomach flips and rolls. *How can kissing a girl possibly feel* this *good?*

I tangle my tongue with hers, feeling heat and a tingling sensation roll up into my chest, and suddenly, this isn't enough.

I pull back and our eyes meet—her gaze is so *hungry,* it makes me breathe a little faster. It makes me want so many things all at once.

My hand slides up to her breast, cupping her softly over her bra, and she releases a slow breath, her eyes closed.

I've never seen a real girl topless although I've copped my share of feels. To be honest, I've never really wanted to—breasts are cool playthings, but they're a means to an end—a happy ending, if you know what I mean.

But not Holly's.

I want to see hers for some reason. To feel them and to watch as her nipples harden when I—

Holy fuck is this easier when my dick isn't dominating the conversation!

Normally, he's clamoring for his so loudly, I can hardly think straight, and I do what I need to in order to get there. But not today. I'm hard as a rock, but the ache isn't there, so I can focus on other things.

I slide from the couch and kneel between her knees. She may not know I'm about to worship her body, but I certainly do—it's something I've never wanted before, and it's both frightening and exhilarating. I place my hand on her stomach, catching the hem of her shirt with my thumb and rubbing it slowly across the bare skin beneath. Her stomach muscles quiver under my touch, and she levels me again with that hungry gaze.

Jesus.

I lift up her shirt, and she raises her arms, her smile there but unsure.

I'll be gentle, Holly. I promise.

Her shirt is forgotten when my eyes fall on—*holy hell, they're* right *there!*

I swallow thickly as my hand hovers over . . . So. Much. Skin. Her breasts are fucking perfect—I can tell even with her bra still on—and I want . . . oh God, I don't think I can wait any longer for what I want.

Although her breasts pull at my fingers like magnets, I manage to slide my shaking hands around her back to free them.

Holly's breath is shaky as she looks downward, but I only have eyes for the delicate pink nipples that are mere inches from my face. The need that wells up inside me is powerful, and as my hands cup that velvet-soft, perfectly shaped skin for the first time, heat flairs in my groin, and I can't hold back a low moan.

I dip my head and circle one nipple with my tongue, completely unprepared for the rush when she arches her back and thrusts it into my mouth. I suck gently, each pull eliciting a moan from her and a twinge of pleasure deep within me.

"Oh God, Nathan." Holly's breathing is shallow, and I can feel my own heartbeat everywhere, from my fingertips to my fucking titanium dick.

I have never been so turned on in my entire *life*.

I move to her other breast—*Jesus, I can't get enough*—and she writhes against me, eyes closed, chin thrust out—*wow, look at the perfect line of her neck*.

My hands take the place of my lips, and I move upward, kissing her heaving chest until I reach the junction between her neck and shoulder. The hunger is nearly unbearable, and I groan as my lips ravish every inch of warm, supple skin with open-mouthed kisses.

Holly's panting heavily, and as her hands slide down my sides, I have the overwhelming urge to—to—to do something *more*. I move a little further down her chest and suck *hard*, pulling her skin between my teeth as my dick twitches, and pleasure roars through me.

Holly cries out—a mix of pain and pleasure that pulls me out of my lusty haze enough to look up at her.

"Jesus, Nathan." Her pupils are so dilated, she looks like she's high, and satisfaction surges through me.

"What time is your dad working until again?" I mumble between kisses. It's hard to think coherently when my head feels like it's floating, but I know this couch is *not* where I wanna be right now.

"Midnight. He'll be home about one. Why?" Holly asks, clearly irritated that I'm asking banal questions when I should be tongue-fucking her.

"Are you sure?"

"*Yes.*"

"Um, do you wanna go upstairs, then?"

That gets her attention.

"Up . . . upstairs?"

Her eyes widen, the haze of lust diluted by a touch of fear.

"We don't have to . . . I mean, I just wanna—"

"No, it's okay. You took me by surprise, that's all. I wanna take you upstairs."

What happens in my groin when she says those words has to be a crime in a few states; it feels that fucking good. I close my eyes and let it wash over me, but the next second, Holly's grabbing my hand and leading me toward the stairs, and I'm grinning like an idiot.

Bloody hell, I wish my little fireman weren't on the fritz. If I don't fuck this up, maybe we can do it again when I can enjoy it like a normal guy.

Even though it feels different, desire has been building in me until I feel like I wanna crawl out of my own skin.

I need to touch her somewhere—everywhere—right now!

As soon as we cross the threshold of her room, I spin her around and meld my lips to hers as I walk her backward toward the bed. My hands are everywhere—skimming over her soft, warm skin as the need to be *closer* pulses through me.

When the backs of her knees hit the mattress, she grabs both of my hands and holds them together in front of me.

What the hell? I—I need—

But as I look into her eyes, I can see the fire there. *This isn't over.*

Her hands move to the hem of my shirt, and my stomach muscles quiver and tighten.

"Can I see?" she asks in shy schoolgirl voice, and I'm ready to strip like a fucking porn star.

I grab my shirt and whip it over my head, my hands groping for her jeans before it even hits the floor.

"I wanna touch you. *God*, can I please touch you?" I beg, completely at the mercy of my own need.

"Yours come off, too," she says, smirking. I think she's realized exactly how far gone I am.

Right now, I'd find a way to suck my own dick if it'd make her happy.

Frantic hands strip us both down to our underwear, and the sight of her little white satin panties and the dark hair underneath pushes me over whatever edge I've been riding.

I pull her close, and we both groan as she melts against my chest.

Warm—soft—hot—fuck!

And suddenly, we're on the bed, and I'm hovering over her, plunging my tongue into her mouth as she explores my bare chest.

I roll to the side and grab hold of her, pulling behind her knee until her leg is on top of mine, opening her to me. A shudder rolls through her as I splay my hand on her stomach, my fingers brushing the lace of her panties.

This is Red Five. I'm going in.

Hopefully, what happens at the end of this will rival the destruction of the Death Star, and I'll be a fucking hero.

My hand inches downward, and I have to draw a steadying breath when my fingers slide into a bed of soft curls. Holly, however, is not breathing at all—her eyes shut in ... *anticipation?*

I graze over her clit, and she jumps, but I know better than to start there. That's where the finish line is. That fuckstick I call a brother did manage to teach me *something.*

So I trace around the edge instead, then move in, exploring her folds by touch as she struggles to breathe. She moans when I approach her slit, so I rub in circles there, watching her eyebrows and lips twitch and quiver in pleasure.

She gasps when I enter her with one finger, the sound and feel tightening something deep within me. We both need *more.*

I move my finger out and then in again, and her hips rise off the bed.

"Nathan," she whispers between breaths, and the urge to thrust is there, even for my fucking finger.

I add another one and set a rhythm, my fingers becoming slick as she pushes against them, driving me deeper.

"Nathan, please!" Holly pants, and I know she doesn't even know what she's asking for, but I know how to give it to her.

Oh God, am I gonna enjoy giving it to her.

I curl my fingers just a little bit, and Holly cries out and grabs my bicep.

"What the hell did you just do?"

"Did you like it?" I ask, smug as the cat that ate the canary. *Score another one for* The Fuckstick's Guide to Girls.

"Oh *fuck!*" She gasps as I do it again, and I know I've found what I was looking for.

Houston, we have a G-spot.

"Don't stop!" Her tone is pleading, and I am *more* than willing to accommodate her.

Holly whimpers, eyes closed, her every move in response to my touch.

So warm. God, she's so tight; what will it be like when—

My dick twitches as if he's trying to pull in her direction, and my teenage-boy, ridiculously vivid, sexual imagination takes over.

As Holly fucks my hand, my own hips move in the rhythm, thrusting forward as I can almost feel all that heat and soft skin surrounding me.

Jesus.

I add a third finger—moving a little faster and grazing that magic spot as often as I can.

"*God*, Nathan."

She's bringing out the deities, so she must be getting close.

"Nathan . . . so much . . . I—you—"

Now for the finish.

I press down on her clit, and she cries out, fucking my hand in earnest as I make slow circles there.

"Oh, I'm—I—"

Her body tightens on my fingers as she jerks and moans—her orgasm is one of the most amazing things I've ever seen. Her whole body participates, and I want to do it to her again as soon as she'll let me.

Damn.

She pants as she comes down, her chest heaving—jiggling those perfect breasts in a way that makes me feel warm pretty much everywhere.

"Fuck," she mutters.

How did I not know how sexy it is when a mostly naked woman curses?

My balls are so blue, I could trade rocks with a Smurf, and there's not a damn thing I can do about it. The ache wasn't there before, but it sure as hell is now, and I have no idea how to ease it.

Holly's brilliant smile pulls me out of my penis pity party, and I know it was worth it despite my aching dick.

She says nothing, but she threads her fingers into my hair as she kisses a gentle trail from my collarbone to my lips.

We kiss and kiss, and it's hot but no longer desperate. It's fulfilling another need now—the need to be close and to feel . . . loved.

The word skitters across my mind, and I run from it, losing myself in the feel of her lips, the swipe of her tongue.

Eventually, we slow down to soft kisses until she falls asleep, her head resting on the arm I have around her. There's a blanket folded at the bottom of her bed, so I snag it carefully with my feet and cover both of us.

As I watch her breathe in and out softly, I know I can't run anymore. The realization is quiet—not at all the trumpets and fanfare I thought big moments in life were supposed to be. But it's quite possibly the best I've ever felt as the truth warms and consumes me.

I'm in love with Holly Ross.

Chapter Eighteen

The best way of keeping a secret is to pretend there isn't one.

– **Margaret Atwood**

NATHAN

I watch her sleep, and it's a religious experience. My finger hovers over her eyebrow—I want to trace it, but I'm afraid I'll wake her up. And her eyelashes are *so* long. *Are all girls' eyelashes that long?* I've never been this close long enough to notice. Her nose is adorable. She wrinkles it like a bunny in her sleep—the same way she does when I do something, and she doesn't understand my reasoning. I wonder if she's solving math problems in her dreams or some shit.

And her lips . . . they're just so . . . fuck, all I know is I wanna kiss them all the time. I've never been in love with a girl before, but I know that's what this is—it has to be. It's the most intense feeling I've ever had, and I'm still in shock that I'm feeling it. It feels so *good*, and nothing has really felt good in so long.

And suddenly, I'm afraid. *What if it doesn't last? What if she doesn't feel the same way about me?* I mean, I know she likes me, and she wants to be my girlfriend, but does she feel . . . *this*? And if she does, what does that mean? In the midst of all the fucked up shit that is my life, can I still have this? Can I just . . . *be* with her and stop being the asshole I've been for so long? What will the consequences be, and can I accept them? Or will protecting myself stand in the way? If it came down to it, would I choose her or keeping my secret?

"What is it?"

I startle when Holly touches me—her hand gently cradles my cheek, and I realize I'm hyperventilating.

Too many things, there's just too much . . .

I close my eyes and focus on breathing.

Get a grip, Nathan. One thing at a time. And as I repeat that to myself, and Holly's soft fingers stroke my cheek, the racing in my mind slows down.

When I open my eyes, Holly's watching me, her brow furrowed. *You're going to have to give her some kind of explanation.*

And so I lie because I can't even begin to sort out what just happened in my head, much less explain it to anyone else—least of all to *her.*

"Bad dream. I guess we both fell asleep," I say, smiling and placing my hand over hers. "I just needed a minute to get out of my head."

She breathes out a sigh, and I know I'm off the hook . . . this time.

"We did," she murmurs, and the smile that lights up her face warms my heart and seems to lighten the load.

My stomach rumbles, and I'm mortified, but Holly just giggles. I need to get home in time for dinner, or Mom's likely to have a bird.

"I . . . uh . . . only had a late breakfast. I should probably head home."

Holly's face falls, and I realize she'll be home alone for dinner and for the rest of the evening. *I wonder how often her dad has to work late?* But I can't

171

invite her over—not tonight. The Evan glare-a-thon will go on until at least tomorrow, and Mom . . . fuck, Mom's gonna follow me around like I'm a toddler until I escape to my room. Yeah, *not* how I want Holly to see my family in action.

"I'm sorry, Holly. Tonight's not really a good night—"

"No, don't worry. I can fend for myself. I usually do," she says quickly. "You should go home—get some more rest before school."

I pull her to me and kiss her, hoping my lips can convey my thanks and my love and whatever the hell else I'm feeling that I don't have words for.

She pulls away long before I want to be done, but then again, I could probably kiss her forever.

"You should go," she says again, although her eyes are telling me something else entirely.

There will be other days, I remind myself because even though she's covered with the blanket I threw over us, I know what's under there, and I just want to pull it back and start all over again.

I reluctantly haul myself up to sit on the side of the bed, and she runs her hand down my back. A shiver rolls through me, and I'm hardening again just thinking about being inside her, about sitting here naked afterward instead of in my boxers . . . So *not helping*.

My jeans are below me so I snatch them up and slip them on before gathering Holly's clothes and my shirt from the floor.

When I turn, Holly's still lying in bed just watching me, the sheet tucked under her armpits so it covers her breasts. *Shy schoolgirl again. Unf.*

She blushes as she takes her things, putting her sweater on sans bra and crawling out of bed and into her jeans with as little skin visible as possible. *Holly, you're killing me.*

We chat about school as she drives me home, but as we pull up my driveway, I realize I don't want to let her go—not yet, anyway.

I slide across the seat, and before she even has the car in park, I'm nibbling on her earlobe and running my hand up and down her thigh.

"Nathan," she says in a whiny voice, but she leans her head back, exposing her neck and making me feel like a vampire about to ravish her.

I move in, but she squirms away playfully, batting my wandering hands away.

"You need to go," she says, smirking at me. *God, I love it when she turns bossy.*

"And I'm going to stay in the car so you make it to the front door."

Does she know I've been fantasizing about putting my hands up her sweater ever since she put it on?

I glance at her chest, and her grin widens. *Yup, she knows.*

"Okay," I say, defeated.

"I'll see you in the morning, Nathan."

I open the door, but I pause, remembering how this day went from shit to awesome, all because of her.

"Today was great."

"Yeah, it was."

I slam the door of her car and watch as it rolls down the driveway until I can't see it anymore. Then I check my watch. *It's ten of five—I'm sure I can at least try to jack off before Mom can get dinner on the table.*

Mom wakes me in the morning because Evan's still being a fuckface, and we avoid each other entirely until we have to get in the car together.

I opt to stare out the window, hoping he'll leave me alone.

"Can we talk?"

So much for that.

"Didn't we do enough of that yesterday?" I snap at him, totally not in the mood to rehash the argument.

"I'm serious, Nathan."

I huff in exasperation. "So am I."

"Look, I'm sorry for going off on you. You scared us, okay? Your seizure didn't seem like it was gonna stop. Mom was crying, *Dad* even looked worried, and I stood there knowing you'd brought the whole thing on yourself! You're not the only one who gets frustrated sometimes, okay?"

He's frustrated. *He's* frustrated? At least a dozen nasty comebacks are on the tip of my tongue, but I bite them all back.

I made Mom cry.

Before I can gather my scattered thoughts into some semblance of an apology, he goes on.

"But that's not what I wanna talk about. I wanna talk about Holly."

Every single muscle tenses, and my stomach does a nervous roll. *I'm not gonna like this.*

"What about her?" I ask, trying to keep my tone even.

"She . . . Nathan, she really cares about you."

I close my eyes and let the warm, fuzzy feeling fill me for a second.

"So?"

"So? Aren't you dating her so she'll keep your secret? This was supposed to be casual, and she was supposed to get bored with you after a while, but I don't see that happening."

Shit. I'm not ready to talk about this yet. I'm barely even ready to think about yesterday's emotional epiphany.

I take a deep breath and let it out slowly.

"I don't know that I'm dating her so she'll keep my secret anymore. I mean . . . not only for that reason."

Evan's eyes widen a little, but he just stares at me. I look away, unable to stand the scrutiny while this is so new and . . . unreal.

"Holy shit, you've got it for her too. Never in a million years did I think—"

"Why not? She's amazing. She's beautiful, and my problems don't seem to bother her, and—"

"Not that. She seems like a nice girl. I mean . . . *you*. You've never let anyone get close to you since all this happened, and you've pushed a lot of people away."

I wish I could say he's wrong, but we both know he isn't. But Holly . . .

"She's . . . different."

"Yeah, she is. And that's why you've got to tell her how this all started."

"What? No!" A shiver of panic shoots down my spine. *Holy mother of fuck no!*

"Nathan—"

"She'll—no, she'll dump me! I can't tell her I started dating her just to keep her quiet! Why the *hell* would I do that?"

"What if she finds out, and you're not the one to tell her? What will she say then?"

"She won't find out. Why would she? Only you and I really know why. No one's ever found out my other secret. I can keep this one too."

"I don't know, Nate. This seems wrong now, somehow. She could get hurt —you *both* could get hurt—"

"No one is going to get hurt," I say, cutting him off firmly, but inside, I'm panicking.

*No! I can't take the risk of her leaving me! Not now that I finally have some-thing—some*one *who makes me happy! Not now that I . . . love her.*

"It'll be fine, Ev. I can handle it."

It'll be fine. I'm good at keeping secrets. She'll never find out, and it'll be as if it never happened. I'm gonna forget it ever happened. I have to.

It never happened. I'm good at keeping secrets. I'm dating her because I'm in love with her.

It never happened. I'm good at keeping secrets.

It never happened.

Evan just shakes his head. "I hope you know what you're doing."

"I do. I promise." *God, I hope I know what I'm doing!*

CHAPTER NINETEEN

The reason as to why we are attracted to our opposites is because they are our salvation from the burden of being ourselves.

– Kamand Kojouri

HOLLY

As we sit down at the lunch table on Monday, I can't help but watch Nathan. I know he's feeling better, but he seemed distracted in chemistry —as if something important were on his mind—just like he is now, in fact, until his eyes widen as if one of us has sprouted another head.

Nathan's gaping at The Gothlet, and she's staring at . . . Ryan? And *he* only has eyes for The Gothlet. Ooey-gooey, lovey-dovey, great big heart-y eyes. He looks like a damn cartoon character, and she's *blushing*. I honestly thought she had ice water or antifreeze in her veins for how pale and sickly she looks at times, but that's not nearly as surprising as the fact that she's blushing over *Ryan*. *What the hell?* The apple in my hand falls to my tray with a *clunk*, and everyone at the table who wasn't already watching this spectacle now gets a clue.

"Hi," Ryan says as if The Gothlet is the only person within a hundred miles.

"Hey," she answers, still blushing, but now a grin threatens to split her cheeks.

Ryan shuffles his feet. "I thought maybe I could—"

"Oh, sure . . ."

Ryan glances around the table, but the only empty seats are the two chairs between Justin and Nathan, across the table from The Gothlet.

The Gothlet turns to Eric and barks, "Move!" and Eric is so startled, he falls out of the chair backward, right next to me.

The Eyes of Sauron disappear as quickly as they came, and The Gothlet actually *primps* her hair as she looks back toward Ryan.

"Here's a seat right next to me."

No one moves, including Ryan, and The Gothlet gives an exasperated huff that seems to start time again.

"What? Doesn't anyone want lunch?" she asks, her cheeks still splotched with crimson.

Ryan slides into the seat, and Eric picks himself up off the floor, scowling as he grabs his tray and takes the seat next to Justin.

And the most awkward silence in the history of awkward silences descends as we all stare at each other.

"So . . . um, did anyone finish their essay for English yet?" Megan asks, and that breaks the bubble and gets conversation flowing again.

Lunch lasts an eternity, but that's probably because I'm dying of curiosity . . . and waiting quite impatiently to give The Gothlet an unholy raft of shit during study hall.

Nathan holds my hand until he drops me at my locker, and I lose track of Ryan and The Gothlet. She hurries into study hall after Megan and I are already in our seats, and she's much more out of breath than I would expect her to be for just coming from her locker to the classroom. *Holy hell—when did all this happen?*

I stare her down from the moment she enters the room, a shit-eating grin on my face, and I can tell by the flick of her gaze to anywhere but me that she can feel it.

And I wait.

After a few minutes, she begins tapping her pen on her notebook, and I know I'm getting to her. Megan is grinning from ear to ear, just watching, knowing that any moment now, The Gothlet is going to lose her shit.

And she doesn't disappoint.

She stills, takes a deep breath, and projectile word-vomits the whole story all over me.

"We hooked up on Friday night after you left the dance, all right? He was drunk; I may have joined him out in the bush for a shot or two, and then . . ."

She stops and her eyes glaze over, and I briefly debate if I really want her to continue. *Oh yes, yes I do, for the sheer satisfaction of watching her blush and squirm the way she's made me do over Nathan.*

"And then?"

"And then we made out and humped each other like wild baboons in heat."

Wow, now there's a picture.

The Gothlet stares me down, challenging me to comment, but I'm still gathering details.

"Did you do it?"

Her expression turns thoughtful. "Nah. We just got each other off with our clothes on. But we could have done so much more."

Full. Stop.

Her idea of more will likely gross me out, scare the hell out of me, or both.

"So let me get this straight. You and Ryan got drunk and juiced each other's fruits, so now he's your boyfriend? After one drunken finger-fuck session?"

"Well . . ."

I raise my eyebrows smugly, and The Gothlet's cheeks flush crimson as she shifts in her seat. *Gotcha! Being put on the spot isn't so much fun, is it?*

"Well?"

"Well . . . we may have spent half of Friday night on the phone sobering up, and then he came over to my place on Saturday."

Damn, she's serious about this! She saw him sober and didn't threaten to cut his balls off for touching her!

"Wow." Megan's eyes are as wide as I'm sure my own are.

"Wow is right! Don't you think he looks like Martin Gore?"

"The singer from Depeche Mode?" I ask, trying to keep up.

"Yes! Is there another one?" The Gothlet pauses her Ryan-gushing long enough to snap at me. "That curly blond hair and those piercing hazel eyes! He even plays the guitar! Did you know that?"

"I had no idea." My sarcasm is lost on her.

"Well, he does! He's hot as hell, and he's mine now," The Gothlet says with a firm nod, but suddenly, her eyes go all dreamy. "I wanna put a collar on him and get him some black leather."

Megan gasps, and I think I do too.

Oh my God, I will never *be able to un-see that mental image.* And I don't think I'll ever be able to look at Ryan again without either laughing my ass off or becoming nauseous. *I hope that boy knows what he signed up for.*

~

The next morning, The Gothlet and I are at our lockers when Megan comes running up the hall.

"Hey, did you see the signs for the winter formal? Justin asked me to go with him!"

We both freeze.

"Really?"

"There's a formal?"

Megan side-eyes The Gothlet and answers my question instead.

"Of course, silly! It's the day after Christmas. The girls wear party dresses, and the guys wear suits and ties. I've never had a boyfriend at this time of year before, so I've never gone. It's going to be so much fun! We can all go together!"

A formal dance?

I glance back at Nathan, but he's not paying attention to our conversation; he's talking to Ryan. *I've never been to a formal. I can't really dance, but . . . does it matter?*

I try to convince myself that the only reason I want to go is to spend time with him, but I know the truth—at least some of it is about being *seen* with him. This is the ultimate in high school relationship status—no one sees most of what we do together, but attending a formal is a declaration of possession.

I know I shouldn't want that, and I shouldn't care, but a part of me wants to see the look on Bitch Face and Bubble Butt's faces when I walk in on his arm . . . to feel like I belong, for once.

I wanna go. I wonder if he'll ask me.

Nathan's eyes catch mine, but I turn around quickly to hide my blush. I have no idea how to explain my feelings to him on this subject, so I'm just gonna hope he asks me, and I can say yes without messing it up in some way.

~

The hallways are abuzz with winter formal talk all morning—girls gossiping over who's going to ask whom or squealing their news of an invitation and boys razzing each other about who will end up taking an ugly girl or no girl at all. Honestly, sometimes I wonder why we talk to those testosterone-riddled assholes.

But that thought exits my head along with every other one as Nathan saunters into the room—white t-shirt, blue hoodie, lickable scruff, and bronze which-god-gave-you-that-amazing-sex-hair to absolutely die for.

He plops down beside me and throws me a smirk, and I swear it hits my chest like some lust-filled projectile and makes me horny on contact.

We're in chemistry—not biology or anatomy. And that porn music is only playing in your head.

He's late—he barely has time to set down his books before Mr. Metcalf begins the lecture, so we don't get to talk like we usually do. I rest my head on my hand, and I don't realize until Nathan grins at me smugly that I'm staring at him instead of my notes.

Dammit! Focus, *Holly!*

I give myself a good shake, but there's too much excitement in the halls today, and my thoughts drift back to the winter formal . . . Nathan in a suit and tie, me in a blue and black satin dress . . . *I wonder if he'll ask me today . . .*

Thump!

"F-f-f-ow!"

I turn and Nathan's cradling his hand, but the look on his face is sheer terror as he stares back at me. His head jerks rapidly to the side, and he's out of his chair and out of the room before I can even blink.

That was a seizure. Just like he had in my car, and it's nearly lunchtime, and now he's gonna have a big one sometime today—

Metcalf stops mid-sentence as Nathan flies from the room.

"Was that Nathan? Ryan, can you go see if he's—"

"Mr. Metcalf?" I ask, but I'm already out of my seat and walking to the front of the room as calmly as I can even though I'm freaking out inside.

Nathan's panicking. Where would he go? I've got to find him so he doesn't have a seizure alone!

"Holly? What—"

I make it to his desk and lean over so only he can hear me.

"Mr. Metcalf, I know Nathan's secret."

His eyebrows rise, but now I have his undivided attention.

"He's going to need to go home. I'll help him call his mom. Please let me go find him."

He draws in a rapid breath, and I recognize the fear in his eyes. *So that's what I looked like to Nathan when I was afraid of him. Shit.*

"I know what to do. Please," I plead, as Nathan on the floor in the grip of a seizure runs on a loop in my head.

Metcalf nods, and I'm out the door, trying to calm myself so I can think.

He'll want to be alone. Where would he go? Think, Holly! Think!

He wouldn't go to the boys' bathroom—too much chance of someone else being there, I think as I walk-run down the hall as quickly as I can.

Empty classroom? No, everything at this end is in use, and he wouldn't go far . . .

I reach the end of the hallway, and I'm already turning to head back when I hear the sound of rapid footsteps. Past the last classroom is a short set of stairs leading to an alcove where the north entrance to the building is. No one ever uses it in the middle of the day, and Nathan's pacing back and forth in that space like a caged animal.

"Nathan!" It's an agonized cry, and he freezes, his chest heaving.

A second later, his arm flashes out in a spasm, and the pain on his face is so palpable, I almost burst into tears.

"Fuck. Fuck, fuck, fuck, fuck, fuck!" He starts pacing again, looking as if he's about to climb the walls.

I don't think he's thinking straight. Hell, I don't think he's thinking at all!

"Nathan, you need to go home. Have you called your mom?" I ask, approaching him slowly.

He stops again, staring at me while he tries to process my words.

"I—no, you're right. Can you call her for me? I'm not sure I can hold my phone right now."

"Okay, give it to me, and I'll call her."

He pulls it out of his back pocket with trembling fingers, and his head jerks sideways again as he hands it to me.

Focus, Holly! He needs you right now!

I dial his mom's number as he stands before me, his gaze trained far away as he gulps in air.

"Hello?"

"Julie? This is Holly. I'm with Nathan at school, and he's having myoclonic seizures. Can you please come get him?"

"Oh, sh—is he all right?"

"For the moment. He's . . . worried. We're at the north entrance."

"Okay, I'll be there as soon as I can."

I disconnect the call, and Nathan hasn't moved, but he's still breathing like he can't get enough air.

"Nathan? I called your mom, and she's coming. It's gonna be okay; I promise. You're gonna be okay."

He startles when I put my arms around him, but suddenly, he's holding on as if his life depends on it.

"Just breathe."

He nods into my neck, and we stand there until his shoulder jerks forward into mine—hard.

"Shit! I'm sorry! I can't—"

"I know, baby; I know. Don't apologize. You didn't hurt me."

"Fuck! Why is this happening? I don't understand, and I can't—I can't breathe!"

His breathing becomes truly rapid, and I start to get scared. I've never seen him this way.

"Just try to breathe slowly. Hold me and breathe. You've got to calm down, or things are gonna get worse," I whisper as I rub my hand over his back in slow circles.

"I'm gonna hold you until your mom gets here, okay? Nothing bad is going to happen while I've got you. Just a few more minutes, and you'll be going home."

As I continue to rub his back, his breathing finally slows down enough that it's no longer coming in gasps. He's still holding me tightly, though, and I can feel his heart thundering against my chest.

"There, you're calming down now. Take deep, slow breaths. You're okay."

"Thank you," he whispers into my shoulder, and I squeeze him a little tighter.

"Do you wanna sit on the steps?"

"Yeah. Yeah, that'd be good," he answers, pulling his head off my shoulder.

His eyes are red, and his cheeks are wet, but I don't say anything as we sit together on the third stair. He stares straight ahead for a few tense moments, but suddenly, it's as if he's just realized where he is and that I'm beside him. He looks over at me, and I try not to react because he looks as if the burden he's carrying is so heavy, he could collapse at any second.

"Thanks for coming to find me. I kinda freaked out totally. I couldn't think straight enough to remember what I should do," he says, resting his head on his arms.

"I know. You looked so scared in Metcalf's room. I knew I had to find you."

"I'll be okay," he says, and I know he's finally come back to himself.

I'm so relieved I could cry.

And I will.

After he goes.

Just then, his mom pulls up, looking as frantic as Nathan did a few minutes ago.

She's through the door and kneeling in front of him before her car has stopped moving, I swear.

"Are you okay, honey?"

"I'm fine, Mom. We just need to go before . . . it happens, okay?"

"Of course. What about—"

"I'll get your books and tell the office you left. I can also let Evan know," I say, rubbing my hand up and down Nathan's arm. "Just go."

"Holly—"

"Just go," I whisper again because I can see it all in his eyes, and he doesn't need to say it. He just needs to go take care of himself.

"Okay. I'll be in touch as soon as I can," he says, squeezing my hand.

And then he's off and down the stairs, climbing into the backseat of the car—just in case.

I sit back down on the stairs, feeling like there's a hole in my chest. *Why is this happening to him?* He seems like he's happy for the first time in a long while, but his damn epilepsy just won't quit. And I spent the morning fixated on something beyond trivial in comparison.

Fuck.

I stay there until the tears stop rolling down my cheeks, then I go take care of all the details left in Nathan's wake.

He doesn't call that night, but then, I didn't expect him to. It's nerve-wracking, but I have to trust that things went as usual; that is, he had his big seizure and spent the rest of the day sleeping. *Julie would call me if something bad happened, right?* I realize I'm honestly not sure. Maybe I should talk to her about that.

I wait out the evening with a book, but the next morning, I'm positively wired in homeroom, waiting to see if he'll show at school . . . and he doesn't. I see Evan in passing throughout the day, but he's always surrounded by other guys or with Lori—neither situation lending itself to any sort of real communication. So I head home alone. Dad's still at work, so I do the dishes, my homework. I even scare up a dust rag and have half the pictures off the mantle when my phone finally rings.

I dive for the coffee table, sighing in relief when I see Nathan's name on the screen.

"Nathan?"

"Hi, Holly."

Evan's voice is unsure, and panic shoots down my spine.

"Wh-what's happened?" I clutch the phone and sink to the floor.

"Oh! Nate's fine! Well, he's not *fine*, but nothing super bad happened." A heavy sigh. "Shit! I'm sorry. I didn't mean to scare the hell out of you."

"I'm just glad he's okay," I say on a long exhale, trying to steady my nerves. "What *did* happen?"

"Well, yesterday wasn't good, so he's upset, and I don't think he's going to call you anytime soon. But . . . I think he needs you. I've tried to snap him out of it, but it's just not working.

"Would you come talk to him? I know he won't bite *your* head off, and once you're here, he's not going to ask you to leave."

I can't help the snort that escapes—the inner workings of Evan's mind are fascinating.

"What?"

"Nothing. Of course I'll come over. Now?"

"Well . . . yeah, as soon as you can. Before he snaps at Mom again and Dad grounds him for eternity."

Oh boy. This is gonna be fun.

"Okay, I'll be there soon."

"Thanks, Holly," Evan says, hanging up before I can respond.

What the hell could have happened?

I'm certainly not going to figure it out sitting here, so I grab my sneakers and a hoodie and head over to Nathan's.

Chapter Twenty

Love is that condition in which the happiness of another person is essential to your own.

– Robert A. Heinlein, *Stranger in a Strange Land*

Holly

As I get out of my car, I hear a ball bouncing, followed by a swishy sound and a harder bounce. The area to the left of the Harris's detached garage is paved, and I see a basketball hit the backboard that's mounted to the concrete wall just before the ball drops straight down through the hoop.

It has to be Nathan.

I've never seen him handle a basketball before despite all I've heard about his skills. I honestly didn't think he played anymore. I assumed it would be too hard for him since he was forced to quit.

I walk over toward the basket but stay far enough over Nathan's shoulder that he won't see me unless he turns around completely.

His lean body makes a perfect line as he releases the ball—red Nike's, muscular calves flexed as he pushes off the ground, black mesh basketball shorts hugging his well-defined ass, white t-shirt slipping down his arms to reveal ridiculously toned biceps.

Swish.

He gets his rebound and jogs back to the very same spot, aiming and releasing in a matter of seconds—no bounces, no time taken to line up the shot—just muscle memory and incredible, effortless talent.

Swish.

Jesus.

I know next to nothing about basketball, but it doesn't take an NBA scout to see the graceful flow of his movements, the precision of his execution, or the fact that he makes each and every shot.

Evan's words from the night Nathan got so drunk reverberate in my head.

"Why the hell does he do this, then?"

"To be like everybody else, I guess. There are so many things he can't do. I guess there's a limit to what he's willing to give up."

He gave this up.

He *had* to give this up because epilepsy leaves no room for high-exertion contact sports.

I can't imagine having to give up something you're this good at. Something you love.

"Has he missed any?"

Evan's voice startles me.

"No."

"How many has he made?"

"I've counted thirty, but that's only since I've been here," I tell him, trying to keep my voice steady.

"Such a fucking waste," Evan says, and I turn to see him shaking his head. "He was the real thing, you know? Even when he was a scrawny thirteen-year-old, he had a golden touch. I really thought he'd go Division I for point guard after high school. He was that good."

"He still is," I say, watching as Nathan nails another effortless shot.

"Yeah," Evan agrees, and that one word conveys so much pain and loss.

"He hardly ever shoots around anymore—only when he's really pissed off."

I nod, not at all surprised when Evan confirms my suspicions. Nathan's disquiet lays across his tense shoulders like a yoke—it's telegraphed in every jerky, too energetic play he makes on the ball.

"What happened?"

"He had yesterday's seizure in the car on the way home. I guess he thrashed around pretty good before Mom could stop and hang on to him; he's got a nasty bruise on the side of his head."

Evan says the words matter-of-factly, but the skin around his eyes is tight as they follow Nathan.

"And this morning, he had the worst headache I've ever seen; there was no way he could go to school. Mom says he's been out here for a half hour, and we should get him to stop before he overheats himself."

I take a deep breath, letting the burden of all I've heard settle on my shoulders.

"I'll talk to him."

"I kinda figured you would," Evan says, clapping my shoulder as he turns away.

I'm nearly thrown off my feet, but I smile as I watch him heading up the walk toward the house. His girlfriend may be a total bitch, but Evan's a good guy.

I step to the side of Nathan's half court—close enough so he'll see me but far enough away not to interrupt his shooting.

He's taking a jump shot when I finally make it into his peripheral vision—nothing but net as he lands squarely, and his head whips to the side.

He sees me, but I'm not sure he wants to because he gets his rebound and continues to shoot. I know I told Evan I'd get Nathan to stop, but something tells me it's not time yet, and if I try to tell him what to do, I'm going to face the brunt of his ire. So I sit down beside the court and enjoy the show.

After about five minutes and only one missed shot, he finally holds the ball and comes toward me.

I try not to react to the deep purple bruising that stretches from temple to cheekbone and encircles his left eye, but his flinch as he approaches is a clear indication I've failed. *Shit.*

"Does it really look that bad? Forget it; I know it does," he says before I can answer.

Oh, yeah, this *is gonna be a fun afternoon.*

"I need a shower," he tells me as he walks past. I still haven't said a word yet, but again, I know better. He's normally so attentive to me, and every thought he's had since he saw me has been about himself. There's too much anger and upset for him to feel anything else.

I follow him into the house, but I stop in the foyer to hang up my coat, and by the time I'm done, he's nowhere to be seen.

Ten minutes later, he walks into the living room in jeans and a soft-looking green sweater, his hair still wet and sticking up in all directions. My heart speeds up like it always does, but he doesn't look at me—choosing instead to stare at the floor between us.

"I'm . . . fuck—"

"You're upset; I know."

"Yeah, but not—"

"Not at me. I know that too."

Nathan snorts, shaking his head. "Is there anything you *don't* know?"

"I don't know why this keeps happening to you," I say, standing up and wrapping my arms around him. "Do you have *any* idea why things are changing?"

Nathan glances down as his lips twist into an agitated frown.

"Yeah, I do . . . now. Mom dragged me to see my neurologist this afternoon. She says it's likely hormones. You know, teenage stuff? Stress and mood swings and girls . . ."

He won't look at me, so I assume the worst.

"This is my fault, then?"

His head snaps up, and he grasps my forearms, suddenly focused and intense. "No, of course not! Your finding out was stressful, but the rest has been—and she said this happens to a lot of her patients. Eventually, it might make things better, but right now—"

"It's making them worse?"

"Unpredictable." He corrects me, looking down again. "Now, I don't know what's going to happen or when—as if this shit isn't hard enough to deal with!"

He breathes a heavy sigh and wraps his arms around my waist, resting his head on my shoulder.

"Thank you for what you did yesterday. I really lost my shit, and I probably would have had the seizure in the middle of the hall if you hadn't gotten me out of there."

I don't respond. I only hug him tighter, and it's as if I'm squeezing the words out of him.

"I'm so scared and angry and confused. And I just can't calm the hell down. It's like . . . like I want out of my own skin. Like it's too tight, and I need—"

"What do you need?"

"A way to escape," he says, his words so soft I almost miss them as he mumbles them into my shoulder.

"How have you escaped before?" I whisper against his neck. "I know you've been stressed out in the past—"

"Basketball. But that was back when I could play. Just shooting is too automatic. I'm still trapped in my head, and it makes me even angrier—"

"Anything else?"

"I also play the piano."

"Wow." I did notice the baby grand the other week when Nathan whisked me toward the kitchen, but I never thought . . .

"I started a few years ago. It's . . . kind of a left-brain, right-brain thing, you know? It's supposed to help with—"

"Fewer seizures?"

"Something like that."

"Why don't you play, then? See if it'll help? I can leave—"

"Don't leave. I *want* to be with you. But I need—"

"I know. How about I sit where you can't see me? That way, I won't distract you."

He nods again and pulls back from me, his steps slow and weary across the open floor to the piano in the front room. When he reaches his destination, he just stands there, one hand resting on the side of the instrument.

I relax into a leather chair nearby, watching him breathe deeply, the set of his shoulders taut and painful to watch. Then he slides onto the bench and stretches his long, nimble fingers over the keys, and I breathe in with him as his fingers make contact, and he raises his head.

Holy.

Freaking.

Shit.

When I envisioned Nathan playing the piano, it was with music in front of him, playing some tune well enough that I would recognize it.

194

That image is so different from what's happening in front of me, it's actually laughable. And maybe I *would* laugh . . . if I could breathe.

His touch is so gentle—he caresses the keys, but the sound coming from them is so powerful in its sadness that it takes my breath away.

He plays with his whole body—eyes almost closed, shoulders hunched over the keys—as if he's channeling everything he's feeling out the tips of his fingers, purging himself.

I'm absolutely frozen in place as I watch him pouring out his heart and soul in the form of angst and sorrow. It's beyond beautiful. In this moment, *he's* beyond beautiful.

The scene before me is so intimate—I realize with a pang that maybe I shouldn't be here. But wait, *he* asked me to be. He asked me to sit and watch; he wanted to share this with me.

The tears brim up and roll slowly down my cheeks, but I don't wipe my eyes, not wanting to lose sight of him for a second.

The piece meanders on, wandering through valleys of sorrow and great heights of anger, finally landing on a gentle resolve. As the last notes echo in the room, Nathan lays his hands in his lap and bows his head, and I'm still too stunned to do anything but stare in wonder.

He clears his throat.

"That was, um . . . Rachmaninoff. I like to play that one when things are frustrating me."

His voice releases me from the music's spell, and I take a gasping breath, startling him. He whips his head around, his eyes making contact with mine before lowering to the floor as his cheeks flush crimson.

"Say something," he mutters, and I'm not sure if it was to himself or to me, but suddenly, my power of speech returns.

"Christ, Nathan," I whisper, standing on shaky legs, my breath still coming in pants to match my racing heart.

"That was . . ."

I nearly trip in my eagerness to get to him, and Nathan turns to face me on the piano bench, but I reach him before he can stand, stepping in between his knees.

"That was the most beautiful thing I've ever heard," I tell him, cradling his cheeks in my hands.

I can't take it anymore—my lips just *have* to be on his—so I lean down and place a kiss on the corner of his mouth.

My head is still spinning, trying to take in everything I've witnessed today —the talent he was forced to walk away from and the one he discovered and honed with his grief—and casting a shadow over it all, the illness that dogs his every step.

He's . . . amazing. And it has nothing to do with his popularity or his sex hair or the persona he assumes at school. I'm talking about who he is—the *real* him. The boy I don't even think he sees.

I want to do everything, say everything I'm feeling all at once, and I don't know where to start, except I know I need to be closer. So I crawl into his lap on the piano bench, my thighs over his legs, hands buried in his hair as I pull his lips to mine.

I think I'm falling.

When our lips meet, it's not the usual explosion of lust but something deeper, higher. It's in my chest and not between my legs, and it's powerful, pulling me closer to him in every way possible.

He's hesitant, but my tongue is insistent, pushing its way into his mouth and tangling with his, searching, hoping.

His moan is low and urgent as he gives in, his arms wrapping around my waist, legs shifting under my thighs.

His kiss is desperate, hands groping, tongue surging, as if he wants to crawl inside me and never come out again, but I meet him with slow, steady strokes, confident and reassuring. I'm dizzy, and now I feel the heat between my legs, but what's in my chest is still stronger, brighter.

I want to love him—with my lips, tongue, and fingers—with everything I have so he understands. I don't even really know what I want him to understand, but I know he has to. He has to feel what I'm feeling right now and give it back to me with everything *he* has.

Our mouths find a rhythm, and suddenly, he's with me, giving back steady and even, pulling me closer as his hands grip instead of scrabble, his tongue caressing and claiming.

We continue for minutes or hours, our conversation silent but saying more than our words ever could. My heart, my whole chest, is full and bright, the euphoria so giddy and overwhelming, I'm almost shaking with it. Maybe I *am* shaking.

I need to be closer still, so my one hand slides down his chest and around his back while the other glides down his cheek. But it's the wrong cheek, and he winces, pulling back as he scrunches his eyebrows together.

I pull in a gasping breath as if I've been underwater all this time and am only now realizing I need oxygen, and he does the same, but the surprise in my eyes isn't reflected in his. His are filled with sorrow as he raises a hand to his cheek, gently moving mine away from his deeply bruised skin.

I can't let it end this way.

After what we've just shared, I can't let his pain come back, so I place my lips to the side of his chin—a featherlight kiss, gentle but full of everything I'm feeling.

His eyes close, so I take that as permission, moving slowly up the mottled skin, loving every bit of it until I reach the side of his eye.

His exhale is shaky, his swallow difficult, and my nose brushes the wetness on his cheek as I return to his lips, kissing him chastely until he opens to me again.

And when he does, he's the one who's giving this time—and it feels just like what I was giving him moments before.

I know what this is, but does he? Has he felt it before, and does he have a name for it? I've felt it before but only in bits and slivers, and I've never given it a name.

It scares me.

For a million reasons and only one, but I push it all away and just *feel*.

I've never felt so much in my entire life and never all for one person, overwhelming and all-consuming.

He grabs my hands, rubbing his thumbs over the backs of my fingers as he stares down at them.

"Thanks for putting up with me. I know I can be a dick when I'm pissed."

His admission startles a laugh out of me, and his grin is not entirely contrite.

"You weren't a dick—"

Blue eyes flick up to mine.

"—well, not to me, anyway. Now, I don't know what you did before I got here . . ."

Nathan chuckles, then takes a deep breath.

"Yeah, I may need to apologize to my mom . . . and Evan . . . and whatever was in that box I kicked the shit out of when I was looking for my ball—"

I laugh and so does he, and it's a beautiful sound. It would be the most beautiful sound I've heard all day if he hadn't just played for me.

"But really, thank you," he says, his hand cupping my cheek and his eyes pulling me in, warm and content.

Our lips meet, gentle and soft, but the feeling is electrifying.

He's *happy*.

We kiss for a few moments until he suddenly pulls back, those deep blue eyes pinning me with their intensity.

"There was something I wanted to ask you yesterday, but then everything went to shit, and I didn't get the chance. Would you, um . . . there's this dance thing over Christmas break—"

"The winter formal?" I blush as I realize I've run right over his proposal in my eagerness.

"Yeah, that," he says, chuckling. "Would you go? With me? I don't know—"

"Yes!" I all but yell, interrupting him again.

I attack his lips because now *I'm* the one who's happy, and we kiss in our little bubble until a wolf whistle makes us jump apart.

"Dammit, Evan!" Nathan swears, but Evan doesn't scowl in return; he laughs.

"Glad you're feeling better," he says, shooting me a wink as he passes by, and Nathan looks at me in confusion.

"How *did* you end up here anyway, Holly?" he asks, his eyes twinkling.

"Oh, I just really missed you at school today," I answer, preserving Evan's secret. Not all secrets are terrible ones, after all.

CHAPTER TWENTY-ONE

You know, Hobbes, some days even my lucky rocket ship underpants don't help.

— Bill Watterson

NATHAN

"You gonna be okay today?" Evan asks, and although I'd rather punch something, I just nod.

I missed half of Monday and all of yesterday, so that's weird to begin with since I usually only miss whole days to "skip school," but on top of that, I've got this massive bruise to explain.

Monday's seizure was terrifying. Before Monday, the seizure Holly saw was the only one I've ever had outside the house, and that day, it came on so suddenly, I didn't really have time to panic.

But not this time. This time, I'd had the panic attack at school, so I was already shaky and worked up. When the aura hit, I froze. I couldn't move, couldn't breathe—I knew I should lie down across the backseat or at least move away from the car door, but none of that happened.

When I woke up, my throbbing head was in Mom's lap, and she tried not to cry as she told me the pain was from where I'd bashed my head into the door as I seized in the moving car.

In the fucking *moving car.*

I pinch the bridge of my nose, trying to hold back everything I'm feeling and to relieve the residual ache. Yesterday's headache was so bad, I took as much codeine as Dad would give me and knocked myself out until afternoon, but then I had to face everything, including the damage to my face.

I pull down the car visor and look at myself in the mirror for what has to be the hundredth time since Monday—I had no idea bruises could get this dark. I'm pretty sure I hit the hard plastic next to the window with my cheekbone—that's where most of the pain and tenderness is, anyway—but the bruising has spread completely above and below my eye.

I look like Evan decked me.

And if he hadn't protested, I definitely would have used that as a cover for what happened.

"It doesn't look that bad," Evan says, glancing over as I poke and prod at the mottled skin.

I pause long enough to roll my eyes at him.

"Come on, it makes you look tough."

I can't contain my sarcastic huff. *If only that were the case.*

"No one will know what happened," he goes on, oblivious to my growing frustration. "And I'll—"

"I've got it, Evan." I all but growl.

He purses his lips but says nothing more. Even *he's* smart enough to know when I'm about to lose my shit.

And except for the few hours Holly was at the house yesterday, I've pretty much felt like I'm about to lose my shit the entire time.

Holly.

She saved my ass on Monday and then swept in yesterday like Mother Teresa of the pissed off, pulling me out of my misery just by listening to me bare my soul—anger and sorrow in words and notes.

Keeping *that* secret seems like a piece of cake right now compared to keeping my seizures hidden.

I startle when Evan's hand lands on my arm.

"You ready for this?"

We're in the parking lot already; I hadn't even noticed.

"Yeah, I'll be fine," I tell him . . . and myself.

I put on my sunglasses and wear them all the way to my locker, but the minute I take them off . . .

"Holy shit! What happened to your face?"

Okay, Nathan, it's showtime.

I smirk at Tyler as I glance over my shoulder.

"You should see the other guy."

"Who *was* the other guy?" he asks, but I shake my head.

"I don't kick ass and tell."

Tyler chuckles, and by now, everyone within earshot is listening.

"And here I thought you *didn't* kick ass, Nate. You never seem to around here." Chris's gaze is hard, daring me to contradict him.

"Well, he did on Monday. It happened on school grounds, so he was suspended yesterday, dumbass. Didn't you know?" Ryan's tone is sarcastic and mocking, and I nearly fall over as what he said sinks in.

Chris's face goes red as the guys around him try to stifle their snickers, and Tyler walks away, shaking his head.

Ryan waits for me while I grab my books, and we head down the hall before Chris can come up with a suitable retort.

"Thanks, Ryan," I mutter, feeling better than I have since the weekend.

"You gonna tell me what happened?" he asks, cocking his head at me.

Fuck. That didn't last long.

"Um . . ."

"Forget it." He turns his back on me before I can come up with a suitable lie, and my stomach plummets to my shoes as I follow him into homeroom.

The rumor of my "suspension" spreads, and by the time chemistry rolls around, everybody's heard it. The junior and senior guys think it's hilarious, while I've seen some of the younger guys looking at me with what I'd consider adoration. The girls just feel sorry for me, and I've had to avoid multiple fawnings this morning because I don't want Holly to get pissed off.

But I didn't see Amber coming.

She sits in Holly's seat while I'm digging in the desk drawer for a pencil, and when I straighten up, she's *right there*, her hand extended to my cheek.

"Aww, Natey, can I kiss it and make it better?" she says, her voice dripping saccharin sweetness just as Holly walks into the room.

Her fingers brush my skin, and I try not to grimace—at her words or the pain.

"I believe that's my . . . *seat*," Holly says, her tone low and dangerous.

"Oh, is it?" Amber answers, still staring at me. "Not very good at *keeping* it, are you?"

She hops off Holly's stool lightly.

"I'll see you in Spanish, Nathan," she says, flipping her hair over her shoulder, and I close my eyes and count to ten, not at all looking forward to what's coming.

"Nathan?"

We're in a room full of witnesses—I shouldn't have to cover my balls, right?

"Yeah?"

"How's your head? Any better?"

I didn't just imagine *Amber sitting here flirting with me, did I?*

"Um . . . it's okay. My cheek is still sore though."

"Aww . . . can *I* kiss it and make it better?" she asks, a devilish light in her eyes.

How the hell am I not in trouble for this? Amber was in Holly's chair!

I shake my head until I remember that fucking hurts.

Just go with it. Who cares why?

"Sure," I say, grinning as I lean toward her.

Holly glances over her shoulder, staring until she catches Amber's eye, then she leans over and gently places her lips on my cheek. I can't help but turn my face until her lips meet mine, and we kiss until the bell brings us back to reality.

I stare at her in a daze, trying to catch my breath, but Holly looks over her shoulder and puckers her lips in Amber's direction.

Whack!

Amber's book hitting the desk perfectly covers the sound of Holly's giggle as she turns back around, grinning like a cat that's swallowed several canaries.

"Don't get mad; get even," she whispers, and while I have to stuff my fist in my mouth to keep from laughing out loud, I can do nothing about the bulge rapidly growing in my pants.

Smartass Holly is sexy as *hell*.

~

The rest of the day isn't so bad. By afternoon, everyone's seen my face and decided what they want to believe, so the gawking and hushed whispers have died down. Spanish is an exercise in looking straight ahead, but I can feel Amber's eyes on me the whole period, and by the time the bell rings, I'm ready to jump out of my skin.

I bolt, wanting to grab my shit and be at Holly's locker by the time she makes it up the hall from physics, but nothing in my life ever goes as planned.

As I straighten up to hoist my bag on my shoulder, an arm wraps around my waist, and I know in a heartbeat it's not Holly's.

"When are you going to ask me to the winter formal, Nate?" Amber whispers in my ear, and it takes everything I have not to spin around and punch her.

Instead, I grip her arm and turn, unwinding her from me as I put a reasonable distance between us.

"I'm *not* going to ask you. Why the *fuck* would you think I was?" Just thinking about the way she treated Holly this morning has me seething.

"Oh, come on, Nathan. Who else would you ask? Holly? I thought you'd have gotten in her pants and would be over it by now. Certainly you'll be done playing with her by Christmas and want to be seen in public with a respectable girl on your arm."

My blood boils so quickly, it's a miracle I'm not vaporized, and this time, it's the thought of my mom's face if I get suspended for punching a girl that keeps my fists at my sides. But just barely.

"Amber!" I yell, and I have to take a few deep breaths and clench my fists to stay in control. "I'm dating Holly. I've already asked Holly to the dance, and we're going together. Why can't you get it through your head? You and I have never *been* together; we're never *going to be* together! You think you're respectable? You've fucked every jock in the junior and senior classes, except for my brother, and that's only because Lori would kick your ass!"

"Nathan—"

Amber's eyes are as wide as saucers, and I can see the tears in them, but I don't fucking care. I'm so sick of all the bullshit I have to deal with, I can't take one more thing, and I have to make her understand once and for all.

"I don't want you, Amber! I never have! I'm with Holly, so leave me the fuck alone. Leave *her* the fuck alone!"

I'm right up in her face, and I'm so focused on keeping my own hands down that I never see hers coming.

The slap hits my bruised cheek and snaps my head to the right, and I see stars, leaning over and gasping from the pain.

"You're wrong, Nathan. You and I were meant to be together, and I'm going to prove it to you!" Amber yells, and she spins on her heel and stomps off down the hall.

"Fuck!" I bellow, and when I look up, I notice the large crowd staring at me like I owe them something. I feel like my head is going to explode; the blood is pounding in my temples so fast, and I'm panting like I've run a marathon. I snap up my bag, and my fist finds my locker door, slamming it hard enough to rattle the entire row.

Suddenly, my arm feels like it's in a vise grip, and Evan's propelling me up the hall.

"Fuck off!" I yell, but Ev just grips tighter.

"We need to get you out of here." Evan's reply is little more than a growl as he moves me bodily out the north-end door. Instead of heading for the car, though, he rounds the steps and takes me up the grassy hill, finally letting me go when we're almost behind the building.

"What the fucking—"

"Is there Xanax in your bag?"

I glare at him like he's deranged.

"Nathan! Is there Xanax in your bag?"

I'm still hyperventilating, shaking with rage, and his question makes absolutely no sense to me.

He rips my bag off my shoulder with a frustrated growl and paws through it until he finds my pill bottle.

"Take one. Take fucking two before you have a goddamn seizure!" Evan thrusts the pills into my hand, and the fear in his eyes suddenly makes sense.

The rage pumping through my system turns to an ice-cold deluge of fear.

"No . . ."

"No?" Evan asks, but I just shake my head, toss the pills into my mouth, and swallow them dry.

"Not here," I whisper, still gulping for air, but now it's from panic and not blinding anger.

"Here, sit," Evan says, maneuvering my shoulders until my back touches the brick wall of the school, and I slide down, crossing my arms over my drawn up legs and resting my head on them.

"Just breathe and try to calm down. Don't think about anything else."

I focus on my breathing, trying to will everything else away.

In. Out. In. Out.

Slowly.

Ev stands over me, positioned between me and the side of the school so that anyone coming around the corner would see him and not me.

It takes about five minutes, but finally, the block of ice in my chest thaws, and I can freely take in oxygen. Normally, this would mean I'm no longer lightheaded, but a double of Xanax is roughly equivalent to my limit in Heineken.

"Are you all right?"

"Yeah, just . . . high. One Xanax probably would have done the trick."

"Oops. I'll remember that for next time," Evan says, and I can hear the smile in his voice.

"Help me up so I don't fall on my ass?" I ask, peering up at him with one eye closed.

"Sure."

And suddenly my feet are under me, and I'm holding Evan's arm.

"You okay to walk?"

"Yeah. Just grab me if I stumble. Sometimes Xanax makes the sidewalk come up and hit you in the face."

Evan chuckles and walks down the hill beside me while I focus on putting one foot in front of the other.

"Nathan!"

I hear my name as something solid propels me backward, but it turns into softness as Holly clings to me, holding me up.

"Oh my God, are you okay? I stayed after physics, and when I came up, you were gone, and somebody said Amber *slapped* you?"

"She did," Evan says, nodding. It all comes back to me, and I wince as I touch my cheek.

"Oh, baby! What happened?" Holly exclaims, taking a step back, and when she lets go, I stagger backward until Ev shores me up.

"Have you been *drinking*?"

"No! I got so pissed at Amber that Ev thought I was gonna have a seizure, so I took two Xanax."

Holly goes completely still.

"What did that bitch say?"

"Why don't we go sit in my car so no one has to hold Nathan up," Evan says, and I have to agree with him on that one. The world is pretty wiggly right about now.

Holly throws my arm over her shoulder, and although I'm sure it looks like I've just slung my arm over my girl to anyone who sees us, she's supporting a good bit of my weight and leading me in a straight line.

We get to the car, and I manage to get myself in, laying my head back and closing my eyes as Holly climbs in next to me.

Her hand brushes my bangs off my face, but her words are hard.

"Spill it, Harris."

"She, um . . . wanted to know when I was going to ask her to the winter formal. So I told her fucking never because I'm with you. And then she slapped me and said I was wrong, and she'd prove it to me."

There's no sound from next to me, and even in my altered state, I know that's a *very* bad thing.

I raise my head and slowly turn to look at her, and even *I'm* scared.

Holly glares, her lips a thin line, her nostrils flared with her heavy breathing. Her cheeks are a ruddy pink, and her brown eyes burn with dark fire.

"I'm going to kill her."

Ev pipes up. "Nathan thought about it. Good job not decking a girl, bro."

We fist bump, but Holly still hasn't moved.

"Holly?"

"I'm going to knock her right on her ugly little ass, and then I'm going to—"

"Holly—"

"What?"

I scooch over to her, wrapping my arms around her and laying my head on her shoulder. "Please don't. I know she deserves it—"

"Nathan, what would you do if a guy slapped *me?*"

"I'd bury him under the school flagpole after I tore him limb from limb, but this is *different.*"

Holly huffs, but I stay where I am, holding her and trying to keep up my end of the conversation.

"You're better than her. You care about me and don't just want me as some trophy on your arm, and you know the truth about . . . well, everything. I need to get out of the spotlight at school as quickly as possible, and your having a catfight with Amber is just going to drag this out. And I know you don't want to hear it, but I don't need a girl to fight my battles for me."

"It has nothing to do with that. She touched what's *mine,*" Holly says, grazing her cheek against my head, and even in my relaxed state, my dick starts to harden.

"I *am* yours, and she sees it every day, and she'll see it at the formal. Please, just stay away from her. I told her to leave us alone, so we need to leave her alone too. Please?"

"Dammit!" Holly's still pissed, but I know I've won, so I cuddle into her a little closer.

I tilt my head up and kiss her neck, then whisper in her ear. "Do you know what your being all protective makes me want to do to you? How much it turns me on?"

Holly softens against me, her hushed whimper a breath against my forehead.

I lift my head, and the world spins, so I shut my eyes tightly.

Fuck.

"But I really need to go home and sleep off this Xanax high that Evan was nice enough to give me."

Holly kisses my cheek, and I grin drunkenly.

"I'm sorry your day sucked."

"It really did," I say, thinking back to Chris this morning and then Amber McBruiseslapper.

"You go home, and we'll talk more about this tomorrow, okay? I promise I won't lay a finger on Amber."

"Thank you," I say, giving her what I know are sloppy kisses, but I'm too fucked up to do any better.

"Evan, you'll take care of him?" Holly asks, and Evan nods, giving me a small smile.

"Then I'll see you tomorrow." Holly gives me one last kiss on my forehead, and then she's gone.

"Dude, you are one lucky man to have a girl who actually listens. My Lori would be in orange right now if that were me, and there's not a thing in the world I could do to stop her."

Your Lori couldn't keep a secret if it was tattooed between her tits.

But I say nothing and just put my head back, letting the motion of the car lull me to sleep.

Chapter Twenty-Two

Life shrinks or expands in proportion to one's courage.

– Anais Nin

Holly

I told Nathan I wouldn't lay a finger on Resting Bitch Face—I didn't say anything about keeping my mouth shut.

How *dare* she fucking *slap* him, and in the middle of the hall for the whole damn school to see? That was over the line and below the belt right there, but on top of that, she made sure to hit him where he was already hurting? If I hadn't made a promise to Nathan, I would have driven right over to her house and—

No, you wouldn't have.

The thought echoes in my head as I stalk down the hall, and I hate to admit how much truth there is to it. The only person in this school I've given a piece of my mind to is Nathan himself, which makes no sense because I actually *like* him. Why can't I just *speak up* when the situation calls for it? Getting Amber's attention while I was kissing Nathan yesterday was the ballsiest thing I've ever done, and that was only because I was pissed beyond reason, and it didn't involve actually talking.

But today? Today I'm gonna give that bitch an earful if it's the last thing I do. She needs to know Nathan doesn't belong to her, and he never ever will.

I slam my locker door, and Megan jumps beside me, flinching when she sees the look on my face.

"I guess you heard about the Amber and Nathan standoff, then?"

I glare at her, and I'm caught off guard when she throws her arms around me and pulls me close.

"Don't let that bitch bother you. You know Nathan wants nothing to do with her."

"Yeah, but she *slapped* him. She hurt him in a way he couldn't defend himself, and she hit the bruised cheek too. She touched what's *mine*."

"That's not all she did."

The Gothlet saunters up, hands clasped behind her.

"What?"

"She insulted you too. I was there."

"You *saw* it?" I gasp.

"Of course I saw it. Half the fucking school saw it! I would have chased her down after if she hadn't been surrounded by so many witnesses!"

Megan raises her eyebrows, but I shake my head to table the topics of chasing down and witnesses for later. Hearing Bitch Face's words from a credible source is *much* more pressing.

"What did she say?"

"*Well,*" The Gothlet says, leaning forward conspiratorially, "she said you weren't respectable enough for him, and Nathan was only with you to get in your pants."

The first one makes my blood boil, but the second one hits so close to my own original thoughts that it turns my stomach a little.

"Respectable? Who the hell does she think she is, the way she sleeps around!" I'm flabbergasted, but The Gothlet just giggles as she nods at me.

"That's exactly what Nathan told her."

"What?"

"Oh, Holly, he was brilliant! He got right up in her face and told her they would never be together! If she hadn't clocked him like that, he would have been the clear winner of the bitch-off. I don't know how he managed not to swing right back."

I do. It involved incredible restraint followed by copious amounts of Xanax.

". . . but you can't let her get away with it," The Gothlet says, looking at me expectantly.

"I know! But I can't slap her around either. I promised Nathan."

The Gothlet gapes at me, but of course, I can't explain why I can't rearrange Bitch Face's face. Suddenly, her lips curl into a wicked smirk, and her eyes blaze like some possessed anime character.

"You only promised *you* wouldn't touch Amber, right?"

"Yeah, but—"

"Nathan can't control what *I* do. Leave this one to me, Holly," The Gothlet says, rubbing her hands together.

"Lucy . . ."

"Oh relax, Megan! I won't put her in the hospital or anything! It was only that one time, and it wasn't even my stiletto!"

The Gothlet turns on her heel and stalks down the hall, leaving Megan and me bewildered in her wake.

"She put someone in the hospital . . . with a shoe?" I ask.

Megan just shrugs.

The Gothlet's past is definitely a scarier place than I thought.

Murmurs swirl around Nathan all day, but he weathers it all, tight-lipped and tense, clearly embarrassed by having to allow himself to be shown up by a girl. By sixth period, the whole thing is wearing on him, and he's disappeared to the nurse's office, claiming he has a headache.

Thermodynamics and I aren't getting along, so I get back to my locker late, and the hallway is almost empty.

"If you have something to say to me, Holly, don't send the crazy Goth bitch after me. Have the balls to do it yourself."

I jump, dropping my bag with a loud thud as her words shoot adrenaline down my spine. *This is it. This is my chance.*

What the hell did Lucy do?

I turn around slowly.

"I've got plenty of balls, and I didn't send anyone anywhere." That's what I want to say.

Instead, my cheeks sting with heat as I mumble, "I d-didn't—"

"He's too good for you. I don't know why he's with you, but it's not because he really likes you. That's not the way he operates. I don't know what his game is, but when it ends, he's going to dump you, and the whole school is going to be laughing at you. Why don't you just save your-self the trouble, and let him go to the dance with me?"

"No . . ."

No, I won't let him go? No, he's not like that? Or no, it can't be true?

"He *will* be mine." Bitch Face sneers, taking a step toward me, but suddenly, The Gothlet is between us.

"I *told* you to leave her alone, but you didn't take me seriously, did you?" The Gothlet says in a quiet, deadly voice.

There's a flash of silver, and Bitch Face's eyes widen.

"Holy shit! You're fucking crazy!" she yells, taking a few steps backward.

"Stay. Away. From Holly!" The Gothlet yells back, stomping her foot loudly and feinting as if she's about to launch herself at Bitch Face, who takes off sprinting down the hall.

Holy hell, is that a—

I gasp as The Gothlet turns toward me, folding a shiny black knife blade back into its handle.

"Jee-*sus*!"

"What?" she asks nonchalantly, now cool as a cucumber. "Like I'd actually *knife* her in the middle of the school hallway. What a moron."

"Yeah." My reply sounds like a squeak, followed by a high-pitched giggle.

The Gothlet's eyes shoot up to mine. "Oh come on, Holly! It's just a small stiletto! His name is Ivan."

Well, this explains a few things about our previous conversation. Mental note: tell Megan that The Gothlet did not *attack someone with a shoe. And that we are stupid.*

"Ivan?"

"Yeah," she says, grinning, and I jump three feet and nearly piss my pants when she releases the blade again to show me.

"Gosh, you're jumpy, Holly. What did she say to you?"

Gee, could I possibly be jumpy because you're waving a freaking knife around?

I breathe a sigh of relief as she sheaths Ivan again.

"Nothing she hasn't said before. Thanks for . . . uh . . ."

Knifing your way in?

Saving me—scary Goth style?

"... jumping in when you did, but I was okay. I was gonna tell her what to go do with herself," I say with as much confidence as I can muster, but I know it's not true. I was gonna stand there and let her tongue lash me like I always do.

Anger flairs in my chest, and I know I need to be alone right now.

"Lucy, I gotta go. Can we talk about this tomorrow?"

The Gothlet assesses me, her head cocked to the side, and if she sees the yellow streak down my back, she chooses to ignore it.

"Okay. If you're sure you're all right."

"I'm fine. I'll see you in homeroom tomorrow," I say, turning to retrieve my bag.

Lucy walks away without a word, and I'm so lost in my thoughts I hardly even notice.

Why am I such a coward? What is it that ties my tongue when I need to stand up for someone—when I need to stand up for myself?

I have no answers, and that makes me even angrier. It's all there in my head, planned and ready to deliver, but it just stays there, mocking me.

"Argh!" I yell, slamming my palms against the steering wheel as I sit in my driveway.

You're no different. You're nothing special—what does Nathan see in you anyway? Why would he change "the way he operates" for you?

Bitch Face's words come at me where I'm weak, and they take hold.

Nathan has a way he operates? What does that even mean?

It means he's never been serious about anyone, my subconscious helpfully supplies.

But I know this. He can't let anyone get close because they'd find out about his epilepsy.

Is that the real reason—the whole reason?

Yes. It has to be because I . . . I love him, and I think he loves me.

Giving that feeling of . . . *everything* a name loosens the knot in my stomach, and I cling to it.

Everything. He's my everything.

I'm in love with him.

My heart flutters and expands in my chest, but my head is still speaking in the voice of Bitch Face.

I glance at my house, and I realize I can't go in there. Dad is working second shift, and if I go in there alone, that little voice in my head is gonna taunt me and tear me down and convince me that Nathan is using me, and I'm not worthy of anyone's love, let alone his.

What I need . . . is him.

I need Nathan.

I need him to look at me the way he does—like I'm the only girl on the planet.

I need him to touch me, like I'm something to be worshipped, and he can't believe he's with me.

I need him, and I need him *now*, and I can't even call him and take the risk that he'll tell me it's not a good time. I just have to go.

I fly across town, thinking of nothing other than getting there, but once I'm in his driveway, sanity smacks me in the face, and I realize I have no idea what I'm going to say to him.

Hi, Nathan. Amber told me you're going to fuck me and run. Is that true?

Hi, Nathan. My head says I'm not good enough for you even though I've just admitted to myself that I'm in love with you. Can you convince me otherwise?

I rest my head against the steering wheel. *I should just go home.*

I scream as a loud tap sounds next to my head. Nathan is standing next to my car, cringing in apology as I hold my hand over my pounding heart.

"Sorry!" he exclaims as I roll the window down. "I didn't know how to get your attention without scaring the shit out of you. What are you doing here?"

And there it is—deep blue eyes drinking me in as if I'm the only girl he's ever seen. His gaze sends a shiver down my spine that has nothing to do with how cold it is, and I know this was the right decision—even if it goes downhill from here, and I come off as the crazy stalker girlfriend for showing up unannounced and uninvited.

And now I drink *him* in—burnished copper hair scattered carelessly but oh so perfectly across his forehead, eyebrows slightly drawn together in confusion, but a soft smile still drawing up his lightly scruffy cheeks. He's happy to see me, no matter the reason.

"I . . ." I feel the tears well up, and when I close my eyes, they spill over, and suddenly, the car door is open, and I'm in his arms.

I press my head against his chest and clasp my hands around his neck; and he cradles me, his arms encircling low around my waist.

"What is it? I couldn't find you after school, and you didn't answer your phone, so I came home with Evan—"

I sob against his chest, letting all my fears and frustrations go in a torrent of gasps and whimpers, and he just holds me, squeezing me tight every few seconds to try to calm me.

"Hey," he says, tipping my chin up so I'm tossed into troubled seas of mesmerizing blue, "did something happen?"

A sudden shiver rolls through him.

"It's freezing out here," I murmur, grateful for the excuse to deflect his question. I don't know how to begin to tell him everything that's swirling in my head, and I honestly don't know if I can or should.

"I should go—"

"Can you stay?"

Our words overlap, and I can't help but smile at the concern I see in his eyes. There's no way he's going to let me go without knowing what's bothering me.

"Are you sure?"

"Yes! Please, Holly?"

After the week he's already had, I can't bear the thought of causing him any more stress, so I nod, and Nathan turns off my car and pulls me into the house.

I slide onto his bed, one leg bent in front of me, and he mirrors my position, taking my hand.

"What happened? Please tell me?"

"Amber—"

"What the fuck did she do? I *told* her to stay away from you." Nathan's agitated now, fingers combing through his unruly hair the way they always do when he's stressed.

"Did she lay a hand on you? So help me, I'll—"

"She didn't touch me," I say hurriedly, although it would have been satisfying to hear him finish that sentence even if he wouldn't have actually done it.

"She just said some things . . ."

Tell me she's lying. Tell me she knows nothing about us.

Nathan huffs in frustration; I can see he's getting worked up, but he's trying to hold it in check. He places his hands on my cheeks, his gaze pulling me in and holding me.

"I don't like Amber. I never did. We fooled around last year, but it wasn't serious—I wouldn't have wanted her to be my girlfriend even if I could have."

I stare into his eyes and find no deception there, and relief washes over me in a welcome wave.

I believe you. You can't fake what I see in your eyes. This is real.

"Amber's not—I mean—she's not even *close*—"

"She's not . . . what?"

He smiles and looks down, his cheeks suddenly reddening.

"She's not . . . *you*. I don't even really know what that means," he says, chuckling awkwardly.

I do. It means you love me, but you don't know it yet.

"But I know I've never wanted . . . *really* wanted . . . a girlfriend before you. I just . . . and you worry about me, and you make it all so much easier to deal with . . . and you're so . . . *Jesus*, what the fuck am I saying?"

"I know what you're saying," I tell him, and he glances downward, smiling as he shakes his head.

"I bet you do. You always seem to know—that's one of the things that's so great about you."

That one hits me right in the chest—square in the heart—and radiates happiness in every direction, but he doesn't see it because he's still looking downward, his lips drawn tightly in a frown.

"I'm so sorry, Holly. You shouldn't have to put up with any shit over me—"

"Hey," I say, grasping his chin because I want him to see how happy he's made me, but he pulls away.

"I mean it. I come with so much fucking"—he throws his hands in the air —"baggage, and you shouldn't have to—"

"I don't care," I tell him, squeezing his hand.

I love you.

I want to say the words so badly, but I know after I do, there's no turning back. My heart already knows it belongs to him, but my head is still trying to protect me, and once I tell him my heart is his, the only way I'll ever get it back is in pieces, so I have to be sure.

God, I'm so sure.

But my yellow streak doesn't only apply to angry words and snotty bitches. So I take another path.

"You shouldn't have to deal with this either. I wish Amber and the seizures and all the stress would just disappear. I wish I could make that happen, but I can't. What I *can* do is be with you. That's all I want to do, Nathan, just be with you."

I can't tell him any more with words, and I think I'm afraid of any response he might have, so I reach up and grab his face, and before he can say anything, my lips are pressed against his. I kiss him slowly and deeply, my fingers sliding up into his hair as my lips worship his, and when he slips his tongue into my mouth, I eagerly welcome him in.

I'm sure he's hard, but the moment doesn't feel sexual. It's more about emotional connection because, although he's as close to me as he can get, he doesn't grind against me or push for anything more.

Somehow, we end up lying facing each other on his bed, our lips idly exploring as he brushes my hair from my cheek.

He closes his eyes, and I'm struck by how relaxed he looks. I bet he's adorable when he's asleep.

"I should go," I say, but his eyes snap open, and he captures my wrist as I make to sit up on the bed.

"Don't go yet," he says softly, but his eyelids are droopy, and the shadows under them look dark.

"Stay for just for a little bit." His puppy-dog eyes implore me, but his half-smile tells me he knows he's already won. "So, who do you think is gonna end up on the Iron Throne?"

I can't help the chuckle that escapes my lips—Nathan is usually pretty turned on when I talk nerdy to him—I don't know why he's wasting this on a night when he's too tired to unsheathe his Valyrian steel.

"Well, we know Dany will be a major threat to the Seven Kingdoms . . ."

As I expound upon my theory, Nathan's eyes slowly drift shut, then pop open as he does battle with the gravitational forces attacking his eyelids. I lose my train of thought, but I keep spewing random nonsense about Westeros just to keep my voice even so I don't disturb the sound that's lulling Nathan to sleep.

Once he loses the battle with gravity, his chin slips down toward his shoulder, and he sighs as if the weight of the day has been lifted from him.

I slide off the bed inch by inch, but Nathan is out cold—he mumbles something unintelligible and curls on his side as I stand up.

I can't resist the urge to brush the hair back from his forehead, lingering for a moment as I let the warmth spread and consume me.

My heart belongs to him, and I need to work up the courage to put him on notice, come what may.

Bitch Face can go fuck herself. He's perfect, and we're good enough for each other.

CHAPTER TWENTY-THREE

The difference between sex and love is that sex relieves tension and love causes it.

– Woody Allen

NATHAN

"You ready yet?" Evan hollers from downstairs.

Am I?

I look myself over in the mirror—black suit, black dress shirt, blue tie, and matching handkerchief in my pocket to go with Holly's dress. I *look* ready, but anxiety is still churning in my gut, heightened by the knowledge that anxiety can bring on seizures. I should be good. I just had one three days ago, but tonight I've got to get through Lori's charming attitude since we're riding with her and Evan, seeing Holly's dad again when we pick her up for the dance, and then asking Holly to stay over at my house tonight.

Yes, you heard that right. Mom went to Chicago early to see my grandparents, and Dad is working the night shift, so Ev and I have decided to have a little slumber party after the formal. I doubt there'll be much sleeping however. Or at least, I'm *really* hoping not.

My dick twitches, but it's a feeble attempt—too much other shit to worry about between now and when his copulatory dreams might come true.

"Nathan!"

"Yeah, Ev, don't get your balls in a twist! I'm coming!"

I hurry down the stairs, but I have to catch myself on the post at the bottom—I've got one Xanax on board and one in my pocket, just in case. I'm a little woozy, but it's better than hyperventilating over another encounter with Chief Feed-My-Balls-to-the-Bears.

I skid to a halt in the kitchen, and Ev and I look each other over.

"You look like Justin Timberlake on a bad hair day."

"And you look like a baboon in a burrito."

"Fucker."

"Asshole."

I duck as he swings an arm to grab me, but I know he won't. Normally, I hate that and try to get him to take a swing at me anyway, but tonight, I did spend a pretty long time trying to tame my hair.

"Let's go. Lori gets bitchy when I'm late."

"Blame it on me; she hates me anyway."

Ev looks like he wants to say something, but he just shakes his head. Lori's attitude toward me comes straight from all the things she can't know, and we both know that.

Ev grabs our little flower things from the fridge, and we haul ass to Lori's house. As he parks, his eyes find mine in the rearview mirror.

"No drinking tonight. I'm not leaving early; I'm not babysitting your ass; and if you piss Lori off somehow, and I don't get mine, I'm going to tell everyone I caught you and Ryan making out."

"That's pretty harsh! Why would you do that to Ryan? He could do so much better—"

"Nate."

"All right! I wasn't planning on drinking anyway because we have to fly tomorrow. Dad will be pissed if we have to cancel, and a seizure on an airplane sounds like a pretty accurate definition of hell."

"Good," Ev says, nodding. Then his eyes flick downward. "And later on . . . just . . . bag it up, yeah?"

My eyes widen, and I swear my eyebrows brush the roof of the car.

A sex talk? From the lech of the locker room? Seriously?

"Fucking hell, Ev! You gonna tell me about the birds and the bees too? *You* bag it up!"

"I do!" he exclaims, his cheeks now a furious red. "Not that it's any of your damn—"

"Yours either!"

"Okay, okay! I'm just looking out for you, asshole!" Ev yells, palming the back of his neck.

"Consider me looked out for." I huff as I cross my arms.

When we finally get to Holly's house, her dad is looking out the front window as if he's waiting for me. My heart rate skyrockets, and breathing becomes my main focus. *Who knew his ability to strike fear in my heart had this kind of range?*

So many secrets. And tonight? Tonight, I'm hoping to play Texas Hold'em with his daughter's V-card. If I still can, that is. My dick feels like it's turned into a raisin. *Who'd want to hit that?*

"Nathan?"

Evan's voice registers, but my eyes are glued to the chief's until something draws his attention, and he looks away. I exhale in a *whoosh* and clutch at my chest. *Shit.* I may have just peed a little.

"I'll walk up with you, okay?"

Relief floods through me until—

"You've *got* to be kidding me! He can't go get his own date?"

Despite feeling like I'm about to pass out, rage and stubbornness flare in my chest and force the words out of my mouth.

"I'm fine, Evan. I'll be back in a few."

My anger thrusts me out of the car and all the way up to the door, but once I'm there, my hands start shaking. What little air I can get is choppy and ragged, and if I don't get more soon, I may just take a dive on the chief's porch.

I ring the doorbell out of desperation more than anything else, and it swings open immediately to reveal Holly's dad standing there with an evil grin on his face.

The chief takes a step toward me, and my heart falters in my chest.

"Good evening, Nathan," he says pleasantly enough, but his eyes are sending me another message entirely—one that starts with assault and battery and ends with murder one.

I'm gonna pass out; the chief's gonna think I'm drunk; and I'm gonna wake up behind bars with Willie the town wino for company. *How did this night go to hell so fast?*

As I'm about to let the darkness take me, Holly ducks under her father's arm and everything stops—my fall, my breathing, my heart.

"Nathan!"

She steps past dear old dad and wraps her arms around me—I'm sure she can tell I'm shaking, and my heart is pounding so hard, it's got to be knocking against her chest too.

"Breathe," she whispers. "I'm here."

I release a shaky breath into her shoulder, and I can't help but inhale the sweet fragrance of her shampoo as my nose buries itself in her hair.

And suddenly, I can breathe again. The two deep breaths I take restore function to my brain and strength to my knees, and my lips move to Holly's of their own accord.

I kiss her, and it's as if everything fixes itself at once, and none of it matters —not secrets, not murderous public servants, not Lori, not anything but the girl who means everything. *Is* everything.

Holly pulls back before I have the sense to, and as I step back, I realize I'm gazing at the most beautiful thing I've ever seen.

She's . . . stunning. Gorgeous. Transcendent.

Tiny little sleeves barely cover her shoulders, and her perfect breasts poke out against a shiny top covered in blue roses. A bow of the same material draws in her slim waist, and a skirt of silky see-through stuff flows down to just below her knees.

"Beautiful," I whisper.

"Isn't she?"

The chief's words reverberate like a sonic boom as his hand clamps down on my shoulder, and he gives me a little shake.

"You two should be going. Nathan, take care of my daughter tonight. I just couldn't *bear* it if anything happened to her."

As if his choice of words weren't enough to remind me, he winks and I nearly swallow my tongue. Holly glares at him as if she could melt him with her eyes.

"I'll be home around lunchtime tomorrow, Dad. Let's go," she says to me as she grabs my arm and marches us out the door.

I don't look back, but when I hear the door shut with a snap, my breath comes a little easier.

Holly stops and turns to me.

"Are you all right?"

And my mind, heart, dick—and every other part of me that's ever registered an opinion—are silent.

Because now that she's with me, I am.

CHAPTER TWENTY-FOUR

I don't know the question, but sex is definitely the answer.

– Woody Allen

NATHAN

We talk. We dance. Holly looks absolutely gorgeous, and my dick is a steel rod the entire time. If it weren't for black slacks and a very dark room, everyone would be able to see that I'm toting around a fucking utility pole —complete with the occasional shower of sparks when Holly brushes a little too close.

I almost lost it the first time we danced. I have absolutely no idea how I kept from spunking all over my dress clothes—and I would have, too, because my balls feel like I'm carrying a third world nation. I'm not in pain though. Maybe Santa gives out red balls instead of blue—a teenage boy's Christmas miracle.

Speaking of miracles, or events that I hope are miraculous, I haven't asked Holly to stay over yet. My heart knows she'll say yes, but my mind is being a total pussy about it. *What if she says no? Does that mean she doesn't want to have sex? Now? Ever?*

And don't get me started on what my dick has to say about all this.

I'm so fed up with my own inner musings that the next time a slow song comes on, *I'm* the one to approach and pull her out onto the floor.

As we sway to the music, I go through a million ways to ask her and nearly talk myself out of the whole thing, but I'm too worked up at the very idea of her in my bed to turn back now.

"Uh . . . I know you're supposed to go to Lucy's, but . . . um . . . would you spend the night? With me?"

I lower my chin to meet her gaze, and her eyes bug out of her head.

"How—"

"My mom left already, and Dad has an overnight shift. Lori's spending the night too, I'm pretty sure."

"Like . . . as in . . . in your bed? With you?" She's floundering, still trying to wrap her mind around what I'm actually asking.

"Well, yeah. And I was kinda hoping we might . . . do more than sleep?"

And that's when she stops breathing.

"We don't have to go all the way if you don't want to." I blurt the words out in a rush. "I mean, I—I'd love to, but . . . we could just touch each other and cuddle and . . . please?"

I give her my best puppy dog eyes, and the smile she gives me radiates through my chest and in every direction.

"Yes."

The word is so powerful, it even manages to drown out the wails of anguish coming from my dick, and I pull her even closer and crash my lips into hers. We kiss until the song ends, and . . . maybe a little after because we're just about alone on the floor when I finally come up for air.

But the exhilaration in her deep brown eyes when I step back is worth every second.

"We'll continue this later," I say with a smirk.

The clock seems to tick backward, but finally, they're playing the last song, and she's in my arms again, her cheek resting on my shoulder.

"I had such a good time tonight," she murmurs, and heat flairs in my chest as I tighten my arms around her.

"I did too," I tell her, and I really mean it. No drinking, no drama, just a beautiful girl so close and warm, her adoring eyes finding me no matter where I was in the room.

"But . . . we're not finished yet, are we?" My voice is shaky as my heart thumps in my chest, but her blush calms me even before her words.

"No. No, I don't think we are."

Her smile is real, and some of my fear dissipates. She *does* want to be with me, and we'll figure this out together. Power pole in my pants twitches his agreement—I hope Holly can't see that I'm currently sporting a sparkler.

"Are you ready to go?"

"Yeah," Holly says, smiling again as I settle my jacket over her shoulders before following after Evan.

The ride home is quiet, and everything's good until we reach the top of the stairs, and my heart starts to thunder in my chest. Holly's been in my room before but never with the intent that we'd . . . It's an entirely different feeling—both exhilarating and terrifying.

I walk over to my dresser and put down my wallet and keys, and when I turn around, Holly's standing beside the bed, fidgeting. She's as nervous as I am, and that's good and bad—good because I feel like less of a pussy, but bad because it's no help in calming *me* down.

Okay, Nathan, time to man up.

Crossing the room on unsteady feet, I take her hands and bring them up to my chest.

"Hey."

"Hey," she murmurs, but the second her eyes meet mine, my fear starts to fade away.

"Nervous?"

"N-no."

"Liar."

She smirks and looks away as her cheeks flush, and my own nerves settle a bit more.

I grasp her chin and bring her gaze back to mine. "It's just us, and we won't do anything you don't want to. I just want to be with you, okay?"

Her eyes light up, and suddenly, she's kissing the shit out of me. I have no idea why, but at this moment, I couldn't care less. My hands find their way to her waist as heat flairs in my groin, and I feel like I have no control as my fingers squeeze her ass and push my throbbing dick against her . . . mother*fucker*.

Nathan gasps against me, and I don't know if it's surprise or relief or lust, but I don't care because now his arms are pulling me close, and his waist is sliding between my legs, and the feeling shooting through me is like a beacon into space.

His lips are warm and soft as we move against one another, and the second I feel his tongue touch my teeth, I thrust mine into his mouth, moaning as my stomach does a somersault.

"Ohh," he groans needily, his fingers sliding into my hair as he pulls me closer still.

"You're so . . . *God*, Holly, I just want to . . ."

His lips move hungrily to my throat, and I thrust my head back, allowing him better access as he kisses every inch of exposed skin. I'm panting, my hands sliding up his sides as his jacket falls from my shoulders.

Less clothing—yes! That's what we need!

Suddenly, I'm itching to touch him—to run my fingers over his quivering abs, to suck a nipple into my mouth because, although he does it to me all the time, I've never been brave enough to see if he likes it. But right now, I want to know . . . desperately.

I reach blindly for his tie because it's hard to do when you're panting and he's ravishing and . . . *there* it is!

His lips vanish from my skin, so I look down, at a loss, but a wave of hot lava rolls through my belly when I meet his dark, hungry eyes, and I know in that moment—

I'm going to give him everything.

He grasps his tie, loosening it as he rips it over his head, and my fingers are already at his buttons, revealing inch after inch of warm, heaving chest.

God almighty, he's so freaking gorgeous!

His shirt goes down and then off, and my hands span his pecs, teasing his nipples. His head rolls back with a deep inhale that ends in a groan, and I shiver, goosebumps breaking out on my skin. He hisses when my tongue makes contact with the hard little nub, and then I begin to suck, just like he does to me.

"Ohh, Jesus, Holly! What are you—ahh . . ."

His dick twitches so hard, I can feel it against my leg, and he melts against me, his hands sliding up my back to hold my mouth against his chest.

"Yes, *fuck*!" he exclaims as I suck even harder, and he presses his cock against my thigh.

His hands squeeze my back, but suddenly, they begin to scrabble frantically.

"I . . . I . . . I need this off. How do I—can I? Oh God, *please*."

If he's ever been this worked up before, I've never seen it, and that's saying something. My stomach twinges, and I squeeze my eyes shut as heat rolls through me. I release his nipple with a pop, and his gasp mirrors it exactly.

As I turn around, our eyes lock—his lust-filled, mine playful—and my smile widens as his fingers fumble and shake as they lower my zipper.

He's quicker with my strapless bra, and both fall as his hands cup my breasts, and his cock presses against me. I shiver violently as warm breath and warmer lips caress my shoulder.

"Fuck, Holly, you're . . ."

His words are just a mumble as his fingers squeeze and tweak, and my head falls back on his shoulder as I rub my ass against his cock.

His hands and lips are everywhere, and for a moment, I lose myself to sensation. The next thing I know, I'm on my back, and he's naked and hovering over me, about to take my nipple into his mouth.

"Mmm." I hum and writhe as he laves at my skin, groaning when he sucks hard.

"Nathan . . ."

I wanna see her naked. She's seen my dick and every other part of me, but she's always kept her panties on or the lights off—eating a girl out in the dark is like some sort of culinary cave expedition.

But tonight, when I closed the door, I flipped on my little desk light, hoping I'd get the chance to see all of her. And, by God, *right now* is my chance.

I slide my hand down her side until I reach her silky white panties, but she tenses when I grip the material.

It sucks to let go of the nipple I'm currently trying to swallow, but she needs to be okay with this. If she can't even let me look at her, we have no business fucking. I don't want her to regret this; I need to know she's doing it for *her* and not just for me.

I raise my eyes to her, and I'm disappointed to see a bit of panic there.

"Holly, I want to see you—*all* of you. You've seen me—"

She snorts, and I know what she's thinking.

"Okay, so maybe I wave my dick around like it's the greatest thing there's ever been—"

Her laughter chases everything out of my head, and the warmth I feel has nothing to do with my fantastic dick—it's all coming from my heart, and I know it.

"Yes, you're quite proud of your . . . endowment," she says, unable to hide her smile. "But you're right, and I *want* you to see me."

Her own hand helps me slide her panties down, and I stare at her from top to bottom—soft, flowing hair splayed out on my pillow; deep, brown eyes that see right to my soul; amazing, perky, fucking awesome tits just the size of my hands; and now, the pussy of perfection—cute little dark curls hiding what's bound to be my dick's new favorite place.

"Fucking gorgeous," I murmur, unable to take my eyes off her.

Um . . . hello? my dick calls out, waving frantically. *Can we quit the romance novel shit and move on to the porn flick?*

I wanna eat her out, but I want her lips, too, and my dick wants to get as close to that pussy as possible. I just want everything, and I'm . . . stuck, so Holly makes the decision for me, pulling me up to smash her lips to mine.

Every inch of our bodies makes contact with no clothes in between, and it feels as if I've been struck by lightning. I writhe against her, rubbing my dick on her thigh while my hand explores those soft curls, and my tongue massages hers, reaching as deeply as I can.

Damn, she's wet already. My fingers spread her, and I insert one, and my dick weeps tears of joy against her leg as all that wetness spreads and engulfs me.

Holy mother of fuck, that's what it's going to feel like around my . . . when I . . .

· · ·

Nathan thrusts a single finger in a few times, but I'm ready for more, and I let him know by bucking against his hand.

A second finger follows, and although we've done this many times before, it feels different . . . better. I try to keep kissing him, but my lips are getting sloppy as I focus on the heat that spreads outward from every place he touches, every thrust of his fingers stoking the flames a little more.

He pulls back and inserts a third finger, and I throw my head back, the coil inside me tightening.

"Oh, Nathan." I moan, feeling myself stretch, and his fingers just about reach that spot—the one that sets off the fireworks.

"You're so fucking—ohh!" The rest of whatever he was going to say is lost in the moan that takes over as he grinds his dick against me, and the sound of his pleasure lifts me a little higher, just a little closer.

"Nathan, please!" It comes out as a breathy plea, and his lips return to devour mine as he curls his fingers and hits that spot . . . over and over and . . .

"Oh, *fuck!*" His thumb makes a single circle on my clit, and I explode, bucking against him as I quake with wave after wave of unbelievable pleasure.

I lie there feeling spent, and I realize that while my breathing is returning to normal, Nathan is still panting like he's just run a marathon.

When I open my eyes, I find him staring, a look of wonder on his face, but then I lower my gaze and see his hand curled around his cock, stroking slowly as pre-cum leaks from the tip.

And this is the moment. There's so much love in his eyes—I don't know if he's breathless from need or from what he's feeling, but time seems to slow down as he reaches out and strokes my cheek.

"Holly, I . . ."

"Make love to me, Nathan."

His sharp exhale is all I hear.

"Really?"

"I want you," I say, pulling him between my legs, and it feels right, as if it were always meant to happen this way.

He pulls away but only to reach for his slacks and pull out a string of condoms.

"Big plans for tonight?" I ask, smirking at him, and he gives me that killer grin of his.

"No harm in being prepared," he answers, rolling one on and then settling between my legs again.

I wait, eyes closed, yearning for the feeling of him entering me, and when it doesn't come, I open my eyes to find him hovering over me, holding his weight up by his hands.

"Um . . . I think you have to help me with this part," he says, and I flush in embarrassment.

"Oh, I didn't know . . ."

"Well, neither do I, but I don't think—"

"What?"

"What, what?" he asks, furrowing his brow.

"What do you mean, you don't know?"

"Well, nobody talks about this part, and since I haven't done it before . . ."

Hold up now.

"Haven't done what?" *Is he saying he's a* virgin?

"This," he says, sounding frustrated. "I don't think my dick is just drawn in there like a magnet—"

"You're a . . . a virgin?"

"Of course! What the hell are you talking about?" he asks, backing up a bit.

"No . . . you're not a *virgin*, virgin," I say stupidly. "I heard you did it with at least six different girls."

"Did you hear it from *them*?" His tone is demanding as he quirks an eyebrow at me.

"Well, no . . ."

"Holly, I haven't ever been with anyone like this before. I've fooled around, but that's all," he says, caressing my cheek. "All this time, you thought I'd . . . Why didn't you just ask me?"

"I didn't want to know," I tell him petulantly. "Whoever you've been with in the past is your business—"

"But I haven't been with anyone, and I don't want to. I want to *make love* to *you*," he says, and I positively *melt*.

Holy shit, he's a virgin! I thought I was the only one, and . . . Whatever, there's nothing I could do about it anyway, but now . . . now this is only mine, and I get to go where *no* girl has ever gone before—the warmth that spreads through my chest is positively unreal.

Merry Christmas to me*!*

But I'm still embarrassed I thought he was a man-whore.

"I'm sorry—"

"No, I'm sorry. Being a guy, I'd never correct those rumors, but I should have told you—"

"I should have asked." Although I'm still over the moon that I'm his first, I'm tired of this conversation, so I grab his dick and give it a few pumps.

"Christ," he mutters, lowering himself until his tip brushes against my clit.

I hiss at the sensation, but then he drops a little lower, and I help guide his cock home with my hand.

I slide in, but oh, so slowly. *Oh my God, she's so* tight, *I'm gonna explode before I even get all the way in.* But it feels so fucking good, I can barely bring myself to care right now. I push in until I can't go any farther, but my dick is still halfway out. *Isn't it supposed to go all the way in?*

We're both panting, but hers sound almost painful.

"Are you okay?"

"Yeah. Are you?" she asks, and it still sounds as if it's painful for her, but I think she's trying to move beyond it, to feel the amazing shit I'm feeling.

"I'm . . . *fuck*, you feel so good. I'm trying not to come," I mutter, and her pussy is gripping me so tightly it takes everything I have not to explode.

"Let's just breathe, okay?" she tells me, her eyes squeezed shut, and I try to do what she says, *just breathe*, but oh my God, this is the best thing *ever*.

The urge to plow into her is almost overwhelming, but I know there's more to it than this, and now I remember Evan telling me long ago that the first time, you have to break through some kind of barrier in the girl's . . . whatever.

"Holly, I'm gonna move, okay?" I say, trying to keep my shit together as my body demands that I thrust.

Her eyes are shut, but she nods, so I pull out, and push in a little harder. She yelps as I hit resistance again, and I think we both see stars—her from pain and me from trying to hold back.

And I know I just have to get it over with.

I pull out and thrust as hard as I can, and although Holly cries out again, I'm now buried to the hilt inside of her.

"I'm sorry," I whisper. "It'll be easier now."

"Okay," she says shakily, and although I'm concerned about her, I know we've made it through the hard part.

I start to move slowly in and out, and she's squeezing me so tightly, I can barely think straight.

"All right?" I ask, teeth clenched, and she nods, thank God, because what's building inside me is so big and so strong, I can't hold it back anymore.

I start to thrust in earnest, groaning more deeply with each stroke, but the pressure in my groin builds so fast that I only make it five thrusts before I'm struggling to keep going.

"Holly, I'm . . . oh God . . . oh, *fuck*!" I explode without warning, buried as deeply as I can be as I pulse inside of her, pleasure surging through me again and again until I feel like I can't come anymore . . . like, ever.

I collapse next to her, a panting, quivering mess. My dick is belting out "We Are the Champions" so loudly that it's hard to think around it—he does a pretty decent Freddie Mercury, I must admit—but as I come down from my high, embarrassment sets in. I came way too fast, and I have no idea if Holly enjoyed that or—fuck!—if she's even all right.

My brain is still in orgasm-induced fragments, so I have no idea what to say to her.

So we both stare at the ceiling for a while.

Finally, she reaches over and threads her fingers into mine.

"That was . . ."

". . . not awesome."

"Huh?"

"I mean, it *was* awesome, but . . .

She's looking at me now, and I scramble to get my brain into some kind of working order.

"I came too fast."

"It hurt."

We blurt out our thoughts at the same time, and I feel like an instant asshole for thinking about my own pleasure and hers and ignoring the fact that I *broke* something inside of her.

"Are you okay?" I ask, rolling to my side and reaching up to caress her cheek. "I didn't mean to—"

Her laughter cuts me off.

"Yes, you did, and I wanted you to. I'm okay. It hurt at first, but then it started to feel better."

"And then I came like a twelve-year-old jackin' it for the first time."

She laughs again, and I have no idea why that makes me feel better.

"Why don't we try again? When you're ready, that is," she says, and I can't help the smirk on my face. My dick was a pleasure-drunken member of Queen a few minutes ago, but he's stirring and beginning to harden again already, eager for an encore.

"I mean, it has to be . . . more awesome than that."

"Evan always says it is," I tell her, hoping I sound confident as I roll to my side to lean over her.

"Ugh," Holly mutters, grimacing. "No offense, but don't ever mention your brother and sex in the same sentence again."

While I'm thrilled she's not attracted to baboon boy, it's odd since most girls fall all over him.

"Evan doesn't do it for you?"

"If he did, I think he'd break me in half!"

Her cute little nose wrinkles in distaste, and I fall to my back, laughing my ass off.

Holly smacks my arm, and my eyes pop open to find her glaring at me.

I bust up again, but this time I roll toward her, and I laugh even harder as she tries to wiggle out of my grasp.

Until I realize she's rubbing against my dick.

And my nipples.

And every other part of me, and suddenly, our lips crash together, and our hands are everywhere.

My dick is hard as a rock, and my balls already feel full and heavy as I grind against her—I have to stop this, or I'm not going to last any longer than I did the first time.

I break contact, but before she can protest, I pull one of her hardened nipples into my mouth. I *love* to play with these bad boys . . . err, girls . . . whatever, I just love them, okay?

I massage with my tongue until everything becomes so freaking soft, and she sighs, both of her hands finding their way to my hair. When I start to suck, four things happen simultaneously, and I fucking love it: her nipple peaks into a perfect little nub; she hisses and arches her back, thrusting her tits farther into my face; her fingers tighten on my skull, scratching and rubbing in time with my pulls on her breast; and, *oh yeah*, my dick twitches so hard I swear I feel the earth move.

"Oh, *Nathan* . . ."

Her words are breathy—I can almost feel the pleasure dripping off them, and *fuck*, *I'm* the one doing that to her. Heat rolls from my chest down into my groin, and I can't help but press my dick against her.

Oh God, that feels so good.

My dick is beside himself—incoherent and pulsing because we're *so close* to Pussytown, but I don't let my body take over—not this time.

Before, I was scared and so worked up, I could hardly think straight enough to put my dick in the right hole, but this time, I want to make love to her, for real.

I release her nipple and look up into her impossibly deep brown eyes, heavy-lidded with the pleasure my lips just gave her.

So fucking beautiful.

"Holly, I wanna make love to you."

Her gasp is soft, but *yes* is written all over her face as she pulls me up even with her, hands on both my cheeks.

"I wanna make love to you too," she says, and it feels like a volcano erupts in my chest—I love her so damn much, and all I want to do is spend the rest of the night showing her, worshiping her, telling her in every way possible.

My lips find hers, and it's gentle, but there's more behind it now—so much more. My tongue slides against hers, and I feel the pull in my groin, the need building in every part of me to get closer to her, become one with her, make her feel everything that's exploding inside of me—the heat and the love and the—oh *fuck*, I don't know what it is, but I *have to* make her feel it too.

She moans into my mouth, and the vibration sends waves of heat through me; the feel of it makes me shiver. I move just a little, and my dick slides against her thigh, smearing pre-cum over the tip—*oh my God, I don't think I've ever been this turned on before.*

"Holly, *please*," I murmur against her lips, need gnawing at my dick and heart and fucking soul—need for whatever of herself she's willing to give me.

With a smirk, she reaches for the condoms this time, and I jerk away when she starts to stroke my dick.

"Shit, if you do that, I'll—"

"I know," she says, palming my balls as I bite my lip, struggling for control. "I just like touching it."

Jesus.

Fucking.

Christ.

I'm dead.

How I manage not to jizz all over her is a mystery I'll ponder for many a sleepless night to come . . . as I masturbate to the mere thought that Holly likes touching my *dick*.

"*Fuuuuck.*"

Holly's laughter brings a smirk to my lips, and I fall just a little more in love with her.

"That's funny, huh? Trying to make me jizz with the shit you say?"

I hiss as Holly rolls the condom on me, and her ensuing giggle more than answers my question, but I keep talking to buy some time to get myself under control.

"You are one evil little vixen, you know that? But two can play at that game."

She gasps as I run a finger from one end of her slit to the other, making a lazy circle around her clit. I pull my hand back, and her look of outrage makes me snort out a laugh; the smack I receive for it is equally funny.

But the break bought me the time and distraction I needed—I no longer feel as if my load is gonna 'splode.

When I slip between her legs and position myself over her, all teasing is gone from both our expressions.

Her hand guides me as I stare into her eyes, and I slide in easily, but I can't ignore her wince.

"Holly—"

"I'm fine; it'll feel good in a minute, just like it did last time."

Oh thank God.

She's so warm and tight, but this time, I'm ready for it, and I only need a few seconds to quell the flare of arousal that threatens to undo me.

And I spend those few seconds kissing her, reveling in the fact that we're joined—as close as we'll ever be.

Her hips flex under me, and I start to move without realizing it, thrusting to the rhythm her hips set as they rise from the bed.

She tears her lips from mine to pant into my shoulder, eyes closed, lips slack with pleasure.

"Nathan, *yes.*"

And I'm high.

I listen to the sounds of our love: skin slapping as we come together, Holly's soft grunts when I push against her deep inside, my moans every time her hot wetness squeezes me so fucking tight.

I feel her warm breath on my shoulder, the flex of her hips as she welcomes me in, the pulse of my dick as I try to hold back the massive orgasm that feels like it's been building for days and days even though I know I came less than an hour ago.

Her fingers digging into my back tell me she's feeling passion and not pain, and I lose myself to the feeling, my own hands gripping the sheets as I push in deeper, thrust a little harder.

This is what making love is, and I know she feels it too.

It's fucking perfection.

I want to stay focused on her, but suddenly, moving inside her feels so good, I can't pay attention to anything else.

"Oh *God*, I . . . uhhh!"

I thrust faster as I squeeze my eyes shut, pressure and pleasure and something almost like pain building so quickly I can barely contain it.

"I want you to come," I blurt out, wanting Holly to feel as amazing as I do, but I'm so drunk on pleasure, I have no idea how to make it happen.

But Holly does.

One hand leaves my back, and I feel it slide between us. I jerk my head up when she moans, and the realization that she's touching herself sets off fireworks in my groin.

"Oh, *oh* . . ."

Her breathless moan is so sexy, but everything in the world stops as all of her tightens around my dick.

"Oh my *God*—"

"Yes!" Holly cries out, and I lose my fucking mind.

She pulses around me, squeezing and pulling, and *oh my God, I'm going to—*

I explode deep inside her, pleasure roaring through me for the longest, strongest orgasm I've ever had. I pulse and pulse until it feels as if all the jizz there ever was just spewed out of my dick, and my arms feel so heavy, I can't help but collapse onto Holly's chest.

I lay there, panting, with no idea how much time goes by before I can focus on something outside my own body again.

And the first thing I'm aware of is the softness and warmth of Holly, her chest still heaving under mine.

I'm still in space somewhere, floating in this perfect moment. *It was amazing!* He was so gentle and sensitive—worried that he'd hurt me when I know his body had to be screaming for him to plow into me.

But he didn't.

And, wow, the way it felt and the sounds he made—the pleasure I know he was feeling. From being with *me*.

It *was* more than sex. It was love; I'm sure of it.

The feeling wells up in my chest and spills over, sending tingles and shivers to the very tips of my toes and fingers.

I can't hold it back anymore—I've given him all of me—all that I am and all that I have, and the only thing left to do is tell him what his body and mine already know.

"Nathan, I . . . I love you," I whisper, and as I close my eyes, I feel the tears escape and roll over my temples.

He pulls in a sharp breath and his muscles tense, and I know it's not the right time for him—I took him by surprise.

"Holly—"

"No! Don't say anything. I don't want you to say it just because I did, and if you're not gonna say it, I don't wanna know right now. If . . . if you feel the same way, say it sometime when I'm not expecting it. That way I'll know it's true."

I open my eyes, and he's staring at me, his look a combination of wonder and furrowed eyebrows. I don't know what it means, and I'm too happy to try to sort it out right now; I'd rather just lie here and feel my love for *him*.

"I love you, Nathan," I say again, and he kisses me. He tells me with his lips and his tongue and the gentle caress of his hands over my shoulders, and I'm content.

Our kisses become languid then stop altogether, and I find myself staring at his sweet, boyish face as his breathing evens out into sleep.

I surrender to sleep myself, basking in the warm glow that still lingers from what was given and felt and said this night.

Everything is perfect.

CHAPTER TWENTY-FIVE

If you tell the truth, it becomes a part of your past. If you lie, it becomes a part of your future.

– John Spence

HOLLY

Nathan calls.

Nathan texts.

Nathan is all I think about for every minute of every day he's away to the point that Dad has threatened to arrest Nathan for breathing if I say his name one more time. And the only reason he's that calm about it is he knows we can't possibly be having sex if Nathan is in Chicago.

It's been the longest week of my entire life, but it had some bright spots too. Watching Nathan come is fantastic, but listening—being able to focus on every ragged intake of his breath, every moan of pleasure, every grunt as he pulses, losing his shit over my dirty mouth and the strokes of his own hand—phone sex needs to be a weekly occurrence from now on, and I won't be taking no for an answer.

I float to school on Monday morning. Down the stairs, out of the house, down the noisy hallway—my toes don't touch the ground until I need them to raise my lips to Nathan's.

"*Fuck*, Holly, I think I've missed every single thing about you."

The kiss is brief, but the heat of his arms and the smell of his cologne and the feel of his cheek against my forehead go on and on and on . . . until the bell rings.

The day passes quietly. Stolen kisses at my locker, Nathan's hand in mine all through lunch, and giving him a hard-on in chemistry by passing him dirty notes drives all non-Nathan thoughts out of my head . . . until after school.

The warmth of Nathan's last kiss is still on my lips—he's already gone outside to track down Evan and tell him that he'll be going home with me. Dad is on night shift tonight, so Nathan and I have the whole evening to get naked—err, reacquainted. *Oh, who am I kidding? I was right the first time!*

Warmth floods through me, and I can't help but smile and pack my books a little faster. Visions of naked Nathan dance in my head as I close my locker and shoulder my bag, but everything stops when I nearly bump into Bitch Face, arms crossed and blocking my path.

"*Excuse* me," I say, with as much irritation as I can muster, and it's a pretty good amount, considering she's standing between me and my next orgasm, not to mention the gorgeous guy I'm in love with.

"Oh, not so fast, Holly! We haven't had a chance to catch up. Did you have a good time at the Christmas dance?" she asks, grinning at me as if we're best friends, except for the evil gleam in her eyes.

I stop and take a step back. *What the hell is she playing at?* I can't imagine why she'd ask me that, but for once, I have a response that'll knock that prissy grin off her face, and even though I know I shouldn't, I can't resist the temptation.

"I had a fantastic time, both during and *after* the Christmas dance. I spent the night at Nathan's." Her eyes go wide, and before she can formulate a response, I continue. "I wonder what we did that night. Oh, *now* I remember! We had mind-blowing sex, and he told me he loved me."

It's a bit of a lie because he hasn't actually said the words yet, but I know he's going to, so it's all good.

Bitch Face's hand flies to her chest, and she gasps, looking horrified, but then a slow smile spreads across her face and she giggles.

Has she lost her mind?

"Oh, this is beyond perfect! He actually slept with you and told you he loved you to convince you to stay with him? What could he possibly need from you that would make him go that far?"

I freeze, and although her words make no sense to me, ice shoots down my spine.

"What are you talking about?"

"*Well*," Bitch Face says, pulling a folded paper from her pocket as she leers at me. "I *told* you he's too good for you, but you just didn't listen, did you? He's only been with you because he needed you to do something for him. I knew it was just a game, and this note Evan gave Lori proves it. What did he need you to do for him that I can't do, Holly? What makes *you* so special?"

Oh my God.

It feels like all the air has left the hallway as I snatch the note out of Bitch Face's hand. I glance at the *To* and the *From*, and then my eyes zero in on Nathan's name halfway down the page.

DON'T WORRY ABOUT NATHAN. HE'LL BE BUSY DATING SOMEONE HE NEEDS A FAVOR FROM. MAYBE HE'LL EVEN GET SOME.

A favor.

What makes you *so special?*

I flinch as the answer fills my head—there's only one thing that makes me special when it comes to Nathan. Only one thing I know that nobody else does.

The words swim before my eyes as my stomach goes into freefall. *No . . .*

Bitch Face stands there watching me, a satisfied, cold smirk on her face. "Were you a virgin, Holly? Did he tell you he was too? That's the oldest trick in the book, you know."

I want to just curl up in a ball and die, but I'm not about to give Bitch Face the satisfaction of seeing me break down. I crush the note in my fist and force myself to walk away, my back straight and my head held high. Her cruel laughter follows me down the hall, and I wince as the gaping hole in my chest rips open a little wider.

No, it can't be true.

I don't know where to go—what to do. The school bustles about me as if nothing's wrong, conversation and laughter echoing in the hallways as my world crashes down around me, and I struggle to breathe. I open the note and read the words again, but the hole in my chest is so large I can't feel anything. I don't want to believe it, but there it is in black and white, and the voice in the back of my mind softly whispers, *I told you so.*

I shift my bag and walk out the front doors of school, and as the cold air hits me, so does the realization that Nathan's supposed to come to my house today, and he and Evan are waiting for me.

My eyes scan the parking lot, and I see them both standing beside Evan's car. Nathan's laughing as he gives Evan a playful shove, and suddenly, the hole in my chest explodes. It's like a volcano, spitting red-hot rage and embarrassment, seething with betrayal. I storm across the parking lot, barely able to contain my fury as heat blazes up my neck and cheeks. Evan catches sight of me and flinches, grabbing Nathan by the shoulder and turning him to face me.

Nathan smiles as he recognizes me, but he freezes when he sees my furious blush and the fire in my eyes.

I grab him by the arm, pulling him toward the trees.

"Holly, what—"

"We need to talk—*now*." I grit the words out, and he glances helplessly at Evan. Evan shrugs and crosses his arms, leaning against the car to wait for us.

I let go of Nathan as soon as we're out of sight of the parking lot and round on him, tears streaming down my face.

"How *could* you!" I scream at him, pounding my fists on his chest. He grabs me under the elbows, and I wrench my arms out of his grasp, turning and wrapping them around myself.

"How could I . . . what?"

I realize the note is still crumpled in my fist, and I throw it at him. He's unprepared but he bends down and catches the paper before it hits the ground, a bit of fear now registering on his face.

"I should have *known*! You were willing to do anything—*anything*—to protect your secret! I should have known it was all an act! But I fell for it! And I—I *slept* with you!" I rage, pacing back and forth.

"Oh, I bet you and *Evan* had a good laugh about *that*! 'Poor, dumb Holly! She's stupid enough to date me *and* to let me in her pants!'" I say mockingly as the tears continue to pour down my face.

"No—" comes the whisper from behind me.

I whirl around to find Nathan staring at me, all the color drained from his face, the little white paper visibly shaking in his hand. At least he has the decency to be upset that he's been caught rather than be even crueler to me.

"No *what*, Nathan? No, you didn't brag to Evan? No, you can't believe you got caught? Spit it out so I can get the hell out of here. I don't know why I'm still here anyway!" I yell, my hands coming up to cover my face.

"No, it's not like that," he says quietly. I just stand there, shaking and crying, cursing inwardly for my inability to make myself leave. I can't look at him, don't ever want to see his face again because I know every time I do, my heart will break all over again because I love him.

I hear the crunch of leaves near me as he comes closer.

"Holly, it's not like that. I'm with you because I care about you . . ." He swallows painfully. "I'm with you because I love you. I've been trying for weeks to figure out how to tell you—even *before* you said it to me. This certainly isn't the way I would have chosen." He's trying to remain calm, but I can hear the tremor in his voice.

His words just make me even angrier. *Is this how far he's willing to go to protect himself?*

"Is this not true? Look me in the eyes, Nathan, and tell me you didn't start dating me to make sure I kept your secret." I realize I'm actually pleading with him. I want, to the very depths of my soul, for him to explain this— for there to be some way he truly isn't capable of *this*. I look up at him, and I have my answer before he even opens his mouth. His eyes mirror his guilt, and my heart shatters into a million pieces.

"It's true, but it was only true at the very beginning! It changed, and I fell in love with you, and I never wanted you to find out how it started."

"Would you ever have even *looked* at me if I hadn't been there that day?"

He looks like he's going to throw up, and that's exactly the way I feel.

"I'm sorry, Holly! I'm so fucking sorry! I was wrong! I should never have done it in the first place, and I should have told you the truth when I decided I wanted to stay with you. Please, *please* forgive me," he pleads, putting his hand on my arm.

I jump back as if I've been burned. "Forgive you? *Forgive* you? I don't even *believe* you! Why should I? I know you'd do anything to keep your secret, so why would I believe you wouldn't do this too? You've already admitted you *used* me to get what you needed—why wouldn't you go all the way?"

"Holly, please, just listen—" He reaches out to me again.

"*Don't* touch me." I snap at him, my eyes flashing.

"What can I do?" he asks, the sorrow and pain plain in his eyes. It looks genuine, but then so has everything he's done over the past few months. He's a good liar—he has to be.

"You can stay away from me, and never talk to me again!" I yell, turning on my heel and shaking off his hand as he tries to stop me.

I run headlong toward the parking lot and don't slow down until I get to Evan's car. I barely glance at him as I fly by, calling, "Nathan needs a ride home," over my shoulder.

Chapter Twenty-Six

The first rule in keeping secrets is nothing on paper.

— Thomas Powers

NATHAN

As she turns and starts to run, my knees buckle, and I land heavily on the fallen leaves. I know there's no point in following her. She's furious, and she has every right to be. I lied to her, and she found out my secret—the second secret she's found out about me, and by far the worse of the two. I'm still reeling, the note clutched tightly in my fist. I recognized the handwriting immediately, but my brain isn't putting together how this happened. I can't get past the anguish in her eyes and the fact that she didn't believe I'm in love with her.

I can't breathe. It's as if a weight has been dropped on my chest, and it's slowly crushing me, inch by agonizing inch. Sweat beads on my forehead as I struggle for breath, and the forest spins dizzily.

Suddenly, waves of nausea wash over me, and I lurch forward on my hands and heave the contents of my stomach onto the forest floor. I stay there, panting and gasping for a few minutes, but I know I have to get away from here. I wipe the back of my hand across my mouth and push myself unsteadily to my feet. My mind feels sluggish—I just can't put the pieces together. Something tells me I shouldn't see Evan right now, so I turn away from the parking lot and stumble farther into the woods.

I was happy. Holly made me happy. The last few months were the best of all of high school, and I know she was the reason. The freedom of not having to hide anything from her was incredible, and she's so sweet and kind to me. She's the best thing that ever happened to me, and now . . .

My stomach turns as I see the look on her face in my mind again, and I wrap an arm around my middle to steady myself. I tried so hard to forget how all this started. Everything was so good lately—it was easy to ignore that it had all been based on a lie. I look down at the note in my hand like I've never seen it before and open it one more time to read the words that drove Holly away from me.

Don't worry about Nathan. He'll be busy dating someone he needs a favor from. Maybe he'll even get some.

The rest of the note isn't about me, and I have no idea what—wait, who did he write this to? I look at the top of the paper and see for the first time that it was Lori. Evan wrote a note to Lori, telling her that I was dating Holly to get her to do something for me and to get in her pants.

What.

The.

Fuck?

Suddenly, everything's crystal clear. Evan. *Evan! Jesus H. Christ, why did Evan write a note to Lori about why I was dating Holly?* When did he do it, and how the hell did this note find its way into Holly's hands? White-hot rage boils through my veins until I truly think I'm going to explode. And then I hear it—Evan's voice behind me, calling my name.

I turn and race toward the sound, my fury growing with each pound of my feet against the unyielding ground. By the time Evan comes into view, all I can see is red, and I launch myself at him, throwing the hardest punch I can at his face. His eyes widen as he sees me coming, and he's able to move in time so that my blow only glances off his jaw. It's still enough to turn his head, but the majority of my force lands on empty air. I turn to throw another punch, but now he's ready for me, and he easily grabs my fist before it makes contact. What he isn't ready for is the intensity of my desire to hurt him. While he holds my right hand in both of his, my left lands a punch to his kidney, and he springs backward in surprise.

"Nathan, what the hell—" He manages to stammer before I'm on him again, swinging with all I have. With a growl, he grabs my nearest fist and twists it behind my back, forcing me to my knees in front of him. I try to wrench from his grip, and he growls again, digging a knee into my back and driving me to the ground until I'm laying with my cheek pressed into the dirt, my arm forced upward painfully behind me, and his knee on my back.

"Get the fuck off me!" I bellow at him, twisting in his grasp and trying to free myself.

"Not a chance until you calm the fuck down!" he yells just as loudly. Still, I struggle, and Evan shakes me until my teeth rattle.

"What the hell is the matter with you?" His harsh demand gets my attention, and I become still under him. "First Holly runs out of the woods as if the hounds of hell were chasing her, looking like somebody died. And then you don't come back, so I have to search for you, and now this. What the hell happened?"

"Let me up," I say coldly.

"Are you going to talk instead of swing at me? Because there's not a chance I'm letting you move until you're calm enough to talk and not attack," he answers, tightening his grip on my wrist.

I take a few deep breaths to try to convince both of us that I can be civilized. "Yes, I'll stop swinging," I reply through gritted teeth.

I feel his knee leave my back and wince as he lets go of me. With all the struggling I've done, I think I just about dislocated my shoulder because pain shoots down my arm as Evan releases it. I rub it as I get to my feet, my eyes never leaving Evan.

"Now why the hell are you trying to hurt me?" he asks, making a visible effort to check his own temper.

"What the fuck is this?" I wad the note into a ball and fire it at him.

He flinches as the paper bounces off his chest, but as soon as he realizes it's only paper, he scoops it up from the ground and unfolds it. His eyes widen as he reads it, and all the color drains from his face.

"Where did you get this?" he whispers.

"From *Holly*, right before she told me she never wanted to see me again!" I yell, and I launch myself at him again. This time, he just deflects my force as I get to him, and I end up overshooting, my momentum propelling me past my mark. I'm out of my mind with rage, and my eyes fall on the nearest alder tree about ten feet in front of me. I keep running toward it, roaring my fury as I slam my fist into the trunk with all the force I can muster. I feel several pops as lights flare behind my eyelids, and I cry out as pain explodes in my hand. Falling to my knees, I cradle my injured hand to my chest, squeezing my eyes shut as a stream of expletives pours from my mouth.

"Dammit, Nathan!" Evan exclaims, hurrying over to kneel down next to me.

My hand is already swelling spectacularly, and I know I've broken it in several places. The pain is intense, and nausea licks at my insides.

"Is it broken?" Evan asks, stretching out his hand toward me but knowing better than to touch me.

"Never mind," I say between clenched teeth. I open my eyes and glare at him, waiting for an explanation.

He flinches, glancing down at the note he still holds in his fist. "Fuck, Nathan, I am *so* sorry about this," he says gravely, the skin around his eyes tight.

"When?" The fury is gone; now I just feel dizzy and lightheaded. I shift my legs underneath me, pulling my knees up and wincing as I bring my aching hand to rest across my thighs. I lay my forehead against my knees, wondering if I'm going to pass out.

"Months ago," Evan says. "This note was written before you even decided you were going to date her—that first week after she saw you have a seizure. I can't believe Lori kept it! What the fuck was she thinking? Did —did *she* give this to Holly?"

"I don't know how Holly got it. She didn't say. Does it matter?"

"You bet your ass it matters," Evan replies hotly. "If Lori is responsible for this, even indirectly, she won't be my girlfriend anymore."

"Why, Evan? Why would you write that down?" Tears begin to prick my eyes as the pain in my hand and the pain in my heart fight for dominance.

"I don't know. In the beginning, this all seemed so simple, like it was a good plan. I'm sorry I ever convinced you to date her, and I'm even sorrier that I *didn't* convince you to tell her the truth when you really started to care about her. I thought there was no way she'd ever find out, and you could go along and be happy."

"Me too," I whisper.

"I'll tell Holly it's all my fault. I made you do this, and you shouldn't have to suffer for it."

I snap my head up, a flare of anger overriding everything else.

"Fuck you, Evan! I don't want your pity!"

"Pity? You think that's what this is?" he says incredulously.

"Of course, that's what it is! You never let me take the fall for anything because you think I can't handle it. This is my fault, Evan. *Mine*! I didn't have to listen to you, but I did, and now I have to deal with the consequences. I'm just as capable as anyone else—my epilepsy has nothing to do with it!"

"I don't help you because I think you can't handle it," Evan says, his tone dangerous.

"Well then, why, Evan? I've never understood it. I can't stand that I never get in trouble for anything, and Mom and Dad always blame you! You all think I'm so weak—that I'm going to fall apart or something! I try so fucking hard to be just like everyone else, but you guys cut me off at the knees before I can even get started. Just *stop* it!"

Evan leaps to his feet, his fists clenched as he stares down at me. "Goddammit, Nathan, how can you *think* that? I cover for you *not* because I don't think you can handle it, but because you have so many fucking things to handle! Why did this happen to you? Why not someone else? Why not me? Don't you think I think about that every time I get in the car to drive you somewhere, every time you have to miss school? Every time I step onto the football field, I think about how you'll never set foot on the court again! It's not fair! And I can't do a damn thing about it! The only thing I *can* do is try to make things a little easier for you! I don't know how the hell you handle it all because I know I never could! You think I'm the strong one, but you're wrong—it's *you*! Fuck!"

He turns and stalks away a few steps, breathing heavily. I just stare at his back in stunned silence. I can't process it—too much has happened in the last hour, and I can't take in any more. Now that my anger is again fading, the pain in my hand becomes almost unbearable. I do know one thing though—right to the depths of my soul and for so many things today.

"I'm sorry," I whisper as the tears finally roll down my cheeks.

"Don't be fucking sorry." Evan snaps at me, but a moment later, he's on his knees again. He squeezes my shoulder and then as I sob, he pulls my head against his chest in a rough embrace, the way he did when I was little and hurt and Mom or Dad weren't around to comfort me.

We stay that way until I calm down, then he releases me.

"We've got to get you to Dad to have your hand looked at. The longer we wait, the worse it's going to be," Evan says gently.

"Yeah, I know. I don't know if I can—"

"I'll help you," he says, getting to his feet and putting a hand under my armpit. I struggle to my feet, swaying as waves of dizziness wash over me, and my stomach threatens to revolt again. Evan puts a shoulder under my arm and holds me around the waist, and I cradle my injured hand tightly against my chest as we walk. I rest my head against my own shoulder and close my eyes—it makes the dizziness easier to deal with—as we slowly make our way back to the car.

Evan calls ahead, and Dad is waiting for us in the ER. As Evan explains what happened, Dad takes one look at my red-rimmed eyes and vacant expression, and he knows better than to say anything just then. My mother is a completely different story. After she finds out how I've hurt myself, she lays into me until Evan and Dad both step in—Evan to defend me and Dad to keep her from screaming at the both of us.

After my argument with Evan, all the fight is gone from me. I just want to be numb. What I want is alcohol, but since I can't have that, Percocet is a good substitute. I cry out and nearly jump off the exam table the second Dad tries to even touch my hand, so he gives me a hefty dose and waits until it takes effect before he proceeds.

Once I'm drugged up, all the pain is muted—both the pain in my hand and the pain in my heart. I still scream when they set the bones in my hand and wince as they do the casting, but for the most part, it's nothing compared to the way I felt out in the woods earlier this afternoon. What I really need to do is sleep. I can't wait for the sweet solace of oblivion, and the minute we get home, I go right up to my room and curl up on my bed.

It feels late when I wake as Mom pulls off my shoes and spreads a blanket over me. She sees me watching her and pauses, reaching out a hand to brush against my cheek.

"How are you feeling?" she asks, and I just stare up at her as the tears well in my eyes. I close them and feel the drops escape down my cheeks, and I turn my head away so she won't see.

"Why don't I get you some more medicine? I bet your hand is hurting," she says tenderly, and I just nod, my eyes still closed. My hand hurts like a motherfucker, but it's nothing compared to the ache in my heart and the tightness in my chest.

While she's gone, I get up and go to the bathroom, and when she gets back, I take the pills she brought, and she helps me change into pajama pants. As I lie down, she sits next to me, stroking the hair on my forehead as the tears again creep down my cheeks.

Mercifully, she says nothing, and oblivion takes me before I can think too much.

Chapter Twenty-Seven

When you care about someone, you can't just turn that off because you learn they betrayed you.

– Paula Stokes, *Liars, Inc.*

HOLLY

It's been two days.

Two days since my world froze and then shattered, and the pieces tore into me like shards of glass as I ran from the woods.

Two days since I ate and slept.

Two days since I've allowed anyone but Dad to talk to me.

Two days since I've seen . . . *him*.

Has it only been that long? It feels like a lifetime.

Megan and The Gothlet cocoon me with concerned looks, but they haven't said a word since I threw a hand in their faces as I struggled not to sob. They don't know, but they do.

Resting Bitch Face has been positively giddy, but she's confused too—she doesn't know where her conquest is or what happened between us.

Two days.

Where the *hell* is he?

I hate myself for every step I take up the hallway, passing *his* locker and *our* hallway and the entire junior and senior classes.

I walk up to Evan, and I know at least half the senior boys are watching—a few of them with smirks on their faces, elbowing each other as I walk by. But I have to know, and this isn't any worse than every other waking moment of the last two days.

Evan snaps his head up, his eyes widening as they fall on me, then narrowing as they take in the leering crowd surrounding me. He takes me by the elbow and leads me to the end of the hall, casting warning glances at the snickering boys all around us as we go.

Once we're out of earshot, he turns and looks at me nervously.

I swallow past the lump in my throat, reminding myself that I only have to get out one little sentence, and then I can walk away. "Is he all right?" I say roughly, staring at Evan's sneakers.

Evan's quiet for so long that I risk a glance up at him, and he's staring at me the same way I've sometimes seen him stare at Nathan when Nathan doesn't know he's watching. It's tender and sorrowful.

He nods. "He's okay. He was really out of it yesterday, and today is a 'vacation' day," he says, looking at me significantly. Of course, I know that means today is a seizure day. *Dammit. But what was that about yesterday?*

"Wait, why was he out of it yesterday?"

"He . . . um . . . he broke his hand after you left, and he was in a lot of pain, so Dad had him pretty doped up," Evan says uncomfortably.

I try not to react, but a gasp escapes my lips, and my hand flies to my mouth before I'm even aware I'm doing it. *What the hell did he do?* I don't know why I care, but somehow I do, and my shattered heart breaks just a little more in spite of myself.

I turn to go, but Evan grabs my arm, turning me back to face him. "Holly, I am *so* sorry for my part in this. Lori is a bitch, and I dumped her. I can't believe she'd do something like that."

"It's all right," I say mildly. "It's not your fault your brother is an asshole."

Evan looks as if I've punched him. He takes a deep breath and meets my eyes, but I hear his breathing accelerate and see the red creeping up his neck.

"Yes, this *is* my fault because I put him up to it. I was the one who suggested he date you so you'd keep his secret."

My jaw drops, and I stop breathing. I can't take any more hurt, so the words wash over me numbly.

"Holly, I can't tell you how sorry I am! As soon as I saw how much you cared about him, I told him to break it off with you—that you were going to get hurt—but he told me he cared about you, too, so I thought everything was going to be okay."

His words come out in a rush now, and I can feel his desperation to convince me.

"He really loves you, and he's *so* sorry he did this—and that you found out —and that he didn't tell you in the first place . . ."

His words fall on me like rain—sliding along my skin but not penetrating —rolling down my cheeks like the river I've already cried.

"I don't . . . believe you."

The hurt in his eyes looks so similar to what I saw in Nathan's two days ago that I have to look away—I can't watch the tentative friendship Evan and I have built crumble.

"He really *is* devastated, Holly. He wanted to kill me when he brought me the note, and he ended up hauling off and punching a tree when I wouldn't let him thrash me, and he broke his hand in three places. He spent that night in the ER getting his hand casted, and he hasn't left his room since."

God*damn* my traitor heart! How? *How* can I feel pain for *him* after what he did to me? Why is the first thought in my head how much pain he must be in? *Why* am I wondering how bad today's seizure was, given that they're always worse when he's under stress? *Fuck!*

Anger roars through me, and it feels so much better than being numb. It feels *alive*—something I haven't felt since a scrap of paper destroyed everything.

"Good!" I shriek, and Evan flinches.

"I hope it fucking hurts! He deserves it! He deserves that and so much more! How could he *do* this to me just to protect himself? He's the most selfish, self-centered *asshole* on the face of the earth!"

"Holly, he—"

"No, Evan! He's still playing the game! He doesn't know how to do anything else, and he's fooled you too! Maybe he's even fooled himself! I don't know, and I don't even care! I can't trust him, and I oughta—"

I stop because even though I'm furious, I can't voice that thought. I'm *not* that person, and no matter what he's done to me, I *won't* let him turn me into that.

Evan tenses. He knows exactly the precipice I stand upon.

His eyes widen, and as the words dare to leave his lips, I explode.

"You wouldn't—"

"No, I wouldn't. I never would have in the first place! That's the whole fucking point! I *never* would have, even if Nathan never spoke to me again after that day! I wouldn't because I'm not that kind of person, and I never will be!

"I'm not a self-centered *asshole* who would do anything for my own gain!" I roar at him, all my anger coalescing into a single declaration.

Evan's gaze hardens.

"You have no idea what it's like—"

"*Don't* defend him, Evan. Don't you dare defend what he's done!" And I realize that even now, he's taking one for team Nathan, standing here and letting me rage at him.

"Fuck *you*! Fuck *him*! I wish I'd never met either of you! I'm done! I'm just so fucking done!" I scream, turning on my heel and tearing down the hall.

The entire senior class stops and stares as I run by, but I don't care—all I care about is getting as far away from any connection to Nathan as possible. There's no way I can manage any more school today. If Resting Bitch Face even *looks* at me, I swear I'll rearrange her face. So I grab my shit and sign myself out without another word to anyone.

I drive until it's dark outside, not really thinking about anything, just trying to outrun the hollowness in my chest.

It doesn't work.

Defeated, I go home, force myself to eat a banana, and follow it up with a double of Benadryl. I can't spend another night lying awake and trying not to think.

I pass out pretty quickly but not before my pillow is damp.

∼

Shit.

It's gonna happen today.

It should have happened two days ago, but Nathan's absence slowed it down. A lot of it probably happened already—there's no way my tearing out of the school yesterday wasn't noticed and talked about, and it wouldn't take much to put that together with the rumors already circulating in the senior hallway.

But it's definitely gonna happen today because . . . because *he'll* be there today.

I doubt it'll be a rough day for him. He has that great facade, that amazing ability to hide everything inside and to lie so convincingly, but I have none of those skills, and it's gonna be all over my face. It's *been* all over my face for *three days* now, but no one cared enough to see it. That's about to change.

I'm about to be the center of attention.

The slut who fell for Nathan Harris's classic maneuver.

The breed 'em and street 'em.

The fuck 'n run.

The wham, bam, thank you, ma'am.

The drive-by.

I honestly don't know which is worse—him leading me on so I'd keep his secret or doing it to get in my pants. Maybe he did both; or maybe getting in my pants was just a lucky bonus. The floating cherry in his Pacman game. Son of a bitch, it *was* my cherry!

But it was his cherry too, wasn't it? The thought echoes in the back of my mind, but I quickly squash it. Guys don't give a shit about who they lose their virginity to, and the whole school thinks Nathan's slept around anyway. No one will know I was his first.

But you do. Why would he admit that? He certainly didn't have to.

Who the hell knows? Maybe he thought it would help him get in my pants. Maybe it was a lie too, just like Bitch Face said.

The thought rings hollow even though I wish it rang true. I *was* Nathan's first, and it was—

I curl in a ball to try to escape the pain, but it feels as if my chest isn't even there. It's just a hole where my heart used to be, a tightness in my throat that leads to . . . nothing. There's nothing until the anger or the tears come. And I can't control which one it's gonna be from one moment to the next. And I don't even really care.

I roll out of bed and stalk to the bathroom. *Let's get this shit show of a day over with.*

The stares begin before I even make it to the upperclassmen's end of the hall, and the whispers give me a preview of what I'm about to be subjected to.

"Yeah, I heard he slept with her and then dumped her right after the dance."

"Why would she date a jackass like him anyway? He's gorgeous and popular, but everybody knows he just uses girls for sex."

"I never understood what he saw in her, unpopular as she is. Must have just been the promise of pussy."

That last one makes me stumble because it's so damn close to the truth, and the laughter of the sophomore boys chases me up the hallway.

All I want to do is grab my books and slink off to homeroom, but when I get to my locker, The Gothlet is standing there, breathing fire like a Balrog of Morgoth.

"I'm gonna kill him! I'm gonna cut his balls off and stuff them down his throat until he chokes! That goddamn son of a bitch! Even *that's* too good for him, I—"

"Lucy," I say, and it's meant to be an admonishment, but my voice breaks, and it comes out as a pitiful whimper.

And I'm knocked back a step by the force of my suddenly human-again friend crushing me in her embrace.

"I'm so sorry, Holly. What really happened?"

The lack of sound catches my attention, and I lift my head from her shoulder to see everyone around us staring and listening.

"Not now," I say, quickly rubbing the back of my fist across my cheek to wipe the tears away.

The Gothlet nods, and she and Megan wait and walk on either side of me to homeroom, chatting about this and that to distract me from the continued barrage of stares and whispers.

But their seats are near the front of the room, and as I walk back alone between the desks of the popular crowd, it's like running some sort of abuse gauntlet.

"All alone today, Holly?" Bitch Face asks, cocking her head with the sweetest smile as Bubble Butt giggles her frizzy little head off. "Where *is* Nathan anyway? Now that he's single, I'm sure we'll be the *very* best of friends again."

I roll my eyes at the stupid bitch—if Nathan is dumb and desperate enough to crawl back to *that*, then maybe they *were* made for each other. But pain still echoes through the emptiness in my chest, and I hate that I just can't stop caring.

I collapse into my seat, leaning back and letting the weight of my pain crush me for a moment, but I nearly jump out of my skin as warm breath hits my ear.

"Nate may have gotten your cherry, but when it's my turn, I want the whole pie. How 'bout it, Holly? I've got something long and loose and full of juice right here for you."

Ice shoots down my spine as I propel myself forward to lean over my desk as far away from Sean as I possibly can. Bile rises in my throat as he chuckles behind me, and for the first time, a different type of shame washes over me.

All this time, I've been feeling ashamed that I fell for Nathan's lies, that I allowed myself to be blinded by my own feelings enough to believe him. But now I realize what I've done has branded me as a slut, and these assholes are expecting that I'll let them pass me around like some goddamn flavor of the week.

I want to vomit.

I want the earth to swallow me up, and I want to go back to Amarillo, and I want to turn back time to September so I can do this all again and avoid the jackass who broke my heart at all costs, but I can't.

I can't even avoid that asshole today.

I shiver when I feel his eyes on me, and a fresh wave of pain squeezes at my chest. I don't want to look up, but there's no way I'm not going to—my eyes have been drawn to his perfect face every day since I first saw him walk through that very door.

He looks like complete and utter hell.

His hair is more disheveled than I've ever seen it—and not in a sexy way—in a haphazard way as if he's been pulling at it. There are dark smudges under his eyes, and his face is as white as a sheet, his lips drawn tightly as if he's in pain.

He's hunched over, curling his body around his right arm, which is immobilized in a high sling across his chest. And I can certainly see why—his thumb and first two fingers are purple and ridiculously swollen, and the rest of his hand and forearm are encased in a blue fiberglass cast.

I draw in a sharp breath, meeting his gaze out of habit, and I nearly fall out of my chair.

His eyes are wells of pure sorrow edged with more pain than I've ever seen, and they speak to me as they always have—telling me how sorry he is as they grow glassy with unshed tears.

And so many desires and emotions overwhelm me that I feel like I'm gonna explode.

I want to throw my arms around him and comfort him, do whatever I can to erase the haunted look in his eyes.

I want to slap him so hard his ears ring and then kick him in the balls.

I want to make love to him again as if none of this had happened.

I want to scream and rage at him for lying to me, for breaking my heart, for making me love him.

And I want to kick my own ass for falling for his lies, for daring to believe that he truly *was* interested in anything more than protecting himself.

I can't control the tears that roll down my cheeks, and I hate myself for letting him see what he's done to me. His eyes soften, and I see so much longing there. I can't even define the twisted emotion it evokes in me, so I just stare at him in misery.

"Nathan! What happened to you?"

Bitch Face's screech breaks the spell between us, and we break eye contact as she pops up from her desk and rushes to take Nathan's books.

He composes his face immediately, and I feel sick to my stomach.

I can't watch, and I don't want Bitch Face or anyone else to see my tears, so I stare down at my desk as they take their seats.

"Holy shit, man! Repetitive motion injury?"

The populars snicker at Sean's comment, and even Nathan manages a chuckle.

"Nah, Evan was working the heavy bag Monday night, and like a dumb fuck, I decided to take a few swings without taping up. Damn thing hurts like a motherfucker, and I've been high as a kite on Percs for the last two days."

The lie rolls off his tongue with no hesitation, and it's accepted without question, just like every other one he's ever told. Just like all the ones he told me. And suddenly, all the crazy emotion I've been feeling morphs into anger.

I grip the edges of my desk, seething, and it takes every ounce of control I have not to jump up and tell everyone that the dumbass punched a tree after I dumped him. But that would raise so many other questions, and I don't want anyone in my business, and I know they'd never believe me over him anyway.

"Oh, you poor thing! How awful! What can I do to make it better?"

Bitch Face's saccharine-sweet voice scrapes at my brain like nails on a chalkboard, and I'm both dying for and dreading Nathan's response. The morning bell sounds, and Mr. Harper settles the debate by calling the room to order, and at this moment, there's only one thing I'm sure of—this is gonna be one hell of a long and painful day.

CHAPTER TWENTY-EIGHT

Tell a lie once and all your truths become questionable.

– Anonymous

NATHAN

"Nathan, honey, wake up."

Mom's voice and a killer headache—my favorite combination. But why is my hand throbbing like the bones want to break out of my skin?

And then it all comes rushing at me like a tidal wave, and the pain that erupts in my chest knocks the wind out of me.

Holly.

Oh God, no.

I watch in horror as the pieces click together in my mind: the note, the hate and sorrow in Holly's eyes, my white-hot rage at Evan, the excruciating pain in my hand. And then, the need to forget—as many Percocet as Dad would give me, sleeping and waking in misery, the panic attack I worked myself into when I finally sobered up.

The ice pick in my temple tells me a seizure must have followed. Without warning. Again.

Holy mother of . . . I don't know any words strong enough for this almighty clusterfuck.

I roll to my side, cradling my throbbing hand to my chest while the other presses against my skull, trying to relieve . . . something, even the tiniest bit of misery, but instead, I just start feeling nauseous.

I *feel* like finding what's left of yesterday's Percocet and checking out until Easter, but I have to go in today. I have to tell Holly how much I love her and convince her to forgive me.

The icky I used to feel over my deception of her has gained a hundred pounds and rests in my stomach as dead weight—except for when it rises in my chest and chokes all the breath out of me. I have to find a way to make this right.

I struggle through my morning routine, one-handed and codeine-trippy, and I tuck my entire stash of Xanax in my bag as I leave my room. I want to see her so badly, but I have no idea what will happen when I do and if I'll be able to handle it. I can't afford another panic-induced seizure at school today.

Wouldn't that just be karma, after everything I've done to—

I squeeze my eyes shut against the thought. I can't even contemplate the fact that I may have lost her. I know what she said, but it's just not possible.

I—I can't live without her.

The weight in my gut threatens to rise and choke me, and I have to stop and take a few deep breaths, convince myself that I can fix this. *I have to be able to fix this.*

I walk into the kitchen, and Evan is sitting at the table cutting up a stack of waffles dripping with syrup. Across from him is a glass of OJ and two strawberry frosted Pop-Tarts on a plate.

"What's this?"

"I made you breakfast—*not* because you can't do it for yourself but because I thought it would be a bitch to do with just one hand."

My cheeks grow hot as I remember what I yelled at him in the woods on Monday. Although he's sat with me over the last two days, I was either high or in a shitload of pain—not exactly the best time for apologies.

"I'm sorry, Ev. I—"

"No, *I'm* sorry. I got you into this mess—"

"No, you didn't," I say, huffing out a breath. "It may have been your idea, but I'm the one who decided to do it. It was my choice, and I'll take the consequences."

Ev closes his eyes, his lips set in a firm line.

"I dumped Lori. I should have done it long ago, but I honestly never thought she'd do something like this."

"She didn't know—"

"Doesn't matter. Your life is none of her business, and she should have butted the hell out when I told her to. She was a bitch to you, and I shouldn't have let it go on as long as I did."

I stare at him, and before I can answer, he rambles on.

"And I have no idea why I wrote that in the note. In September, I was a dumb fucker with pussy on the brain and my head being ground into the turf every day at practice. I am *done* writing notes to girls. They keep that shit like pack rats—"

"Ev, stop! Jesus! I don't think I've heard you say that much at once since the Seahawks lost the Super Bowl!"

He stops and stares at me, his eyes as wide as I've ever seen them.

277

"I know you didn't mean to do it. But *fuck*, I really wish you hadn't," I say, running the fingers of my useable hand through my hair.

"Me too," he says, closing his eyes as he frowns.

We're both silent as we finish our breakfast, and I allow Evan to clean up after me and carry my bag out to the car. His words from Monday echo in my head, and I see every time he's ever covered for me in a new light. I knew he was a good brother, but *damn*, he's a *really* good brother.

I carry my own bag into school, but Evan stays with me with a hard look on his face—he can't shield me from the stares, but nobody says a word. I let him unpack my shit and hand me my books too. I'll be able to do it for myself, but today my headache is so bad, I get dizzy when I bend over, and even the slightest nudge to anything on my right side sends pain radiating through my hand. I'm a fucking mess.

But all that fades into the background as I head toward homeroom.

Will she even look at me? And God, what will I see in her eyes if she does?

My breath freezes solid in my chest, and I duck into the bathroom as a wave of nausea rolls over me.

It's okay. You're okay. You love her, and she loves you. She told you so. You can fix this. You can make it right.

I repeat the words in my head like a mantra, and it takes a few minutes, but my stomach eventually settles, and I'm able to take a full breath. I know I shouldn't do it with codeine in my system, but I fish a Xanax out of my pocket and swallow it dry.

I wait until the first bell, hoping enough time has passed for the drug to do something for me, and my first wobbly step down the hall confirms that Xanax has joined the party.

I'm so focused on putting one foot in front of the other that I don't even register when I step into homeroom until I look up and see Holly.

Oh God, she looks like hell.

There's no color in her cheeks, and her lips are pale—she looks like a china doll that they haven't finished painting—and she's gripping the sides of her desk as if her life depends on it.

I meet her eyes, and pain and sorrow explode in my chest with the force of a nuclear bomb. And I just manage to keep the tears from rolling down my cheeks.

I'm so sorry, Holly. I never meant to hurt you. I love you so much—you just have to *know that.*

Her eyes blaze at me, and there's so much emotion there that I don't know if she wants to kill me or kiss me, but then a tear rolls down her cheek, and my heart splits in two.

Oh Holly—

I struggle through physics and English, but by the end of second period, I'm so drowsy I can't even see straight. I head to the nurse's office to rest for a little bit . . . and wake up four hours later to the sound of the dismissal bell, groggy and in pain.

As I head for my locker, I make eye contact with no one.

I have yet to spot Holly, and the junior/senior end of the hallway is starting to clear out, so I head for the window to have a look at the parking lot. Her car is still here, so I go back down to her locker to wait.

Between my nerves over the conversation I'm about to have and the effects of the codeine, I'm a bit shaky on my feet, so I slide down her locker until my backside is on the ground. My hand is still throbbing, so I pass the time by examining my swollen fingers . . . until I feel her eyes on me.

Her face shows no emotion—a mask, just like the one I wear so often.

"Move."

"We need to talk," I say as I scramble awkwardly to my feet.

"I have nothing more to say to you."

Her words are an arrow straight into the center of my chest, and I don't hide their effect on me. I will *never* hide anything from her again.

"Then just listen, *please*," I beg, extending my hand toward her but not daring to touch.

She closes her eyes, and the mask crumbles for a second, but it's replaced with anger.

"What? What could you possibly have to say to me right now that I would want to hear? You—you put on a show with me. You lied to me from day one, pretending you were interested in what I had to say. And like a fucking *idiot*, I fell for it! I let myself believe that someone from the popular crowd, this gorgeous boy, could be interested in me for *me* and not to keep me quiet about—about what I saw!

"And as *you* kept lying to me, I kept lying to *myself*! I convinced myself that I was the one person you never lied to. But I'm just like the rest in your eyes—someone to manipulate, someone to give you what you want. I'm nothing special."

I stare at her, not even knowing where to start trying to untangle the mess I've made. All I know is, I have to make her believe me.

"No. It was real. All of it was real! And you *are* special!"

"Oh yeah? It was real when you apologized to Megan for the pictures? It was real those first few conversations in chemistry? The first time you talked to me in the library?"

She spits the words at me, her eyes demanding answers, and dammit, I said I wasn't going to lie to her anymore. I drop my chin because I can't look her in the eyes.

"No, it wasn't real then. I was afraid you'd tell everyone my secret, so I decided I had to get close to you, to make sure you didn't."

The words hurt *me*, so I can't even imagine what they're doing to her.

She snorts derisively. "I would have been one of your targets, wouldn't I? Just like Megan and Lucy. One of the misfits you did awful things to, to keep the focus away from you!"

Just tell her the truth. If you tell the truth, you can fix this.

"Yes, you probably would have been."

"Then what more do we have to say to each other?" Holly says, sounding half-angry and half-defeated, and I make the fatal mistake of looking up into her beautiful brown eyes that are drowning in tears and heartbreak. *God, I love her so fucking much! How could I do this to her?*

"I have to get out of here."

As she moves toward her locker, I snap out of it and realize this isn't going well at all—I haven't told her any of the things that really matter, and telling her the truth about the things I have hasn't helped. The panic starts to rise in my chest—I have to do something to turn this around—

"Holly, wait! I love you! As we spent time together, I realized how awesome you are, and I wanted to be with you! I fell in love with you, and I just wanted to forget how it started—can't we do that? I love you, and you love me—does anything else matter?"

She stops, and she's still for a whole minute before she raises her eyes to me, weary and desolate.

"Yes, Nathan, something else matters. What matters is that if you hadn't lied to me, I would still be a virgin, and we wouldn't be standing here. You built everything on a lie, and I'm reliving everything—trying to figure out where the lies stopped and the truth began, if it even began at all. We both know that keeping your secret is the most important thing to you, and I believe you would even go *this* far to keep it, to keep me close to you and to keep your secret safe."

Her bottom lip quivers, and my heart breaks into a thousand pieces as she bites it, and fresh tears roll down her cheeks.

"You know what the worst part is? You never had to do any of this because I never would have told anyone what I saw. I'm not that kind of person, and I never *will* be, but *you* are, and I see that now. You only think about yourself, *your* gain, so you assumed I would too, that I would use what I knew to put you down and raise myself up. Even now, if what you're saying is true, *you* love me, so *you* want me to ignore how all this started.

Have you *ever* done anything for anyone other than yourself, Nathan? I don't think you have."

She covers her mouth, her whole face crumbling into a sob behind her trembling fingers.

"Goodbye, Nathan."

Her words shatter . . . everything. My heart and my head and *oh* shit, *I can't breathe!*

She's gone, but Evan . . . *Ow, fuck! My arm! Can't breathe, can't breathe . . . No! Not here! I can't—*

~

It's dark, and I don't know what day it is. My head is likely to split open at any second, my hand is throbbing, and my chest feels like it's been hit by a mortar shell.

Holly.

Everything flies at me at once—the lockers, Holly's emotionless face, her tears and her eyes and "Have you *ever* done anything for anyone other than yourself" and "Goodbye, Nathan." The panic attack. The ceiling of the boys' bathroom and Evan's terrified face leaning over me right before I black out into the seizure.

My body is making demands: my throat is dry, I'm starving, and I have to piss something awful; the pain is urging me to find codeine or Percocet— or a shot of whiskey from the bottle buried in my closet—

But I don't care . . . about any of it.

All I want to do is not feel and not think. I want to sleep—permanently, if I can manage it. But all I can do right now is roll over and try to pass out again, and I can't even have that. The tears come instead, and I weep until I don't know who I am anymore.

I don't think I ever *did* know.

Chapter Twenty-Nine

The truth will set you free, but first it will piss you off.

– Gloria Steinem

NATHAN

"Come on, Nate. You haven't done anything outside the house in weeks. I'm going, and I don't have a girlfriend. I'm just gonna hang with the guys and shoot the shit."

"*She*'ll be there."

"So what? She's there at school every day. You can't just sit in your room all the time and mope. It's not healthy."

I roll over to find him frowning at me from the doorway of my room in his favorite Nike shirt and jeans.

"Maybe she'll talk to you."

"*Don't*, Evan." My warning is stark as I glare at him. Holly hasn't even so much as looked at me since the day after my last seizure, and that was over a week ago. I'm not gonna get my hopes up.

"All right, all right! But come, okay? Mom sent me up here to get you to go, so you know she's not gonna give you a moment's peace tonight if you stay. She'll drag you downstairs and try to play Scrabble with you or some shit."

Evan does have a point—Mom has been regularly hauling me out of my room and trying to get me to engage in . . . anything. At least at the dance, I can disappear and be left alone if I want to.

"If I agree to go, will you stop trying to cheer me up?"

"Except when Mom or Dad make me," he answers, but I can still see the worry in his eyes. I'm doing everything that's expected of me, but when I'm not doing that, I'm here, lying on my bed—asleep, if at all possible. Sleeping is the only way to escape how miserable I feel.

"Fine, I'll go."

"That's the spirit!" Ev says, and the goofy grin on his face almost makes me smile.

I walk into the caf with Evan, and this dance is the same as all the others. Girls in the middle of the room bouncing to the beat while the guys hang out in the dark corners, shooting the shit or doing their best to hide whatever they're drinking or smoking until a slow song comes on, and girlfriends materialize beside them to drag them out to dance.

What the hell am I doing here?

I sigh and follow Evan to where the football team is hanging out, smiling and nodding in all the right places, but I'm not really there. I stand with my back to the dance floor, not allowing myself to scan the room for her or any of her friends. I'm only here as a way to pass time until Ev says we can leave; if I keep my back to the dancing couples, I can forget that some people here are feeling the things I felt the last time I was here. That love is happening in this room and first kisses and—*fuck!* I tuck the memories carefully away before they can play behind my eyes, and I run my hand through my hair.

"Let me do that."

And suddenly, there are fingers in my hair that aren't mine, and I whip around to find myself face to face with Amber. She reaches up to paw me again, but I grab her hand with my good one and force it back down.

"Ooh, we can hold hands instead," she says, gripping my fingers and grinning lazily. *I wonder how many beers she's had.*

"What the fuck do you want, Amber?" I ask, tearing my hand out of hers.

"You, silly," she answers, touching the tip of my nose. "I've always wanted you, and now that Holly is out of the way . . ."

She tries to put her arms around me, and I elbow her away, but then I freeze. Something's not right about what she just said. She didn't say, "now that you dumped Holly" or "now that Holly broke up with you." She said Holly was "out of the way." As if . . .

As if maybe she had something to do with it.

I plaster a smile on my face and touch her arm, as much as it repulses me to do so. "She *is* out of our way, isn't she?"

"Yeah." Amber's whisper is a contented purr as she reaches for my hair again, and this time, I let her. "What did you need from her anyway? There's nothing she has that *I* couldn't give you."

She's read the note.

"Amber, did . . . did you give that note to Holly?"

Her eyes widen—even in her drunken state, she knows she fucked up.

"You did, didn't you?" I ask, tightening my grip on her, but she doesn't have to answer because her eyes are telling me everything I need to know.

Oh my God.

Amber threw that note in Holly's face. She had to have . . . on the day Holly dragged me into the woods—

And all this time, I've been letting Amber help me—

"You bitch!" I yell, shoving her away from me. She bumps into one of the senior boys but manages to stay on her feet, and I wish I'd shoved her harder. Rage surges through me. I charge up to her, and the only reason my fist doesn't connect with the side of her head is because Evan grabs my arms from behind.

"You ruined *everything*!" I scream, but I can't get any closer to her—Ev's arms are like a vise grip.

"She's not good enough for you!" Amber's sneer has me struggling to get loose so I can rearrange her stuck-up face. "She's a whore who hangs out with the losers and misfits. I've loved you all this time, but she just . . . showed up and took you away from me!"

"I was never yours, Amber! Never was, never will be, and you better stay the *fuck* away from me, or I swear I'll knock your teeth in! Do you hear me?" I roar, and for once, she actually looks scared, as if she believes me.

She gasps and runs toward the stairs, and I suddenly notice the crowd gathered around us.

"What the—"

Evan loosens his grip in the confusion, and I pull forward, breaking my arms out of his grasp. I bolt from the caf and into the woods, my thoughts and emotions—everything—spinning out of control.

Amber made Holly break up with me. She was jealous of Holly, so she ruined our lives.

I'm so fucking angry I don't know what to do with myself, so I keep running until I hear rustling and voices. As I slow down, I realize my feet have brought me to the clearing where the guys usually drink.

Yes.

I burst out of the woods, startling Tyler and Chris, but they relax when they see it's only me.

"Hey, Nate, what's—"

I tear the bottle of vodka from Tyler's hand and tip it back, guzzling until my nose burns too much for me to breathe.

"Now that's what I'm talkin' about." Chris slurs with a smile on his face, and I tip the bottle back again, hoping the burn will obliterate the anger and the hurt . . . and everything else.

"Nathan. Nathan!"

I moan as Evan shakes me, and although I know he's stopped, I still feel like I'm moving.

Oh my God, I've never felt this bad in my entire life.

Every inch of my body aches; my throat feels like it's on fire, and my head is splitting.

"Nathan!"

"Yeah! Fuck!" I mumble, trying not to move even the slightest bit.

"Mom and Dad are bound to come in here before too long, so listen closely, and don't fuck this up. It's Sunday morning. You and I spent the night at Mark's on Friday, and then you had a seizure when we got home."

I've been trying not to think about anything I remember from Friday, and how shitty I feel at the moment has been a great help in distracting me, but the look on Evan's face makes me think I owe him even more than I think I do.

"I'm sorry, Evan, I—"

"Do you even know what to be sorry for?" His hands curl into fists, and I notice that the knuckles on one are bruised. "Because I'd be amazed if you even remember half of it; you were that messed up."

Shame washes over me like a warm tide. "You said we spent the night at Mark's. I, um . . . don't remember that at all."

"That's because it didn't happen," Evan says, and he takes a second to stare at the ceiling. "When I finally found you, you were face down in the dirt, and Chris and Tyler were laughing their asses off at you."

The memories fly at me, and now that I'm sober, I understand what was going on. *Oh God.*

"Once I was drunk, they kept making me drink more. Chris even held the bottle for me when I was too fucked up to do it myself."

"That asshole! I should have given him more than a black eye!"

"You punched him?"

"Damn right I did! Fucker was drunk himself and had no idea how much you'd had! He could have killed you!"

I close my eyes against the words and images assaulting me, my stomach rolling as I remember how I felt. If Chris had kept giving me vodka, I would have kept drinking it, and I'd probably be dead now.

"Evan, I . . . I'm so glad you came and found me—"

"You . . . you passed out, and I had to carry you out of the woods and to the car. I didn't know what the hell to do—I couldn't take you home like that, or you'd be busted for sure. So I called Dad and told him we were sleeping out, but you're the only one who did any sleeping."

"Oh Christ, Ev." I don't want to hear anymore. The only things I remember are just a few flashes—the backseat of Evan's car in the daylight and sitting on the floor in our bathroom. *Jesus, I blacked out for at least ten hours.*

"I got some water and drove us out to one of the logging roads off Route 6, and I just sat there and prayed you'd keep breathing. You were breathing so slowly—I should have taken you to the hospital, but I didn't want you to get arrested. When you woke up, you started vomiting, so we sat out in the woods for a while, and we went back and forth all night.

"In the morning, I brought you home when I knew Dad would already be gone for his shift, and Mom would be at breakfast. I cleaned you up and put you to bed, but the myoclonics started as soon as you lay down, and the seizure came soon after.

"Goddammit, Nathan! You scared the hell out of me! You were so fucking confused, you didn't even know it was me half the time! If you had stopped breathing out there, there would have been nothing I could have done. I didn't even think about it at the time, but I risked your life—you could have died!"

As Evan gets everything off his chest, mine just feels heavier and heavier.

Holy.

Fucking.

Shit!

I look Evan in the eye, and I can't tell if he wants to hug me or punch me. I've never seen him look so scared.

"*Jesus,* Ev! I'm so fucking sorry! I never meant—"

"What the hell did Amber do to set you off like that—make you want to drink so much?"

My heart sinks because I just don't have the energy to get angry again. I have to swallow hard before I can get the words to come out.

"Lori didn't give your note to Holly; she gave it to Amber. Amber is the one who told Holly I lied to her."

"Mother*fucker*! Lori never said anything about Amber! She protected her—"

"Because they're friends, and Amber thought if Holly was out of the way, she'd have a chance with me."

"Goddamn these girls! They're so . . . evil! Guys don't do crafty, manipulative shit like this—"

I raise an eyebrow at him.

"Well, most of the time, and not unless we have to! If I could dump Lori again, I would! I'd like to punch her right in the—"

"Yeah, I believe that's where you interrupted me with Amber on Friday night," I say, smiling at him grimly.

"Okay, now that part makes sense. Then what happened? You ran out, and it took me forever to find you."

I close my eyes, and an echo of the anger and rage I was feeling surges through me. And the words tumble out of my mouth with no filter at all.

"I was so angry! Amber ruined everything, and if she hadn't done that— fuck! I might still be with Holly. It hurt so fucking bad! I just wanted to forget all of it—put an end to it. I'm so tired of hurting all the time! I ran and I ended up near where the guys usually drink, and I just . . . I drank until I couldn't feel anything anymore. And even then, it didn't feel like enough."

"Jesus, Nathan! Were you actually trying to—"

"No! No, I wasn't trying to, but it might not have been so bad if it happened," I tell him, owning up to what I was feeling then and what I've felt off and on since Holly and I broke up.

Evan goes very still, staring at my comforter for a full minute before lifting blazing eyes to mine. His words, however, are calm and quiet.

"I don't want to *ever* hear you say that again. Do you understand me?"

I have no idea how to answer. I can never say it again, but that doesn't mean I won't be thinking it. I close my eyes and feel tears overflow the lids, and I can't open them again because I'm afraid of what I'll see on Evan's face. His hand closes over mine.

"I'm worried about you, man. Really fucking worried. Maybe . . . maybe it *would* be better if everyone knew your secret. If you just stopped lying and actually told people the truth when it happens—that would show Holly she's more important than everyone not knowing you have epilepsy . . . right?"

"I can't do that, Evan."

"Why not? Would it really be worse than things are now?"

Memories of when I was first diagnosed come flooding back, and with them, the crystal clear memory of the first lie I ever told—a lie I still haven't come clean about. *Maybe it's time.* Maybe telling someone the truth about *something* will lift a little of this weight crushing my chest.

"Yes, I think it would. Do you remember when I was first diagnosed? Dad handled it pretty well because he's used to this kind of shit, but you and Mom? You tiptoed around me like I was gonna explode."

"No, we didn't—"

"Yes, you did. I saw it in your eyes every time you looked at me. You were afraid—afraid that you wouldn't know what to do, afraid of what could happen, afraid of *me*. I couldn't handle it. I know you couldn't help it, but it made me feel like a freak and . . . and that's when the panic attacks started. I told Mom and Dad I was afraid of having more seizures, but that wasn't all of it. That wasn't even most of it. It was the way you guys looked at me. It was like I could feel the charge in the air—everyone on alert for the next time I would fall down twitching. It was suffocating. It stole the air right out of my chest and made me gasp to get it back. I just . . . suffered through it until you guys stopped looking at me that way."

I know I've said way more than I should, but once I started, I couldn't stop. It feels . . . good to get something off my chest, to lay down a weight I've been carrying for so long.

I look up at Evan, and he's staring at me, his eyes glassy and wet. He's hurting and I know I've caused it, and suddenly, I feel like shit because I haven't really laid down this burden. I've given it to him.

"I'm sorry—"

"No! Dammit, Nathan, you will *not* be sorry for anything! I'm the one who's sorry—fuck! I didn't know—"

"I didn't *want* you to know—Mom either—because there's nothing you could do about it, and I knew that. We all needed time to adjust—"

"What? So Mom and I were adjusting, and you were having panic attacks because we were making you feel like a freak? *While* you were dealing with your own fear of the seizures and everything else? Why the hell didn't you tell us? We could have done *some*thing—"

"You were already doing enough, and I was . . . I didn't know what to do, so I kept it to myself. That was the first lie I ever told in all of this."

A tear slips down Evan's cheek, and I break a little more—I haven't seen Ev cry since we were little.

"I'm sorry."

"God, Nathan, please don't be sorry. *I'm* sorry! And I'm so fucking angry; sometimes I don't know how I'm gonna keep it inside anymore! I feel so helpless! Like I'm on the sidelines, and you're out there with the ball and no defensive line, getting sacked over and over. And all I can do is watch. I can't protect you like a big brother should—not from this."

"You *do* protect me. You always have. I didn't realize just how much until the day I did this"—I raise my casted hand—"and you told me why you always cover for me. I never saw it that way. I was an idiot."

"You're *not* an idiot," Evan says, sniffling. "God, what a fucking mess!"

And that brings my thoughts back to the reason for my confession. "But now you see why I can't tell everyone. The whole school will look at me like I'm ticking . . . all the time. Some will be scared, but most will be morbidly curious to see it happen, and everyone will look at me like I'm—like I'm less than human—"

Evan squeezes my forearm, and I realize I'm breathing fast, and my head is starting to spin.

"You're okay. Take a deep breath, and let it out slowly." I close my eyes because it helps to settle my stomach, and I focus on breathing for a few minutes.

"Okay, so telling everyone isn't the answer, but there's got to be one. You still love her, and she still loves you—"

"I don't think so, Ev," I say as my throat gets tight. "She hasn't looked at me in weeks, and I . . . I let *Amber* help me at school. I had no idea she was the one who gave Holly the note, but I'm sure Holly thinks I did it on purpose to hurt her—"

Evan sighs heavily and shakes his head. "Girls. They're so damn complicated and . . . devious and — If they weren't the only way to get pussy, would we really even need them?"

I'm pretty sure he's joking, but then again, Evan likes things simple. But I know I still need Holly, and it has absolutely nothing to do with her spectacular pussy.

"Why don't you go back to sleep for a while? You look exhausted," Ev says, fist-bumping my knee. "We can talk more when you're not—"

"Fighting the hangover from hell?"

"Something like that. Just promise you'll talk to me next time before you go off and do something so totally stupid?"

"I promise," I say, fighting my heavy eyelids.

"Good," Evan responds, nodding as he leaves my room.

Although I sleep the day away, by suppertime I no longer feel like roadkill, and I'm actually hungry. But I feel . . . low. The pain of losing Holly was sudden and agonizing, but the dull ache that clings to me is worse. I hurt her again without realizing it. Why the hell did I let Amber anywhere near me after Holly broke up with me? I *know* why, and now it seems like the lamest reason, but at the time I just didn't care. I didn't care about anything—I was in so much pain, it was as if the world had stopped around me, and I just blindly did whatever I needed to do to get by. But the world didn't stop—only I did—and I hurt Holly even more by not thinking about what I was doing.

I hate who I am. I hate all the lies, and I hate the things I've done to protect myself, the people I've wronged. I've lied so many times, I don't even know what the truth is anymore.

What the fuck *is* the truth anyway?

The truth is I don't want to be anybody if I can't be who I was with Holly. And I can't be that person without her. I just feel so trapped. I can't tell everyone the truth because I'll have a fucking mental breakdown, but I can't think of any other way of proving to Holly that I love her.

Have you ever done anything for anyone other than yourself, Nathan?

And would telling everyone really prove anything to her? I would be doing it for her, but I don't know if she'd see it that way or if it would even matter to her now.

And it's in this state of mind that Lucy finds me on Wednesday after school. I've trudged through the week, avoiding Chris and his black eye and warning Amber away with my glare, but other than that, I couldn't tell you what I did. Every day is the same without the brown eyes and quirky little smile that I never realized made each one worth living.

I'm late, shoving my shit into my bag when the hairs on the back of my neck suddenly stand on end.

"I've been waiting for this. It's taken weeks, but I've finally gotten you alone. I want you to meet a friend of mine. Yeah, Ivan is all ready to cut your balls off so I can put them in a jar and give them to Holly."

I lean my head against my locker because I'm just too weary to have another pointless conversation today.

"You can have my balls, Lucy. Without Holly, I have no use for them anyway."

"What?"

I turn around, and Gothzilla does, in fact, have a switchblade that she's pointing at me, but she looks thoroughly confused.

"I said you can have my balls. And while you're cutting, can you hit a major artery for me, if it wouldn't be too much trouble? Maybe I'll get lucky and bleed to death too."

Goth girl squints at me. "This conversation isn't going at all the way I thought it would."

"Let me guess. You thought I'd make some smartass remark about how my balls are way too good for you, throw in a few other insults, then take your knife?"

"Well, you'd never get Ivan, but something like that, yeah."

I sigh and close my eyes. When I open them again, Gotherbell looks annoyed.

"What the hell, Nathan? You pretended to like Holly for the sake of your balls, but now you're willing to let me cut them off? What about your next conquest?"

I'm so tired of lying, and I don't have the energy to pretend to be who I was before.

"There are no conquests, Lucy. I didn't pretend to like Holly—I'm in love with her—and I didn't do anything just so I could sleep with her. It wasn't even about that. Making love to her was the most amazing thing I've ever done."

Lucy's eyes are so wide, I swear they extend out past the edges of her face, and I think she's choking on her tongue.

"Why don't you sit down before you fall down. I'll join you," I tell her, grasping her elbow, and she plops down on the floor so we're both sitting with our backs against the lockers.

"But Holly said—"

"I don't care what she said; her breaking up with me had nothing to do with sex. She dumped me because . . . because I lied to her."

I close my eyes, but I force myself to keep going. I learned from my talk with Evan that telling the truth makes me feel better, even if it's only for a little while, and right now, I'd do anything to ease the weight pressing down on me.

"I lie . . . a lot. Not because I want to—because I have to. Holly saw something she wasn't supposed to see, and . . . I . . . pretended to like her so she wouldn't tell anyone. But now I know she never would have told anyone because she's not like that, and I only pretended to like her at the very beginning. Once I got to know her, I realized I really did like her—I fell in love with her. But I was so afraid of losing her that I never told her how it all started. I thought she'd never find out, and everything would be okay."

"What happened?" I open my eyes, and Lucy's gaze holds no reproach. Her hand is also resting on my knee.

"My brother wrote a note to Lori about it, and she kept that note and gave it to Amber. And I guess . . . Amber told Holly."

The Gothlet's eyes narrow to slits, and I can almost see the red-eyed hamster of evil running on the wheel in her mind.

"Oh, that girl has had it coming from me for so long, and now she's gonna get it," Lucy murmurs, clutching Ivan-the-knife tighter. "I *told* her to leave the two of you alone, but she just couldn't, could she?"

I manage half a smile, but a pound of flesh from Amber, however satisfying, won't fix anything.

"I didn't know Amber was involved until the dance this past Friday night," I say, although it hurts to do so. "I think I might have hurt Holly even more by letting Amber help me because of my hand, but . . . I guess it doesn't matter now."

"Why wouldn't it matter?"

"Holly doesn't care about me anymore, so—"

"Nathan, *where* did you get the idea that Holly doesn't care about you anymore?" Lucy asks, her grip on my knee tightening.

"Well, she didn't believe me when I told her I loved her, and she won't even look at me anymore—"

"She looks at you *constantly*, just not when you're looking," Lucy mutters, and I raise my eyebrows in disbelief. "*Do* you love her?"

"More than anything. And I would do anything to get her to believe me."

Lucy clasps her hands together and squeals. "I *knew* there was more to this than Holly said! And I'm glad you're not the complete asshole I thought you were."

"Um . . . thanks?"

"Okay. So. What did Holly see that she wasn't supposed to?"

Heat creeps up my neck and chest, and I can feel it spreading across my cheeks. This is the closest I've ever come to telling anyone my secret. My heart starts to thunder in my chest—I wonder if Lucy can hear it.

"Nathan? Are you okay?"

"I . . . I can't tell you." The words come out as a painful rasp over shallow breaths. "I can't tell anyone. Holly found out by accident."

"Okay," Lucy says, rubbing my arm. "I don't think that's the important part anyway."

Oh God, if she only knew.

"The important part is convincing Holly you made a mistake. Everybody makes mistakes, but if you truly love each other, you should be able to see past those mistakes, right?"

"Right," I answer, not at all sure how we're gonna do that, but I'm totally on the "getting Holly to see past my mistakes" train.

"So you started seeing her for the wrong reason, but it turned into love, right?"

"Right."

"Okay, I can work with this. Just give me a little time," Lucy says, starting to get up off the floor.

"Wait! What do you mean?" I ask as I scramble up beside her.

"I don't know yet. I'll figure something out. Thank you for telling me the truth, Nathan. I don't know how, but everything's gonna be okay!"

She bounds upward and kisses my cheek, then skips away like some coked-out cupid. I don't know what just happened, but maybe it'll turn out to be good. Things can't get any worse, right?

CHAPTER THIRTY

Sometimes hearing the truth takes more courage than speaking the truth.

– **Amit Kalantri,** *Wealth of Words*

HOLLY

Nathan got his cast off today. Instead of the royal blue fiberglass, his hand is now encased in a black brace. You'd think he'd be happy about it, but his expression when he walks into homeroom is the same as always—neutral with his eyes on the floor. I look at the calendar in my binder and realize with a start that it's been six weeks since he broke his hand. Six weeks since I broke up with him. How can it seem like only yesterday but also a lifetime ago?

My eyes still follow him every day. The anger is long since gone, but the hurt remains, and somehow, I think it always will. But there are new emotions—concern and confusion—and they're starting to nag at me.

Admittedly, I'm watching from the sidelines, but it seems like he's just . . . existing. He doesn't hang out with Ryan anymore, or anyone, really. He's alone, and I haven't seen him smile—I mean *really* smile—since the day we broke up. And the rumors I heard last week were downright disturbing. I know he had it out with Bitch Face in the middle of the dance because everyone saw it, but I also heard he got really drunk with Ken-doll and Tyler that night, and somehow Ken-doll ended up with a black eye. Nathan didn't have any visible injuries, but I'm sure if he got wasted, he had a seizure on Saturday, and—

And you're still living your life as if it matters to you what happens to him.

I know I'm still in love with him, but the question that's been keeping me up at night is this: is he actually in love with me?

Reason needles at me—he knows that I'd never tell anyone, and he would have gotten over not getting his way by now. And if he wanted sex, Bitch Face would have mounted him in front of the entire student body if he asked her to, or he could have charmed just about anyone. Instead, he walks around looking like a lost puppy, and he's isolated himself from almost everyone.

If he truly only cares about himself and his gain, he's doing a piss poor job of taking care of himself right now.

The Gothlet is next into homeroom, and—*what the hell?* Her gaze falls on Nathan, but it's not the *your-balls-will-soon-be-mine* death glare she usually gives him when she deigns to acknowledge he exists. Her eyebrows are furrowed as if she's concerned, and when he looks up at her, her lips curve into the hint of a smile. I shake my head to clear the hallucination, but her smile lingers as she sits down beside Megan.

I lean forward and fix her with my best *what-the-fuck-was-that* look, but her smile just widens as her eyes twinkle at me. I don't get it, but I brush it off as some sort of cosmic oddity.

Until it happens again.

Megan and I are walking down the hall to lunch on Wednesday, and I glance toward the little hallway by the art room as I always do because that's the place Nathan and I had our first civil conversation, and who do I see there but The Gothlet, deep in conversation with *he-whose-balls-were-promised-to-me*, aka Nathan.

Now I'm pissed. Because unless she's negotiating for his nuts, which I seriously doubt, she's just violated every girl code there ever was and napalmed our friendship.

I stomp down the hall with Megan clueless at my side, but I stop at the water fountain and pretend to drink until they both emerge from the alcove. Nathan heads to his locker, but The Gothlet is coming our way.

"I'll meet you in the caf, Megan. I need to talk to Lucy for a minute."

I don't even notice as she walks off—my eyes are fixed on Baroness Von Backstabber as she skips down the hall.

She's still a good ten feet away when I can longer contain my temper.

"What the fuck, Lucy? What's going on with you and Nathan?"

She looks slightly surprised, but then she smiles—*smiles!*—at me. "So you noticed."

"Of course I noticed! He hasn't talked to anyone for weeks, and now all of a sudden, he's smiling at you, and you're holed up talking in *our* hallway? What the hell is going on?"

The Gothlet sighs heavily. "We need to talk."

A million possibilities are flitting through my mind as I follow her through the lunch line, each one scarier than the last, until finally, we're seated at a table away from everyone else.

The Gothlet turns deadly serious as she faces me, her hands resting palms down on either side of her tray.

"Nathan told me his secret."

"*What?*"

"Well, not the actual secret, but he told me you saw something you weren't supposed to."

My mind is reeling. "How in the *hell* did you convince him to tell you that?"

"I didn't! I finally got him alone to cut his balls off for you, and he spilled his guts instead. Sat down and told me everything . . . well, except for the actual *thing*."

"What did he say?"

"He told me that he has to lie to cover up whatever it is, so when you saw it, he pretended to like you to keep you quiet."

Pain radiates around the edges of the hole in my chest as if it's trying to connect with the heart that isn't there anymore, and I lean back in my chair and press a hand there.

"But, Holly, there's more," The Gothlet says, reaching out to cover my other hand, and I listen to the rest of her words with my eyes closed.

"Once he got to know you, he realized he really liked you. He fell in love with you, and he was so afraid of losing you that he made a mistake—he decided not to tell you how it started. It was the wrong thing to do, and he knows that, but if it hadn't been for that note-saving bitch Lori and Amber's stalker obsession with him, you'd still be together right now."

I sigh and shake my head. "I know all this. He told me the last time we talked. But how do I know his saying he loves me isn't a lie? I know he would do anything to protect himself."

"Holly, it's been six weeks since you broke up. If you haven't spilled his secret in all that time, do you really think he'd be trying to get back with you to protect something you're already protecting for him?"

Her words make sense, and the lovesick part of my brain is nodding furiously. But the voice of hurt is louder.

"After we broke up, he went right back to the populars, and he let Amber help him with everything. How could he do that after she broke us up and humiliated me? He obviously thought what she did was just fine, and he had to know that getting close to her would hurt me."

"No, he didn't!" The Gothlet exclaims. "Lori covered for Amber—only *you* knew who gave you the note. Nathan didn't find out until the dance two weeks ago when Amber screwed up and admitted it to him."

So that's what happened at the dance! I wasn't there, but The Gothlet and Megan told me Nathan was livid, and Bitch Face ran out crying. I haven't seen them speak a word to each other since.

"That doesn't mean he loves me," I say stubbornly.

"He's been miserable since you broke up—anyone can see that."

"Maybe his dick's just lonely."

The Gothlet huffs impatiently. "He's got *one* working hand, and if that's not enough, he's gorgeous and popular enough to have almost any girl in the whole damn town. If he wanted some, I'm sure the cheerleading squad would strip down and build him a pussy pyramid.

"*I* believe he loves you," The Gothlet says, and when I meet her eyes, I see nothing but certainty. "When I threatened to cut his balls off, he asked if I could hit a major artery for him so he'd bleed to death. Does *that* tell you anything about his state of mind?"

Holy shit! Tears choke my throat and gather at the corners of my eyes, but I blink them back. *Is he really that miserable without me?*

"He had absolutely no reason to tell me anything. All I wanted were his balls, and all this tumbled out instead. I think he's just really tired of lying."

"Well then, he should stop," I say with no small amount of heat.

"Can he? With whatever this secret is that he's keeping?"

I think about his anxiety and how hard it was for him to adjust to me, a single person, knowing about his condition, and the answer is obvious.

"No, he can't."

"Well then, is it fair to ask that of him?"

"That's not what I want." I hate to admit it, and although I wish things were different, I know I'd help him keep his secret forever if that's what he needed. "I just wish he hadn't lied to *me*. He's so good at it, Lucy—how can I trust him again? Keeping his secret is more important to him than I am, and that means there's always the possibility this could happen again, and . . . and he's selfish.

"He assumed I would tell everyone what I saw to make myself popular because that's how he operates. That's why he used to bully people, did he tell you that? He put them down so the focus was never on him. Everything he does, he does for himself and no one else."

"No, he didn't tell me that," The Gothlet says, frowning. "But he hasn't bullied anyone since he started dating you, has he?"

"No."

"And he didn't go back to that when you broke up, did he?"

"Well . . . no."

"I think you've changed him. I've known him for years—he stopped being a bully when he started dating you, and since you broke up, he's been a ghost.

"And what about you? I know you still love him. You watch him every second of the day—it's like your world revolves around where he is, and if he's not in the room, then you have no center.

"He made a mistake, Holly. A really bad one, but I think he'd do just about anything to make it up to you. You both love each other—should you really have to spend the rest of your lives miserable because of one mistake? Talk to him. I think you'll see what I'm talking about if you just open your heart and listen."

Fuck. It's as if The Gothlet and every nagging doubt in my head brainstormed and came up with the best way to confuse the hell out of me.

"I don't know, Lucy. I need to think about it."

"I get it," The Gothlet says, squeezing my forearm. "And I hope you don't think that because I talked to him, I'm on his side now. I've just never seen two people so miserable, and I thought maybe I could help."

I want to be angry at her, but my heart's not in it. I'm so tired of feeling angry and hurt, and all she really did was listen to him.

"I'm not mad at you."

"Thank God!" The Gothlet exclaims. "You know, he can be really endearing when he's pouring his heart out to you. I couldn't help but feel sorry for him; he was that pathetic."

A vision of Nathan the day after his near miss of a seizure at school comes to me unbidden, his head resting on my shoulder as he tells me he needs a way to escape.

"Yes, he can be very sweet when he wants to be."

"But if he *did* somehow manage to bullshit me, this time it'll be his *junk* in a jar, and I'm keeping it for myself," The Gothlet says, winking at me as she gets up and heads over to sit with Ryan.

My mouth hangs open but only for a few seconds. I think I'm actually getting used to The Gothlet's way of solving every high school problem with violence.

I rest my head in my hands, my brain going a thousand miles an hour trying to process everything The Gothlet said, while the team Nathan side of my brain flashes only one message: *I told you so.*

The Gothlet made all the points team Nathan has been dogging me with for weeks, but she has one thing my Nathan-loving neurons didn't have— she's talked to Nathan and verified that he's still saying and feeling the same things he did six weeks ago.

Maybe he *is* telling the truth.

Something warm and bright surges through the hole in my chest, and for a moment, I feel as if it isn't there. But only for a moment.

So what if he *is* telling the truth and he *does* love me—can I ever trust him again? And The Gothlet says he's changed, but has he really? Did he stop bullying because he doesn't want to hurt anyone that way again or because it doesn't benefit him as much as he thought it did?

The questions swirl around in my head for the rest of the week, and although I feel Nathan's eyes on me more than once, I can't bring myself to meet them. I feel like I'm standing on some sort of precipice—caught between the need to play it safe and the urge to just jump—and so I hesitate, with uncertainty as my companion.

I don't know what I'm doing here. The Gothlet damn near made me swear a blood oath that I'd show at the dance, but as I walk through the caf doors, I'm already regretting it. I haven't been to a dance since the Winter Formal, the night that was arguably the best night of my life. Even if Nathan and I never get back together, it'll *still* be the best night of my life because everything was just so perfect. I keep those memories in a separate place from the hurt, distancing myself as if I'm watching a movie, the scenes edged with soft golden light.

This dance is nothing like that, and I seriously don't know what the hell I'm doing here. I dance with The Gothlet and Megan, but The Gothlet has a new move added to her groove this evening—she keeps looking over her shoulder as if she's expecting something . . . or some*one*. I'm not an idiot. Her insistence that I come tonight and her pleas that I talk to Nathan add up to a Gothlet-staged Dr. Phil session with the Goth-fairy swooping in to wave her wand or shoot her arrow or whatever to make everything magically okay. Alas, Cupid of the dark side, it doesn't work that way even if it *is* Valentine's Day.

I've been a resident of the land of confusion ever since Lucy confessed to me on Wednesday—my heart and head pulling in different directions and switching places with a frequency you can clock with an egg timer. I just don't know. I want so much to throw caution to the wind and believe in him, but I'm scared. I can't do halfway with Nathan. If I reach out for my heart that's still in his keeping, there'll be no defenses, no caution—I've missed him so much, I know I'm going to grab on with everything I have. So I have to be sure.

And I'm not.

I'm scared that the same selfish person I met six months ago is still lingering under there—that *he's* the real Nathan, not the sweet, sensitive boy who was forced into a personality of self-protection by his own fears and a debilitating illness. *That's* the boy I fell in love with as he slowly and painfully let me into his lonely world. I want that boy back.

I'm fucked.

A slow song comes on, and Justin and Ryan materialize out of nowhere, just like good boyfriends should. I feel a tug in my chest for what was, but I try my best to ignore it.

Lucy looks at me with pity in her eyes. *I don't think he's coming.*

But as she glances over her shoulder, a smile sweeps over her face like the first light of dawn.

He's here.

Chapter Thirty-One

HOLLY

I meet his eyes for the first time in weeks, and it's both brutally strange and achingly familiar. Looking at him straight on, his face looks thinner, and there's more scruff on his cheeks than he ever left there when we were dating. The smudges under his eyes are dark—he looks tired and broken, as if a piece of him is missing—exactly the way I feel. Faded jeans, the soft green button-down with the chest pocket that I used to put Jolly Ranchers into, and—wow—both hands in his pockets. It seems his hand is completely healed.

Can we heal too?

He closes his eyes and takes a slow, deep breath, and it's as if I can see his nerves rattling just under the surface. He's trying to get himself together enough to come talk to me, to break the silence that has endured since I said goodbye to him six weeks—or a lifetime—ago.

And I'm not sure if I want him to or not.

Fear and anticipation surge in such similar ways; it's hard to tell which one I'm feeling as he shuffles across the floor toward me, his own steps far from certain, until he's right here, and I have to raise my chin to meet his eyes.

The tears well instantly, and all the emotions of the past weeks come flooding back, but loss and loneliness and hurt are right on the surface, making me want to throw my arms around him and save us both.

But I don't.

"Hi, Holly."

His voice caresses my name as only his ever could, and I melt a little as I croak out a broken "Hi."

"Can we talk? Please? I have some things I want to say . . . even if it won't change anything."

My heart is thundering in my chest, and I seem to have lost the power of speech, so I just nod, then follow him as he weaves a path through the dancers and up the caf stairs into the main hallway of the school. There's a lunch table against the wall under one of the trophy cases, and he leads me there, leaning against it as he turns to face me.

"Can we sit? I'm a little—"

"Nervous?"

"Nauseous."

He smiles a little as he looks down, and I do the same although he doesn't see it, and I mirror his pose as he sits on the table, one leg bent in front of him so he can face me.

Well, his body is facing me anyway. His face is angled downward so he can stare at his bent knee, and I can hear his rapid, shallow breaths and hard swallows. He's close to panicking, and while I'm trying to come up with ways I can help ground him that won't freak him out even more, he raises misty blue eyes to mine, and his words finally come tumbling out.

"Lying to you was the biggest mistake I've ever made in my entire life. I expected you to be like everyone else because I didn't know you, but now that I do, I know you would never ever hurt someone else to help yourself."

He takes another deep breath, and his eyes shift downward. "But that's what *I* did. I pretended to like you to keep you from telling everyone, and I bullied so many people to keep the attention away from me. I wish I could take that back too. I've done so many awful things in the name of protecting myself, and maybe I didn't have to—I'm pretty sure now that I didn't have to—but I didn't know that at the time, and I let myself become a complete asshole.

"I don't like who I am. I hate all the lying; I hate that no one can get close to me; and I'm so fucking tired of being alone and afraid."

He closes his eyes, and a tear escapes onto his cheek, but he dashes it away. "I hate that I have epilepsy, and I hate that I can't just deal with telling everyone the truth. But I can't.

"The only time—*the only time*—I've been happy since before all this happened was when I was with you." Now his eyes meet mine, and the longing in them is so deep, so powerful, I can feel it in my chest, taste it in the air.

"I love you, Holly, and . . . I like who *I* am when I'm with you. You make *everything* in my life easier to deal with, and you make me feel strong and not afraid. You make me feel like I might be worth something. And I love talking about *Game of Thrones* with you and helping you with physics, and I love dancing with you and touching you, and . . . I just love you. I don't know what else to say. And I would do anything to make you believe me—anything but the one thing I *can't* do.

"And I want to do things for you. I know you think I'm selfish, and you're right, I am, but . . . I don't *want* to be. I want . . . to make you smile and make you laugh. I want to take you on dates and hold your hand and show everyone I'm yours. I wanna be someone you're proud to call your boyfriend because he does such awesome things for you. You might have to help me with that because I'm not used to doing things for other people, but I *want* to."

I look into his eyes, and it's all there—the pain and self-loathing, the confusion and loss, the love that he feels for me, the sincerity of his apology. It's all there, and he's so close, and my hand is itching to reach out and touch him, to tell him it's okay and I forgive him and I love him. I lean forward, and I can feel his breath—I want to kiss him so badly it hurts, and I want to forget what he did, pretend it never happened. He's so warm and *right here,* and it would be *so* easy—he closes his eyes when we're two inches apart and—

"No!" The word flies from my mouth, startling us both. *I need time to think.* He's too close, and I'm thinking with my hormones and not my wounded heart or my head and I . . . *I need to get out of here.*

Wide blue eyes meet mine, brimming with shock and hurt, but this is all happening too quickly, and we need to talk and not kiss, but I can't even begin to think of the words as he stares into my eyes in the semi-darkness.

"You don't believe me, do you?" He says the words as if he's in a daze, and they're not really a question. I know I'm messing this up, but I just can't sort it all out in my head.

"I don't know. I can't . . . I need to go!" I let instinct take over as I leap from the table and tear down the hallway into the main part of the school. My heart twists in my chest with every inch of distance I put between us, but I have to keep going. I need to slow everything down.

I can hear Nathan calling my name, but I don't stop until I get to the main lobby, panting and brushing away tears. I can't stay here because I don't want him to find me—I don't want *anyone* to find me until I've had some time, so I try the gym doors, and thankfully, they're open.

I walk briskly down the stairs and across the floor to the far corner of the bleachers. Even if someone comes in, they won't see me in the darkness.

When I finally sit down, the weight of what just happened falls on me, and the tears begin in earnest. I miss him *so* much, and now that the hormones have been drowned by tears, my heart is begging me to run back to him and fall into his arms and just . . . make everything okay.

Is everything okay?

Lying to you was the biggest mistake I've ever made in my life.

With his words comes the look in his eyes, sorrowful but unflinching, owning what he did, and I know in my heart he really *does* mean it.

I've done so many awful things in the name of protecting myself, and I'm pretty sure now that I didn't have to.

Holy shit, he *did* listen to me. He heard me all those weeks ago when I told him he didn't need to hurt others to help himself even though he denied it at the time.

I don't like who I am. I hate all the lying; I hate that no one can be close to me; and I'm so fucking tired of being alone and afraid.

His voice broke over the words—there's so much pain there. *How* did I not throw my arms around him and tell him he never has to be alone or afraid ever again?

I know you think I'm selfish, and you're right, I am, but . . . I don't want *to be.*

I think you've changed him, Holly.

Lucy's words follow right after Nathan's, and team Nathan seems to be holding its breath and so am I. The precipice I stand on doesn't seem quite so high anymore and . . .

He made a mistake, Holly. A really bad one, but I think he'd do just about anything to make it up to you. You both love each other—should you really have to spend the rest of your lives miserable because of one mistake?

"No."

My answer echoes in the gym, and hope surges in my chest, holding me up as I leap off the precipice and into the chasm of blind trust borne of the love I feel for him—the love I've always felt but was afraid to own because he hurt me. You *don't* stop loving someone just because they hurt you, and if you love them, then you have to be willing to forgive them when they make a mistake—even if it is a horrible one.

And I do.

I love him, and I forgive him.

You don't believe me, do you?

He bared his soul to me, and I *ran away.*

"Oh God, what have I done?"

I dash across the gym floor.

I've got to find him and tell him I love him and forgive him, and—

I let out a squeak, confused as I'm brought to a sudden halt at the bottom of the stairs.

"Well, look what we have here, Chris."

"Let me go!" I yell as I pull to get away, but Sean's grip on my wrist is like a vise. Both of them start to laugh at me.

"Oh, I don't think so, Ross. I've wanted you for a long time."

Rage fills me, and I whirl to face him. He's leering at me, and I'm more disgusted than I've ever been. I take two steps so I'm right in his face and raise my chin defiantly.

"I told you *no*," I say with as much venom as I can muster, and I spit right in his face.

Ken-doll gasps, but Sean just snorts a laugh as he wipes off his face. And before I know what's happened, my cheek explodes in pain, and I'm pressed against the wall of the gym with my hands pinned over my head and Sean's knee between my legs.

"Maybe you don't *get* to say no." The stench of whiskey turns my stomach as I break out in a cold sweat.

Oh God, he wouldn't . . .

"Sean, what the—" Ken-doll slurs as he appears beside us, leaning on the wall.

"Fuck off, Chris! You can either jerk off while you watch or leave—I don't give a shit—but I'm getting mine tonight, and I swear I'll beat your ass if you interfere. You *know* she gave it up for Harris. Now she can give it up for me."

I gasp as Sean raises his knee so it presses right *there*, and fear floods me in a rush of shivers.

"No, Chris . . . help!"

I barely get a breath before Sean's kissing me, and I taste blood as my lip is smashed against my own teeth. I thrash my head, but he follows, thrusting his tongue into my mouth so hard I nearly gag.

I'm panting and crying when he pulls away, and I jerk back when he grabs my chin *hard*.

"Not so tough now, are you? Go ahead and fight, Holly. It just makes me harder."

His hand slides down my neck. I jerk forward as my blouse opens and buttons go flying, and I squeal as he squeezes my breast.

"No! Please! Don't—"

His knee grinds upward again, but suddenly, I'm on the ground, and Nathan is between me and Sean.

I can't see Nathan's face, but I hear his gasp and swear as he shakes out his right hand—the one that was broken.

Sean is bent over, cupping his nose as Nathan turns toward me.

"Son of a bitch." There are tears in his eyes as he kneels before me and takes my hands. "Did he—"

"No." But I'm shaking, and it's hard to breathe.

"But I'm gonna," Sean says, and Nathan pulls us both to our feet as he turns, keeping me firmly behind him.

"Over my dead body," Nathan growls, but Sean just laughs.

"It'll be like foreplay. Holly can watch while I fuck up Harris's pretty face. Chris, come hold her."

"The hell I will," Ken-doll says, coming up beside Sean. "I've wanted to fuck up Harris for a long time now."

Nathan glances over his shoulder, and suddenly, his arms are stretched backward to cage me, and we're moving along the wall toward the glass doors that lead to the parking lot. *He has a plan.*

We're almost there when Ken-doll steps forward, and before Nathan can react, he's nearly on his knees, clutching his stomach and gasping.

"But I still want Ross," Sean says, making a grab for me, but the next thing I know, I'm outside freezing and Nathan is pulling the gym door shut tight between us.

I tug on it and gasp in horror.

It's locked.

Nathan's eyes lock with mine from the other side of the glass, and I can't stop the tears as I beat on the door with my fists. His gaze is everything, and I watch as his pain turns to determination, readying himself to fight.

He mouths one word, then turns to face two angry, drunken boys, outmanned and outgunned.

"Run."

CHAPTER THIRTY-TWO

Love is not what you say. Love is what you do.

– Anonymous

HOLLY

Oh God.

OhGodOhGodOhGod...

The door flies open as Nathan takes a punch, but he pulls it shut again with both hands behind him.

But there are other doors.

Sean's face appears in the glass of the door next to the one Nathan's holding, and I scream as I stumble backward.

Nathan can't defend himself if he's trying to protect me.

Run!

I turn and take off blindly, flying down the hill until I reach the side of the building, and I'm out of sight of the gym doors.

My hand finds the brick wall, and I lean over, unable to catch my breath. The taste of iron sickens me, and I spit out bile and blood, my lip stinging and my cheek throbbing as I gasp for air.

I cringe as Sean's face swims before me, and my wrists ache as if they're still pinned over my head.

And that's when I hear it—footfalls on the concrete. *They're outside.*

"Sean!"

The footfalls stop, and I can't see him as I press my back against the wall, but he's close to the corner—close enough that I hear him swear under his breath. "What?"

"Stop thinking with your dick, and get back here! Holly's long gone. I need you to hold him up!"

Hold . . . who . . . oh God.

I have to get help.

The haze in my brain clears, and I sprint toward the football field, making for the back door to the caf and praying I can find Evan before . . .

We're way past "before" if Sean is holding Nathan up.

"Evan! Evan, it's Nathan!" I screech, slamming into his chest. He catches me by the elbows, his eyes boring into mine.

"Is it—"

"No, it's worse! Sean tried—" *Shit! I can't even say it!* "—but Nathan saved me! Now he's all alone!"

Evan's eyes widen as he takes in my open blouse and the bruise that surely covers my aching cheek. "Holly . . ."

"Just go!"

"Where?" Evan demands, gripping my arms a little tighter as a scowl settles on his face.

"Out front. Hurry!" I yell at him, and he releases my arms and barrels for the doors like a freight train.

I stand there, gasping for air while my mind tries to catch up.

Evan will—Christ, Evan will kill them both for what they've done to Nathan—someone has to stop the fight—I need to get more help.

I look around frantically, and—*oh thank God*! Harper is striding purposefully across the caf, intent on whoever he's about to bitch out.

"Mr. Harper! Mr. Harper!"

He nearly runs into me as I block his path, but as he steps back, his eyes lock on my chest, and his jaw drops.

I glance down self-consciously and see my bra—my blouse is still hanging open, almost down to my belly button. For a second, I flash back to the ping of buttons hitting the floor—

I need you to hold him up!

"Nathan!"

"What the—Nathan did this?" Mr. Harper asks, scowling.

I pull my blouse together and hold it with one hand, shaking my head as I grasp his arm with my other one. "No! Sean, he—and now there's a fight, and you have to stop it!"

"Okay, okay. But what happened—"

"They're out front! Please! I sent Evan, and he'll kill them for hurting Nathan!"

"Shit! Bob? Go on ahead and I'll be there in a minute."

Mr. Metcalf nods and takes off at a jog for the caf doors—I didn't even see him come up to us.

"Holly, are you all right? Your face . . ."

I put a hand to my cheek and wince as tears well in my eyes. "I was alone in the gym, and—and he said I couldn't say no—"

"Sean? Did he . . . uhh—"

"No, but he would have if Nathan hadn't—oh God, *Nathan*! I have to go—"

"Holly, wait—"

He grabs my wrist, but my gasp-wince makes him let go, and I bolt for the caf doors, dodging clueless students left and right. I think I hear The Gothlet call my name, but I don't stop—I can't stop until I get to Nathan. *He has to be okay—he just has to!*

Evan got there in time and kicked the shit out of both of them—

I skid to a halt trying to process what's before me.

Evan is red-faced and screaming curses as he tries to get around Mr. Metcalf, who has both hands planted on Evan's chest and is shoving him backward.

Ken-doll is on all fours, gasping, and Sean is bent over him—

Where's Nathan?

"Oh!" A strangled cry escapes me as I fling myself across the parking lot and fall to my knees beside him. He's on his stomach on the concrete, the side of his face lying against the cold, hard surface.

Blood is everywhere. It seeps from a gash above his right eye and pools on the concrete beneath him. It drips from his busted lower lip, now swollen and angry-looking. And it flows freely from his nose, obviously disjointed and broken. The skin under both his eyes is already smudged reddish-purple. His right eye is swollen shut.

"Oh my God, Nathan!" I wail, wanting to pull him into my arms but terrified I'll hurt him further by moving him. I touch the side of his head gently, and he winces, but the corner of his mouth rises ever so slightly in the hint of a smile.

"Believe . . . me . . . now?" He forces the words out on weak breaths, and my heart shatters into a thousand pieces in my chest.

"Yes! God, yes, I believe you! You saved me. I can't believe you saved me from . . ." I can't finish the thought. I haven't had time to go into shock over what happened to me, and I know eventually it'll truly hit me, and I'll have to deal with it, but right now, my only concern is Nathan and getting him the help he needs.

My head whips up frantically—Ken-doll and Sean are sitting on the curb with Mr. Harper standing in front of them.

". . . we've had an incident at Tillamook High. Yes, send Kevin, and we need the paramedics . . . five injured . . ."

Nathan shifts his bloodied hand and tries to push himself upward but collapses back to the ground with a cry.

"Hurts . . . breathe . . ." he whispers.

"Shh . . . don't try to move. Mr. Harper called the police and the ambulance, and they'll be here any minute. Everything's going to be okay," I say, trying to comfort him.

"Stay . . ." he murmurs, his eye drifting closed wearily.

"Of course, I'll stay," I whisper. "Forever."

~

The wait for the paramedics is an eternity, and I tune out everything around me but Nathan. I hold his left hand because his right is swollen and purple—*I wonder if he broke it again*—and although his eyes are closed, he squeezes my fingers every few minutes to let me know he's still with me.

My chest aches, and I realize it's because I'm barely breathing—trying to hold everything just as it is until help gets here.

The flash of the ambulance lights startles me back to life.

"Here! Over here!" I yell, waving the hand that's not holding Nathan's, and the guy quickly changes direction and jogs over to us.

"He . . . they . . . please help him!"

"Don't worry, I—are you okay?"

I glance up from Nathan, and the guy is giving me a look I should be used to by now—eyes wide and staring at my bra because I let my shirt go to hold on to Nathan.

"I'm fine! Him first—please!"

He nods and focuses on Nathan, gently removing my hand from his and putting two fingers to Nathan's wrist.

"What's his name?"

"Nathan."

"Nathan? Hey, buddy, are you with me?"

"Yes."

"Can you tell me your last name?"

"Harris."

"One of Dr. Harris's boys?"

"Yes."

"Okay, Nathan, I'm going to roll you on to your back so I can check you over. Is that okay?"

"Yes. Whoa, fuck . . ."

"Nathan? Are you still with me?"

"Yeah . . . too fast . . . spinning . . ."

"Were you drinking tonight?"

"No."

"Did you hit your head?"

"Yeah. On the ground . . . I think . . ."

"Holly?"

I startle as someone touches my arm, and I tear my eyes away from Nathan.

"Mr. Harper said you were hurt—"

It's a female EMT, and her eyes do the same thing everyone else's have when they look at me.

"Did one of these boys do this to you?" she asks, her gaze hardening.

"Yes."

"I'll be right back, honey. Stay here," she says before turning and walking briskly back the way she came.

Nathan's cry of pain tears at my heart—the EMT has Nathan's shirt open, and he's poking at a huge bruise on the side of his chest.

"You may have a broken rib or two. We'll move you as carefully as we can, okay?"

Nathan says nothing—he looks like he's out of it, but when I take his hand, he quickly finds me with the one eye he can open.

"Holly . . ."

"I'm so sorry, I—"

"Miss, we need to move him."

"Nathan, I'll see you at the hospital, okay?" I say, squeezing his hand before I let go. "Let them take care of you."

"Holly," Nathan mumbles, but then the EMT is talking to him again.

"One, two, three!"

I cringe at his pained gasp and rapid intake of breath.

This is all your fault.

If you hadn't run away from him, none of this would have happened.

Tears fall as they load Nathan into the ambulance, and I watch as the EMT continues to look him over. The guy lifts Nathan's swollen hand to inspect it, unbuttoning the cuff of his shirt to get a better look. I see him flip Nathan's bracelet over, a frown creasing his brow as he reads it.

Just then, Nathan starts convulsing. "Shit!" the EMT yells. "Brian, tell John we need to get this one outta here now! I'm gonna need you in here with me. Epileptic with a probable concussion; I doubt this is gonna stop."

My heart, my breath, my brain—everything—stops. Oh my God, *those assholes punched him in the face, and he hit his head on the ground.* He can't fight! He can't hit his head!

And he knew all this when he shoved you out the gym door and pulled it shut.

The look in his eyes as he watched me through the glass of the gym door assaults me, and the realization of what he actually did strikes me like lightning.

He risked . . . everything—his very life for me.

Oh, Nathan, you risked your life for me! How could you risk your life for me?

I take a step toward the ambulance, my eyes glued to Nathan's jerking form as my heart explodes in my chest. *No!*

He gave up everything, and he didn't give a shit about the consequences. And you thought he was selfish.

The EMTs pull the doors shut as the sirens wail, and everything inside me twists with a sickening lurch.

"Nathan . . . *no* . . ."

I fall to my knees as it all overwhelms me. Great, choking sobs wrack my body, and even though my eyes are closed, I can still see Nathan seizing in the back of the ambulance as it pulls away.

"Holly? Holly!"

I fly to my dad and cling to him, burying my nose in the familiar smell of his leather jacket.

He pulls me back and holds me at the elbows, his eyes widening as he takes in my open blouse and bruised face. "Nathan!" he roars, looking around frantically.

"No, Daddy, no," I whisper, and I point a shaking finger toward Sean, who's still sitting on the curb talking to one of the other officers. I can't look at him.

Dad's across the parking lot in an instant, his deputies moving to restrain him as he grabs Sean by the throat.

"What did you do to my daughter?" he roars at him, struggling to break free of the guys now holding him.

Sean's white as a sheet as he coughs and clutches at his throat, but once Dad realizes his guys aren't gonna let him commit murder, he shrugs them off and runs back over to me. He tears off his jacket and wraps me in it, covering my chest and the marks I know he can see.

"Holly, are you all right? Did he—"

His eyes are watery and pleading. I shake my head.

"Thank God! But he—" his hand reaches toward my cheek, and I close my eyes. "That bastard! I'll have him locked up! You'll need to give a statement—"

"Kevin."

The female EMT is back, and she puts a hand on Dad's shoulder.

"She needs to go to the hospital. Her lip might need stitches, and they'll need to take pictures."

"Uh . . . right . . ."

The hospital! *Yes, I need to go to the hospital to be with Nathan.*

I startle when Dad touches my chin.

"Oh honey, I—"

324

He pulls me into his arms, and I feel . . . safe. I do my best to ignore the fact that he's shaking—whether it's from rage or sorrow, I can't tell, but I've never seen him this unhinged.

"I have to stay here and deal with *them*, but I'll come to the hospital as soon as I can. Liz?"

He glances over at the EMT, and she responds with a warm smile.

"I'll stay with her, Chief."

Dad squeezes my shoulders and starts to turn away, but my eyes fall on Evan, pacing in front of one of Dad's officers as he's being questioned.

"Dad—"

"Yeah, baby?"

"Whatever they tell you . . . Nathan saved me and fought both of them off alone, and I sent Evan to help him. Nathan and Evan didn't do anything wrong."

Dad's eyes stray to Evan, but he nods.

"Okay. We'll talk about it some more at the hospital, all right?"

"Yeah," I say as Liz shepherds me over to a waiting ambulance.

～

NATHAN

I feel like I'm underwater. I can hear voices, but I can't make out any of the words, and things seem to be getting brighter, like I'm coming to the surface. Suddenly, the light is too bright, and I scrunch my eyebrows together to make it darker. *Fuck, that hurts!* I raise my hand to my forehead, and I cry out as my own touch sends spikes of agony through my head.

Hands are on me instantly, lowering my hand and gently pushing me back as I struggle to open my eyes. I can only open one. I can crack the other one enough to let some light in, but it hurts so much to try to open it wider that I let it close again. My chest aches, and it hurts every time I breathe. My mom is leaning over me, smiling, but she also looks frightened. *What the hell is going on?*

"M-m-mom?" I say, but it comes out as barely a whisper.

Her smile widens. "Yes, honey, I'm here. Don't try to move, okay? You've been hurt, and I don't want you to hurt yourself any further."

I think about that for a moment, or at least, I try to. My head feels all swimmy, and I have no idea how I got hurt.

"W-w-wh-a-a . . . h-h-hap-p-p . . ." I draw in a frustrated breath, unable to finish saying the words. I know what I want to say, sort of, but I can't seem to do it. The more I try to concentrate, the more my head hurts. I close my eyes and try to bring my hand to my forehead, but again, Mom stops me.

"Honey, don't touch your face. Does your head hurt?"

I don't know which is worse, trying to nod or trying to talk. "Y-y-y-e-e . . ." *Dammit! Now I'm starting to get scared.*

"Okay, we'll get you some medicine," Mom says as she glances over her shoulder at someone. *A doctor?* "Nathan, do you remember what happened to you?"

I try again, but I can't seem to hold on to anything. All my memories seem vague and distant. A spike of fear rolls down my spine. "N-n-n-o-o . . ." I huff out another frustrated breath. "W-w-w-h-h . . ." I point at my mouth with one shaking finger, my one eye now wide with fear, my breath starting to come faster.

"Shh . . . calm down, sweetheart, everything's okay. After you were hurt, you had a really long seizure, and Dr. Sutton thinks that's why you can't talk right. It should get better as more time passes."

Holy hell, what happened to me? I raise my hand again to touch my face, and Mom gently holds my arm, but this time, I yank it from her grasp. "T-t-t-e-l-l . . . m-m-m-e . . ." I huff out a breath, the fear that's now coursing through my bloodstream making me frustrated and irritable.

326

Mom turns to the doctor, who I now realize is Dr. Sutton, my neurologist. "Can I just tell him what happened? I know you wanted to see if he remembered . . ."

"P-p-p-l-l-l . . ." I give her a pleading look. *I have to get some answers here.*

Dr. Sutton nods. "We'll have to wait to do most of the assessments anyway since he's experiencing dysarthria."

"Honey," Mom begins, "you got into a fight at a dance at school. You were . . . outmatched, so you got beaten up pretty badly. You have a broken nose and stitches above your eye, which is why we don't want you touching your face. You also have a broken rib and a concussion from hitting your head on the concrete. That's why you had the really long seizure."

I listen as she tells me what happened, but I feel . . . disconnected. I can't remember any of it. *Who did I fight with and why? Am I in trouble now?*

I close my eye as I try to focus, but I just can't. I'm tired and hurting *a lot*, but the thought of trying to communicate what I need is overwhelming. I feel a tear roll down my cheek.

"Nathan, can Dr. Sutton give you some medicine for the pain and to help you rest? I know you want to know more, but it might be easier in a few hours when you'll be able to talk better."

"Y-y-y-e-e-s-s," I answer slowly, my eye still closed.

"Oh honey, it's going to be okay. Things will get better. I know you're confused now, but I promise it'll be better soon," Mom says, but I can hear the quaver in her voice. I lift my hand from the bed, and she holds it between both of hers, gently massaging my fingers. We sit that way as more tears roll down my cheeks until the medicine starts working, and I'm dragged under.

CHAPTER THIRTY-THREE

"No one blames her."

"That never matters," said Alec. "Not when you blame yourself."

– Cassandra Clare, *City of Lost Souls*

HOLLY

They take pictures.

Of the bruises on my face, wrists, and breast.

Of the scrapes on my chest from his fingernails.

Of the stitches in my lip, split open by my own teeth.

Of my damaged clothing.

I probably have bruises in places I don't tell them about, but he didn't rape me, so there's no way I'm letting them take pictures down *there*. Even if he did knee me so hard I saw stars.

When the exam is done, they let me change my clothes. Dad's brought me a new set, and I don't even question it when he bags up everything I had on. Whether it's evidence or not, I don't want to see them again anyway.

He holds my hand as I give my statement, squeezing my fingers when my voice quavers, and I'm not sure if it's in anger or for support. Maybe both.

He wants me to go home, but I don't even consider it. Nathan's been admitted to neurology, and as soon as I'm through with all the bullshit, I head straight there, Dad hot on my heels.

Evan's in the hallway outside Nathan's room. He's bruised, but so much less than Nathan. He's my hero.

"He's still unconscious," he tells me. "They don't know when he'll wake up, and they're only letting one person at a time in there. Mom's hogging all the time."

He laughs, but it's weak and his smile doesn't linger. We both know how serious this could be, but my Dad is clueless.

"Holly—"

"Nathan has epilepsy, Dad. That's why he's up here. They punched him, and he has a concussion from hitting his head—"

Dad pulls me to him, and I cry against his shoulder.

"Jesus. Did you tell Officer Banes?"

"No," Evan answers. "No one knows, and I . . . it's not their business. I would have done the same even if Nathan wasn't . . . and I saw what they did to Holly."

Dad squeezes me a little tighter, and I hold in a wince.

"Thank you. I can't say this on the record, but you got in the shots I couldn't. Those boys will likely press charges, but we'll work something out. There's no way I'm letting you take the fall for protecting these two."

When Dad reaches for Evan's shoulder, I slip out of his arms, drawn to the little rectangular window in the hospital room door.

Nathan lies still, his face angled toward Julie. His nose and lips are puffy, and bruising spreads across his cheeks and around one horribly swollen eye to a line of stitches above. He looks like hell, but I know the worst of the damage probably can't be seen.

Oh Nathan, please wake up and tell me you're okay. You have to be okay.

But he doesn't, and Dad forces me to go home.

I call Evan first thing Saturday morning, and the news is not good. Nathan woke up Friday night, but he had trouble talking and didn't remember what happened to him. He was in a lot of pain, so they knocked him out again with morphine.

He had a seizure in his sleep during the night . . . and then another. Evan tells me he's never had seizures in his sleep before.

I want to go to the hospital, but there's no point—until Nathan's less disoriented and the doctors are able to do a neurological exam—they're not letting anyone into his room but his parents. Evan would be allowed in, but Nathan doesn't remember the fight, and they don't want Evan's appearance to upset him.

Evan promises he'll text me when Nathan's ready for visitors, but I pester the hell out of him for updates anyway.

My phone is blowing up every time I look at it—texts and calls from The Gothlet, Megan, Justin, even Ryan—*and who the hell gave my number to that bitch who always hits on Nathan in calculus?* I ignore them all. All I can think about is Nathan, which is good because the last thing I want to do is relive the events of Friday night—the earlier ones anyway. My brain is stuck on a loop that starts with the one I love lying broken on the ground and ends with him seizing for the longest time I've ever heard of.

Saturday into Sunday, Nathan wakes a few times at odd hours, but he's confused. He's still having seizures. His speech is improving, but slowly. He's groggy and out of it, and he doesn't ask any questions about what happened on Friday. They don't push him. I talk to Julie on Sunday afternoon, and she calls it the postictal state—Nathan's brain is still recovering from the first seizure, and it could take a few days. She tells me not to worry, but I can hear the strain in her voice.

Dad gives me a break and lets me skip school on Monday. I'm not ready to deal with the clusterfuck that's waiting for me, and he'd have to pick me up at lunch to take me to have my stitches checked anyway. When he comes home for lunch, he tells me there won't be any charges against Evan —Sean and Ken-doll agreed not to go after him for assault in exchange for the Harrises not pressing charges against them for the assault on Nathan. The charges for what was done to Nathan would have been more severe, but that would have meant disclosing Nathan's epilepsy, and the Harrises wouldn't do that against Nathan's wishes. So, since Evan's an adult, to everyone else it looks like he got the better end of the deal, but no one knows that Nathan's lying in a hospital bed because he can't remember what day it is, and he's had more seizures in a weekend than he's had all year.

"I got both of them on alcohol consumption, and Sean Murray still has other charges pending. I can't get him on rape, but indecent liberties is still a class A felony . . . if they charge him as an adult. Newman got off because he didn't touch you."

"Chris wasn't going to do anything, Dad."

"He was gonna stand there and *watch*." Dad looks positively scary as he clenches his hands into fists on the table.

I close my eyes, and it feels like Sean is right there in front of me—I can feel his breath on my face. "Dad, stop!"

I cover my chest with my arms, and the abrupt silence is deafening.

When he finally speaks, his voice is quiet and even. "I'm sorry. I'll try not to bring it up again. I'm still pretty angry about it—"

"Me too—"

"—but I don't want to make you go through it again. Since you're a minor, the statement you already gave is enough to prosecute. You won't have to go to court or anything."

Thank God.

"And that . . . boy won't be back at Tillamook High. His parents decided to pull him out instead of dealing with the fallout and the conditions of the restraining order I put in place."

"That's—"

My phone pings, and I grab it—Evan hasn't yet responded to my morning barrage of questions.

Nathan is much *better today. He's asking for you. Can you come?*

Are you freaking *kidding* me? I would have been there every minute of the last three days if I could have!

"Dad, Nathan's awake. I gotta go!"

I bolt from the room, grabbing keys and shoes as I fly through the house and out to my car, and *holy shit, can't this thing go any faster?*

Nathan looks toward me at the sound of the door opening, and the smile that spreads across his face could outshine the sun. It doesn't matter that his right eye is still mostly swollen shut, and the bruises on his cheeks and jaw are purplish-black and angry—it's the most beautiful smile I've ever seen.

I smile back automatically, my joy at seeing him awake far outweighing the pain his appearance is causing me. I rush across the room, ready to throw myself into his arms, but at the last minute, I think better of it and screech to a halt at the side of his bed.

"If y-y-you were g-g-gonna hug me, d-d-don't stop," he says, and my arms are around him before I can even think to consider his injuries. He hisses in pain, but he pulls me closer at the same time.

I can't hold back the tears. It's my fault he's here and his face is broken and his speech is slurred. It's my fault he's having seizures, and he can't remember what happened to him. It's my fault for running away, and *oh God, it's all my fault*!

I weep into his shoulder, and he holds me, his unsplinted hand rubbing circles on my back until I finally stop sobbing.

"I'm s-s-so s-s-sor-r-ry for l-l-ly—"

"No! *I'm* sorry! I shouldn't have run after everything you said to me. I should have thrown my arms around you and told you I forgave you, but I was confused and overwhelmed. I ran so I could think about things, and I was on my way back to find you when they . . ." I can't finish the sentence, and I don't know what Nathan remembers, but he holds me so close that I know he remembers something.

"S-s-so you b-b-believe me n-n-now? That I l-l-love y-y-you?"

"Yes! God, yes, I believe you! I should have never doubted you in the first place—I was so stupid! I love you *so* much!"

We both hold on for dear life, and his sniffle lets me know I'm not the only one crying. Nothing has ever felt as right as this moment—even though so many things are screwed up, holding him is coming home after being gone way too long.

He loosens his hold, and his eyes wander over me, taking in the still-purple bruise on my cheek and the stitches in my lower lip. A shadow crosses his face.

"Are y-y-you o-k-k-kay?" he asks tenderly, and I know in that moment, no matter what he doesn't remember, he knows exactly what he's asking and what almost happened to me.

"Yes, I'm fine. Thanks to you," I tell him, squeezing his arms gently.

"G-g-g-good," he says, his eyes closing for a moment.

"But I thought you didn't remember what happened?"

"I r-r-remember everything up to wh-wh-when I sh-shoved you through the gym d-d-door . . . after that, there's n-n-nothing until I w-w-woke up here. I don't r-r-remember the f-f-fight at all."

"It's probably better that way," I tell him.

"They w-w-won't tell m-m-me about it," he says, his eyes searching mine.

That's because you got your ass kicked by two drunken assholes, and it was probably the stuff of nightmares.

"It doesn't matter what happened. Are *you* okay?" I ask, my gaze shifting to the device on his head. It looks like a gaming headset except, instead of covering his ears, the white plastic bands curl behind them.

He frowns, but his eyes don't leave mine.

"EEG m-m-monitor. So the n-n-nurses know wh-wh-when I'm about to have a s-s-seizure." He huffs out a breath, so I save him the explanation.

"I know about the seizure in the ambulance and that you've had more since. They wouldn't let me in until you weren't so confused, or I would have been here every minute. I've been pestering the crap out of Evan—"

"I'm s-s-sorry it took m-m-me so l-l-long to ask for y-y-you—"

"You were recovering from the worst seizure you've ever had! I'm so glad you're better—"

"N-n-not compl-l-letely. My head is killing m-m-me, and my sp-p-p—da-m-m-mit! I can't t-t-talk right. It's g-g-getting better, but . . ." His voice trails off, and he rests his head back on his pillow, closing his eyes.

I sit beside him and hold his hand, and he's quiet for so long I'm beginning to wonder if he's fallen asleep. Suddenly, he breathes a heavy sigh, and when he opens his eyes, he looks more lost than I've ever seen him.

Icy dread closes around my heart, but I have to ask because I can see the fear in his eyes, and I made a promise to him, even if he didn't hear it, that he'd never be alone and afraid again.

"What is it?" I whisper.

"My epilepsy is c-c-completely out of c-c-control. I'm having m-m-multiple s-s-seizures a day, and they have to s-s-stop them with m-m-medication. And . . . there's no w-w-warning any-m-m-more. No little s-s-seizures. I just f-f-feel the f-f-fear and—"

How will he know when to stay home from school?

"But they'll come back, right? It's probably from the long seizure or the concussion, and once you've recovered—"

"M-m-maybe. It c-c-could be p-p-permanent."

"Oh God." *His secret won't be a secret anymore if he can't predict the seizures.*

"Nathan," I say softly, tears I can't contain rolling down my cheeks as I reach out and gently caress the less bruised side of his face. He leans into the touch and closes his eyes. I didn't think my heart could break any more, but somehow it does, and I struggle to hold back a sob. "This is all my fault. If I hadn't run away—"

"N-n-no!" He opens his eyes and fixes me with his gaze. "Don't s-s-say that. I w-w-would have s-s-saved you from those g-g-guys no m-m-matter what, and if this is the p-p-price, then I'll p-p-pay it.

"I l-l-love you, Holly. There's n-n-nothing m-m-more important than y-y-you."

My heart soars in my chest, but there are so many feelings, I don't know how to contain them. I lean forward—it takes Nathan a second, but as soon as he realizes what I want to do, he raises his head—and our lips meet in a soft, gentle kiss.

The lump in my throat is like a grapefruit, and tears sting my eyes, but Nathan just sighs. *His* guilt was absolved when I forgave him, but mine is painted in black and blue all over both of us, echoed in every slurred word he struggles to speak.

He pulls back and looks at me, but I can't hold his gaze for long.

"When will they let you go home?"

"I d-d-don't know." The frown returns, and he lies back again, closing his eyes. "The s-s-seizures are s-s-still too frequent, and they w-w-won't let m-m-me go until I don't n-n-need b-b-benzos to s-s-stop them.

"I'm t-t-tired," he mutters, and fear and guilt and sadness collide in my chest as I realize how much effort it took for him to have this conversation with me. He didn't ask about charges against anyone for the fight, and I have no idea if he even knows Evan was involved. His only concerns were to make sure I knew he loved me and that I was okay. *Fuck.*

I keep my epiphanies to myself and hope that he won't notice the strain in my voice.

"Why don't you sleep for a while? I have to go get my stitches checked, but I can come back after."

He opens his eyes but doesn't lift his head. "You'll come b-b-back?"

"Of course I will. I'll be here as much as I can."

"Okay," he answers as his eyes drift closed.

CHAPTER THIRTY-FOUR

The oldest and strongest emotion of mankind is fear, and the oldest and strongest kind of fear is fear of the unknown.

– H. P. Lovecraft

NATHAN

"Nathan Harris."

"And what day is it?"

I roll my eyes at the nurse and heave a frustrated sigh. I've had a few hours here and there where my head wasn't killing me, but now isn't one of them, and the pounding in my skull is making me really fucking irritable.

"Nathan?"

"Tuesday, F-f-february eighteenth."

"And where are you?"

"Do w-w-we have to do this?"

Mom raises an eyebrow. "Do you realize that two days ago you had trouble answering these questions?"

I stop to think for a minute, and Sunday is pretty hazy. Saturday I don't remember at all although Mom told me I was awake off and on—yesterday is the first day since Friday that I can honestly say I remember everything that happened. I think. *I guess I should shut up and answer her questions.*

"I'm in the hospital because some assholes b-b-beat me up, and I had a massive s-s-seizure."

"Good enough," the nurse says, nodding and giving me a smile, but I can't return it. Yesterday was all about seeing Holly and making sure she was okay, but today, I'm more than a little worried about *me*.

I can see a little bit out of my right eye, but it's still really swollen. I re-broke my hand on Sean's fucking face, but at least it wasn't *all* the bones, so my hand is only in a splint this time. My ribs ache, and my face and head are just one big throbbing center of pain, but I'm trying to resist asking for more meds because I know they'll make me sleepy. I'm exhausted even though all I've done is lie in bed since Friday—the seizures are knocking me out for hours at a time because they're causing so much neural activity. I've had eleven since the big one on Friday night, and five of them have been while I was sleeping. That's never happened before. And they're not stopping on their own. That's never happened before either.

But the worst part, the part that scares the hell out of me when I even think about it, let alone when it actually happens, is that the big seizures, the grand mals, now come without any warning. I haven't had a myoclonic seizure in more than two weeks, and although I never could have imagined a situation that would make me feel this way, I'd give anything to have them back. Having a big seizure sucks, but having a few hours' notice so I can stay home from school, make sure I'm somewhere safe and private when it happens? I never appreciated what a blessing that was until now.

Now all I'll have is ninety seconds of sheer terror to prepare for what's about to happen to me. I can hardly move in those precious few seconds, let alone get myself somewhere out of sight—*how the hell am I going to go back to school?*

The myoclonics will come back—they have to. Everything will go back to the way it was before.

~

Fingers are running through my hair, and I lift my chin to lean farther into the touch.

"Mom?"

"No . . ."

My eyes fly open—well, one does anyway—and Holly is sitting beside me, smirking. And just like that, everything is right in my world. She loves me, and she forgave me. I wish things hadn't gone down the way they did, but as long as she's mine again, I feel like I can survive the rest of it.

I glance at the window—it's getting dark outside. "What time is it?"

"Well, hello to you too." My cheeks heat as she teases me, and she grins even wider. "It's 6 p.m. Evan told me you had a seizure in your sleep this afternoon, so you've been out ever since."

"Shit," I mumble, closing my eyes. My headache is dull, but I can feel that not-quite-right sensation that lingers after a seizure. *When is this gonna stop?*

"Did they have to stop it with m-m-meds?"

"I don't know," Holly answers, frowning. "Is that important?"

"Yeah. S-s-seizures that stop on their own are my ticket out of here."

"I can go find out—"

"No, that's okay. I'll ask later," I tell her, not wanting to think about it anymore. Right now, what I really want is to do something normal, like

339

kiss the shit out of my newly re-girlfriended girlfriend, but there are a few things I have to do first.

I throw the covers back from the bed, and Holly covers her face with a gasp. *What the hell?* I laugh for the first time in days even though I have to wrap my arm around my chest to support my broken rib. *Ow!*

"Holly! I'm not *naked*."

She lowers her hands so I can see the color flooding her cheeks.

"I didn't *know*!" she exclaims, smacking my shoulder as if we were just goofing around like we used to in my room, and it's the best feeling in the world.

She looks like she's gonna apologize, but I shake my head a little. When she smiles, warmth spreads outward from my chest.

"What are you doing?"

"Well, I'd like to get up and use the bathroom, among other things."

I don't miss her glance at my left arm, and her brow furrows. "Are you allowed?"

I lift my arm to give her a better look. "Were you checking out my jewelry? The hospital was nice enough to add to my collection."

I'm wearing the standard white hospital ID bracelet, but my regular, very discreet medical bracelet has been replaced by a blue silicone band that says "Alert! Epilepsy" in red capital letters, and I'm also sporting a fluorescent yellow plastic one that says "Fall Risk." There's no hiding anything in here, and my arm looks like a fucking party.

She blushes again, and I love it. *God, I've missed just messing around with her.*

"If I yell for you, will you c-c-come help me?"

"Of course!"

Please don't let me have to yell for her to come help me.

"Well then, I can get up," I tell her, although in all honesty, I haven't done this without a nurse yet. *Oh well, there's always a first time for everything.*

I raise the head of the bed as much as I can and gingerly swing my legs over the side. My ribs protest, and everything spins for a minute, so I sit and make sure everything stays where it belongs before I try standing.

Once I'm on my feet, the rest is easy, but I stumble to a halt when Holly whistles behind me. I'm not naked, but I'm only in a hospital gown and boxers, and the breeze on my lower back tells me my ass is quite visible.

"Nice ass!" she calls, and I keep going and shut the door behind me. I want to be freshened up and back out there kissing her as fast as humanly possible.

I take care of business and put paste on my toothbrush, but I stop dead when I raise my eyes to my reflection. I haven't really looked at myself since I've been here. *Holy mother of . . .*

I knew my eye was swollen, but the bruising on my face is spectacular. My nose is taped, so I can't see the damage there, and the stitches above my eyebrow are black and ugly. The EEG monitor on my head makes me look like a freak—*exactly why the hell was I thinking Holly would want to kiss me?*

My semi-good mood takes a nosedive, and although I have no motivation now, I finish brushing my teeth and trudge back toward my bed with my head down.

"Nathan, what happened?"

She's on her feet and at my side in a flash, but all I want in this moment is to be alone.

"Holly, I—"

"What's that smell?" She moves closer and goes on her tip-toes, putting herself right in front of my face. "Did you just brush your teeth?"

"Yeah—"

"Can I kiss you?"

Her request floors me. Now that I know what I look like, my libido is cowering in a corner somewhere—I can't imagine why she'd want to put her lips on any part of me.

"Why? I look like someone should put me out of my misery."

Holly shakes her head slowly and gathers my hands in hers. She walks us backward until my knees hit the bed, and she waits patiently while I sit down with a pained grunt. She stands in front of me, and now that my face is easier to reach, she cradles my cheeks in her hands.

"You're my hero," she whispers, and she begins to brush her lips over where I now know there are bruises.

Her kisses are featherlight and cause me no pain, and the ache in my chest that began when I looked in the mirror starts to ease. A lump rises in my throat as I try to swallow down everything I'm feeling in this moment, and I realize a few tears have escaped when her lips press the wetness to my face.

"I love you, Nathan," she murmurs, and my arms slide around her waist as I pull her between my legs. My lips find hers and I kiss her—softly at first, but I can't hold back what I'm feeling, and soon, my tongue is tangled with hers, trying to tell her everything my fumbling words never could.

We kiss until my nose brushes hers and I wince, immediately sorry that my discomfort interrupted the best thing I've done since we made love all those weeks ago.

"I love you so much," I say, resting my forehead against hers. I want to thank her for making me feel this way, but I don't know how. Maybe she just knows. *God, I hope she does.*

Warm brown eyes meet mine, and I feel a stirring in my groin. It's the first time that country's been heard from in quite some time—I was worried I was a eunuch now.

But now's not the time—my head is starting to pound again, and my ribs are aching. I should probably lie down if I don't wanna have another fucking seizure.

"Are you okay?"

I wanna tell her yeah, but suddenly, I feel like shit.

"Headache," I say, and it seems I don't need to elaborate.

"Lie down," she says softly, and she lifts the blankets so I can slip my feet under them. Once I'm settled, she returns to the chair next to me and takes my hand.

We sit in silence for a few minutes, and my aching head takes my thoughts right back to my fucked up situation—*when the hell will I get to leave here, and what happens then?*

I sigh heavily, and Holly squeezes my hand.

"You *are* getting better, you know. Evan told me you only had one seizure last night and one so far today, and your speech is better than it was yesterday."

"It's not f-f-fast enough. And what am I g-g-going to do about school? Holy shit, what d-d-does everyone *think* happened to me?" It's the first time that thought's even occurred to me, and the realization sends a spike of anxiety down my spine—I'm still not thinking and processing things the way I should.

"Evan and I told them you had complications from a concussion. Your dad came up with it, and no one questioned it when we told them."

So my secret is still a secret. I should be overjoyed that my illness is still hidden, but instead, my chest starts to feel tight. The weight of lie upon lie feels like it's crushing me—*I almost wish . . .*

I gasp in shock as the realization nearly overwhelms me. *I almost wish everyone had found out, and I had no choice but to deal with it.*

I say nothing to Holly—I can't even wrap my own mind around what's going on up there, let alone explain it to her.

"Nathan?"

"Yeah?" I open my eyes, and she's looking at me warily.

"As soon as I told Ryan what happened and that you were still in the hospital, he asked if he could come see you. Lucy, Megan, and Justin said they wanted to come too."

I just stare at her as I think it over. I'd have to hide my epilepsy bracelet, but I could explain away the EEG monitor. As long as I didn't have a seizure right in front of them, there's no reason they'd have to know.

A part of me feels so weary at the thought of the lies I'll have to tell, but I ignore the nagging feeling. *After all, what choice do I have?*

"Nathan?"

"Um, yeah. I'd like to s-s-see everyone." *Shit! My speech is still a bit slurred. I'll have to explain that away too.*

"Are you sure?" Holly asks, eyeing me thoughtfully.

"Yes. I'll have to hide this,"—I gesture to my bracelet—"but I c-c-can explain the rest."

Holly's brow furrows for a moment, but while I'm trying to figure out why, her expression clears.

"Okay, I'll tell them they can come whenever you're ready," she says, but her smile isn't the one I'm used to. Something is off, but my head is pounding, and I'm too tired to try to figure it out right now. *I'll have to ask her later.*

Chapter Thirty-Five

NATHAN

This morning, there's a big meeting in my room. Mom and Dad, my neurologist, the orthopedist, the plastics guy, the speech therapist—pretty much everybody who's been working on putting me back together is there, and the news is pretty good.

My stitches will be coming out tomorrow, and I can lose the nose cast by the weekend. My rib is healing well, and my speech is improving every day. My hand will be splinted for at least six more weeks, but I'm not really surprised. I know I'm still not thinking as clearly as I did before, but I've passed the neurological exam for three days in a row now, so Dr. Sutton is happy with my progress. But the best news is that I had no seizures last night. The frequency is going down rapidly—now if they'd just stop on their own like they used to, I could go home.

"There's only one more thing we need to discuss, Nathan," Dr. Sutton says, but she's looking at my dad.

Dad nods and swallows like he's preparing for something, and my stomach drops like I'm on Goliath at Six Flags.

"I know you've asked the residents if the myoclonic seizures will ever come back, and the answer is we really don't know. But we know that if they do return, it won't be in the same pattern as before. The trauma and subsequent status epilepticus you experienced resulted in changes in your baseline EEG pattern. Changes in your brain's electrical activity are not necessarily a bad thing, but in this case, the changes mean you won't have the myoclonic seizures to warn you of a future tonic-clonic seizure."

I don't understand everything she said, but I'm pretty sure what she means is that my days of having a warning before the big seizures are over.

"So . . . no more warnings before the big s-s-seizures? Just the fear and then a minute or two later . . ."

"Yes, Nathan. Just the way it's been for you this week. You'll still have the aura, but you'll need to make some changes in your school seizure action plan—"

No more warning.

I'd known it was possible, and I thought I could handle it, but the words hit my chest like a cinder block.

Suddenly, there's no air and I'm gasping.

Panic coils around me like a python, squeezing my chest as cold sweat covers my body. My stomach cramps violently, but I couldn't vomit if I tried—my throat is completely closed.

"Nathan, you've got to breathe!"

Dad's voice is distant—soft compared to the roaring in my ears and the pounding of my heart.

"We're going to have to—"

Terror devours the panic, and I arch my back against the sudden change in sensation. Hands grip me, but all I can focus on is trying not to scream as the horrible overload pulls me into darkness.

The next morning, I wake slowly—sore and aching and devastated. For once, it takes me no time to figure out I had a seizure and what caused it. *What in the holy mother of fuck am I gonna do now?*

How can I go back to school? I don't have a lot of known triggers for my seizures, but stress is a huge one, and there's no way I could get within a mile of that building without losing my fucking mind with fear.

I could have a seizure at any moment; then everyone would know what a freak I am. I have no trouble picturing that scenario—me falling down in front of the whole student body, pissing myself if I'm really unlucky, and I can see what comes next even better.

Waking up surrounded by people who are now afraid of me.

Staring at me like I'm gonna fall down and convulse at any moment.

Tiptoeing around me because they can't treat me the way they used to—one wrong word or look, and I'll crumble before their eyes.

Fragile.

Weak.

Other.

Different. People avoid different because they don't understand it. The easiest thing to do is pretend it doesn't exist. Keep it over *there* where it can't interfere with their lives.

The weight of deceit is heavy, but the weight of judgment is so much worse. I've felt it already from those closest to me, and it changed me, broke down my ability to cope—I can't.

I just. Fucking. *Can't.*

My chest aches, and it has nothing to do with my broken rib. *There's no way out.* I'm too wrecked to even panic—that would take energy I just don't have.

I've fought so hard not to be Nathan the epileptic, but this illness clings to me like a second skin. I used to be able to obscure it in a cloak of lies, but now I'm naked, and everyone will see the real me— infected and afflicted with this disease that bends me to its will time and time again.

I hate it.

And I let that hate and self-loathing consume me.

Psych shows up, but I want nothing to do with that bullshit—deep breathing and visualization of my happy place is not gonna stop me from having a seizure in the middle of the fucking school, nor is it going to improve my mood right now.

Mom and Dad drift in and out, but I pretend to be asleep whenever they're in the room, and they leave me alone. By lunchtime, I think they're on to me—they leave right after my tray comes so I can try to eat in peace.

I have zero appetite, but the only way out of here is for my seizures to return to "normal," so I have to do everything possible to encourage that.

I choke down what I can, then buzz the nurse and ask for more pain meds. God knows they owe me some—I've been avoiding the narcotics all week so I could actually stay awake for a few hours. But right now, all I want to do is obliviate myself for as long as I can. Maybe this is all just one horrible nightmare that I'll wake up from if I try hard enough, if I want it bad enough. *A guy can hope, right?*

I curl in on myself and wish for nothing, wish for all of it to go away.

And it does . . . for a while.

When I wake, Evan is beside me, but I'm so low I can't bring myself to care.

"I thought you were gonna sleep the day away," he says, not glancing up from his phone.

"That's m-m-my plan, so fuck off." There's no heat in my words—they're flat and monotone.

"Can't do that. We need to talk."

"There's n-n-nothing to talk about. I'm screwed. There's no way out—"

"That's not true, and you know it. You need to tell your friends about your epilepsy, and you need to go back to school."

I sigh in exasperation, and when I open my eyes, he's leaning forward, staring me down. "I can't."

"What do you mean, you can't? Of course you can! It'll suck for a week or two, but then things will go back to normal."

I snort derisively. "Things will *never* go back to normal."

"Of course they will! You think everyone in that school cares that much about *you*? Once everyone knows, it'll be old news as soon as the next girl fucks and tells."

"Evan, you d-d-don't understand."

"What don't I understand? I think *you* don't understand what all this lying is doing to you. It almost lost you Holly, for Christ's sake, and you want to continue on with it? How the hell would you do it now anyway? You could have a seizure at any moment—how are you gonna lie your way out of that one?"

"I'm n-n-not! I *can't*! I told you I'm screwed! I d-d-don't know what the hell I'm going to do!" My mind spins the problem again and again, and I start to breathe faster. *There's no way out.*

"You're right. I don't understand. All I see right now is a coward who won't man up to his own problems."

Evan's words pierce me like knives, the pain cutting deep into my heart. Tears sting my eyes, and I have to gasp around the painful lump in my throat. But suddenly, it's as if a switch has flipped, and everything I'm feeling—the hurt from his words, all the pain and confusion and hopelessness—all of it turns to seething, white-hot anger.

And I explode.

"I am *not* a *coward*! I've faced these s-s-seizures for years, and you know *nothing* about it! The aura is terror like I've never known, and then I w-w-wake up wanting to cut off my own head and having to figure out what the fuck happened! Could *you* live with that again and again and *again*? I gave up b-b-basketball for this! And driving! And my b-b-best friends! I gave up *everything* I cared about until Holly came along, and I almost had to g-g-give her up too!

"Do you know what it's like to have people treat you like you're a time b-b-bomb? No, you fucking don't, and *you're* one of the people who d-d-did it to me! You and Mom made me so twitchy, now I have p-p-panic attacks! But I made it through all that! Could you, Evan? F-f-fuck . . ."

I trail off because there's no more air, and I'm startled when Evan grabs me by the shoulders.

"Breathe, Nathan. Holly's coming a little later—think about that. Focus on her face, and just breathe."

Evan's gaze is boring into me, but I close my eyes, and Holly appears. Evan rubs my shoulders, and it helps to ground me, but I pretend it's Holly soothing me. It takes a few minutes, but eventually, I calm down and sag against the mattress.

Evan sits down heavily and blows out a breath. "You're right. You're *not* a coward. You *did* do all those things, and you can do this too. Of the two of us, you're the stronger one. You amaze me because I know I could never handle this even half as well as you do. I would have crumbled long ago, but *you* don't. You keep going. That's how I know you can tell your friends about this and let them support you. I know, I *know* Ryan will be right by your side, and so will Lucy and the others. They won't let you down, and if you have them, then fuck the rest of the world. We'll help you—all of us.

"You're not only Holly's hero; you're mine too, and I want . . ." Ev pauses and looks down, and when he looks up again, there are tears shining in his eyes. "I want you to be happy, and . . . and I need to know you're gonna be okay when I'm not here next year."

His words deflate my anger, and I feel empty—exhausted and spent. Tears roll down my cheeks, and I don't even care.

"Ev, I . . . I really d-d-don't think I can," I whisper, curling on my side, and it feels as if my whole body is sagging under the weight of it all.

"You can, but you can't do it alone. Let. People. In. You let Holly in, and it was okay—it'll be the same for Ryan and Lucy and Megan and Justin. You need people you can count on now, and you're lucky that you have some.

"Now that you can have a seizure at any time with no warning, you're going to need to always have someone with you who can help. Holly and I can't be there every minute, but if you let the others in, they can be there for you when we can't."

He looks down, studying his hands, which are folded on the side of my bed.

"I can't even imagine how hard this is for you, but like I said, you're my hero, and I know you can do it. And I'm sorry for calling you a coward. I just wanted you to realize how strong you are, and I . . . I hope it worked."

I reach over and cover his hands with my splinted one. I don't say anything because I have nothing left, but I know he can see my forgiveness in my eyes because he smiles a little. I'm so tired, I pass out right away, but somewhere in my dreams, I hear, "Please let it have worked."

I don't get to sleep long. An hour later, some nurse comes and manhandles me, and my mind goes right back to the mess that is my life.

I'm just . . . tired.

I'm so fucking tired of being in a situation I can't control, and now it's more uncontrollable than ever.

I'm tired of trying to control it. Evan's right—the lies have taken their toll on everything I was, to the point that I don't even really *know* who I am anymore. All I am is a pile of lies, stacked like sandbags to protect myself from a flood that came anyway, and now the lies are useless. They can't protect me anymore, if they ever really could.

I'm terrified. The thought of everyone finding out makes my stomach roll, and I have no idea how to deal with it. But I really don't see how I have any choice. A huge part of me just wants to hide away from the world, but I can't let that part take control because I know I'll lose Holly too.

There's a tentative knock at my door, and a few seconds later, Holly peeks around it. Even though I feel as if I've been through a war today, her smile ignites a comforting warmth in my chest, and I feel a little bit better.

"Rough day?" she asks as she walks across the room and seats herself on the edge of my bed.

"Yeah," I answer, my voice breaking at the end, and her arms are around me, and she's pulling my head down onto her shoulder before I even realize she's doing it.

She's warm and so soft, and even though it hurts my ribs, I pull her close to me, soaking in all the comfort I can get.

"I'm sorry the little seizures aren't coming back," she whispers into my neck, and I completely fucking lose it, unable to contain what I'm feeling. Gently rubbing my back as I sob into her shoulder, she whispers, "I love you" and "It'll be okay" over and over until my sorrow is spent.

"I'm s-s-sorry," I say into her shirt, but she shakes her head.

"You've been through so much this week. I can't even imagine what you're feeling. But I'm glad you love me enough not to hide it from me," she says, and the sharp sting of my embarrassment for crying like a bitch fades away into nothing.

"I don't know how I'm going to d-d-do this."

"Well, you're not going to do it alone," she says, pulling away but only far enough so she can meet my eyes. "I made you a promise. You don't know about it because I never got the chance to tell you that night at the dance, but I promised you'd never be alone and afraid again. I can't control the afraid, but I can promise you'll never, *ever* be alone."

I curl back into her shoulder and hold her tight, unable to tell her with words how much that means to me—how much *she* means to me.

"I know you're afraid everyone is going to look at you like you're a bomb ready to explode, but I don't think that's true. Some will, but the people who really matter won't, and aren't those the important ones anyway?

"The loss of control you have to endure from the seizures breaks my heart, and you can't control how other people react to you, but you *can* control how *you* react to *them*. You can ignore anyone who's asshole enough to give you shit about this, and you can trust and rely on the people who care about you.

"Ryan and Lucy and Megan and Justin—they care about you. They're worried, and they've asked about you every day, and I keep putting them off, but they can tell something is seriously wrong. Let them in. Let them be the good friends to you that they truly want to be—let them show you what you mean to them.

"Start there, Nathan. If you let them in, they're going to stand by you if something happens when you go back to school. They're going to support you. I know it. You'll see."

"Holly, I'm s-s-so scared." It's the most honest thing I've ever said in my life, and I've never felt more vulnerable, but . . . it's okay because she loves me, and I can feel it in the way her arms tighten around me.

"I know you are, but you're also so very brave. Being brave doesn't mean you're not afraid, you know. It means going on *even though* you're afraid. That's what you did when you found out you had epilepsy, and that's what you did when I found out your secret. You go on, Nathan. It's who you are."

More tears escape down my cheeks, but they're not borne of desolation.

It's who I am. Maybe Holly sees me more clearly than I see myself.

"Can you ask Ryan and everyone to c-c-come tomorrow after school?" I'm still terrified, but Holly's right—I need to go on. Maybe it won't be so bad if I'm not alone.

"Really?"

"Yeah."

"What are you going to tell them?"

"Everything," I answer, even though my heart stutters in my chest. "Will you c-c-come too?"

"Of course I will!" Holly exclaims, pulling back to look at me. "I'm *so* proud of you, Nathan. I know you can do this, and you're going to feel so much better after you do."

"I hope so," I mutter as her lips brush mine, and I let go of everything but the sweetness of her kiss.

I really hope I can do this.

Chapter Thirty-Six

Do the thing you fear most and the death of fear is certain.

– Mark Twain

HOLLY

When I walk into Nathan's room the next afternoon, my eyes zero in on his face, and he's ashen, his breathing slow but deliberate, and he's clutching Julie's hand as if his life depends on it.

"Holly!" Julie greets me, but Nathan just gulps down a breath and closes his eyes—my arrival means everyone else will be here soon.

"Hi, Julie."

She smiles, but her eyes are watery and bright, and it nearly brings tears to my own. "Nathan? Why don't I give you and Holly a few moments? I'll go wait in the hall for your friends."

Nathan bites his lip, but he nods slowly, still not opening his eyes. His hand fists as soon as Julie lets it go, and even though he squeezes until his knuckles are white, he can't stop the tremors running down his arm.

Oh, baby.

I smile and nod at Julie, but as soon as she's clear, I grab that shaking hand and clutch it between my own, sitting as close to him as I can on the edge of his bed. He leans forward, and I pull him into my arms—he's shaking all over.

"Oh, Nathan—"

"I'mokay," he says in a rush. "I'mokayI'mokayI'mokay."

I hold him tighter. "You *are* okay. And you're *going to be* okay, I promise."

He nods against my shoulder.

"Did they give you anything for anxiety?"

He nods again. "As much as they could."

Christ.

My heart aches for him, and I want to ask him if he really wants to do this, but I know I can't. He *needs* to do this, and if I give him the out, he might take it, and then he'd have to go through this all over again some other day.

So I just hold him, rubbing his back in gentle circles while he shudders against me.

"Nathan, you're the bravest person I know. You're my hero for so many reasons, but this is the most important one. I'm so proud of you for facing your fear head on. You're amazing."

He snorts, and I feel his arms settle around me. "You make me sound like Superman just for barely holding my shit together."

"So? Maybe this *is* your super power: Super Nathan, the guy who holds his shit together."

Despite the hell I know he's in, Nathan laughs, and my heart soars. *God, I've missed that sound.*

Just then, Julie pokes her head in the door.

"Nathan, your friends are here," she says softly.

Nathan inhales sharply, and his arms and shoulders tense around me.

"I c-c-can't do this. I can't tell them, and they'll just stare at me . . ."

"What if someone else tells them, and then you can see them after?" Julie asks.

"I'll do it," I volunteer, smiling confidently at him. "I think they're more likely to ask me questions than your mom."

"Holly—"

"It gets the job done, Nathan. And you'll still have to face them after. It doesn't matter who says the words as long as they know the truth."

He nods, but he doesn't lift his gaze from his blanket. I've never seen him look so defeated.

"I'm not Super Nathan," he mutters, and although my heart twists in my chest, I still manage to get the words out.

"Oh yes. Yes, you are."

"I'll stay here with you while Holly talks to them," Julie says, rubbing her hand gently up and down Nathan's arm as she takes a seat beside him.

I reassure him as I head for the door. "It'll be fine. I promise. They're your friends, and they're gonna show you how much they care about you."

I turn and walk from the room, trying to gather my thoughts and figure out how I'm going to tell Ryan, Justin, Lucy, and Megan the news that will change their perception of Nathan forever.

Shit. This wasn't the plan, but if I can bear the brunt of their reactions and spare Nathan at least that much, I'll do it in a heartbeat.

They're clustered in the waiting room down the hall. Megan and Justin are sitting together on one of the little couches, holding hands. The Gothlet and Ryan are sitting on the other one, but Ryan's arms are crossed tightly, and there's a worried look on his face. Ryan's been

Nathan's friend since elementary school—he's going to take this the hardest.

When I walk in, they all look at me expectantly, but Ryan is the first to speak. "Something's wrong, isn't it? Why wouldn't Mrs. Harris let us go in to see Nathan?"

I take a deep breath. "We'll all go see him in a minute, but I have to tell you some things first. He's okay—well, mostly, but he's had a secret for a while now, and he thinks it's time you guys know."

"What is it, Holly?" Megan says nervously.

I take another deep breath to steady myself and then look at Ryan as I tell them. "Nathan has epilepsy. He was diagnosed the summer before freshman year."

In my periphery, I see Megan and The Gothlet both cover their mouths with their hands, and Justin drop his gaze to the floor, but Ryan doesn't move.

"That's why he misses school so much," Megan says, dazed.

"Is that why he quit basketball?" Justin asks.

I nod.

"When did *you* find out?" Ryan asks me through clenched teeth.

I close my eyes wearily. I knew Ryan wasn't going to take this well—for a lot of reasons.

"I found out before Nathan and I started dating. He didn't tell me—I happened to be with him during the first seizure he ever had at school. He didn't want anyone to know about this, so I kept his secret for him. He *still* doesn't want anyone to know, but . . . he doesn't really have a choice now."

"What made him decide to tell us now?" The Gothlet asks, and as she does, she covers Ryan's hand with her own.

Now comes the hard part . . .

"Because things have . . . changed. For the last three years, Nathan has always known ahead of time when he was going to have a seizure. There were warning signs, and he would always just stay home. But during the fight, he got a concussion, and after that, he had a really long seizure. Since then, his seizures have been out of control," I say tearfully, closing my eyes to try to keep myself from crying.

"What do you mean 'out of control'?" Justin asks gravely.

I sniffle a bit, but the thought that Nathan's counting on me to get through this helps me focus. "He used to have a seizure every two or three weeks, and he always knew about them ahead of time. Now, he's having them every day, he doesn't get a warning anymore, and they have to stop them with medication. That's why he's still in the hospital. The concussion threw everything out of balance somehow, and they don't know if everything will go back to the way it was or not.

"That's part of why he wants you guys to know. He won't be able to come back to school until he stops having seizures so often, and they're stopping on their own again. And there are other things you need to know before you see him too.

"He doesn't remember the fight at all, and he's not completely back to normal yet. He slurs some of his words when he talks, and he takes more time to think before he answers questions.

"Seizures can have a lot of triggers, but Nathan's biggest one is stress. He was really nervous about you guys knowing—about how you'd react. That's why I'm telling you and not him. He didn't think he could handle the stress of telling you, and his mom and I didn't think so either. So please, *please* try not to upset him when you see him. You can't imagine how hard this is for him after all the time he's kept it secret."

I look around the room, and all I see is sympathy and understanding, just as I expected. *I think they're ready.*

"Are you guys ready to go see him now?"

They all nod and stand up. I walk to the door but stop before going out into the hall. "I should also warn you he still looks pretty bad from the beating he took. I saw him the night it happened, so he actually looks a little better to me, but since you guys haven't seen him, it might be a bit of a shock."

Ryan and Justin nod, but the girls look at me wide-eyed. I hope they won't react, but honestly, it's hard for *me* not to react when I see him, and I've been coming here every day.

I walk in first, and Nathan looks at me tentatively. His mom has moved over to the couch, but he glances at her as if he wishes she were still sitting beside him. I grin at him warmly and nod, trying to reassure him it'll be all right.

His face falls as the others file in behind me, and I know without looking what I'll see on their faces. I wince as I walk over to stand beside him, but I grip his hand and turn to face them with him anyway.

Megan and The Gothlet's eyes are wide as saucers, and each has a hand over their mouth. Justin's lips are pursed into a tight line, and the skin around his eyes is scrunched angrily. Ryan . . . Ryan's eyes are pure sadness and shock, and as I gaze at him, he looks away.

"I look p-p-pretty bad, don't I?" Nathan asks uncomfortably. "I looked a few days ago, but I doubt it's g-g-gotten much better."

Megan recovers first, crossing the distance to his bed with a gentle smile on her face. "Nathan, I'm so sorry this happened to you."

He looks down. "It's okay. I'll heal up from the fight, and I've b-b-been having . . . s-s-seizures for years now, so I'm used to it."

"How are you feeling?" The Gothlet asks, coming forward to stand beside Megan.

"Tired. And I alm-m-most always have a headache. But I'm having fewer s-s-seizures and my sp-p-peech is much better."

The Gothlet raises her eyebrows, but instead of freaking out, Nathan takes it in stride.

"The first time I woke up after the big s-s-seizure, I couldn't talk at all. I knew what I wanted to s-s-say; I just couldn't figure out how to m-m-make the words."

"Damn." Justin shakes his head. "Was it scary?"

"Terrifying."

"Does it hurt? When you have a seizure?"

I flinch as Justin asks the question because I know it will make Nathan uncomfortable but also because I've never asked it. I think I've been afraid to.

Nathan looks down, but then he forces himself to meet Justin's eyes. "No, I'm not aware of it at all—well, I know right b-b-beforehand and then after, but during the s-s-seizure, I kind of black out, and then when I wake up, I'm p-p-pretty out of it and really sleepy."

Nathan's eyes scan the room, taking in everyone's reaction, I'm guessing, but his gaze lingers on Ryan, who's still standing by the door.

"Ryan?" Nathan asks, and I can hear the questions he's not asking.

Ryan closes his eyes and shakes his head slowly, clearly trying to hold his temper, and Nathan starts to shake a little bit. I start to walk toward Ryan to ask him to leave the room, but Nathan catches my arm and holds it.

Suddenly, Ryan fixes Nathan with a piercing look. "Why didn't you tell me? We've been friends our whole lives. I don't understand," he says, the hurt plain on his face as he looks away.

Nathan closes his eyes and takes a deep breath. "Ryan, I'm s-s-sorry. I didn't want anyone to know who didn't absolutely have to. It was easier to deal with when n-n-no one knew."

"But why? I could have helped you. I could have . . . understood. I could have *not* taken the mickey out of you when you quit playing basketball!" he exclaims, raising his voice.

Nathan remains calm, but I can see the pain in his eyes. "You would have treated m-m-me differently. I didn't want that."

"I wouldn't have." Ryan's tone mirrors the fierce look on his face.

"Yes, you would . . . you will. *Everyone* does," Nathan says vehemently. "Do you have any idea what it's like to have p-p-people watching you all the time, treating you like a fucking time bomb? Being careful what they do and s-s-say around you so they don't g-g-get you too upset? I've had to p-p-put up with that from my family for two and a half years n-n-now and from every teacher at school."

Everyone looks at him incredulously.

"Yeah, all the teachers know. They have to because if s-s-something happened at school, I'd be dependent on them to help me. I'm *always* dependent on s-s-someone, and it sucks. Now imagine if everyone knew about this. What do you think that would b-b-be like?"

Ryan looks down, but he's not ready to give up yet. "I'm not everyone."

"No, you're not, but after w-w-watching how everything changed after I was diagnosed, I decided I didn't w-w-want anyone else to know. At school, I c-c-could escape from it—I could feel *n-n-normal*, but at home, I had to deal with it. It was just easier this way."

"What will you do now? Holly said something changed, and you don't know ahead of time when you're going to have a seizure anymore," Megan asks. *Shit. Why does she have to be so perceptive?*

Nathan's jaw flexes, and he closes his eyes as he takes slow, even breaths. He takes his time to answer, but I'm so proud of him when he does.

"Well, I'm just g-g-going to have to take my chances now. Go back to s-s-school and hope for the best."

"How can we help?" Ryan asks, finally moving toward Nathan.

If it weren't such a serious moment, the look on Nathan's face would be comical. "You want to help?"

"Of course we do!" The Gothlet exclaims, taking Ryan's hand. "At least one of us is in class with you even when Holly isn't; we could help you if you need to leave the room. Or if something happens, and people are staring at you, I'll stab them with Ivan!"

The Gothlet's eyes have an eerie glow, and I'm so mesmerized by them I startle when I hear laughter—*Nathan's* laughter.

"I don't think that'll be necessary, Lucy, but thanks for offering to risk p-p-prison time for me."

Lucy just grins sweetly, dropping her chin to her chest and looking through her eyelashes as she winks at him. *God, that girl is so damn scary!*

"Who's Ivan?" I hear Justin whisper to Megan, and I can't contain my snort as she shushes him. I'm sure she'll tell him all about Lucy's pet switchblade later.

"But seriously, Nathan. We'd really like to help," Megan says, putting her hand on his forearm.

Nathan closes his eyes, but instead of freaking out, he takes a deep breath and covers Megan's hand with his own.

"Okay."

I'm so proud of him in this moment, I think I might burst.

After that, the tension seems to dissolve, and everyone starts chatting as if we're not in a hospital room. Nathan even manages to smile a few times when The Gothlet teases him about all those "vacation days" he's taken.

Suddenly, I hear Nathan suck in a ragged breath, and his arm tenses under my hand. His eyes are closed—and he begins to tremble. The room goes silent, but I can hear an alarm sounding down the hallway. Everyone's eyes are drawn to Nathan.

"Seizure?" I whisper softly to him, and he nods jerkily in response.

"Julie?" I say a little louder, and I lift my hand from Nathan's arm to step back.

"S-s-stay." He reaches a shaking hand out for me.

"I'm right here. I'll stay," I tell him, moving back to the side of the bed and taking his hand in mine.

Julie squeezes my shoulder. "Are you okay to stay with him while I see everyone out? The nurse will be here in just a minute."

I nod, my eyes widening a little. I look over at my friends and see the fear and pity on their faces, and that's enough to snap me out of it.

"We'll be fine," I tell Julie confidently.

"Guys, I'll talk to you tomorrow."

As Julie shepherds them out, I turn my attention back to Nathan. His eyes are still closed—I guess that's so our friends wouldn't see the terror there as I did that day in the classroom. That or it's his way of wishing them away since I'm sure he's not ready for them to see this. He lays his head back against his pillow, and I rub his hand gently between mine.

A nurse bustles into the room about ten seconds later and lowers Nathan's bed so he's lying flat. Then Nathan goes rigid for a few seconds and starts to convulse. "Stand back," the nurse says gently, but I realize as I bump into the wall that I was already backing away. I shake myself and step closer again, forcing myself to watch. It's heartbreaking to see Nathan's body so out of his control, but since his seizures no longer come with a warning, I need to know how to handle this.

I want to ask the nurse questions, but I hold my breath for most of the almost five minutes that Nathan shakes, and when he begins gasping for breath, so do I. The nurse moves next to him and gently rolls him onto his side, tucking one hand under his cheek and lifting his chin. She bends one of his legs over the other so his weight keeps him on his side.

"Is that what you're supposed to do for him?" I whisper, and she looks over at me kindly.

"Yes, honey. Let him be during the seizure unless you need to stop his head from hitting something. Then afterward, position him like this to recover, and make sure he's breathing. This is the best way to keep his airway open."

I nod slowly.

"You can touch him now. He'll probably wake up in a few minutes, but he'll be a bit confused. Just reassure him, and buzz me if you need anything," she says as she turns to leave the room.

I walk slowly over to him and run my hand over his copper-brown hair. He looks so . . . peaceful after all the violence I just witnessed. It's hard to reconcile that something so scary-looking can happen to him, and then he can lie here like a little boy, curled up in sleep. I run my hand over his hair again. This time his eyes open, and I stroke his forehead softly. His eyes meet mine but with no recognition, so I continue stroking and whisper to him that everything's okay, and he's safe. After a moment, he closes his eyes again, but I continue, and I feel him angle his head into my hand.

We stay like that for a few moments, and the next time he opens his eyes, I can tell he recognizes me because a lazy smile spreads across his face. "Hey there."

"Hey," he whispers, blinking slowly.

I can't help but smile at him. I missed him so much over the last few weeks, and I'm so happy to have him back. "How are you feeling?"

"Fine . . . I think . . ." he answers, his eyes drooping closed. Suddenly, they pop open again. "I'm s-s-sorry, Holly. What were we talking about? I'm so tired . . ."

"Just rest, Nathan. We weren't talking about anything important. You had a seizure a few minutes ago—that's why you're tired."

"I did?"

"Yes, you did. But everything's fine now, and I'll stay with you. Why don't you try to sleep for a bit?"

"Okay," he mumbles as his eyes again drift shut. I breathe a sigh of relief, not realizing until then that I've been tense, waiting for Nathan to act normally.

"You did it, Super Nathan," I whisper, leaning down to kiss his cheek, and he smiles in his sleep as if he heard me.

Chapter Thirty-Seven

Honesty is the highest form of intimacy.

– Anonymous

NATHAN

When I woke up late Friday night and put the pieces together, I felt better than I have in a long time. Making the decision to tell my friends about my epilepsy was the hardest thing I've ever done, but actually telling them was easier than I thought it would be. Yeah, yeah, I know I wussed out, and Holly told them, but I still faced them afterward and answered their questions, and I feel . . . okay with them knowing, somehow. It's as if the burden of all this is lighter, and I'm not facing it alone. I'm still scared shit-less to go to school, but *one thing at a time, Harris. Baby steps.*

The other good thing about Friday was that the seizure I had in front of Holly stopped without them having to give me medication, and so did the one the next day and the one on Sunday night. The reduced frequency of the seizures and the fact that they're stopping on their own now means I can finally go home.

Holly hangs out with me at the hospital all weekend, when I'm not zonked out from seizures and headaches, that is, and when she texts me on Monday afternoon, I'm more than ready for some time with her. I had a raging hard-on this morning that was more than a little difficult to hide from the nurses, and just thinking of Holly coming over and getting a little alone time with her is making my dick feel like it belongs in the Macy's Thanksgiving Day Parade—thank *God* that long seizure didn't break my dick. I can handle a lot, but permanent limp dick would just break me.

Holly: *Nathan?*

Oh, right. I was texting Holly.

Nathan: *Come over.*

Holly: *You mean to the hospital?*

Nathan: *No, I mean come OVER TO MY HOUSE.*

I can't help my smirk as I shouty-cap text her, and her response doesn't disappoint.

Holly: *No. Freaking. WAY!!*

Nathan: *Yup, they sprung me this morning. I've been lying here on my bed waiting for you.*

Holly: *Five minutes.*

I chuckle as I put my phone down, and Mom raises an eyebrow.

"Holly's coming over," I tell her, and she just smiles. There's nothing more that needs to be said. Since Holly and Evan good cop/bad copped me into telling Ryan and the rest of our friends, Holly can do no wrong in my parents' eyes—particularly my mother's. Maybe she'll even give us that alone time without me having to get whiny about it.

My mind drifts, and I jump when someone touches my arm.

"Nathan?"

Focus, Harris. "I'm s-s-sorry, Holly. I must have fallen asleep waiting for you."

I shake my head to clear it, which is a mistake because it still hurts, and that makes it worse, but I manage to get my bearings.

Door closed? *Check.*

Mom gone? *Check.*

Gorgeous girl in my bed? *Check and mate . . . well, at least I hope to in a little while.*

I pull Holly down to lie on my shoulder, and she snuggles into my side as if that spot were made just for her. *God, this is perfect.*

I let out a contented sigh, and Holly's fingers find their way to my chest.

"Happy to be home?"

"More than you'll ever know." And I wonder if she knows I mean her arms and not my house.

"Can you come back to school now?"

This sigh is a bit less contented. "No, not yet. My neuro wants to see how I do managing the s-s-seizures at home first, and I'm pretty sure I'm still too worn out from last week to stay awake through a full day of classes."

I hate to admit it even to myself because it makes me feel weak, but I'm still exhausted—I fell asleep twice today while Mom was talking to me.

"I bet you'll be ready by next week," Holly says as her fingers part my button-down and begin to wander up and down my chest.

"Probably." I say it as normally as I can, but something tips her off to my growing anxiety because she lifts her head and those warm, brown eyes damn near swallow me whole.

"You're going to be fine. I'm sure of it. Evan, Ryan, me, and everyone else will be there for you. Whatever we need to do, we'll do it."

I close my eyes as my chest tightens, but instead of pushing me, Holly snuggles back into my shoulder, her fingers making soothing circles on my pecs until I feel like I can breathe again. I'm still all sorts of fucked up over what I'm about to tell her, partly because it didn't even occur to me, which tells me my brain function still isn't back to normal yet, but mostly because it's the biggest loss of freedom this damn disease has ever imposed on me.

"Holly, I . . . I can't be alone anymore. Ever. Since I can't predict the s-s-seizures now, someone always has to be with me, in case . . ."

I trail off because I can't say the words, but Holly doesn't need me to say them. She holds me as close as she can, and we lie like that until my muscles slowly relax. I'm nearly asleep when she whispers, "I'm so sorry, Nathan," into my shoulder. She knows what it means to me, but I'm calm now—I'll have plenty of time to work through it some more later.

"You know . . ." Holly says with such a pregnant pause that I shift my chin to meet her mischievous grin. "Not being alone could work to our advantage. Like, 'Dad, I need to stay with Nathan after school to do homework,' or 'Dad, Nathan's parents are busy, so I need to stay with him today.' He already thinks you're awesome because you defended me. I'm *sure* we can get some mileage out of this after everything that's happened."

Huh, I hadn't thought of that.

"Contemplating the possibilities, pervy boy?"

My cheeks warm, but it's not really out of embarrassment—I love when she teases me. And speaking of mileage, I'd like to add a spin around the bed to ours right now.

"Maybe," I answer, giving her my most charming grin. "We're alone, and I feel like I could use some exercise after lying around the hospital for so long."

Holly gives me a blank stare for a few seconds, but when she catches on, her smile makes my stomach do a somersault.

"Exercise, huh? A run around the yard, perhaps?" She blinks at me innocently, but I swallow hard as her hand brushes over Rockhard McEagerdick, who's currently trying to poke a hole in my pants.

"Um . . . I was thinking—"

"You think too much," Holly says just before her lips crash into mine, and witty makes a hasty exit so horny can take over every single cell in my brain.

It takes me a second to catch up, but then her tongue swipes against my lip, and I swear I feel it all the way down in my balls. I open to her hungrily, and the heat that flares and spreads through my chest is like drinking Fireball straight from the bottle but so much better.

She's half on top of me already, but I grasp her thigh and pull, desperate to get her closer to where I need her. Her leg rubs over my dick, and I can't help but moan into her mouth—I don't think it's ever felt this good.

Her lips are still devouring mine, but she flexes her hips to perfectly repeat the motion that just made me see stars, and I feel her smile against my mouth as I moan shamelessly, completely at her mercy. *God, I love a woman who can multitask.*

We kiss and she rubs, and I'm just about to lose my mind *and* my jizz when she suddenly breaks away from my lips.

"Dammit!" She all but yells, and I nearly weep at the loss of my new overlord, the Thighmaster, but it allows me to realize she's been trying to get my shirt off with one hand, and I didn't even notice. *Apparently, I'm the one who can't multitask.*

"Stupid buttons!"

She's on her side now, and both hands make quick work of opening my shirt, my abs quivering as she gently brushes against my skin.

"I need you."

I was already on fire, but those words take me to another place, deeper than lust and so much more important. "I need you too," I tell her, and as I cup her cheek, she's unbuttoning her blouse, her eyes never leaving mine.

I'm so aroused, I feel like I'm gonna explode, and we still have our clothes on. *Calm down, Super Nathan. You're the guy who holds his shit together, remember?*

I feel like I could just burst out of my clothes like The Hulk, but that's not gonna happen—in fact, I can't even wiggle out of them because of my broken rib. *Dammit, can't I have a little time outside of reality?*

With a final caress of her cheek, I gently roll away from her, hissing in pain as I push myself up to sit on the side of the bed. I can hear her moving closer behind me, but I stand up before she can reach me, wanting to get naked and back to touching her as soon as possible.

I turn to face her, and she's kneeling on the edge of the bed, topless. *Lord, have mercy!* my dick cries out, straining against my shorts with all his might. *Down, boy! I'm getting there!*

Holly gasps as I shrug my shirt off, and I'm surprised by the horrified look on her face. For a second, I'm worried I've grown a third nipple or some shit, but when she extends her hand, I realize she's staring at the still-dark bruising on my side where those assholes kicked me.

Tears well in her eyes, and I can feel the mood slipping away, but I can't let it—not like this.

I close the distance between us and cup her face in my hands. "Holly, please, *please* just let it go. The b-b-bruises will heal, and I just want . . . I want *you*, and I don't wanna think about any of that today. I want . . ."

I don't have the words, so I pull her even closer to me and do my best to tell her with my lips. The kiss is wet at first from Holly's tears, but she calms quickly, and I know we're right back where we were when her hand slips down and squeezes my ass.

My hands slide into her hair as my tongue explores, and fireworks explode everywhere except where I want them to—out of the tip of my dick. *Her* hands make short work of my shorts and boxers, and I nearly lose it when she grabs me, and her stroke feels like a vise grip from root to tip.

"*Christ.*" I pull back before she can do it again—way too close and yet too far away all at the same time. *I need . . . I want . . .* I want to eat her pussy, suck on her nipples, and fuck her into oblivion, but since I can't do all that at once, my warring desires grind my brain to a halt. But there's one thing every part of me can agree on: *Holly's still wearing too many clothes.*

Ooo . . . north or south? She has no notion of the pivotal debate taking place in my head.

Those gorgeous, perfect tits win out, and I sample one of her nipples right through her bra while I reach behind her back to release the boobsy twins. I expect her to moan as her nipple peaks between my teeth, but the whimper I hear is actually my own as my groin tightens and releases a fresh wave of heady pleasure.

"Yes, Nathan!"

The words fall from her lips as she arches her back, and suddenly, I've got a whole mouthful of soft flesh to suck on as I knead the other one with my fingers.

Her hands skim down my back, making me shiver and trying to draw my focus away from Tit-topia, but I won't be deterred. I switch sides and suck her other nipple into my mouth as I clutch her to me with both hands.

I work her up with my teeth and tongue until she's writhing against me and trying to furrow her hands between us to get at my dick. But I don't want a handjob. I want to be inside of her again, like I should have been all these months. I want to make love to her.

I grasp her hands as I release my favorite tit, and although we're both panting for breath, when she meets my eyes, she seems to understand. She sits back and slides off the underwear that are pooled around her knees —*how the hell did those get there*—and scoots backward up the bed until her head is resting on my pillow.

With a seductive smile, she spreads her legs for me . . . and I completely lose any sense I ever had. *My God . . . my bed . . . hair eyes tits naked, she . . . she . . .*

"Mmm-beh," is my intelligent response to the perfection laid out before me because language is a skill for those with brain cells, and all mine just went supernova.

She blushes in places I didn't know she could blush, and her soft giggle makes me feel weak in the knees.

"Come here, Super Nathan," she whispers, and as I'm moving to hover over her, her eyes stray from mine to the new black watch I'm wearing just above my med alert bracelet.

"I can't take it off," I tell her, and as her eyebrows furrow, I realize just how much I *don't* wanna talk about this right now.

"Wha—"

"Later." I snap at her, but I feel like shit when I see the hurt in her eyes. "I promise," I say more gently, caressing her cheek with my hand and, once more, taking in the stunning view below and in front of me.

"So beautiful."

Holly's smile is brilliant, and she lets it go, like she always does, and her gaze snaps back to mine.

It's time.

My balls are tingling, my heart is racing, and when the tip of my dick brushes against so much warm softness, I have to force myself to breathe so I don't pass out or go off.

"Make love to me," Holly whispers, and I push forward slowly, biting my lip and scrunching my eyes closed.

God, so warm and so fucking tight.

By the time I'm all the way in, I'm panting, and Holly's soft moan does nothing to help me maintain any sort of composure—I'm seconds from exploding and becoming a card-carrying member of the one-thrust club.

"Oh *fuck*—"

"Nathan?"

"I just . . . I need a . . ."

Her hand cups my cheek, so I focus on that as my breathing slows, and my dick backs away from three seconds to midnight. *Sometimes, I think she can read my mind.*

I open my eyes, and she's smiling up at me, waiting patiently for Super Nathan to get a grip on his shit, and I know, I *know* in that moment— she's it for me. She's all I'll ever need.

"What?"

I answer her by pulling out and pushing slowly back in, and the look of bliss on her face makes me feel giddy inside. *I made her feel like that.*

The urge to move is overwhelming, so I do, but I can't hold in my wince as my side pinches and starts to ache.

Goddamnmotherfuckingsonofabitch! Why can't I just—

"That hurts, doesn't it?"

I'm in full-on toddler-pout mode in under a second, and I have no idea what might come out of my mouth, so I nod with my lips tightly closed.

My dick is having an epic shit fit, and I'm so busy trying to control the disappointment in both my heads that for a second, I forget about Holly entirely.

"Nathan!"

"Yeah?"

She looks concerned, but somehow she's smirking at the same time. "Stop feeling bad about it, and come back to me. I want to try something."

We can't make love, but she wants to try *something? What in the holy mother of—*

"Nathan." This time she grabs my chin. "Trust me."

As far as I'm concerned, this can't get any worse.

"Okay."

"Good. Now, get up and then lie back down right where I am."

I'll do as she says, but if it's cuddle time, I swear I'm gonna cry.

I lie down, spread out like a starfish because I'm pissed off and grumpy, but instead of curling up beside me, she kneels between my legs.

My dick is at half-mast, but she takes care of that by stroking me until my legs are quivering, and my hands are fisted in the sheets.

"Now, put your legs together."

She straddles me, and it's not until she lifts up that I finally get a clue.

Oh. *Oh.*

My dick hardens to a steel rod, but as she lowers herself down on me, I feel like I'm melting.

"Is this okay?"

Pork chops are okay. Reading a book is okay. This? This is fucking *divine.*

"So much better than okay," I say, and her grin is impish.

"Let's try some more, then."

She lifts up slowly, but she comes down harder and faster this time, and I think I see my brain as my eyes roll back in my head.

"Oh, ssshhhit . . ."

The next time, she leans forward a bit, and on her way down, I thrust up to meet her. It's her turn to moan and swear this time, and when she rolls her head back, I'm struck dumb by how amazingly beautiful she is in this moment.

It doesn't last, though, because suddenly her eyes meet mine with a hunger in them I've never seen. She leans forward like before, but this time when she goes there and back again, she doesn't stop.

My upward thrust to meet her is automatic, and the jolt of pleasure is unbelievable. I try to look down to make sure everything's still intact, but my eyes never make it past Holly's glorious tits, which are swaying and bouncing *right in front of my face.*

Oh, *wow.*

No one ever told me there was a sideshow when a girl rode you. This must be the best-kept secret in all of sexual experience. Evan is gonna get smacked upside the head for—

"Ohhhh, fuuuuck . . ."

My hands are full of spectacular tits, my dick is molten heat and fan-fucking-tastic pressure, and my balls are so damn tight, I can't believe I haven't blown a hole in my bed yet.

But then her eyes meet mine, and it all becomes something . . . more. She's sweaty and panting, but her eyes are steady, boring into mine and telling me with every roll and rock of her hips that she's mine and no one else's. That this moment is mine and only for me.

"I love you." I'm desperate to hold my shit together for a few more moments so I can touch and feel and breathe her in before this part is over, and I get a slice of heaven before coming back to earth.

"I love you too," she whispers, then she drops her hips so she's bucking against my pelvic bone with every roll.

"Oh . . . Nathan . . . I'm . . ."

Her walls squeeze me and then flutter, and *oh fuck, I have to thrust, it's so fucking good I'm so full I have to—*

"Ohh . . . ohh . . . ohh . . . ohh . . ."

I moan with every pulse of my dick, and it seems to go on forever until, finally, I'm exhausted and spent as I shake and shiver with the aftershocks.

Holly's here somewhere, right?

I open my eyes, and she's spread out on the uninjured side of my still-heaving chest, a mass of flowing chestnut hair and warm, soft, perfect *everything.* My hands are drawn to her, and when I start to gently tickle up and down her back, she lifts her head and looks so content that it seems to seep from her right into me. And at that moment, I realize . . . she's truly in this for the long haul. Whatever happens, no matter how badly things go at school or if my seizures get worse—she'll be here.

And that's all that matters.

I pull her down and cuddle her into my shoulder, away from my eyes so she won't see the wetness there, and when I squeeze her against me, we both sigh.

No words need to be said. I could tell her how fantastically amazing that was, but the words don't seem adequate, and I *know* I have no words for the revelation I just had. I squeeze her against my side again, and she hums another soft sigh. She pulls the sheet over us and we lie that way until we're both languid and dozy.

My hand is nestled under her arm, and I've been playing with her boob for a few minutes already when she runs her fingers over my watch. She's asking without asking . . . *Fuck, I might as well get this over with.*

"That was a parting gift from the hospital—the latest in epilepsy tech. It detects repetitive shaking motion, like when I have a s-s-seizure, and it sends a signal to my phone to text and call Mom, Dad, and Evan and give them my location. That way, they can come help m-m-me if I happen to be alone somewhere."

Holly raises her head to look at me.

"Wow. That's amazing! Why didn't you have one of these before?"

I shrug sullenly. "I didn't need one before."

Holly's face falls for a second, but she huffs out a breath, and her smile returns.

"What else can it do?"

Her fascination with it makes me chuckle for some reason, and for the first time since I put it on this morning, the thing doesn't seem like such a damn burden.

"Well, it has a button, right here, that I can press to call for help if I n-n-need it, and it also records all this data during a s-s-seizure like heart rate, duration, s-s-severity, and it sends it to my doctor through my phone."

"Daaamn," Holly says, eyes wide. "It's like you're Tony Stark or something."

I laugh out loud until my side starts to hurt, and she sits up and just watches me over her shoulder, the sheet clutched under her arms to cover her breasts.

I can tell she's missed this. Missed *me*.

The warmth that spreads through me has nothing to do with my dick for once.

"So, I really am Super Nathan now?" I ask as I pull myself up to lean against the headboard.

"Absolutely!" Holly exclaims as she lifts my wrist again. "I always knew that's who you were!"

She studies the watch for another moment, and when she meets my gaze this time, she's turned serious.

"Um . . . can you set your watch to contact whoever you want when you have a seizure?"

"Yeah, it'll text half the town if I want it to," I say sarcastically, unable to look at her.

"Not half the town . . . how about . . . just . . . me?"

Oh.

My gaze shoots back to her, my mouth dropping open in shock and wonder and a few other feelings I don't have a name for.

"You want to be notified when I have a s-s-seizure?"

I know she and the others said they would help, but I've been avoiding thinking that through to its logical conclusion for obvious reasons.

"Yes. I want to know whenever you have one, but . . . I also helped you on Friday at the hospital. The nurse taught me what to do, and I could help you again if you needed me to . . . at school or wherever else, if that's what you want."

This girl.

My heart.

"You would really do that?" I ask, unable to keep the quaver out of my voice or the sting from my eyes.

"I love you, Nathan! Of course I would!"

I gather her into my arms and just hold her there, too choked up to speak and too emotional to think about anything but how much I love her.

"I promised you'd never be alone, and this is part of that. Will you let me help you?"

I nod into her shoulder because I've truly lost my shit over this, and for once in my life, it's a *good* thing. A very, very good thing.

CHAPTER THIRTY-EIGHT

There is no illusion greater than fear.

– Lao Tzu, *Tao Teh Ching*

HOLLY

I startle awake in the middle of the night, and I have no idea why. I lay there for a few seconds, and I'm almost back to sleep when my phone buzzes against my nightstand.

*That must have been what woke me up. Who the hell is texting me at—*I pick up my phone—*three-sixteen in the morning?*

And then I see the alert bar at the top.

NATHAN: ABNORMAL MOTION START: WED, FEBRUARY 26 3:15 AM

It takes me a moment, then understanding washes over me in a chilling wave.

Holy shit, Nathan's having a seizure.

Right now.

I bolt upright and click on the banner, which opens my messages and shows the full text including a Google maps link that I click on with shaking fingers. The pin falls in the middle of nowhere, but when I zoom out, I can see the River Loop, so I know he's at his house.

I sit frozen, tears rolling down my cheeks as the memory of Nathan seizing in his hospital bed plays on repeat in my head. I want to call—him, Evan, his parents, 911—anyone, so I can feel like I'm doing something to help him.

I nearly drop my phone when it buzzes again.

NATHAN: ABNORMAL MOTION END: WED, FEBRUARY 26 3:18 AM

Now I'm wondering if he's woken up yet and who's with him. Does he even really wake up when he has a seizure at night? I'll have to ask him.

I sit with my knees drawn tight to my chest, my head and my heart ten miles away, but unfortunately, my eyes and the rest of me are right here, so I have no idea what's going on. My thoughts chase each other in ever-tightening circles—I know there won't be any more sleep for me tonight until I know he's okay. It's another five minutes of mental-anguish gymnastics until I can't take it anymore.

I'll text. I'll send Evan one text just to make sure everything's okay.

Holly: *Is Nathan all right?*

I'm three seconds from calling when Evan's text comes through.

Evan: *Holly? What the hell are you doing up?*

Holly: *I'm on Nathan's alert list, and I woke up when I got the alert. Is he all right?*

Evan: *Oh, gotcha. Yeah, he's fine. He's asleep now, actually. He's the ONLY one in the house who is. That alert system works pretty well.*

I laugh as all my tension rolls away, along with a few tears down my cheeks.

Holly: *Thanks, Evan. I'll see you tomorrow.*

I flop back on my bed, exhausted and relieved and so freaking happy just to know what's going on. For the first time, I feel as if everything between Nathan and me is completely open, and I fall asleep with a smile on my face.

～

On Wednesday afternoon, everyone comes to my house, and we spend a couple of hours learning all about epilepsy.

We watch YouTube videos. We learn the steps for putting someone in the seizure recovery position, and we practice on each other until all of us can do it without hesitation. We add Nathan, Evan, Nathan's parents, and each other's numbers to our phones if they weren't already there, so any one of us can reach any of the others for help. And when we're done, I feel like I have some power to combat what epilepsy does to Nathan. I can't stop it, but I can make sure he's never alone, and the ability to keep my promise to him makes me feel ten feet tall.

Nathan never mentions his impending return to school, and I don't bring it up either—I'm pretty sure he's intentionally blocking it out to keep himself from agonizing over it all week. We have a good plan, but the closer Monday gets, the more I see him fidgeting and zoning out. I bring him back with my words, and sometimes my lips, but I can tell his fears are weighing on him.

Saturday morning, my phone goes off with a seizure alert from Nathan, and although my heart aches for him, he hasn't had one since the early morning one on Wednesday, and that's the longest he's gone without a seizure since everything changed. Evan texts me as soon as it's over to let me know Nathan's okay and resting, and I raise my eyes and thank God that Nathan was given such an amazing brother.

Sunday is hell.

Nathan woke late Saturday night, an anxious, restless mess, so Dr. Harris gave him a sleeping pill that knocked him out until midday.

When I finally make it there Sunday afternoon, I find him curled up in his bed, but the shiver that rolls down his back as I watch him tells me he's far from sleep. I close the door, turn the lock, and slip off my shoes, and although I'm sure he hears, he doesn't move until I crawl into bed behind him, and then his only acknowledgement is to pull my arm around him and hug it tight to his chest.

I hold on and just breathe him in for a few minutes. There are a million things I could say, but none of them will help, so I whisper the only thing I can offer.

"I'm here."

Nathan pulls me tighter against him.

"I know."

I bite my lip to keep the tears at bay—there's so much in those two words: *I'm scared. I'm frustrated. I'm hurting. I'm glad you're here. Thank you.* I hear it all and more, and I can't do anything to comfort him. Not really anyway.

"Does your head hurt?"

He nods slowly but doesn't offer any more.

We lie in silence for a while longer, both lost in pain and helplessness— together yet alone because I can't even fathom what he's feeling as he faces his biggest fear.

"I know there's nothing I can say to make this any easier, but I'm so proud of you for what you're doing. I know you're scared, but you're doing it anyway because you're not willing to give up your life to epilepsy.

"You really are my hero, Nathan, and I love you so much."

I can't hold the tears back anymore, and when he turns to face me, the first thing he does is wipe them from my cheeks.

His eyes are wet and glassy, and when he brushes my hair behind my ear, a few of his own tears escape.

"I love you so much too. It means a lot to me that you're here. That you've *been* here every day since the fight. I'm so sorry I ever lied to you about anything."

I look into his eyes and see the sincerity there, and I feel like a fool for not seeing it sooner—for not realizing that it didn't matter. Not after everything else we shared.

But we can't go back. He can't take back the lie any more than I can take back running away from him, so we both need to let it all go and not look back.

"It's in the past, Nathan. You can't change it any more than I can change what happened in the gym and everything that came after. We've forgiven each other. Now we have to find a way to let go and move forward. And honestly? I think we already have."

He smiles and my heart flutters.

He's gonna make it through this. We'll make it through this together.

His nerves seem to have settled a bit, but as I look away from him, mine are just starting. I need to tell him what Evan and I have done, but I don't know how he'll respond—I hope it'll be a comfort and not another burden he has to bear.

A gentle finger guides my chin back to him.

"What is it?"

"I . . . well, Evan and I . . . Do you remember last week when Ryan and everyone said they wanted to help?"

Nathan nods, but his smile fades.

"Well, I know you'll need people around you at school who know how to help you if . . . if you have a seizure, and Evan and I can't always be with you."

Nathan swallows hard and closes his eyes, and I can feel his muscles tense. *Out with it, Holly! He's anxious enough as it is!*

I take a deep breath and spit it out in one go. "Evan and I taught Ryan, Lucy, Justin, and Megan how to put someone in the seizure recovery position this week, and we all added Evan's and your parents' numbers to our phones so no matter who's with you, we can all help you or get more help if you need it."

My own eyes have closed, and my chin has dropped as I spoke, and Nathan's silence is making me feel sicker by the second.

He's upset. This was the wrong thing to do, and I've made it worse. Dammit, Holly! Why are you so stupid!

"I'm sorry, I thought—"

"Stop."

He nudges my chin up, and when I try to drop it again, he enfolds my cheeks in his hands. I can't help but meet his eyes, and what I see there dazes me for a moment. He's . . . happy. His lips are curled in a small smile, but his eyes tell me so much more. He's looking at me so tenderly—I can't help but take a gasping breath.

"You did that . . . for me?"

"Well . . . yeah. I want you to feel as safe as possible, and so does everyone else."

"And they were willing?"

"Nathan, they were eager! We all feel so helpless—I thought this was something we could do to make you feel less alone. I'm sorry if I—"

"I do," Nathan says. His smile grows wider, but I'm just more confused.

"You do . . . what?"

"I do feel less alone. I've done my best to avoid thinking about this all week, but today, everything hit me, and I had no idea what I was gonna do if I had a seizure, and you or Evan weren't there. I mean, the teachers know, but it would be a disaster if . . ." He trails off and shakes his head.

"But you . . . you fixed that for me . . . days before I even thought about it. Why didn't you tell me what you guys were doing?"

"Well . . . I knew you were trying not to think about tomorrow, and I didn't want to stress you out. I thought it would be easier on you if we just did this, and then I told you, but then I was worried because I was keeping something from you—"

"You were right," Nathan says, closing his eyes briefly, but then those brilliant blue eyes have me in thrall again, and this time, they're soft and smiling.

"Thank you. I didn't think anything could make me feel better today or make me less anxious about tomorrow, but *you* have. You're so caring and thoughtful and—fuck, I don't have the words except to tell you that I love you, and I'm *so* happy you're mine."

My heart melts to a mooshy puddle in my chest, and I pull him close, needing to give back even a fraction of what he's just given me. Our lips meet, and his soft moan electrifies me—head, heart, hoo-ha, and everything in between.

His hands are roving—through my hair and under my shirt and up my sides and back, but his kisses are gentle and not hungry, and his fingers never find my waistband.

Right now, I'd like to ride him until we actually *see* some cows come home, but he's just not there today, and whether it's because of yesterday's seizure or his headache or limp dick from Xanax—*shit, I'm glad he's at least up for kissing and touching.*

We make out until his lips lose focus, and his hands are doing that start-and-stop-suddenly-then-start-again thing you do when you're trying not to fall asleep.

I reach up and run my fingers through his hair, and he's out almost instantly, but I keep doing it until my hand grows tired, and I fall asleep beside him.

～

It's 7:30 a.m., and I'm sitting in Nathan's driveway. I've been here for a half hour because although I had no trouble falling asleep last night, I woke up at five, and my mind started running through all the ways today could go, and that was it for me and sleep.

I'm so nervous and worried for him, but I can't let him see it because it'll only compound what I already know is going on in his head. He'll think it's fear of him having a seizure today, but it's not that at all. I know he's going to have a seizure at school—it's merely a question of when. What I'm worried about is how the students at Tillamook High will respond. Will they be immature assholes about it? Treat him like a pariah as he's always feared? He needs to learn to only pay attention to the people who really matter—those who care about him—but the rest of these jackasses could make life a living hell for him for a while.

The front door opens, and Evan steps out, throwing me a nod and a grin that I can't help but return . . . then my eyes fall on Nathan.

He looks absolutely awful. I've gotten used to the fading bruises on his face, but the mottled black and green on his cheek and around his eye has a sickly yellow cast to it today—probably because the rest of him is white as a sheet. He gaze is hollow and haunted—as if he's being led to the gallows, and there's no escape—it's like he's not even really here.

He trudges mechanically toward Evan's car, but I scramble out of my mine and intercept him before he can get to the front passenger door.

His hand is cold and clammy as I clutch it between mine, and although he raises his eyes to me, he seems dazed and allows me to lead him toward the backseat.

I shoot Evan a worried glance over the top of the car, but he just sighs and shakes his head.

"Dad hit him with the max dose of Valium about a half hour ago, and he's been out of it ever since. This is better than how he was earlier though. Trust me."

I want to ask, but I'm more concerned with how Nathan is *now* than how he was then, so I drop it and open the car door.

Nathan climbs in, and when I sit beside him, he burrows his head into my shoulder, and I twine our fingers together so we're holding hands.

And that's the last moment of peace we have.

As Evan drives, Nathan's breathing accelerates, and he increases his grip on my hand until it actually hurts.

"Nathan—"

"Talk to me. Distract me before there's not enough air, and I pass out!"

I've never seen him like this, and I'm so shaken up, I can't even think how to make a sound, let alone what to say to him.

"*Please!*"

He's almost gasping now, so I do the only thing I can think of—I press my lips to the side of his head and run the fingers of the hand he's not crushing through his hair.

He truly *is* gasping now, but I keep kissing and stroking, and the words well up and escape in a torrent from my lips.

"Shh . . . you're okay! You're fine. I'm right here with you, and nothing bad is gonna happen. I'm gonna be right here, and I'm never gonna let you go. I love you, Nathan. You're my hero, and you're so fucking strong."

He's holding on to me for dear life now, but I just keep caressing him with my lips and fingers, whispering my love for him and praying silently that he'll make it through this until, finally, his grip on me begins to loosen.

His breathing is still ragged, and the moment the car stops moving, he scrambles away from me, leaning out the open car door and taking great lungfuls of air as if he's been drowning.

Evan gets out and stands in front of the open door, blocking Nathan from the view of any curious onlookers.

We stare at each other over Nathan's heaving back, neither of us knowing what the hell to do now, until Nathan speaks up.

"I'm . . . all right. I just needed some air. I'll be okay . . . in a minute."

He's shaking, and I can't help but reach out and rub soft circles on his back. It takes a few moments, but Nathan's breathing slows, and he sits back in the car, letting his head fall back against the seat. He looks exhausted, and this awful day hasn't even really begun yet.

"Are you sure you wanna do this?" Evan asks, and after what we just went through, I have to agree, but Nathan nods slowly.

"I have to. I need to stop thinking about it and just do it, okay?"

"Yeah, okay," Evan says, clasping Nathan's shoulder, and Nathan puts his hand over his brother's as he raises his head.

"Holly?"

I think I'm still in shock over how bad his panic attack was, but if Nathan thinks he can soldier on, I'll be damned if I try to hold him back.

"Let's go," I tell him, nodding and giving him a smile, and the grin he gives me in return is weak, but it warms everything.

He stands tall as he gets out of the car, and he has me fooled until I take his hand and discover he's trembling.

But there are things he can't keep hidden. He stumbles more than once as we walk through the parking lot, and it has me worried until I remember the day he was high as a kite because Evan made him take too many Xanax. He grips my hand and lets me steady him as we make our way up the stairs, and I know I'm right—that Valium has him all messed up.

But it's better than having another panic attack—or worse—in front of everyone, right?

We make our way down the hall, and people are staring, but Nathan doesn't notice—he's too focused on trying to keep his breathing even and not tripping over his own two feet.

All of our friends are congregated around where my locker is, but they follow us up the hall, silently offering their support.

Nathan's hands are visibly shaking when he tries to open his locker, and Evan shoots me a concerned look as he continues up the hall. I wave him on with more confidence than I feel, but he can't exactly escort Nathan to class, now can he?

Ryan makes short work of the locker door and gathers Nathan's physics books for him while Justin and Megan just watch, at a loss, but The Gothlet shakes her head and saunters over to Nathan.

"Hey, Nathan, I'm so glad you're back! Did Holly tell you what we did last week? I wanted to make us all 'Team Nathan' t-shirts, but she wouldn't let me."

Nathan actually *chuckles*, and I'm floored for a second, but then I realize The Gothlet's done the best possible thing at this moment: she's made Nathan feel normal on the most abnormal day he's ever had.

"I think I have to agree with Holly—Team Nathan should remain incognito," Nathan says with just the smallest quaver in his voice, and again, I'm amazed at his composure. Even though he's used to hiding his condition at school, he has to be using all the skills he has right now to keep his anxiety at bay.

Ryan carries Nathan's books for him, and I hold his hand to steady him as we walk to homeroom. His grip on me tightens with every step we take, and his breathing is again becoming rapid.

This is it—he thinks he's gonna have a seizure in homeroom, I realize with a start, and I rub my fingers up and down his arm to try to keep him grounded.

He pauses just before the doorway and swallows hard, but his hesitation doesn't even last for a moment. He raises his head and walks into the room, and I've never been prouder or more in awe of anyone in my whole life.

Everyone is looking at him, but he only has eyes for the fourth desk in the row, and as soon as he falls into the seat and Ryan puts his books down, Nathan lays his head down on his desk.

The five of us look at each other helplessly as Mr. Harper calls the room to order. Harper's eyes pause on Nathan as he takes silent roll, but he says nothing, and I breathe a sigh of relief.

Nathan's trembling, and I can hear his shaky breaths from here—this is the moment he's been dreading, I just know it. And there's nothing I can do for him, so I hold my breath and wait for it to happen.

But then . . . life just continues on. Nathan doesn't have a seizure. Mr. Harper reads the announcements. After a few minutes, Nathan slowly raises his head, and his breathing is slower and more even. *Nothing happened.*

I sigh in relief when the bell finally rings, and I'm at Nathan's side in an instant. He looks up at me in confusion, but I just grin back at him.

"You're okay," I say, and it's not exactly a question, but he nods anyway and gets to his feet. He seems a little more relaxed, but his grip on the desk tells me he's still trippy and off-balance.

First period is the only class we don't have together this morning, so I give Ryan ample warning.

"Keep an eye on him walking down the hall," I tell him, jerking my head toward Nathan. "His dad lit him up pretty good."

"I'm fine, Ryan," Nathan says, narrowing his eyes at me playfully. "Just make sure I don't fall on my face, okay?"

"You got it," Ryan answers, grinning at both of us.

"I'll see you in English," I tell Nathan, and he pulls me in for a soft, chaste kiss before turning and following Ryan out of the room.

God, I hope I don't see him before then.

I hold my breath and keep my phone on my lap all through first period, but it stays quiet, and when Ryan delivers Nathan to his locker, he looks worn out, but he's smiling.

And the morning continues: English, calculus, chemistry—Nathan seems to relax a little bit more with every passing hour, and by lunchtime, it's as if nothing has changed. *Almost.*

Everyone has stayed close to Nathan all morning, limiting his contact with everyone else so he wouldn't have to answer their questions and glaring at anyone who had the balls to stare at him. By the time we get to the cafeteria, Nathan's return is old news, and everyone is going on about the short skirt Mrs. Gibbs is wearing today.

"Do you think she's trying to impress Mr. Metcalf?" Megan asks, and the boys all chuckle at the same time.

"I don't think 'impress' is really what she's going for," Ryan says, elbowing Nathan, but Nathan's gone strangely still.

When his eyes widen in terror, it's like I'm back in Gibbs's room last fall, and everything freezes—my heart, my brain—everything but Nathan.

"Oh God!" he exclaims, and it's as if his deep breath pulls all the oxygen from the room. His arms start to shake, and by now, everyone at the table is staring at either him or me.

"Holly!" Ryan demands, and now it's as if everything is moving *too* fast.

I turn to Nathan, but he's closed his eyes. *I have to get him out of here.*

"Nathan! Can you stand?"

"N-n-n-o-o-o," he mumbles, his breath coming faster, and I don't know if that's an answer to my question or a denial of what's happening.

"C-c-can't-t-t."

"Okay, let's get you down on the floor then," I say, shoving back my chair, and everyone at the table springs into action.

Ryan moves the chairs out of the way while I pull Nathan down onto the floor, and out of the corner of my eye, I see Megan dart off toward Mr. Harper.

Nathan grips my hand tightly as I lower his head to the floor, but when I start to run my fingers through his hair, he jerks away from my hand.

"N-n-n-o-o-o—"

His moan ends in a sharp cry, and I skitter back as he starts to convulse. His head hits the floor with a dull thud, and I curse myself for my stupidity as I scramble forward again and pull his head into my lap.

"Fuck off!"

I tuned everything out while I was taking care of Nathan, but Evan's angry shout breaks through my focus. I look up and see the backs of Ryan, The Gothlet, Justin, and Megan arranged in a circle facing outward from Nathan, with Evan standing in front of them, tall and imposing. Chairs are scraping, feet are shuffling, and the cafeteria is emptying, but I can hear their words as I watch Nathan helplessly.

"What's going on?"

"He's having a seizure!"

"Holy shit! Harris is a freak!"

That last one brings tears to my eyes, but I have no time to worry about it because Nathan abruptly stills and starts gasping for air. His color gets better with every breath he takes, and when I shift his head out of my lap to sit beside him, Evan's right there to put his folded jacket under Nathan's head.

There's commotion as Evan stands up to talk to someone, but I block it all out as I position Nathan's arms and roll him onto his side just like we practiced at my house. When I tilt his chin back, I can't help but run my fingers through his hair until his eyes finally open.

"You're okay. Everything's fine," I croon softly, knowing it's the sound of my voice that's important since he doesn't know it's me and might not be able to understand my words.

His eyes close again, and I can't keep the tears back anymore because I know he's going to lose it when he realizes where he is. I keep stroking his head, though, dreading the next few moments more than any in my existence.

He opens his eyes, and I smile through my tears, caressing his cheek, and he smiles back at me so trustingly. Then his eyes focus on the ceiling above me, and I watch in agony as his face contorts in shock and horror.

"No . . . no . . . no, no, *no!*"

He curls in a ball, hands gripping the back of his head as he sobs, his body shaking from anguish now instead of illness.

And I cover him—with my arms, my tears, with everything I have and everything I am because I know beyond any doubt—this is the worst moment of his life.

CHAPTER THIRTY-NINE

No one can hurt you without your permission.

– Mahatma Gandhi

NATHAN

I wake with a shudder and a groan. My head is pounding, and the memories assault me before I even think to look for them—Holly's face looking down at me with the cafeteria ceiling above her, curling in a ball and fucking bawling until I passed out, Evan carrying me to Dad's waiting car.

It happened.

I had a seizure at school in front of *everyone.*

Why couldn't it have been in homeroom? Twenty-two kids I could have handled, but *all* the juniors and seniors? *Who are you kidding, Harris? You can't handle any of this.*

But . . . I think I kind of can. It happened. It's over. And now I have no choice but to deal with the aftermath, whatever it is. I *hate* when things are out of my control, but I realize I don't feel frustration right now.

I feel resigned and sort of . . . still.

I open my eyes, and Evan is there, smiling at me like he always does.

"You shoulda woken up ten minutes sooner. Dad just kicked Holly out."

"Kicked her out?"

"Told her to go home. It's going on eleven, and you've been sleeping like the dead the entire time she was curled up on your bed tonight. Dad thought you might not wake up until morning, and he wanted her to get some sleep."

I wish she were still here. I feel empty, and I could use a hug, but Evan's tree limbs around me just wouldn't feel the same. And while getting a hug from your brother is all right, asking for one is just weird.

"What happened? I remember the aura at the table and Holly helping me get down on the floor . . ."

Evan takes a deep breath. "Well, when I heard the commotion, I knew it had to be you, so I ran over, but everything was under control. You were already seizing, but Holly had your head in her lap, and Ryan, Lucy, and Justin had made a little circle around you to block everyone's view. Megan was talking to Mr. Harper, and he started yelling at everyone to clear the caf. Holly was taking care of you, so I just stood in front of the others and glared at anyone who dared to try to see around me or say anything."

I've pictured having a seizure at school so many times, I swear it's tattooed on the underside of my eyelids, but none of my imaginings were anything like what Evan just described. In all those nightmares, I was completely alone, but when it finally happened, I had six people helping me.

Six people who truly care about me and want to protect me.

Including one who loves me enough to forgive my stupidity and all the hurt I caused her.

"Then what happened?"

"Once the caf was cleared, and you had come to, Holly was finally willing to let go of you long enough so I could carry you to Dad's car. Holly had to stay at school, but I think she was here before the final bell finished ringing, and she sat with you all night, hoping she'd be here when you woke up."

"Shit."

"Eh," Evan says, shrugging. "I told her I'd be here if you woke up, and she looked exhausted. You won't be awake for that long anyway."

I'd like to say he's wrong, but I can already feel the fatigue dragging at my eyelids, and I'd do just about anything to get some relief from this headache.

"Here," Evan says, picking up a tray from the floor beside him. "Gatorade, PB and J, and some codeine, courtesy of Dad. I can go get him if you want."

I love my parents, but the last thing I want is to be pitied and fawned over —Dad would be fine, but he and Mom always come as a package deal.

"Nah, just tell them I woke up groggy and went right back to sleep."

"You got it, bro."

I scarf down the sandwich, pop the pills, and chug the Gatorade, eager to get some relief and give in to my exhaustion, and when I curl on my side, Evan covers me with my blankets.

"What you did today took some serious balls," he says, looking toward my dresser. "After the car ride . . . I know *I* couldn't have pulled my shit together and gone on, but *you* did, and I . . . you're pretty fucking amazing, ya know?"

"Holly says I'm Super Nathan," I tell him, chuckling. "My super power is that I keep my shit together."

Evan laughs loud and long, and I join him until my headache lets me know it's time to stop.

"Holly . . . that girl is one in a million, you know that, right? I didn't think so at the time, but now I think . . . well, I think her seeing you have a seizure might have been the best thing that could have happened to you."

I ponder his words, and I realize there's truth in them. If Holly hadn't come along and pissed me off enough that I literally lost my mind right in front of her, I'd probably still be keeping my secret—alone and isolated from everyone I now know cares enough not only to accept me but to help keep me safe.

"I think you're right," I mumble as my eyes start to close, but the warm feeling in my chest and the grin on my face follow me into slumber.

And my last thought before sleep takes me? *Wow . . . brothers can hug you without even touching you.*

I'm up well before dawn, mostly because I had to piss but also because my head still feels like a damn warzone and because today's gonna be another fan-fucking-tastic day in the land of newly outed epileptics, population: me.

But I'm not panicking like I was yesterday morning. I panic when I don't know what's going to happen or when I'm afraid something might happen, but I know *exactly* what's going to happen today.

I'm going to be stared at.

I'm going to be feared.

I'm going to be regarded as the freak that I am, and everyone I've ever put down is gonna come and take a shot at me.

I deserve it—I really do—but that's not going to make it any easier. Getting your just desserts isn't like a trip to Dairy Queen.

But that part, I think I can handle. The parts that are harder to handle are the stares and the fear. At first, it'll just suck, but over time, it's gonna make me twitchy like it did with Mom and Evan. And then it's gonna make me paranoid and on edge all the time, and the panic attacks will start.

I don't want this to happen again. Fuck!

I jump up from the couch and start pacing because I suddenly can't sit still anymore. Anger and frustration form the bars of my cage, and I'm restless in their confines, but there's nothing I can do about what I'm going to go through today.

Come on, student body, give me your anger and your abuse . . . just don't look at me like I'm an alien creature and act like the guy who's sat next to you in physics all year is now suddenly gonna explode.

Don't tiptoe around me.

Don't treat me like I'm made of glass.

And, for the love of God, don't stop treating me like a person.

I'm a human, not a disease. I'm not some automaton that starts shaking like clockwork and should be avoided from now on—I'm still *me*. And epilepsy is just a small part of me, but for some, that's all they're ever gonna see from now on when they look at me: Nathan, the guy with epilepsy.

I promised myself I would never let this condition own me, but now it's going to do something even worse—now it will define me.

I start to breathe faster, but resignation and hopelessness shut it down before the panic has a chance to take hold—there's really no point. I can't take back yesterday. All I can do is move forward.

I still have more energy than I know what to do with, and I really want to punch something, but Mom's pretty fond of most of the walls, and I already have one messed up hand, so I head for my room, hoping I can find something there to distract me for a while.

I glance out the front window on my way up the stairs, and I do a double take when I see Holly's car in the driveway.

What the hell?

It's 7 a.m. and if I hadn't looked out, she'd be sitting there for another half hour at least until my lazy-ass brother decides we should probably head out for school.

As I approach, I can see that she's gripping the steering wheel with both hands and resting her forehead on it, and my heart sinks, my own frustration all but forgotten. Yesterday was hell for her, too, and I didn't even call her when I woke up last night. I hope Evan sent her a text since I was apparently too lost in my own shit to think about anyone else.

I stand next to her window and tap softly, but she still jumps a mile and clutches her chest as she raises her eyes to me.

My smile is involuntary, just like it is every time I look at her, and I watch as relief rolls over her and transforms her weary face from fear to her own soft smile.

I barely have time to back up before the door swings open, and she's in my arms, holding on as tightly as she can, and it's my turn for relief and peace. And something funny happens in my chest—it feels squishy somehow— gooey and warm and just . . . home.

"Thank God you're okay! Yesterday was so hard, and you were so upset after the seizure—I didn't know what to do for you and—wait! *Are* you okay?

My smile widens at her babbling, and I can't help but chuckle as her head comes flying up from my shoulder, her hands gripping my biceps as those deep brown eyes bore right into my soul, demanding nothing less than the absolute truth.

And the absolute truth is . . .

"Yeah, I'm okay. My head is killing me, and I don't wanna go back there today, but I'm okay."

And it *is* the truth. At least, it is in this moment.

Her hands cradle my cheeks, and fireworks go off in my groin as her lips brush mine, but before I can deepen the kiss, she's already pulled back.

"You were so brave yesterday! I still can't believe you stayed even after the panic attack and how freaked out you were in homeroom. And then the seizure—I'm so freaking proud of you!"

When she stops to take a breath, I capture her lips, and when she relaxes against me, I know she's gotten the message that I'd rather kiss her than talk. Her fingers slide into my hair while my hands slip down to cup her ass, and the heat between us builds with every swipe of our tongues.

I pull her tighter against me, moaning shamelessly as my dick becomes the meat in a Holly-Nathan sandwich. I want to rub myself against her so badly, but it's freezing out here; I can't get her off in the middle of the driveway, and I probably won't even be able to get off myself because it's the day after a seizure.

Holly shivers, and I reluctantly detach my dick from her thigh before he can convince me to try to start a fire between us.

"You're freezing. Why don't we sit in your car?"

She glances behind her—the ancient beast is idling, and the door is still open—and her blush is adorable.

"I was a little anxious to see you."

That should make me smile, but it brings out the guilt as we climb into the warmth of the car.

"I'm sorry I didn't call you last night. I woke up not long after you left, but I was only awake long enough to have a sandwich and take some codeine."

"No panic attacks?"

"No, I pretty much know how today's going to go. I usually only panic when I don't know what's going to happen."

"And what's going to happen?" she asks, and my nerves kick in, sending tension through every muscle in my body.

"Everyone I've ever wronged is gonna come and take a shot at me." I have to swallow hard around the lump in my throat to rasp out the next part. "And the rest are going to stare at me and treat me like a freak."

Her arms are around me before I can even finish what I'm saying.

"No, Nathan—"

"Yes!" I yell, and it takes all my restraint and the shock in her eyes to make me dial it down a few notches. "I deserve it. I made fun of people all these years to keep the attention away from me—and now it turns out *I'm* the one who's the freak. Why wouldn't they *all* take a shot at me?"

"You are *not* a freak!" Holly yells, and it's my turn to startle in shock. "God*damn* it, Nathan! I am so tired of hearing you say that! You have an *illness*! It's not your fault! If you had diabetes or . . . or cancer, would you consider yourself a freak?"

"At least *those* illnesses don't come with public performances!" I yell back, my stubbornness getting the better of me.

"So what? You didn't choose this! Why do you have to take it in and—and *own* it as if it's your dirty little secret? It's not *you*. It's something that happens *to* you. It's not who you are!"

"Yes, it *is* who I am! To *them* anyway! And it's all I'm ever gonna be to them from now on—Nathan, the guy who has epilepsy! Don't you understand, Holly? That's all they're gonna see!"

"So? Who gives a shit about them? They're not the people who *matter*. The people who matter are your friends—the ones who see you for the person you are. They won't be afraid of you or treat you differently because they see *you*.

"I've told you so many times before—you can't control how other people react to you, but you *can* control how *you* react to *them*! If they're gonna treat you like a time bomb, don't let them get to you, Nathan, because they don't *matter*! They're nobody, and they can't hurt you unless you let them!"

Holly's words echo in my ears, and suddenly, her car is too small, and I can't keep still. I burst out the door like a sprinter from the gate, making for the front door until a vision of Mom's concerned face pops up like a stop sign, and I veer to the left, running around the side of the house. I can hear Holly calling me, and I know I should stop, but I keep running through the back yard and down the trail until I get to the big log by the river—a place where I've come to think so many times before.

I'm out of breath and overheated and *so . . . fucking . . . angry*! I have to find a way to calm down, or I'm gonna have another seizure, and going to school will be the least of my worries.

I throw myself down onto the log, elbows on knees with my palms pressing into my forehead.

Breathe. Breathe. Why am I so angry?

But no answer comes, so I just try to empty my mind and stop hyperventilating.

My chest hurts. At first, I think it's my rib, but it's not. It's my heart—a deeper pain that penetrates to the center of my being.

Why me?

I've never asked that question, but now it's the only thought in my head. *Why did this happen to me and not someone else? Why am I the one who has to deal with it? Why not Evan or Ryan or that bitch Lori? Why am I the one who has to suffer through this?*

And in the silence of the woods, I realize there's no answer.

There is no *why*.

It just happened. Or, maybe there is.

"I don't know how the hell you handle it all because I know I never could! You think I'm the strong one, but you're wrong—it's you*!"*

". . . maybe this is your super power*: Super Nathan, the guy who holds his shit together."*

"You go on, Nathan. It's who you are."

Evan's and Holly's words swirl in my head, and for the first time, I really *hear* them. I *can* handle my epilepsy and all the shit that goes with it. It's not easy by any means, but I've had it for almost three years now and made it through everything it's thrown at me. I'm still in school. I have a girlfriend. I have friends who care about me and will help keep me safe.

And nothing else matters.

The weight drops from my shoulders, and I swear I hear it hit the ground and crumble like concrete dropped from a great height. I flex my shoulders and draw in a deep breath, and I feel so much lighter than I did just a minute before.

Nothing else matters.

Holly's right. *Fuck* those assholes who can't separate me from this disease. They don't matter. The only people who matter are the ones who can see me for *me*, the ones who look at me and see a person and not an illness I didn't choose. I *don't* need to own this. I don't need to hide it. It's not *me* —it's something that happens to me.

Holly.

I raise my head, and she's sitting beside me, her hand on my back, and I didn't even know it.

"I'm sorry—"

"No, *I'm* sorry! You're right—you're right about all of it—what those assholes think doesn't matter. I shouldn't care, and I don't want to, but it's gonna be . . . hard. It's hard to be stared at, and it's hard to have people walk on eggshells around you. I don't know if I can help letting it get to me."

Holly's arms encircle me, and I rest my head on her shoulder, tired and aching, and this day hasn't even really begun.

"You won't be alone," she whispers. "Just like yesterday, we'll all be there for you. If those assholes stare, then I'm gonna stare right back, and Lucy'll probably stab their kneecaps."

"Because she's not tall enough to reach their eyes?"

"That's right!" Holly exclaims, and I can't hold in my laughter.

"There you are!" She grabs both of my cheeks and gives me an exaggerated peck on the lips, and when she pulls back, her smile is so bright, it's like the sun came out.

I can't help but grin back at her, but I still don't know how this is gonna go. *Can I really tune out all their whispers and ignore their gawking stares?* I've deflected attention away from myself for so long. Can I really handle it when all of it is focused on me? I just don't know.

We get to school, and it's bad. We're almost late, which means hardly anyone is in the parking lot, but nearly everyone is still in the hallway, getting their shit together for first period.

And they all stop and stare at me openly as we walk by.

I'm flanked by Holly and Evan, but they can't protect me. My cheeks are flaming, my palms are sweating, and I can feel their eyes on me like bugs crawling all over my skin.

All the whispers are behind us because Evan would deck anyone who dared say anything to my face, and they all know it.

"There he is—I heard he had a seizure yesterday."

"He looks okay, but is he gonna have another one?"

"Damn, that must suck. I'd hate to be a freak."

I draw in a sharp breath as Holly puts a hand on my arm, but Evan whips around, glaring at everyone. No one meets his gaze.

"Who said it?" He's daring someone to own up, but suddenly everyone has something better to do, and the prickly feeling on my skin dissipates.

"Let's just go," I say, tugging on Evan's sleeve, and he huffs out a breath but resumes stomping up the hallway.

When we get to my locker, I can tell he doesn't want to leave me, but Holly and the others are here, and I have to figure out how to handle this in a way that doesn't involve Evan getting arrested for assault.

"I'm good," I tell him, but my voice breaks. I know he can see right through me, but he keeps walking anyway because he knows he has to.

I'm not alone. I'll be okay, I tell him with my eyes, and I repeat it to myself under my breath, and it helps a little.

But as soon as he's gone, the staring and the whispers start up again, and I grip the back of my neck as the prickles return, and I start to sweat.

They're all watching me.

"What if he has a seizure right now?"

I start to breathe faster, and the word "seizure" seems to pop out of every conversation I overhear.

The prickles slide down my spine to the base, and I can't stay still—the fear and tension are mounting, my stomach is churning, and I feel like I want to jump out of my own skin.

I'm going to have a panic attack.

I swear I jump a mile when Holly touches me; I was so focused on my breathing and fighting desperately to slow it down.

She slides into my arms, and I cling to her, trying so hard to get a grip before everything spirals out of control.

She rubs my back, and her lips brush against my neck, dropping soft kisses there before she whispers, "They don't matter."

Her lips go right back to kissing my neck, and as my body starts to respond, my breathing slows. The prickles down my back now head straight for my groin and bloom into heat there, and I let go of Holly's shoulders to slide my arms around her, pulling her as close to me as I can.

Our tongues tangle, and I moan as my dick rubs against her thigh, and I start to move her backward, looking for a surface to lean on so I can grind against her.

"Holy shit, guys! Get a room!"

My lips leave Holly's with an audible pop, and all the sounds from the hallway come rushing back in as my head spins, trying to process what the hell is going on.

Holly's arms now sit at my waist, and she's smirking at me, her eyes sparkling with mischief.

"See ya in homeroom, Super Nathan," she whispers before she lets go, sashaying away with an exaggerated swing to her hips as she heads back to her locker.

Ryan smiles at me, and I find myself smiling back. We gather our books, and I turn around to walk to homeroom, but everyone's eyes are still on me, and I flinch back in surprise. I was so distracted by Holly that I didn't even notice, but they're all still whispering and staring.

Ryan stands in front of me, taking up my field of vision.

"They don't matter," he says, looking intensely into my eyes, and I suck in some much-needed air with a gasp.

I close my eyes and breathe for a second, willing the prickles and the voices away, including the one in my head insisting that it's time to lose my shit.

"They're assholes. They're all too damn nosy, and they can go fuck themselves," Ryan says, gripping my forearm. "Actually, some of the girls? I wouldn't mind seeing them fuck themselves."

I bark out a laugh, and it completely derails my path to hyperventilation.

"Don't tell Lucy I said that though. She's liable to introduce Ivan to my balls."

Now I'm laughing for real because I know a close encounter for Ivan with some guy's balls has to be on Lucy's lifetime goals list—although I doubt she's planning it to be Ryan unless he manages to fuck up big enough.

And that's how things go all day long. Everyone stays close to me, and when I get lost in my head or I start paying too much attention to the assholes around me, one of them reminds me that they don't matter and distracts me somehow.

I like Holly's method the best though. I was dreading going to lunch all morning, and when we got close, I locked down and started hyperventilating for real. I honestly thought that was it, and I was gonna have a panic attack followed by another seizure, but Holly grabbed me and dragged me into the closet in an empty classroom and . . . well, let's just say my balls are now a nice shade of "fuck, that was awesome" instead of blue.

And I made it through lunch although I did eat quickly and try to persuade Holly that we'd forgotten something in that closet, and we really needed to go get it. She knew I was lying, but it was worth a try, right?

And I made it through study hall and government, and by the time I decided to dodge Spanish for a nap, either the number of people staring was diminishing or my brain was finally on board with them not mattering because I hardly noticed anyone as I made my way to the nurse's office.

~

"Nathan."

"Wha—?"

I open my eyes slowly, and Holly stares down at me, her eyes shining. "It's the end of the day, Super Nathan. You made it."

The obnoxious noise of students from the hallway confirms it, but it's not too bad because my headache has eased a bit.

Warmth spreads through my chest and into my smile, but I realize it's not just because the most beautiful girl in the world is making eyes at me. I'm *proud* of myself for today. No seizures, no panic attacks, no lies. I haven't had a day that didn't involve one of the three musketeers of misery in almost three years. And it feels *good*—so good that I feel more alive and more in control than I have in a long time.

"Come on. Everyone's waiting for you," Holly says, and I follow her out of the office.

But there are other people waiting for me.

As we walk up the hall, I see Chris standing with a few of the sophomore boys, and I try not to flinch as we pass him. The teachers have separated us in all of our classes for obvious reasons, so this is the closest I've been to him since the fight, and the few hazy memories I've managed to recall are kind of awful.

"I always knew there was something wrong with you, Harris," Chris calls out, and the hallway goes silent.

I freeze, and anger, hurt, embarrassment, and every other emotion I've bottled up since that night roar through me at once.

"But I never guessed you were hiding that you were a freak."

A shit-ton of things happen at once and so fast that it takes me a few seconds to process them all.

As I turn to face Chris, I see Ryan coming up the hall with Lucy hot on his heels, Ivan in hand. Holly grabs my arm to keep me from lunging at Chris, but Ryan goes right past, and while I expect him to throw Chris against the lockers, when my eyes finally make it to Chris, it's Tyler who has him pressed up against the wall, arm at his throat.

"Did you just call Harris a freak?"

Silence.

"*Did* you?"

"Yes." Then he gasps, his face turning red as Tyler presses harder on his windpipe.

"He has epilepsy, you fuck! Just like my mom. It's a sickness, not a choice. And *you're* the freak for making fun of people who are sick, you fucking asshole! You probably made things worse for him when you and Sean kicked his ass, so maybe I should—"

As Tyler draws back his fist, I find myself grabbing his arm. Tyler's eyes are murderous when he looks back, but they shift to confusion when he sees it's me.

"He's not worth it, Tyler. You'll just get suspended, and he'll still be an ignorant ass. What he thinks doesn't matter though. Not to me."

"Well, it does to me." Tyler snarls as he focuses his attention back on Chris. "The only reason your head isn't bouncing off this wall right now is because Nathan doesn't want it to. But this is the only pass you get. You say another word or lay a hand on him again, you're gonna have to answer to me as well as Ryan. Got it?" he asks, giving Chris a good shake.

Chris nods, eyes wide, and only now do I notice that Eric and Justin are restraining Ryan, and Holly and Megan are trying to calm a wild-eyed Lucy. *Holy shit, I've got a security flash mob!*

Tyler gives Chris a final shove, and he takes off down the hall, locker still open behind him.

Now Tyler turns to me, still trying to get his breathing under control. "What an asshole! He's known about my mom for years, but he thinks he can stand here and call *you* a freak? I always thought he acted like a jerk for fun, but now I can see that it's who he actually *is*. What a fuck."

"If you ever feel a seizure coming on, and these guys aren't around, let me know, okay? I help my mom all the time."

"O-k-kay." My answer is tentative, my head still trying to process what just happened.

And then something even more amazing happens.

"I can help too. My little brother has epilepsy."

"And me. My dad used to, but his seizures stopped."

My eyes, wide as saucers, land on the girl and boy who have stepped out of the crowd. I never even considered how many people around me might be living with epilepsy as part of their lives.

Tyler fist bumps my arm and then walks away, and the crowd dissipates except for my friends. I look at each of them in turn, and I have to swallow hard around the lump in my throat as I'm overwhelmed with emotion— I'm truly not alone, and . . . maybe I never was.

Maybe I never will be.

Holly puts her arm around me, and I drop my head to her shoulder, trying to keep my shit together but for a completely different reason than I'm used to. This time, I'm falling apart with relief and gratitude and a feeling of coming home.

"Are you okay?" Holly asks, nuzzling her nose under my chin.

"Yeah," I respond without hesitation. "I think I'm gonna be okay."

Epilogue

"Maybe happy endings are real, as long as you understand that they aren't endings, but steps on the road."

– Katharine McGee, *The Towering Sky*

Holly

The first few weeks were hard.

Even though he had Team Nathan to help him, and he now knew there were others around him whose lives are touched by epilepsy every day, Nathan had a hard time letting go of his fears. He couldn't help it—he could feel the stares and hear the whispers of the few assholes who seemed to think he was a sideshow act, and his anxiety was through the roof. He had another seizure the first week and two the following week, and the last one was triggered by a panic attack to boot. At least for that one, I pulled him into an empty classroom, and no one saw anything.

But then, something amazing happened. After about a month, the extra attention directed toward Nathan just stopped. I don't know if Tyler got to them, and Ryan has never admitted to any involvement, but *something* definitely changed. Maybe everyone just got used to what was happening. After all, how many times can you point and stare and call someone a freak before no one gives a shit anymore?

And that's when things got better. The seizures didn't stop, but he only had one or two a week, and sometimes he was lucky enough that they happened at home. The little seizures have never come back, and he still has seizures in his sleep—his seizure pattern had changed, but it stabilized. *He* stabilized.

Without the constant attention, Nathan was able to focus on the people who really matter to him and to ignore the occasional jackoff acting like he might shatter. I swear I could see a change in his posture—as if the weight of all the lies and the fear was lifted off him and left him able to stand tall again.

But the most important day of all was just a random Tuesday in October during our senior year when Nathan came to school sporting a new piece of jewelry. Gone was his old medical bracelet with the very subtle caduceus in the corner—replaced by a black and brown braided bracelet with a black nameplate displaying a large caduceus inside the star of life and the word "epilepsy" in bold white letters. That was the day I knew he'd finally made peace with who he was, epilepsy and all.

I startle and nearly drop my knife as the *Game of Thrones* theme blares from my phone—it's still Nathan's ringtone, and I suspect it always will be.

"Hello?"

"Hey, Sasha and I are running a little late, but we should be home in ten."

"That works. I'm running late on dinner too."

"Okay, beautiful. See you soon."

Warmth flutters through my chest, and I grin. I still melt when he calls me beautiful.

I wonder what held him up? His class was over forty-five minutes ago, and it usually only takes him fifteen to get home, even with Sasha.

I smile and shake my head—Sasha probably slowed him down. She's good at that, but I can't be upset about it. She's the apple of Nathan's eye, and she's made such a difference in our lives, especially Nathan's. There are times I feel almost jealous of her, but that's silly, isn't it?

By the time I finish the salad that goes with our fettuccine, Nathan's key is jiggling in the lock, and he and Sasha come bounding through the door. He must have roughhoused with her out front for a bit because she playfully paws at him as he hangs up her leash—she clearly knows she's off-duty, as much as she ever is anyway.

As soon as he drops his bag and keys, he gives her the attention she's been begging for, ruffling her ears as she sits in front of him, tail thumping on the floor so hard I don't know how it doesn't hurt.

"Who's a good girl? Who's a good girl? That's right! You're a good girl!"

They are absolutely adorable together, and Nathan loves her as much or even more than he depends on her. Sasha is the miracle we never even knew to hope for—a dog who can alert him to an oncoming seizure.

Team Nathan was fantastic for high school, but as our senior year progressed, and the frequency of his seizures settled to at least one a week, Nathan started freaking out about how he could possibly go to college. Even if he and I went to the same school, unless we took all the same classes, and I followed him into the men's room every day, there was no way he could manage not to be alone for some portion of the day. And that just wasn't a viable option, given the sudden onset of his seizures. His watch would alert us, but if one of us was more than three minutes away, he could have bashed his head open on the sidewalk by the time we got to him, or worse, depending on where he was. No one was willing to take that risk, given what happened after his concussion—status epilepticus and its aftermath was something Nathan never wanted to experience again.

So, the research began. Nathan already knew about service dogs that can help someone after a seizure, but it was never something he'd even considered because of the predictability of his seizures and, of course, the fact that he'd kept them a secret.

But now, it seemed like the best addition to his care plan—a dog could go to all his classes, the bathroom, everywhere—without raising any eyebrows, and they could assist him in that critical time between the onset of a seizure and the arrival of qualified help. A service dog could be trained to draw attention to Nathan or bring someone from nearby to help. They could alert someone to his condition by showing them his epilepsy bracelet during the aura when Nathan is too deeply in the grip of terror to communicate effectively. And in the worst case, they could guard him during a seizure and act as a brace to try to prevent injury if no help was nearby.

It wasn't a perfect solution, but it was enough to offer him some independence from Team Nathan and, hopefully, provide him with enough peace of mind to go it alone when he needed to.

What we got was so, so much more.

Dr. Harris researched a lot of service dog organizations, and we learned that among them, the debate rages about whether dogs can actually detect a change in a person's scent prior to a seizure and alert them. Some epileptics swear by it; some say that dogs can't alert for shit, but even the possibility that he could get his early warning system back had Nathan eager to try. Even if a dog couldn't alert him, he'd still get all the assistance benefits, so what did it hurt to look for a dog that could?

Enter stage left Little Angels Service Dogs and Sasha. There were interviews and consultations. Then a customized training plan for the dog had to be constructed to meet Nathan's needs, including training for alert capability. Then came a contract and a big-ass check because although Little Angels never asks anyone to pay for a dog, Dr. Harris covered the cost because he had the means. And then we had to wait for a dog to be identified and trained—an activity that took six months, and that was only because Nathan got a dog that had already begun its basic training. The training time for service dogs can be up to two years.

I'll never forget the day Nathan met Sasha. Once she was ready, we had to go to San Diego to get her, and Nathan had to stay at service dog training camp for two weeks to learn how to work with her. Nathan's dad and I flew down with him because he was nervous as hell, but I could tell the moment he saw her, his fears just fell away. Sasha is an English Cream Golden Retriever, and everything about her is warm and soft—deep, brown, soulful eyes, creamy white fur, and the sweetest disposition I've ever seen in an animal. She walked right up to Nathan, sat down in front of him, and put her paw on his leg. No one missed his sob of relief. It had taken so long, and he had been anxious that this wouldn't work out, but Sasha pushed all his fear away with one swipe of her little paw.

And then the miracle happened. Nathan had two seizures the first week of training, and before the second one, Sasha started whining and pacing in front of him. When Nathan had a seizure twenty minutes later, the trainers knew what was going on. The following week, the same thing happened, and Nathan was over the moon—Sasha could give him twenty minutes' warning of an oncoming seizure.

To say Sasha changed our lives would be a gross understatement. Since August I've watched the two of them bond and Nathan gain a confidence I haven't seen since I first met him, but even better because there are no lies weighing him down. We both started at Portland State in September, and Nathan and Sasha attend classes on their own, but Evan and I are within twenty minutes' walk of Nathan at all times in case he needs us.

Now that he's gotten his class schedule down, Nathan and Sasha have been working to identify safe spaces where they can go if he can't get home before a seizure, and that seems to have boosted his confidence even more. Nathan is honestly as happy as I've ever seen him.

Warm arms surround me from behind, and his lips at my neck send a shiver down my spine.

"And how's my other good girl?"

How in the hell does he make those fireworks explode in my chest every. Damn. Time? I melt back against him, eyes closed and chin raised, and his lips caress and explore just as I knew they would. *God, I love this boy and the man that he's becoming*—right before my very eager eyes.

I miss his lips the minute they're gone, and he doesn't seem to notice that I almost fall over backward when he slides away to steal a carrot from the salad.

He looks downright sexy today in his green Vikings t-shirt and jeans—he's grown almost two inches since the end of our junior year and filled out in all the right places. I believe I have Ryan to thank for that. Once he knew everything, he and Nathan became thick as thieves again, working out together and even playing some pickup games, although Nathan never felt comfortable enough to don a jersey for Tillamook High. But that's in the past, and he's happy now, and Lucy and Ryan are coming down from Seattle to visit this weekend.

"Hey, salad stealer! That's *my* carrot!" I scold him, but he sidesteps me before I can grab his arm.

His grin is pure mischief. "It's mine now, and besides, I'm an equal opportunity food thief. I believe I took your cherry a while back."

Now *that* thought sends warmth and tingles to a few places and a smirk to my lips. "That carrot is *definitely* yours," I tell him, appraising it as if it's his manhood, "but I believe I got your cherry too!"

"Mmm . . . yes. I will *never* forget that. Maybe we could *bone up* on our thievery skills again soon."

He wiggles his eyebrows suggestively, and I dissolve into laughter. "Boys. Your bone is all you think about."

"Who's getting boned?" Evan asks as he breezes into the kitchen, stealing *another* one of my carrots. I should have known thievery ran in the family.

"Um . . . I think we're the ones who are going to get it if we don't get the hell out of the kitchen and let Holly finish dinner," Nathan tells Evan, correctly interpreting my glare.

"Sorry, Hol," Ev says, crunching noisily, and the two of them beat a hasty retreat to the couch.

Nathan's condition got him out of having to live in the dorms, so he and Evan got an apartment together just off campus. I store my stuff in a dorm room a short walk from here, but it's only for show when Dad visits. I hate to have him waste the money, but he was adamant that Nathan and I not live together our first year so I could "make friends." Well, I'm doing fine in the friend department, and Nathan and I are counting the months until this officially becomes my home too. Besides, how would these "bone" heads eat anything but ramen and takeout without a woman around the house?

Dinner is the usual raucous affair with the boys shifting topics from sports to classes to the hot girl who lives upstairs whom Evan is trying to get up the courage to talk to. Kate is nice, and she's a bit sweet on Ev, too, but I think I'll let him suffer a bit longer.

Evan was thrilled when Nathan and I chose PSU for school, and he jumped at the chance to share a place with Nathan when the opportunity arose. It was awful for Evan the year before when he left for college. It was supposed to be an exciting time for him, but he felt like he was abandoning Nathan. I can see how happy he is that he's able to help again, and the brothers have become even closer, if that's possible.

After dinner it's homework time because we *are* in college after all, so I lounge on the couch, reading a novel for English Lit, while Nathan sits at the table and works on something for his music theory class. He's exploring the idea of double majoring in behavioral science and music, with the goal of studying how playing music affects the brains of people with seizure disorders and maybe even developing a program that will help ease their symptoms. It's a lofty goal, but Nathan's been there and done that, so who better to help others in the same boat?

As for me, I have no clue what I'm doing here. I'm working on my gen eds and waiting for inspiration to strike. Maybe I can find a way to help Nathan with his idea. Who knows?

My first sign that homework time is over is the sound of Nathan's book closing. Sasha is curled up at his feet, and I see her ears perk, but she doesn't even open her eyes as Nathan gets up and makes his way over to the couch. He's still close enough for her to keep an eye on, and she's got to be pretty used to this by now.

Nathan kneels on the floor beside me, cozying up as if he's going to read over my shoulder. I work hard to contain my smile as he nuzzles his chin into my chest and drapes an arm around me, but it's basically a losing battle. So I grin and ignore him even though his breath is tickling my chest, and his warmth is all around me, setting certain parts on high alert and others into overdrive. *Damn sexy bastard!*

Then, Nathan really begins in earnest. His other hand creeps under my shirt, settling on my stomach and rubbing gentle circles there as if he's debating which direction he wants to go. I shift my glance to his face, but it's expressionless—as if he's completely focused on reading and not about to molest me—the only giveaway to his mischief is that I can feel his heart beating rapidly against my shoulder.

His path north is blocked by my book, so he heads south, slipping his hand into my sweats and giving me goosebumps as he slides over all the sensitive spots, landing with one finger poised at the top of my slit. I can't help my rapid intake of breath, but I keep reading as that finger ventures on, sliding between my lower lips and rubbing until it's drenched, and *everything* down there feels smooth and wet and so very warm.

I spread my legs to give him better access, but I'm still trying to maintain the charade that I'm reading even though I've gone over the same sentence three times, and my left brain is merrily debating my right over how hard Nathan is right now.

Two things happen at once, and I'm done for—Nathan thrusts a finger inside me just as his lips begin worshipping my neck, and I throw my head back with a low moan as I bend my knees. My book falls from my suddenly nerveless fingers, and Nathan snickers in between thrusts and kisses, adding a second finger as mine scrabble against the couch cushions for purchase.

He tosses the book as he rises up on his knees, pulling my lips to his as he continues to thrust those talented fingers into me. They curl and brush that oh-so-sensitive spot as I push and writhe against his palm, rubbing my clit against the fantastic frictional surface he's provided.

The heat builds between my legs and flares upward as Nathan's tongue enters my mouth, and I cling to him, one hand buried in his hair and the other digging nails into his back. He brings me closer and closer to the edge, but I don't go over until he moans deeply into my mouth, unable to contain his own pleasure as he rubs himself against the front of the couch.

Oh God, Nathan orgasms are amazing, is the only thought I can hold on to as I pulse and quiver, panting his name into his chest as he pulls me close.

When I can breathe again, I open my eyes lazily, and his smiling, smug-as-hell face fills my vision.

"Hi, Holly. How's your book?"

Cheeky, cheeky boy!

"I just got to the sex scene apparently. You. Bedroom. *Now.*"

He tries to look innocent, so I run a hand over his crotch and he hisses, rubbing up and down until I pull my hand away, making him whine in his throat.

"Oh, *that* sex scene. Why didn't you say so?"

I roll my eyes and give him a shove, hard enough to make him catch himself with his hand but not enough to knock him over. He's on his feet in a flash, and Sasha is too because she knows what comes next, and she's not gonna like it.

She beats us to the bedroom, and when we arrive, she's curled up on the bed, head down between her paws and giving us the saddest eyes. But if I ever decide I want a threesome, it's not gonna be with a dog, so Sasha just needs to suck it up and deal. Or at least, that's what I thought until today.

Nathan hangs back by the door, giving me a sheepish look. I have a sneaking suspicion what's coming, and *I'm* not gonna like it.

"I talked to Robin today, and she said Sasha's pacing and barking when she's in her crate are definitely signs of separation anxiety. She suggested I don't crate her for a week or two and see if she calms down."

"Even when we're . . ." I give a rough approximation with a gesture, and Nathan nods.

My face must be doing something because Nathan comes toward me, arms outstretched and eyes pleading.

"She's been so good lately. I'm sure she'll just lie on the floor, and we won't even know she's there. I don't like it either, but I hate the thought that I'm hurting her by keeping her away. She does so much to help me."

I love Sasha. I really do. She's given Nathan his independence back, and she's become the baby in our little pseudo-family—she's been with him every minute since San Diego except when we're intimate. We've kept that time as just ours, and we've been putting her in her crate, but she's become increasingly agitated—so much so that Nathan felt it was necessary to call Robin, her trainer, to find out what our options are.

Apparently, our option is to let her join us. No big deal, right?

Oh hell, I am about to have a threesome with a dog.

"Nathan—"

"Let's just try it, all right? If it's too weird, we'll come up with something else."

"Like?"

"I don't know. I'm sure this won't be an issue when we have our own place and can leave the bedroom door open. Sasha's not interested in watching us have sex—she just doesn't want to be kept away from me."

"Are you sure?"

"Hol-lyy!" Between Nathan's whining and the damn puppy dog eyes, I know I'm not going to win here. The irony that they're both giving me the same look isn't lost on me.

"Fine." I huff as Nathan gathers me into his arms; he grunts softly when his dick comes into contact with my thigh. He's still hard as a rock—the thought of his new best friend watching us isn't even a slight turn-off for him. I guess that honor only applies to elder female family members . . . or my dad.

Before things can heat back up, Nathan backs away from me and walks to the other side of the bed. He fixes Sasha with a serious look, points to the floor, and says "Down" in a commanding voice.

Sasha doesn't flinch, but she obeys immediately, taking up the same position on the floor at his feet.

Nathan bends down in front of her, and I have to stand on my tip-toes to see him cradle her head and talk to her, nose to nose.

"You don't have to leave, but you've got to be a good girl and stay on the floor, okay? Don't let me down."

Sasha stares at him solemnly, and the warm, gooey feeling in my chest has nothing to do with the anticipation of sex. Someday we'll have kids, and I can see just from the way he is with Sasha that Nathan will be an incredible father. I can't wait to watch those chapters of our life unfold. But *this* chapter comes with lots of happy endings and no bundles of joy—just a sexy boy and his canine voyeur.

Nathan stands before me again, and I forget all about dogs and babies as he takes my face in his hands and plunders my mouth with his tongue. My arms curl around the backs of his shoulders, pulling him closer until his deep hum of pleasure lets me know I'm putting enough pressure in just the right place.

He rubs against me, his arms shimmying down to reach the buttons of my flannel, exposing my chest so he can put his lips everywhere. I roll my head back, panting as he lavishes my breasts with soft nips and open-mouth kisses, working his way around until he sucks a peaked nipple into his mouth. I moan shamelessly as he sucks, feeling the pull rocket down between my legs, and I hold on to him tighter as my knees turn to jelly.

The sound flips a switch in Nathan because, suddenly, I have no shirt on, my sweats and undies are around my ankles, and he's moving me toward the bed.

"Oh no, you're not getting on the bed like that," I tell him, eye-fucking every inch of him from his fantastic sex hair all the way down to his adorable socked feet.

His t-shirt is over his head in a flash, but I go for the jeans, pressing this way and that just to hear him moan as I slowly unbutton each button until he growls and shoves them down over his hips.

I hear the jingle of a dog collar, but I can't see Sasha, so I continue on, sliding his boxers down and listening to him hiss as his erection springs free. My hand is on him instantly, rubbing and stroking as he struggles to step out of his pants, not giving him a second free of pleasure to allow him to focus on the task.

He nearly topples over, so I cut him a break and ease off to allow us both to get naked, but as soon as all the clothing is on the floor, I pounce on him, pushing him down on his back and covering his body with mine.

I writhe against him as I thrust my tongue into his mouth, and his hands find purchase on my ass cheeks, squeezing and kneading as we make love with our tongues. It feels fantastic, but Nathan is grinding my hips against his, and I can tell from his groans into my mouth that he's gonna come pretty quickly if I don't slow things down.

So I pull back a bit and shift my body to his side, but his whimper ends in a pant when I pull his earlobe into my mouth and suck, curling my tongue just behind the shell into that spot that drives him wild. He tries to turn on his side, but I stop him, straddling his waist just above his dick and smothering his neck with kisses.

"Oh *fuck*, Holly," he mutters, giving up his bid for dominance and going limp on the bed, arms spread and chin lifted high to give me all the access I need.

I work on his neck until he's squirming beneath me, then I slide lower, spreading his legs so I can kneel between them as I lavish his chest with equal attention.

He knows my ultimate destination—I can see the lust and desire in his eyes just before I swirl my tongue over his nipple.

"Ahh . . . keep going."

I don't know if he means toward his dick or with this nipple, so I switch sides and lick and suck until he's pushing downward on my shoulders, unable to keep still in anticipation.

Greedy, bossy boy.

But he knows how that shit turns me on.

His ab muscles are tight as I kiss my way down to his waist, but they spasm as I kiss lower and lower—until my chin brushes against the tip of his cock.

"Let me suck your cock, Nathan," I say as I level him with my stare, and his dick twitches hard in response.

"Oh God, *please.*"

His eyes are desperation and heat, but mine are lust and satisfaction as I take him all the way in, his tip brushing the back of my throat.

His groan is low and deep, making all the right places tingle as I suck my way back up to his tip, swirling my tongue around the head when I get there. The sound I hear is more of a whimper this time, and it's followed by a jingle and half a bark.

I pretend I didn't hear anyone but Nathan, and I repeat the maneuver that led to my recent crowning as the "goddess of head" until he's moaning on every suck and bucking his hips. His hands are buried in my hair, but when I cup his balls, one hand disappears, and . . .

"Oh, Christ!"

I'm smug for a second until I hear, "Down, Sasha!"

I open my eyes and look up to see Nathan's arm stretched out and his fingers flailing . . . in front of Sasha's nose and paws that are perched on the edge of the bed, an inch from his reach.

Oh, hell *no! There isn't a creature alive that can distract a man from* my *blowjobs!*

So I redouble my efforts until Nathan's writhing, Sasha's whining, and I'm desperate for something to fucking give . . . or give way to fucking because that's exactly what happens.

One minute, I've got his dick in my mouth, and the next, I'm on my back with Nathan hovering over me, his gaze desperate and hungry. I give half a nod, and that's all he needs to plunge in to the hilt, making us both cry out in pleasure. He wastes no time, angling his thrusts to hit my clit with his pelvis because he's got to be oh-so-close after the fantastic fellatio I gave him—that or he thinks Sasha is going to jump on us before we get to finish.

Speaking of Sasha, she's now on her feet with her paws stretched across the bed, staring at us as if she's trying to determine if Nathan is in danger. For his part, Nathan's doing his best to ignore her, eyes closed as he works to bring us to orgasm.

He loses his rhythm, thrusting harder as he begins to grunt every time he hits my pelvis, and Sasha starts to whimper after every sound he makes. I can't pay attention to that now, though, because I can feel my own build starting, the sensation winding tighter and tighter every time Nathan makes contact.

"Ohh—"

As I pulse around him, Nathan's whimpers turn to moans, and Sasha is half-barking again, but I'm still too lost in my own pleasure to see or care what she's doing. Seeing Nathan come is one of life's true pleasures, so I open my eyes as soon as I can to watch my favorite show.

Nathan is thrusting in earnest, eyes closed with a sheen of sweat on his brow, and his moans are crescendoing like a porn star's—he's seconds from the big finish. I can pinpoint the exact instant he starts to come and, apparently, so can Sasha because the air is punctuated by a soulful howl.

Oh my God, she fucking howled. We've never heard her howl before—even when Nathan has a seizure, she doesn't *howl*.

My attention snaps back to Nathan as he falls forward, laying his head on the side of my chest like he usually does, but his breathing's not right. He's not panting, he's . . . laughing?

He turns to face me, and yes, he's definitely laughing—quite hysterically, in fact.

I shove him, and he rolls in Sasha's direction, and as soon as he's flat on his back, her paws are on his chest, and she's licking his neck and face.

Dammit, that's my *post-coital bliss! Take a walk, Sasha!*

Nathan pets her head roughly. "I'm fine. I'm *fine*! I promise! Now will you let me go back to Holly before she kills us both? *Down*, girl."

Sasha resumes her position on the floor with a thump, and I want to be angry so badly, but I just can't. She howled when Nathan had his orgasm, and I swear she was ready to jump between us if she thought for a second that I was truly hurting him. *Now that's dedication.*

Nathan rolls so his back is to Sasha—naked, sweaty, and flushed from exertion *and* embarrassment.

"Um . . . was it good for you?" he asks, face puckered and already bracing for my wrath.

When I pull him in for a kiss, he obliges but pulls back after a moment in confusion.

"You're not mad?"

"Well, I'm not *happy*, but at least, I know one thing."

"What's that?"

"You'll never be able to cheat on me because I'll be able to hear that howl no matter where you are."

"Oh hell," Nathan mutters, but I just kiss him some more. Secrets are a thing of our past, but howlingly good sex is our future.

If you loved Me Before You and The Fault in Our Stars, Come Back Tomorrow is your next angsty romance must-read.

William Everson, Jr. is young, he's dying of terminal cancer, and he's all alone. I meet him through my hobby of befriending terminal cancer patients with no family, but it takes me much longer to meet "Will" and to learn anything about his family, his friends, and why he has a DNR order in place.

"Can I come back tomorrow?"

That's always my question at the end of our visits, until it becomes his question, and it changes both of us forever. Will's given up on life; but I won't let him go without a fight. But is our love enough to change Will's mind about the rest of his life?

Come Back Tomorrow is the first book of the Embrace Tomorrow Duet.

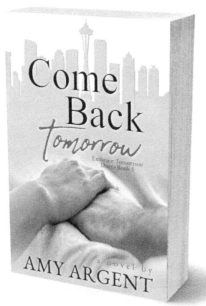

Available Now

Purchase Come Back tomorrow

ACKNOWLEDGMENTS

Jared, thank you for always supporting me no matter what I try to do and for patiently handling all my IT and art requests. You're a trooper, truly. I'm so lucky to have you as my best friend and husband!

Noah and Tori, thank you for your hugs, your pats on the head, and your unwavering belief in me. And for reminding me what it's like to be a teenager.

Mom and Dad, thank you for always being in my corner and cheering me on. Your support means the world to me.

Sue, this one's for you! Thank you for your edits, your graphs and charts, and your gentle persuasion when I try to dig my heels in. But most of all, thank you for being there any and every time I reach out and for talking me off the ledge, repeatedly.

Sally, Aimee, Jennifer, Belynda, you guys were my team on this one. Thank you for your perspectives, your revisions, and most of all, your encouragement.

Thank you also to my "little group" who take the time to give me opinions whenever I ask: Sally, Jennifer, Belynda, Sue, Teresa, and Beth. Making decisions isn't my forte, so you guys are lifesavers!

Thank you so much to Mayhem Cover Creations for the stunning cover! LJ, you made my Nathan come alive so beautifully!

Thank you to everyone who read, reviewed, and discussed this story in its first incarnation, both in my group and elsewhere on the web. That journey with you was brilliant—I hope you enjoyed it as much as I did.

Dear reader, thank you for spending this time with Nathan and Holly. I hope my words made you laugh; I'm sure some of them made you cry, but most of all, I hope they showed you the amazing things love can do. I hope you have a Holly in your life—we all deserve unconditional love.

And to the fifty million people worldwide living with epilepsy, I hope I have managed to make some small contribution to raise awareness, help dispel stigma, and encourage understanding. I hope you realize you're not alone—you never were.

About the Author

Amy Argent is a reader and writer of contemporary romance. Amy can honestly say she writes day and night—clinical trial documents as a medical writer by day and contemporary romance as a novelist by night . . . and possibly into the wee hours of the morning. She has a PhD in Genetics that she agonized entirely too much over, but it did result in a fascinating day job—the details of which tend to creep into her fiction.

Amy can be found in Raleigh, North Carolina, with her husband, two teenagers, and two hedgehogs, where she's most likely planning her next departure from reality—destination: Dragon Con, the closest Renaissance Faire, or the nearest book.